LIVING A LIE

Also by Josephine Cox

Queenie's Story

Her Father's Sins
Let Loose the Tigers

————

The Emma Grady Trilogy

Outcast
Alley Urchin
Vagabonds

————

Whistledown Woman
Angels Cry Sometimes
Take This Woman
Don't Cry Alone
Jessica's Girl
Nobody's Darling
Born to Serve
More than Riches
A Little Badness

LIVING A LIE

Josephine Cox

HEADLINE

First published in 1995 by
HEADLINE BOOK PUBLISHING

10 9 8 7 6 5 4 3 2

British Library Cataloguing in Publication Data
Cox, Josephine
Living a Lie
I. Title
823.914 [F]

ISBN 0-7472-1328-3

Phototypeset by Intype, London
Printed and bound in Great Britain by
Mackays of Chatham PLC, Chatham, Kent

HEADLINE BOOK PUBLISHING
A division of Hodder Headline PLC
338 Euston Road
London NW1 3BH

For
Hilary and Bernie

Fate brought us together.
Friendship will keep us close.
Luv you!

CONTENTS

PART ONE

1975

Choices

CHAPTER ONE

Riddled with guilt, the young woman kept her gaze averted.

Beneath her calm and elegant manner seethed a terrible secret, a dark and dangerous intent that no one there could have foreseen, least of all the dark-haired girl hurrying along beside her.

It was 1975. To the sober-suited commuters waiting for the train to London, Lucinda Marsh was a ray of sunshine, a vision of loveliness in high heels and a red tight-fitting two-piece. With her trim figure, mass of wavy golden hair and smiling blue eyes, she was a welcome distraction.

The platform was crowded. Only a short while ago there had been the usual daily chatter about the state of the government and Margaret Thatcher's emergence as new Tory leader, the awful February weather and the train being late yet again. The meaningless chatter subsided with the arrival of the young woman and the girl.

At first there were admiring glances, then admiration gave way to curiosity, then almost to a sense of expectancy.

Pausing by the edge of the platform, Lucinda glanced nervously at the middle-aged man standing nearby. He was holding a newspaper in front of his face, but his eyes peeped over the top and he smiled at the girl with Lucinda – a delightful creature with coal-black hair and earth-coloured eyes. When, embarrassed, she looked away, he bent his head to read, but like the others was captivated by Lucinda, strangely moved by her beauty and her manner. There was something secretive about her, something oddly bewitching.

Gripping the girl's hand, the young woman made her way to the far end of the platform, the tips of her heels echoing against the cold hard ground, her outer composure belying the

3

turmoil inside and the questions, always the same, only this time more urgent. Was she right? Was she wrong? This was not the first time she had made a decision to escape, but then she had always changed her mind, deciding she should give it another try, for Kitty's sake if not for her own.

This time, nothing on God's earth could make her change her mind. Today was *her* day. This time she was in control. For too long she had endured agonies in the name of love. Soon the agony would be over. Not his though. To hell with him!

Dressed for the occasion, she was ready for the long journey. As she mentally prepared herself, she could feel Kitty's hand in hers and her heart warmed with love.

Pausing to look down on that trusting young face, she was shaken by the dark eyes that returned her glance: dark brooding eyes, incredibly beautiful. Her father's eyes. Yet where Bob's intense gaze instilled fear in her, Kitty's inquisitive glance created only a sense of terrible guilt.

Stooping closer she asked tenderly, 'Are you all right?' While she talked, her long manicured fingers toyed with the girl's rich black tresses.

Kitty was twelve years old. She loved adventure, and she adored her mother. 'Where are we going?' she asked for the umpteenth time. Last night her parents had quarrelled again. As she had so many times before, Kitty had sat on the stairs listening, afraid to go in, yet wanting to stop them. But *how* could she stop them? She was only a girl, and they were adults.

Lucinda too was reliving the memory of last night. 'You shouldn't ask where we're going,' she gently chided.

'Are we going to London?' Delightful visions of parks and palaces filled her mind.

Her mother laughed softly. 'We'll see.'

'Sarah wanted me to call for her this morning.' Kitty and Sarah Jenkins had known each other for ever. 'We're playing clarinet in the school concert.'

'You're very fond of her, aren't you? And her brother Harry.' Lucinda smiled knowingly. 'Has he taken up music lessons yet?'

'No.' Kitty was only a little disappointed. 'He'd rather play football and swim in the school team.' Her young heart bubbled with joy. 'But he's coming to listen to me and Sarah play in the concert.' A terrible thought struck her. 'We *will* be back in time for the concert tonight, won't we?'

Yet again Lucinda questioned what she was about to do. This morning she had been so sure. Now she could hardly suppress the niggling doubts that crept up on her. 'There are more important things than school,' she said finally. 'Do you know what happened last night? Did you hear your father?'

Kitty lowered her gaze. 'You were fighting.'

'You don't ever want that to happen again, do you?'

'No.'

'Kitty?' The voice was softer now. 'Look at me.'

Kitty didn't want to look up. Whatever her mother said, it *would* happen again. It always did.

'Kitty?' There were tears in the voice, and something else, something that intrigued the child. 'Please . . . look at me.'

Kitty raised her dark eyes and what she saw made her ashamed. Her mother was crying. 'I'm sorry,' she murmured. It wasn't her fault, but she felt responsible somehow.

'Do you love me, Kitty?'

'Yes.'

'And you want to come with me?'

'Yes.'

'Kitty?'

'Yes, Mother?'

'I don't want you to hate your father. Especially not today.'

There were times when Kitty *did* hate him, but mostly she tried not to think about it. 'I wish you wouldn't fight.'

'Do you think it's my fault?'

'Not all the time.'

'Your father won't let us live in peace. You do understand that, don't you?'

'Yes.' Kitty recalled the many times when she and her mother would come home from shopping and there would be a furious row. Her father would say cruel things, accusing her mother of meeting some man or other, then he would shout and scream. The last time he hit out with his belt, cutting her mother's face and making it bleed.

'Some men are bad, Kitty.'

'Why?'

'They like to hurt.' Gently fingering the bruise on her temple, Lucinda confessed, 'Your father hit me again last night . . . see?'

5

Gingerly lifting a strand of hair, she revealed an angry red weal that stretched from brow to temple.

When she realised that the man standing nearby was watching, she quickly covered up the mark and looked away. 'I wish the train would come!' she snapped. If it didn't come now, she might lose her courage.

'Does Daddy know where we're going?'

Lucinda began to think more clearly. She mustn't upset the girl. Maybe she should have left Kitty behind, but then what? Too soon she would be a woman. Then she could meet a man like Robert Marsh, a man who would rob her of her dignity and make her feel inferior, a man who might beat her until she was black and blue ... a man who would think nothing of taking what he wanted, then treating her like so much dirt beneath his feet. She could *never* let that happen to Kitty. 'No, sweetheart,' she answered kindly, 'Daddy doesn't know where we're going.' When Bob came home there would be a note waiting for him, a note that told him everything. He would not understand. He never did. But it would be done and, rightly or wrongly, he must share the blame.

Suddenly she was nervous. Suppose Bob came home early? Suppose he found out where she'd gone and came looking for her? The idea made her tremble inside.

When the destination of the approaching train was announced over the tannoy, Lucinda Marsh quietly addressed her child. 'Stay close, sweetheart.' Her voice was soft and caressing as she ran her fingers over the black wavy hair, brushing it back from the girl's forehead and smiling lovingly into those dark trusting eyes. 'When the train comes in, you must keep hold of my hand.' Fearing that Bob might find them before she could carry out her intent, desperation betrayed itself in her voice.

When Kitty looked up inquisitively, she bent to kiss the girl on the forehead. 'Trust me,' she whispered hoarsely. '*You mustn't run away.*'

Suddenly, and for no reason she could think of, Kitty was afraid. She asked again, 'Where are we going?'

'Where we can never be hurt again,' her mother answered. 'Where we can always be together.' She didn't look at Kitty. She too was afraid. Afraid those dark eyes might make her change her mind. 'Remember now, stay close.'

The girl's reply was lost as the train came into sight. People began surging towards the platform's edge. In that moment Lucinda glanced over to where the man had been standing. He was nearer now; his newspaper neatly folded and tucked into his jacket pocket. If he stretched out his arm he could touch her.

Suddenly, gripping Kitty's hand so hard she made her wince, Lucinda started walking down the platform, towards the train. With some way still to go before it entered the station, it was approaching fast. 'I'm not afraid,' she murmured, 'I'm not afraid.' But she was. And yet, at the same time, she felt exhilarated.

With the train speeding towards them, she waited for the inevitable. 'Keep hold of Mummy's hand, sweetheart,' she urged. She could feel Kitty pulling away, as though she sensed something terrible. Lucinda's grip tightened. 'It won't be long now,' she promised. For the briefest moment she closed her eyes and softly prayed.

Most people remained at the centre of the platform. As the train came speeding into the station. Lucinda prepared herself. Only another minute and she would be free. The words of an Abba song sped through her mind; she actually began singing them . . .

A last smile at the daughter she adored, the sign of the cross to keep the devil away, and with one almighty leap she threw herself on to the track.

Kitty's screams echoed along the platform. With her mother's hand wrapped tightly about her own, she felt herself being propelled forward. Her feet left the platform. All she could recall later was the train driver's eyes, wide with horror, and a searing pain across her neck. Then it was dark, and all feeling was gone.

Shocked and tearful, the passengers gave their versions of what they had seen. 'She was so beautiful,' said one. 'Disturbed,' said another. 'You could see the madness in her eyes.'

The man who had been closest watched the first ambulance leave. It went at a steady pace. There was no emergency now. It was too late for that. 'How could she want to take an innocent child with her?' he cried, groaning with pain when the

7

ambulance man strapped his injured wrist. His shirt was torn and there was a kind of madness in his own eyes as he told how he had watched mother and child fall beneath the train. 'All along I had an idea she meant to do something crazy.'

The police officer thanked him for his statement. 'If it hadn't been for you, there would have been *two* dead people,' he reminded him. 'It took courage to do what you did.'

When his wrist was made comfortable and the police officer had gone to speak to other witnesses, the man walked over to where a second ambulanceman was tending the survivor. She was sitting bolt upright on the ground, wrapped in a rug, her wide eyes filled with terror. Droplets of blood dripped from the gash on her neck, falling on to her bare arm where they made a crimson trail. *He* had done that. It sickened him.

Looking at his finger, he saw the ring that had sliced into her neck. The gold sovereign had been one of his most valued possessions. Now it was contaminated, the rim thick with gouged skin. Filled with disgust, he ripped it off and threw it down. Addressing the ambulanceman, he asked, 'Will she be all right?'

'She'll be fine,' came the answer. 'Thanks to you.'

That was all he needed to know. He left then. Like all true heroes, he wanted no reward. It was enough to know he had saved a life.

Kitty watched intently. 'Please! Where's my mother?' she pleaded. First her mother had been beside her, then it was dark; now it was light again and her mother was gone.

'All in good time, young lady.' They settled her into the ambulance. 'First we'll get you to hospital . . . let the doctors look at this gash, eh?'

In the ambulanceman's opinion she had had a miraculous escape, with no bones broken and no serious injury, apart from the shock which would take its course. He had cleaned the deep neck wound and, though he was sure it would scar, it posed no threat. He smiled at her. 'You'll have to be brave,' he warned, though he didn't tell her the worst. He didn't say her mother was never coming back.

CHAPTER TWO

Kitty sat on the stairs. This time it was her father and her aunt who were fighting. 'Like it or not, she's *your* responsibility. It's up to you to take care of her.'

'For God's sake, woman, don't you think I've tried!' Bob Marsh paced the room, eyes downcast and shoulders hunched as he contemplated the future. 'I thought you of all people would help.'

'Well, you can think again, because I've enough kids of my own to take care of.' Glancing towards the door, Mildred lowered her voice. 'Where is she, anyway?'

'Who knows? Since she came home from the hospital, she hides herself away.' Straightening his shoulders, Bob looked at her in appeal. 'These past weeks have been a nightmare... finding that note... realising what Lucinda meant to do... all the questions afterwards... the inquest and then the funeral.' He paused, sighing aloud, filled with self-pity. 'The girl is no help either.' He made a sour expression. 'She blames me, you know? The little cow has the gall to blame me!'

'And you want her to believe it was all Lucinda's fault? Is that what you're saying?'

Enraged he slammed his fist against the wall. 'Damn it all, Mildred, anybody would think I *threw* her under that bloody train!'

There was a short silence, until she answered in a hard voice, 'You might as well have.'

His violent reaction took her by surprise. Swinging around, he slapped her hard on the face. 'You bitch! You're no better than she was.'

'And you're the worst kind of coward.' Wiping the blood from her mouth she taunted him, 'You enjoyed hitting Lucinda too,

9

didn't you? Time and again you hit her, put her in hospital, took pleasure in making her life a misery.'

'I gave her everything!'

'Oh, you gave her money, I'll not deny that. Clothes and jewels and this fine big house.' With a wave of her hand Mildred encompassed the handsome rosewood furniture, the tall display cabinet filled with silver and crystal; above the inglenook fireplace hung a splendid oil painting, and the carpets were the plushest money could buy. 'But it meant nothing, don't you see that? She wanted your trust... a love that was as deep and loyal as hers. She needed tenderness. She needed a man who could take her in his arms and love her for what she was, not for what he wanted her to be.'

'She was a bloody tart!'

Mildred gave a short laugh. 'Lucinda Marsh was never a tart. She was too attractive for her own good, yes, and she was like a kid at heart. She hated arguments and fighting. She wanted nothing more than to be a good mother and wife, and you made her suffer for it. She was the minnow and you were the shark. You took advantage of her soft nature... used her as though she was your personal property. You showed her off to your cronies, then slapped her good and hard if they dared to look at her in a certain way.'

'You don't know what you're talking about.'

'Well, now, that's where you're wrong. Lucinda came to me time and again after you'd beaten her up. She was desperately unhappy, yet still she adored you... begged me not to confront you.' She spat out her next words. 'If any man treated me like you treated her, I'd cut his balls off while he slept!'

Laughing in her face, he replied, 'It's just as well we're brother and sister and not man and wife, then.'

'You really are a swine.' Picking up her coat from a chair she told him. 'You'll never find a woman to love you like she did. How could you do it, Bob? How could you torment her... accusing her of being unfaithful when she wasn't... saying Kitty wasn't yours, when you know damned well she is. God Almighty! You've only to look at the girl to see she's your flesh and blood. Lucinda didn't want other men. She loved *you*... and you knew that. Yet you never let up on her, did you?' She crossed the room to stand before him. 'If the girl blames you, then so do I.'

10

'I think you've said enough.' His eyes brimmed with tears, yet he was not sorry. If anything, he was angry, feeling neglected and unloved, as always.

Mildred stared at him for a moment. He was her brother, and she wanted no part of him. No part of him, and no part of his daughter. He alone had created this tragedy and he alone would have to deal with it. In slow deliberate tones she told him, 'When Lucinda threw herself under that train, it was because *you* made her life unbearable!'

'GET OUT!'

'Oh, don't worry, I'm going. I may be your sister, but so help me, I can't stand being under the same roof as you.'

'Get out before I throw you out.' His voice was low, trembling with hatred.

Kitty sat tightly huddled on the stairs, head bent and her heart breaking. The row brought back too many memories. Now her mother was gone and nobody wanted her. Not for the first time since that awful day she wished she had died with her mother.

When the sitting-room door was flung open and the small fair-haired woman emerged, Kitty raised her head. She didn't speak but her sad eyes told their own story.

Her aunt was not surprised to see her there. 'I'm sorry you heard all that,' she apologised. 'But it had to be said.'

Still Kitty gave no response. There were so many questions in her head, and she could find no answers to any of them.

Aunt Mildred came to sit beside her. 'I can't take you home with me,' she explained. 'I've got four demanding kids of my own, and Len's just lost his job. As it is, I don't know how we'll manage.'

'I thought I told you to get out?' Bob's voice called up the stairs.

'I'll go when I'm ready.'

The sitting-room door slammed, and he could be heard swearing and complaining. 'He knows better than to cut up rough with me,' Mildred told the girl.

Still Kitty said nothing. Instead she gazed at her aunt and wished she could go with her. 'Like I say, Kitty, money's in short supply and I've too many mouths to feed.' Grimacing at the sound of something breaking downstairs, Mildred said, 'I

11

expect *he* would pay me to have you, but it would be like blood money.'

Kitty wondered what 'blood money' was. But she didn't ask. There were other, more important, things here she did not understand.

Putting her arms round Kitty, Mildred murmured kindly, 'If I can't do anything else, I can at least give you some advice.' When Kitty didn't respond she went on, 'There will come a day when you're old enough to marry. When that happens, think hard about the man you choose. Some men are born bullies. Like your father, they only feel good when they're hitting a woman . . . it gives them a sense of power. But they're not real men, they're just cowards – not worth the time of day.'

Looking at the girl with renewed interest, she realised with a little shock that Kitty had a special kind of grace; blessed with dark and sensuous looks that would attract men like moths to a flame. 'With your beauty you should be able to pick and choose,' Mildred remarked thoughtfully. 'But, for pity's sake, child . . . don't make the mistake your mother made. Find a man who is gentle . . . a man who will share your love and treat you like a woman. They're few and far between, so if you do find such a man, stick with him through thick and thin. Oh, he'll probably have his little faults, we all do. But I promise you, Kitty, you can face anything in life if you have a partner who truly loves you.'

Silently she marked her aunt's words, but all she could think about was now. In a desolate voice she pleaded, 'I don't want to stay here, Aunt Mildred.' She recalled the screaming arguments, that had always ended in her mother crying and her father storming out of the house. In her mind she could see the angry mark her mother had shown her just before she jumped.

Feeling only the smallest flush of guilt, and adamant that she would not make life easier for the man who had caused all this, Mildred told her firmly, 'Now you listen to me, Kitty Marsh! Your place is here with your father. This is your home and you've had enough upheaval with all that's happened. Besides, I've already explained why I can't take you.' Realising how disturbed the girl was, she had to reassure her, 'You have my word, he won't lay a finger on you. He knows I'm on to him, and he'll be wary of that.'

'Please, can't I come home with you?' Kitty had tried so hard not to blame her father, but she couldn't love him. Not any more.

'You can't come with me, and that's an end to it.' Fearing she might get dragged in over her head, Mildred gathered her belongings and hurried down the stairs. At the bottom she looked up, thinking herself as much a coward as her brother. 'I've got to go now. Be a good girl, Kitty. Remember what I've told you, and everything will be all right.'

'Aren't you coming back?' With her mother gone and her father thinking only of himself, Kitty was feeling very lonely.

At the door her aunt paused to look once again at that small dejected figure. 'No, I won't be coming back,' she answered truthfully. She didn't feel responsible, nor was she prepared to make her own life more complicated by taking on other people's problems.

However, there was one more thing she could do to put Kitty's mind at ease. Retracing her steps to the sitting room, she flung open the door. 'You'd better know this before I leave,' she said. 'If I find out you've raised a hand to that girl I'll have the authorities down on you so fast your feet won't touch the ground.'

Sprawled on the settee, Bob Marsh stared her out. 'Don't tell me what to do in my own house . . . with my own kid.'

'I *mean* it, Bob.'

'Piss off out of it.'

'One bad word from me and they'll take the girl from you.'

'They're welcome to her.'

'You're a hard bugger!'

'And you're asking to be thrown through that door.' His angry eyes were like black slits. 'I've told you . . . piss off out of it, before I forget myself.'

As she went from the house, he chuckled softly. Hearing Kitty move on the stairs, he called out in a harsh voice, 'I KNOW YOU'RE THERE, DAMN YOU! GET YOURSELF IN HERE!'

Her first instinct was to run after her aunt. But it was suppressed as she dutifully delivered herself to the sitting room, where she stood at the door, a solemn little figure, her dark eyes sparkling with unshed tears.

13

'Get in here.'

Reluctantly she took a step forward.

'Here, damn it! In front of me.' With one vicious kick he sent the coffee table flying; the shattered glass top flew in all directions. 'Are you bloody stupid or what?'

She was standing before him now, visibly trembling, her dark eyes upturned to his.

Her fear seemed to please him. 'Are you frightened of me?'

'You hit her.'

Leaning towards her, he clenched his fist and held it in front of her face. 'Oh? And you think I'm going to hit you, is that it?'

'Aunt Mildred said you wouldn't dare.' Her dark gaze was unflinching. All she could think of was her mother and what he had done to her.

He laughed out loud at her boldness. 'Oh? Did she now?'

When Kitty continued to look at him with accusing eyes, the laughter died and his face crumpled. For a while there was an awkward silence while he studied that small perfectly shaped face with its full mouth and those dark magnificent eyes; they were sad now, but he knew the sadness could not last. He knew there would come a day when those same eyes would turn any man inside out.

Confused and humbled by her silence, he told her in a small voice, 'One day, you're going to be a real beauty.'

'I want to go now.' She didn't like the way he was looking at her.

'Go where, eh?' Enraged, he roared like a man demented, '*I'll* say when you can go!' Reaching out, he grabbed her to him, pressing her to his body until she could hardly breathe. 'Your mother was a beauty too... oh, not dark like you and me... a china doll she was, with eyes blue as the sky and hair like a summer's day.'

Terrified, Kitty fought to free herself, but she was held too close. She couldn't cry out because her face was squashed to his breast and his arms were like steel bands round her shoulders. He rocked her backwards and forwards, his tears rolling on to her face. 'I loved her, you know,' he was saying. 'Whatever else I did, she knew I loved her.'

Suddenly he thrust her away. Gasping, Kitty struggled to

break his grip on her shoulders but he held her fast, his face twisted with loathing as he shook her hard. 'You were there when she went under that train. Why couldn't it have been you instead of her, eh?' Tears were flowing down his face and his sobs were terrible to hear. 'You could have stopped her! Why didn't you?'

Kitty was sobbing, too. 'I didn't know!' she called. 'Please, Daddy, I didn't know.'

With a fierce blow, he sent her crashing across the room. 'IT SHOULD HAVE BEEN YOU!' Stumbling across to the drinks' cabinet, he took out a bottle of whisky and turned to her again. But she was gone, and all he could hear was the front door closing behind her. 'Good riddance,' he snarled, then took the top off the bottle and drank until he almost choked. 'Doesn't matter to me if you never come back,' he muttered to himself, and settled down to drain the bottle dry.

Linda Jenkins was a kind soul. When Kitty arrived at her door, afraid and confused, her heart went out to her. 'Stay here for a while,' she insisted. 'As soon as Mr Jenkins comes home, he'll have a quiet word with your father.'

A large woman with wild red hair and small brown eyes, she prided herself on being able to handle every little crisis. But this was different. A man had lost his wife and a child had seen her own mother leap to her death; had nearly gone with her too by all accounts. 'You're not to worry,' she reassured Kitty.

It took only a few minutes to brew a pot of tea and pour it out. When that was drunk and Kitty was more composed, Linda urged tactfully, 'Sarah's gone to the shop. I forgot to tell her I needed an uncut loaf . . . if you go now, you can catch her on the way back. Go on.' Ushering Kitty to the door she told her, 'It'll be all right, you'll see.' But she couldn't be certain. Bob Marsh was known for his bad temper. He wouldn't take kindly to others poking their noses into his business, and that was a fact.

Once she had seen Kitty safely down the road, Linda returned to her chores. There was the evening meal to get and a pile of washing to fetch in. 'Rain forecast,' she muttered, rushing about and falling over the dog as she fled outside. 'Bloody weather.'

The Jenkinses lived only a few hundred yards from Kitty's

home. Ron Jenkins earned his living as a mechanic at one of Bob Marsh's two garages. The Marshes' house took pride of place in Woburn Sands High Street, while the Jenkinses lived across the road in a terrace of older, more modest dwellings.

Linda Jenkins ran a happy household. There was herself and her husband Ron, fifteen-year-old Harry, twelve-year-old Sarah, two cats named Bill and Ben, a budgie with one leg, and a spaniel named Jasper – a mad creature who spent his days chasing cats and his nights howling to get out so he could cock his leg up the clothes' line.

'Over the years, me and mine have had more than our share of troubles,' Linda muttered as she folded the dry washing. 'There have been times when I wished things could have been easier. But I know this much ... I would never have swapped places with Lucinda Marsh, not in a million years I wouldn't!' Like everyone at the top end of the street she had heard the shocking row between Kitty's parents on that last night. 'Bob Marsh is a bad bugger deep down, and she were always too good for him, that was the pity of it.' Growing angry, she absent-mindedly flung the washing in a heap. The dog ran off with a shirt and she gave chase, swearing like a trooper when she went flying over the clothes basket.

As Kitty turned the corner of the High Street she caught sight of Sarah going into the Co-op. The same age as Kitty, Sarah was slightly built, with carrot-red hair, droopy hazel eyes and a face peppered with freckles. She also had what her mother called 'a wicked temper'. Her moods blew hot and cold, so you never really knew where you stood with her.

Cheered by the sight of her friend, Kitty went at a run along the street, screeching to a halt when a miserable old man confronted her at the doorway. 'Get out of my way, you little sod!' he bawled, poking at her chest with his cane. The impact made her gasp. Opening the door for him, she apologised, but his answer was to push her aside. He went out, muttering all the time, 'Bloody kids! Nearly knocked me arse over tip, she did.'

Sarah had seen it all. 'It wasn't your fault,' she said. 'Anyway, how did you know where I was?'

'Your mum told me.' Kitty walked alongside her. 'She says you're to get an uncut loaf.'

Sarah was surprised. 'She already told me that.' Eyeing Kitty suspiciously, she remarked. 'You've been crying. It's your dad, isn't it?'

Reluctant to discuss it here in the shop, Kitty lowered her gaze. When she raised her dark eyes it was to glance around. Seeing there was only one other customer, and she was too far away to hear their conversation, she softly confided, 'There's been another row. Dad and Aunt Mildred.'

Sarah reached up to the top shelf and took down a tin of beans, 'I know,' said Sarah, 'I heard it.'

Taken aback, Kitty was curious. 'How could you hear it?'

Grabbing a packet of cornflakes, Sarah told her, 'I called for you. There was so much yelling I don't expect you heard me knocking on the door.' Shrugging, she explained, 'It doesn't matter. I just thought you might come shopping with me, that's all.' Placing her hand on Kitty's arm, she continued, 'She's a hypocrite.'

'Who?'

'Your Aunt Mildred.'

'How did you know it was her?'

'I saw her come out, that's how.' Going to the cheese counter she pointed to the display. 'A pound of red leicester please.' Lowering her voice she told Kitty. 'That old biddy doesn't want you, does she?'

'*Nobody* wants me.' The truth was like a fist squeezing her young heart.

'You're wrong, Kitty.' Sarah's soft voice reprimanded. '*I* want you, and so does Harry.'

Kitty's eyes swam. 'I know,' she said simply. 'I didn't mean that.' Eager to put things right, she explained, 'I meant my dad and Aunt Mildred.' A thought crossed her mind, 'Do you think your mum and dad would let me come and live with you?'

Sarah shook her head. 'I expect Mum would, but Dad says we have to look after ourselves and not bother about others.' Shrugging her shoulders, she made a sour face. 'He's a real misery lately.'

'Why doesn't he like me?'

''Course he likes you!' Sarah had already gone through all the arguments with her parents. 'It's just like I said ... he's frightened to get on the wrong side of your dad. He told our mam we shouldn't poke our noses in where they're not wanted,

in case he gets the sack and we're all put on the street. That's
what he said, but our mam told him he was talking through his
arse.'

'I see.' But the only thing Kitty saw was that she was on her
own.

'You wouldn't really want to live with your Aunt Mildred,
would you?'

If she had been asked, Kitty might have gone with her aunt
that morning, but now she gave it a little more thought and her
answer was resolute. 'No. I'd have to move to Bedford, and she
might not let me visit you.'

'Don't worry,' Sarah told her with the wisdom of youth,
'you and your dad will be okay now, you'll see.'

The lady had finished cutting and wrapping the cheese. After
marking it with a big black pen she instructed kindly, 'Pay for
it at the till.'

A passerby watched the two girls walk away, still deep in
conversation. 'Kids! They never cease to amaze me,' she
remarked when the next customer came to the counter, 'Look
at them two . . . like a pair of old women discussing the ways
of the world.' She chuckled then in more serious voice explained
that Kitty was the daughter of 'that poor young woman who
threw herself under the train'. She went on to add that the two
girls had known each other since primary school, then, in hushed
tones, revealed every snippet of conversation she had just overheard. 'The dark one seems to think nobody wants her, and the
carrot top seems to think it will all come right in the end.' She
shook her head. 'All I can say is . . . I'm glad it's not *me* who
has to live with Bob Marsh!'

The other woman agreed. 'Poor little bugger. Lost her mother
and left with a father who wants no part of her.' As Sarah and
Kitty went up the street, earnestly talking, she murmured softly,
'It's a good job she's got a friend.'

Ron Jenkins was on edge. 'They've been up there long enough,'
he told his wife. 'It's time the girl went home.'

Linda looked at the wall-clock; it was quarter to nine. 'I
suppose it *is* getting late.'

''Course it's getting late!' Irritated, he took a great gulp of
his tea then placed the mug on the table, announcing in a firm

voice, 'I want her out of this house. Now!'

'Surely she won't hurt for another few minutes? They're watching that *Top of the Pops* tape our Sarah videoed.'

'Do you want Bob Marsh coming round here?'

'That's the last thing I want.'

'Then get the girl out, that's all I'm saying ... otherwise he just might come banging on the door, demanding to know why we're harbouring his kid.'

'All right.' Going to the door, Linda added, 'Though it's hardly likely he'll come looking for Kitty ... not when he's already told his sister he doesn't want her. Our Sarah heard them going at it hammer and tongs.'

'None of our business!'

'That's what too many people say.' Before he could answer, she was up the stairs, telling Kitty, 'It's time you went home, love. Your dad will be worried about you.'

Kitty might have said he wouldn't care if she never came home again. Instead she thanked Mrs Jenkins, promised Sarah she would see her tomorrow, and with a heavy heart made her way up the street.

Harry was just turning the corner. His face lit up when he saw her. 'Are you coming back later?' he wanted to know.

Kitty shook her head. 'I seem to make your dad uncomfortable,' she said.

Harry was nothing like his father. While Ron Jenkins was short and round with pale eyes, Harry was tall and dark-eyed. He was also athletic and good-natured, while his father fell into the chair minutes after he'd had his tea, woke up later with a sore head and never had a good word to say about anybody.

Harry was also persistent. 'Fancy a walk?'

Kitty shook her head. 'Better not,' she answered. 'Dad's in a foul mood.'

He studied her for a while. It hurt him to see her so unhappy. 'Kitty, I want you to know I'm here, if you ever want me.'

She was more grateful than she could say. 'I know that.'

Bob Marsh was sprawled out, his long legs dangling over the arm of the settee and his hand still clutching the empty whisky bottle. He had drunk himself into a stupor. 'Dad!' Kitty tried to wake him. 'Dad, I'm going to bed now.' Though she had too often witnessed the violence in him, she had never before seen her father like this.

She shook him, yelled at him, even put a cold wet cloth over his forehead. He stirred and murmured Lucinda's name.

Realising she would not wake him, and subdued by the sound of her mother's name on his lips, Kitty locked all the doors and went upstairs. Here she had a long lazy bath. Afterwards she put on a clean nightie, brushed her long black hair and slid into bed. For a long time, she couldn't sleep. The room was dark, but through the open curtains she could see the night sky; it was incredibly beautiful, a vast expanse of black velvet streaked with starlight. She wondered if her mother was up there, watching her. The idea both excited and terrified her.

Restless now, her frantic thoughts recalled what her mother had said: 'Stay close . . . don't run away.' It seemed inconceivable to Kitty that her own mother had wanted to kill her. 'Why didn't you stay with me?' she asked the darkness. 'We could have run away together . . . found somewhere to live, just the two of us.' Her words echoed in the silence. A moment passed, before she heard the sound of soft laughter; for one leaping heartbeat she thought it was her mother laughing.

Going to the window, she saw a young couple strolling down the street arm in arm. They were meandering from side to side as he bent his head to kiss her full on the mouth. Kitty was fascinated, the sparkle in her dark eyes shaming the stars above. 'When I grow up I want a man who will love me like that,' she murmured dreamily. She thought about what her aunt had said: 'find a man who is gentle' . . . 'stick with him through thick and thin'. The words were on her lips. When she went to sleep they echoed in her mind, etched there like a blueprint for the future.

Somehow, amidst all the confusion, Kitty had found a purpose in life. Aunt Mildred had promised there were such men – men who could be gentle, men who would love and protect her. It was small consolation for what she had lost, but it brought her comfort.

In her dreams she was suffocating, lost in a swirl of dark fog, her lungs hot and burning. Asleep, she fought against it. She opened her eyes but couldn't see. 'DADDY!' The fog tasted sour, forcing itself into her mouth, her body. While her senses weakened, her desperate screams grew louder: 'DADDY, HELP ME!'

Suddenly he was there. 'Don't be afraid,' he told her softly. 'Hold on to me.' Echoes of her mother's voice haunted her. 'You mustn't run away... keep hold of my hand.' She was afraid he meant to hurt her too, but she couldn't fight him, she couldn't breathe, *'Please don't kill me, Daddy!'* Her eyes closed and she was at his mercy.

Kitty woke to a worse nightmare.

When the cool night air revived her, she saw what her father had done. People came from everywhere to look. 'He must have been crazy with grief,' they said.

Linda Jenkins took Kitty in her arms and together they stood in disbelief, watching as the house burned. Flames leapt high into the air, while the awful sound of crackling and the smell of burning hung over everything and everyone. In the distance the wails of sirens splintered the night air as rescue vehicles raced to the scene. Spectators stepped aside to make way.

Suddenly a cry went up. 'For God's sake! Marsh is still inside!'

Kitty raised her gaze to an upstairs window. When she saw that tall familiar figure silhouetted in the firelight, she screamed out: 'NO!' Fighting to keep him in sight, she struggled like a thing demented. He seemed to hear her tortured cries because, in those last few seconds, he blew her a kiss. His mouth moved as though he was saying something to her. Then he smiled and was gone.

'He saved your life,' they said afterwards. 'He got you out of the house.'

Kitty wondered about that. She wondered why her father who'd always seemed to resent her, should want her to live, while her mother, who'd loved her dearly, had wanted her to die.

It would be many years before Kitty could even begin to understand.

CHAPTER THREE

An order was given for Kitty to be placed in a home. 'I'm sure it won't be for long,' Linda Jenkins promised her. 'Some kind family will foster you. Be patient. Everything will come out right.'

For a while Kitty believed her. But that was at the courthouse, before the enormity of her situation had sunk in; before she was brought to the outskirts of Bedford, and her new 'home'.

The thin-faced woman climbed out of the car first. 'Come along, Kitty,' she instructed in a firm crisp voice. 'The sooner we get you settled in the better.' When Kitty paused to look at the unfamiliar red-brick building, the woman stood by, fidgeting and visibly harassed; presently she took hold of Kitty's hand to propel her forward. 'I don't want to rush you,' she apologised, 'but I have to be back in court this afternoon, and I have three home visits to make before then.' Not for the first time she wondered whether she had chosen the right profession. 'A social worker can never afford to waste time,' she complained. In fact she didn't care for children very much, but in the short time she had known Kitty she had taken a liking to her. 'You'll be all right here,' she said in a kinder voice. 'The woman in charge is a good sort.'

In fact, 'the woman in charge' was a formidable figure. Miss Davis was built like a Churchill tank; six feet tall with miniature eyes, miniature spectacles, and a hairy chin. 'Well then, my dear,' she said, ushering Kitty and the social worker into her spacious office, 'I hope you're a good girl?'

Kitty nodded. She didn't know what to say. The sight of this huge woman had been another shock.

The social worker stepped forward. 'Speak up, Kitty. It's rude not to answer when spoken to. Are you a good girl, or not?'

She smiled at Miss Davis, and the two of them looked at Kitty who wished the earth would open and swallow her up.

'I suppose I am a good girl.' She tried hard not to stare at the dark stubble on Miss Davis's chin, but it was difficult. At school there had been a box filled with old comics, to be read at your desk on rainy playtimes; in one of the comics there was a character called Desperate Dan. *He* had stubble on his chin, just like Miss Davis; in fact, he and Miss Davis looked much alike, except he wore a cap and she had a big roll of grey hair.

'Well, now, that's a good thing,' Miss Davis's smile was quite frightening, 'because I don't welcome naughty girls into my house.' Turning to the social worker she said pertinently, 'I expect you're in a rush to get away?'

'Well, yes, I do have a tight schedule.'

'You'd best get off then. Don't worry about Kitty. We'll take good care of her.' She turned to smile at Kitty. 'You're not worried about being left with me, are you, child?'

Strangely enough, Kitty felt safe with her, 'No, Miss Davis.'

The younger woman placed her hand on Kitty's shoulder and said softly, 'I'll be back tomorrow, to see how you're settling in.' She looked down at Kitty's upturned face and was deeply moved by the confusion in those beautiful brown eyes. 'Don't worry,' she murmured, 'we'll try to get you fostered out, into a real family. That's what you want, isn't it?'

Kitty knew it was impossible, but in spite of the awful rows and all the fighting, there was just one thing she wanted more than anything else in the whole world. 'I want to go home.' Suddenly it was all too much and she was sobbing uncontrollably.

The women looked at each other and felt uncomfortably helpless. 'It's all right, my dear.' Miss Davis hurried to Kitty's side. Wrapping her great arms about that small frame, she comforted her. There were tears in her own eyes as she told Kitty, 'That's it, my dear, you just cry it all out.' Glancing at the social worker she gave her a sign to leave. In another minute Kitty was alone with the big woman. It was the first time she had cried in such a way and somehow it seemed to drain some of the pain from deep inside.

Later, when the tears had subsided, Kitty was shown round the big house. Downstairs there were six rooms: the spacious modern kitchen; a large dining room with a long sideboard, four round tables and enough chairs to accommodate the twenty children in care; a lounge with a television and a bookcase filled with all manner of literature, mainly teenage reading but with a selection of comics and magazines; further down the hall was a games room with a billiard table, two computers and a splendid old juke box that was still functional though the sound output had been governed by the caretaker. There was also a tiny cloakroom, Miss Davis's office, and then her own private sanctuary at the back of the house.

Upstairs were three bathrooms, two small bedrooms allocated to the women who supervised the children, a larger room where the boys slept, and a long wide dormitory which had once been three rooms and was now the girls' sleeping quarters, furnished with beds, lockers and bedside cabinets. It was a pleasant room with big windows and lots of cheery posters on the walls.

'Here we are, Kitty.' Taking her to the far end of the room, Miss Davis pointed to a narrow bed and the locker and cabinet beside it. 'This is your own little corner.' Glancing at a bed further along she revealed, 'That one belongs to Georgina. You'll like her.' She lapsed into thought before adding smartly, 'In fact, I shall assign her to look after you.'

Kitty wasn't sure about that. 'Is she the same age as me?' She had visions of being bossed about by someone older, someone she might not like.

'A good two years older.' Chuckling, Miss Davis said wryly. 'She's fourteen going on a hundred, but she has a wise head on young shoulders. She's been allowed home on a two-day visit, but she'll be back later tonight.' Her expression clouded when she recalled how these 'home visits' always upset Georgina. She hoped this time it would be different. 'She's not very talkative, and it will take you a while to get used to her, but I'm in no doubt – Georgina Rogers is the one to keep you out of trouble.'

In fact 'trouble' came looking for Kitty that night.

At dinner she was publicly introduced to everyone and when the introduction was over they all clapped and she felt sick with embarrassment.

The two women who lived in were friendly souls. Meg Austin, a fat lady who wobbled when she walked, was a widow who said very little but smiled a lot. The younger, Dorothy Picton, was thin and nervous but with a look that could slay Goliath. She also had the kind of voice that put you at ease straightaway. Kitty liked them both.

The children were an odd mixture. There were four boys ranging from a baby in nappies to a snotty-nosed sour-faced eight year old who kicked everyone under the table and was eventually sent to his room in disgrace. Of the girls two stood out in Kitty's mind; both tall and well built, with plucked eyebrows, they wore multi-coloured Sinbad trousers. One of the girls had long blonde hair; the other had dark hair cropped almost to her scalp, and big green eyes which, throughout the entire meal, stared threateningly at Kitty.

At eight o'clock the younger children were sent to their beds. It was nine-thirty when Kitty and the older girls made their way upstairs. There was a frantic rush for the bathroom, a few heated arguments, and a telling off from Meg Austin when two girls started throwing water around in the showers.

While she waited her turn in the bathroom, Kitty checked her belongings; the writing pad and blue biro she had been given by the social worker, and the clothes, books and toiletries allocated to her by Miss Davis. She put them all away in her locker and bedside cupboard.

All around her the girls chatted and giggled. Occasionally someone would smile at Kitty, but no one went out of their way to make friends with her. The two girls who had earlier caught her attention kept staring at her and furtively whispering before collapsing into fits of laughter. Kitty was in no doubt that they were laughing at her, and the loneliness was almost unbearable.

Half an hour later she had bathed, cleaned her teeth, brushed her hair and fallen exhausted into bed. It had been a long unsettling day.

She was woken from a deep sleep by the sound of a whisper in her ear. 'Get up, slut!'

Shocked and disorientated, she hitched herself up on one elbow. Rubbing the sleep from her eyes, she peered hard. At first she couldn't make out the face, but then in the half-light she saw it ... big green eyes, narrowed like a cat's, staring at her, just as they had done all evening.

Kitty sat up, her strong angry voice belying the fear inside her. 'What do you want?' Her dark brown eyes met the other's gaze, and there was a conflict of wills.

'That's no way to talk to your betters, is it, eh?' Prodding Kitty on the shoulder, the dark-haired girl taunted, 'You're an orphan, aren't you?'

'What if I am?' Kitty hated the fact that she was an orphan.

'You know what an orphan is, don't you?' Seeing she had touched a raw nerve, her tormentor wouldn't let go. 'An orphan is something nobody wants.' Sneering, she pointed along the beds. 'They're two a penny in here, and you're just another.'

'I want you to go . . . get away from me.'

The girl laughed softly. Turning to her pal, she whispered scathingly 'See what I mean? Orphans are nothing but trouble and this one doesn't seem to like us at all.'

The girl with the blonde hair leaned forward to touch Kitty on the face. As she drew her hand away she scratched her nails along Kitty's neck. 'Whoops! Clumsy me.' Her face was wreathed in a wicked smile. 'Hope I didn't hurt you?' she asked with feigned innocence.

The dark-haired one playfully pushed her, 'Silly bugger!' she chided. ''Course you hurt her. Look . . . she's bleeding.' Wiping her fingers along the scratch she smeared them with blood. 'That's blood, isn't it?' she asked the other slyly, 'I mean . . . it *looks* like blood.' In the half-light she stared at the crimson stains on her fingers, then raised them to her nostrils, and sniffed. '*Smells* like blood.' Putting them into her mouth, she sucked noisily. '*Tastes* like blood as well.'

Kitty thought they must be mad. 'Go away,' she snapped. 'Leave me alone.'

'Well now, that's not very friendly, is it?' The green-eyed one began stroking Kitty's hair. 'We could be tucked in a nice warm bed. Instead, we've come to say hello . . . introduce ourselves. And all you can say is "Go away".' Suddenly she was pulling on Kitty's hair, long agonising tugs that almost wrenched it from the roots. Her voice trembled with rage. 'You'd better learn how things are here. Sometimes me and my mate go out at night . . . through the window and back the same way. Nobody knows 'cause nobody tells.' Twisting the hank of hair in her fist, she thrust her face close to Kitty's. 'Nobody tells because they know

27

what they'd get. You see, we don't care much for tell-tales.' Grinning, she said, 'We put them in the shower . . . wash their mouths out with soap. That usually does the trick.' A look of horror came over her face. 'Oh! Have I frightened you?' Grinning at her friend, she protested, 'Honest to God, I didn't mean to frighten her.'

'Why don't we show her what we mean? Then she'll see it isn't so bad after all?'

Kitty felt herself being dragged from the bed. She kicked out, making them gasp when several blows struck home. But it only made them madder, more determined to teach her a lesson. She had the feeling that all the other girls were awake and listening, watching, but too afraid to do anything.

As they stripped off her nightgown, Kitty's own fear exploded into anger. Fetching her fist up, she struck the fair girl on the face. Suddenly there was a scuffle and everything happened at once: the lights went on, and the dark-haired girl was sent reeling backwards. Astonished, Kitty looked up to see the other girl struggling with someone she didn't recognise. In a matter of minutes the two offenders were making off, urged on by the threat, 'Next time you go after her, you'll have to come through me first!'

Even though she was shocked, Kitty had to giggle at the speed with which those two made their escape. This was to be her introduction to Georgina Rogers: a wayward girl with a heart of gold, a lifelong friend in the making.

'Call me Georgie.' Taller than Kitty, with a large plain face and honest grey eyes, Georgina walked her back to her bed. 'They won't bother you again,' she promised. 'They may be big and ugly, but they're cowards at heart.'

Kitty felt that here she had a true friend. 'I'm Kitty Marsh. Miss Davis says you'll be taking care of me for a while.' Climbing in between the sheets, she was surprised when Georgie sat on the edge of the bed. She was even more surprised when she glanced down to see deep meandering scars on the other girl's arms. When Georgie saw her looking, she pulled her cuffs over the marks. Embarrassed, Kitty quickly turned away.

There was an awkward silence before Georgie spoke. 'Don't be embarrassed,' she entreated. 'I made those cuts a long time ago.'

There was a faraway look in her eyes and something like regret in her voice as she went on, 'Don't ask me why I did it ... they've all asked me that ... so-called therapists and quacks ... people who wanted to look inside my head and see what made me tick.' She chuckled. 'Just as well they *didn't* know what I was thinking, or they'd have been shocked. Most of the time I was thinking about *them*, and how wonderful it would be if they were suddenly to blow up like balloons until they exploded.' Making a big round circle with her arms she blew out her cheeks and made a funny face. When she gave a full-throated laugh, Kitty had to laugh with her.

'I like you,' Georgina told her.

Kitty's heart felt lighter already. 'And I like you.'

'Goodnight, Kitty Marsh.'

Kitty held on to her hand. It was a lifeline in this strange unfamiliar place. 'Good night, Georgie ... and thank you.'

'What for?'

'For chasing the bullies off.'

Georgie smiled. 'Looked to me like you were doing all right before I came along.'

'Still, if it hadn't been for you ...' Kitty knew it would have been only a matter of minutes before they overpowered her.

'Would you have done the same for me?'

'Yes.' Though younger and smaller than Georgie, she would not have hesitated if the other girl was in trouble.

'There you are then. No thanks needed.'

'Georgie?' Kitty wasn't sure whether she should ask, but she needed to know.

'Go on,' Georgie sensed her dilemma. 'I won't bite you.'

'Have you been here a long time?'

Georgie took a deep breath. 'It seems like all my life.'

'It isn't though, is it?' Kitty had visions of being here until she was old and grey.

Georgie laughed. 'No.' She raised her eyes to the ceiling and began counting on her fingers. 'One ... two ... three ... four, no ... *five* years.'

'FIVE YEARS!' Kitty thought Georgie was right after all. It *did* seem like a lifetime. 'Are you an orphan too?'

Georgie shook her head. 'No, I'm not. More's the pity.'

Kitty was shocked. 'Why do you say that?'

'You might say it too, if you had a mother like mine.'

'Don't you love her?'

'I've never been with her long enough to find out. To tell you the truth, I don't really know her that well. She ran off when I was four. My dad brought me up. Five years ago he was killed in an accident, and I've been in here ever since.'

'Miss Davis said you were on home leave?'

'That's right. You see, my mother came back after my dad was killed. She rents a house, and I'm allowed to see her every other weekend.'

'Doesn't she want you home for good?'

'Yes, but the welfare won't allow it.'

'Why not?'

'Because she's a prostitute, and they think I'll be at risk.' She laughed, but it was a cynical sound. 'Between you and me, they're right an' all. She tried it on last night . . . brought a bloke into my room and asked me to "be nice to him".' On the bedclothes, her fists clenched and unclenched. 'So now you know. *That's* what my old woman thinks of me, and that's why I wish I was an orphan.'

Kitty wanted to hug her new friend, but something in Georgie's manner cautioned her. 'Can't you be fostered?' she asked hopefully. To her shame, part of her was hoping Georgie could not be fostered, because then Kitty might never see her again.

Taken aback by the question, Georgie laughed aloud. 'I'm too bleeding old to be fostered! People want cuddly babies and pretty little girls with golden curls . . .' Realising how her words must be hurting Kitty, she was quick to add, '*You'll* be all right though, with your big black eyes and pretty face. And you're only what? Nine? Ten?'

'I'm twelve, and I don't think I want to be fostered.' Suddenly the thought of some stranger taking her away was more frightening than the idea of staying here with Georgie.

'I was fostered once.'

'What happened?'

'They said I was too much of a handful.'

'And were you?'

''Course! It was the only way I could get out of there.' She chuckled as she recalled the couple who had taken her on. 'They were a right pair of crackpots! He used to call her sweetie-pie and plait her hair, and she thought I was her own personal slave.' She wouldn't forget that pair as long as she lived. 'Every-one thought they adored each other, but I saw what was really going on.'

'What do you mean?'

'They were like Jekyll and Hyde. During the day they were all sweetness and light, but when the door was closed and the curtains drawn they filled that house with hatred... I mean, they really hurt each other. Once, he locked her in the bathroom and left her there all night... said she smelled and needed a wash.'

Thoughts of her own parents filtered through Kitty's mind. 'Why would he do that?' she asked. 'Why would he pretend he loved her when all the time he wanted to hurt her?' It was her own father she was really asking about.

Georgie thought for a minute before answering in a voice old beyond her years, 'People are are strange, that's why. I'll bet there's at least one house in every street in every town where things go on behind closed doors no one would ever guess.'

'If they don't love each other, why do they go on living together?'

'Because sometimes it's easier than breaking up and finding a new life alone. Sometimes a bad partner is better than none at all.' She gave a wry little smile. 'What I'm saying is... some-times it's easier to live a lie.'

Kitty's mind fled back to that fatal morning. Suddenly it all spilled out. 'My mother killed herself because she and Daddy fought all the time.' The memory was too much. Her throat tightened and the tears rose.

Georgie gently touched her hand. 'I'm sorry,' she said, 'but, right or wrong, there are times when we all have to make choices. Tomorrow morning I'm going to tell Miss Davis what my mother tried to make me do. I know I'll never be allowed to go home again, but I don't care. That's *my* choice.'

She hesitated then went on, 'What your mother did was *her* choice. You have to accept that, Kitty, or it'll drive you mad.'

Kitty couldn't speak for a minute. She swallowed her tears. 'I wish she hadn't done it, though. I miss her so much.' Funny how she didn't miss her father.

'Would you rather she'd lived a lie like that other unhappy couple?'

'I don't know.' Kitty wondered why it had to be one way or

the other. 'But why couldn't she have run away? Why didn't she find some place for me and her to live? We would have been happy ... without *him*.'

'Only your mother could answer those questions, so we'll never know, will we? Maybe she did try other ways. Maybe she loved your daddy too much to leave him ... but couldn't live with him any longer. Maybe they talked about it and he threatened to take you away from her. Who knows what goes on in somebody's mind?'

Sensing Kitty's distress, Georgie brightened her voice and smiled cheerily. 'Anyway, you're here now, and I'm going to take good care of you, so buck up, eh? You and me have each other, don't we?'

'I'm glad you're here.'

'You might not be when I start to get bossy.'

'I hope you don't get fostered again.' Kitty felt so comfortable with this delightful person, almost as though she had known her all her life.

'Not much chance of that, thank God! To be honest I'm not fourteen yet, but it's near enough and nobody wants to take on that sort of responsibility. Besides, in a little over two years' time I'll be on my own. They throw you out when you're sixteen.' With that she bade Kitty goodnight. 'I won't be too far away ... just four beds down from you. Sleep tight. See you in the morning.'

Kitty lay in bed, her eyes turned towards that capable figure as it made its way down the room. 'Goodnight, Georgie,' she murmured. Then she turned over and closed her eyes. For the first time in a long while her young heart was quiet. She had the feeling of being wanted, of being warm and belonging. Tomorrow she would see Georgie again, and the morning couldn't come too soon.

Miss Davis entered the dining room with the two bullies in tow. Her stern face told its own story. 'When you've had your breakfast, I'll see the pair of you in my office.' She waited for them to be seated then swung round and marched out. 'Old cow!' muttered the dark-haired girl. 'Big mouth Rogers!' grumbled the other. 'I bet it was her who split on us.'

'That's right.' They didn't see Georgie come in. 'I told her what you did. Want to do something about it, do you?'

'Why don't you piss off?' suggested the blonde.

'Better still, drop dead!' snapped the other.

Georgina's reply was light-hearted and infuriating. 'I reckon you two are slipping,' she said, 'Kitty Marsh is only half your size, but she gave you a real fight, didn't she, eh?' Grinning as she brushed by, she added insult to injury. 'I hope your arse is sore where she kicked it.'

Catching sight of Kitty, who had watched the little fracas, she collected her breakfast tray and made her way to the table. 'Sleep well, did you?' she asked. Setting her tray on the table, Georgie began on her scrambled eggs until a stern glance from Dorothy Picton prompted her to take the plate off the tray. 'They'll be watching us like hawks today. The place has to be spick and span when we have callers,' she told Kitty. Aware that Miss Picton was still watching, she put the tray on the floor beside her chair, out of everyone's way. 'It's visiting day today,' she explained. 'Is anyone coming to see you?'

Kitty shook her head. 'Nobody's said anything to me. Anyway, there's only my aunt, and she won't want to see me.' In fact, since the court had committed her to the care of the authorities, Kitty had neither seen nor heard from her Aunt Mildred.

'What about friends?' Georgie dropped a sausage on the floor and kicked it under the table.

Kitty could hardly stifle her laughter when another girl kicked the sausage back and Georgie indulged in a game of footsie. 'There's only Sarah – and Harry.' Just the sound of his name on her lips made her young heart glow.

Georgie was all ears. 'Oh! A boyfriend, eh?' she teased. 'What's he like . . . this Harry?'

A pink blush suffused Kitty's cheeks. 'He's not my boyfriend.' She had never thought of him that way before, but now the idea was thrilling.

'If you say so, but I still want to know what he's like.' She playfully dug Kitty in the ribs. 'I'm naturally nosy, you'll have to get used to that.'

Kitty had been eating a piece of toast, but now she replaced it on her plate and let images of Harry flood her mind. 'He's really nice, and he's got these dark eyes that crinkle when he laughs.' She missed him almost as much as she missed her mother, but in a different way. 'He's got thick black hair and it's always in a mess.'

'Good-looking, is he?'

'I think he is.'

'Tall?'

Kitty remembered when Harry teased her by saying he could tuck her under his armpit, and related the incident to Georgie. 'We were fishing in the brook. I slipped into the rushes and he carried me out.'

'Sounds romantic to me.'

Kitty blushed again. 'He makes me laugh.'

'Older than you, is he?'

'He's fifteen.'

'Do you think he'll come to see you?'

Kitty's smile fell away. 'I don't think so. His dad doesn't like me.'

Georgie scooped up a forkful of scrambled egg, swilling it down with a gulp of tea. Grimacing, she asked Kitty, 'Do you want to know what *I* think?'

'Yes.' Kitty took a gulp of her tea and realised why Georgie had grimaced. 'Ooh! It's stone cold!'

'I think your Harry will try and see you, whatever his dad says.' Taking her tray from the floor, she put the soiled crockery on it. 'Do as I do,' she said. 'And for God's sake don't drop the tray or we'll have to wash the floor from one end to the other.'

Georgie was right. At four-thirty that afternoon, Kitty was sent for by Miss Davis. 'Go to the day room, Kitty . . . there's some-one to see you.'

She couldn't believe her ears. 'Who is it?'

'Get along and you'll find out.' Ushering her out of the door, Miss Davis reminded her, 'Visiting finishes at five o clock. That gives you half an hour. Miss Picton is already in there. She'll see to you.'

'Over there,' said Miss Picton, pointing to the far end of the room. 'If you need me, I'll be here.' She sat down again and left Kitty to find her visitors.

The lounge was full to bursting; outsiders and inmates had taken almost every available chair, and at first Kitty couldn't see who had taken the trouble to visit her. Weaving her way in and out of the furniture, she made her way to the far end of the room.

'Kitty!' The voice was thrillingly familiar. She raised her eyes and there he was, tall and good-looking just as she had described him to Georgie. 'Kitty, it's good to see you!' He had her in his arms and they were hugging. She was crying and he was laughing, and his dark eyes drank her in. 'Oh, Kitty! I thought I'd never see you again!'

Kitty clung to him for a full minute before she saw Linda Jenkins out of the corner of her eye. The sobering glance she received made her step back a pace.

'Sarah won't be coming,' she murmured as they walked over to his mother. 'She's got a touch of flu and didn't want to spread it.'

'That was thoughtful.'

'How are you, Kitty?' Linda Jenkins felt ill at ease. She wouldn't have come, only Harry had threatened to visit Kitty on his own if she refused. As it was, his father had warned her against it. 'Best to keep out of it,' said Ron. 'I knew all along there would be trouble in that family.'

'I'm all right,' Kitty answered. 'Only I don't like this place much.'

Harry was troubled. Turning to his mother, he asked softly, 'Why can't you persuade Dad to have Kitty with us?'

'You know very well why!' They had been through this so many times, and each time Linda found her son and herself growing further apart. 'Your father won't hear of it, that's why.'

Sensing a disturbing undercurrent, Kitty intervened. 'It's all right, Harry . . . really. The people here are nice and I've made a friend. Her name is Georgie.'

Grateful for the reprieve, Linda remarked, 'That's nice, dear. And have you got your own room?'

Kitty shook her head. 'No, but we have our own little area, with a comfortable bed, and a bedside cupboard and locker.' She didn't want to talk about these unimportant things. She wanted to talk about her parents, and how her whole world had been turned upside down. She wanted to tell them that she wished everything could be the same again, even the rowing. Now it was all different, her parents were gone, she was in here, and she could never go back.

As though he could read Kitty's thoughts, Harry asked, 'Has anyone else come to see you ... a solicitor or someone like that?'

She shook her head. 'No.'

'So they haven't told you about the house? Or your dad's business?'

'No.' Kitty was intrigued. 'What about them?'

Linda interrupted. 'I don't think we should be worrying Kitty about all that,' she said, giving her son a warning glance. 'It's for the authorities to tell her.'

'Well, they haven't told her yet, and she has a right to know.' Addressing himself to Kitty he told her, 'Your Aunt Mildred showed an estate agent round the house. He was taking pictures and everything. Then yesterday she went to the garage and spoke to the manager. He told my dad she was after selling the business.' His brown eyes grew serious. 'I thought she would have told you all about it?'

'Be careful what you say, son.' Linda was more concerned about what her husband would say. 'Your father told me that in confidence. We can't be certain what Kitty's aunt is up to.'

'She's up to no good, that's what she's up to!' Urging Kitty to think about it, he added softly, 'By rights it's all yours ... the business and everything else. It's strange that your aunt hasn't even been to see you.'

A bell sounded, and Linda stood up thankfully. 'Looks like they're chucking us out, dear,' she told Kitty. 'I don't know if we'll be able to make another visit, but take care of yourself anyway.' Gathering her bag, she joined the visitors heading towards the door. 'Come on, Harry,' she called impatiently. 'We've a bus to catch.'

In fact the bus wasn't due for another fifteen minutes, but after what her son had told Kitty, she couldn't get out of there quick enough. For once her husband was right. Least said, soonest mended in this case.

Harry held on to Kitty's hand far longer than he should have. 'Oh, Kitty, it's not the same without you,' he said. 'Every time there's a knock on the door, I'm hoping it might be you.'

Her heart ached. 'One day it will be,' she promised.

'Are they really taking care of you in here?'

'I suppose so.'

'And are you getting over it ...?' He hesitated, not wanting

36

to mention it, but knowing it had to be brought out in the open '. . . your mum and dad and everything?' He squeezed her hand and it gave her courage.

'It wasn't my fault, was it, Harry?' She had to believe that.

He shook his head and his smile warmed her. 'No, Kitty. You mustn't think it was your fault. Your mum and dad did what they wanted to do. I don't believe anything you said would have made any difference.'

'Georgie told me that.'

'Then she really is a friend.'

'You'll like her.'

'I like her already.'

'Harry?'

He didn't speak, but inclined his head to one side. His gaze was enough.

Kitty's heart was racing. She didn't want him to go, but neither did she want him to stay. This place was *her* punishment, not his. 'Do you think I'm too young?'

'Too young?' Not quite certain what she meant, he quietly regarded her. He had always thought Kitty very beautiful, with her dark hair and wonderful eyes. She was gentle in nature, with a sense of humour and a strong bold heart, yet she had a certain vulnerability that made him feel protective towards her . . . made him feel like a man. 'Too young for *what*, Kitty?'

Her grip tightened in his, and her eyes clouded over. 'I don't know,' she replied softly. 'Only I don't *feel* too young.' She paused to assemble her thoughts. 'I feel lost, and afraid. Sometimes I cry myself to sleep like a baby. But I don't feel too young.' In fact she felt old, almost as though her life had already been lived.

When she shuddered, he took her in his arms. 'You've been through a lot, Kitty,' he reminded her. 'It's no wonder you're lost and afraid.' Easing her from him, he looked down into her face. 'What if I told you *I* cried myself to sleep?' It was difficult for him to confess that fact to anyone, let alone Kitty. But if it helped her then he could swallow his pride. 'I cried once when they took you away, and again last night when I knew I was coming to see you.'

Kitty was so astonished she laughed and cried at the same time.

'So you see, you're not alone, and you've nothing to be

37

ashamed of.' Placing the tips of his fingers under her chin he raised her gaze to his. 'And, for whatever reason you need to ask . . . you are *not* too young.' It seemed all his life he had loved her, and never more than in that moment when she looked up at him with soft dark eyes.

'Will you come and see me again, Harry?' If he said no, she couldn't bear it.

'Try and stop me.'

'Your dad might try and stop you. He doesn't like me.'

'No one will stop me from seeing you, Kitty.' His voice was hard. She had never heard him talk like that before.

'Goodbye, Harry.' Reaching up, she meant to kiss him on the cheek.

He held her away for a moment, then bent his head and kissed her full on the mouth. 'Goodbye, Kitty,' he whispered. 'I love you.'

Long after he'd gone, those words echoed in her head. 'I love you', he'd said. Did he mean he loved her like a friend? Did he mean he loved her because he was sorry for all that had happened to bring her here to this place? Did he mean he loved her like a brother? Or did he mean he loved her in the way grown-ups loved each other? She wasn't sure she wanted that. After all grown-ups started out loving, and ended up hating.

Kitty decided to take Harry's love as being the love of a friend. Yet, deep down, somewhere so deep she could barely recognise it, Kitty sensed that the love between her and Harry would carry them through all the years. She knew instinctively that what they had would never turn to hate, and that somehow the same strong love that flowed between them now would endure and survive, in spite of any obstacles life might put in their way.

From now on, that would be Kitty's dream . . . that one day, she and Harry would be together for all time. It was to be a dream that would light her way through the darkest years to come.

PART TWO

1977

Chances

CHAPTER FOUR

'I have some good news for you, Kitty.' Miss Davis had a soft spot for Kitty but knew better than to show it in front of the other children. Leading her to the far end of the television room where they could sit quietly, she handed Kitty a letter. 'Read it,' she urged, her face beaming from ear to ear.

Intrigued, Kitty glanced at the envelope. 'But it's addressed to you.'

'Ah, yes! But it's to do with *you*, my dear.' Retrieving the envelope, she withdrew the letter from it. 'There! Now read it and tell me what you think?' Holding out the letter, she waited for Kitty to take it from her.

Something in Miss Davis's manner told Kitty the letter contained news she had been fearing. 'It's from *them*, isn't it?' Her heart sank at the reply.

'If you mean Mr and Mrs Connor, then yes, it is.' Her smile stiffened then disappeared altogether as Kitty's expression told its own story. 'I see.' Miss Davis stared into Kitty's face, her voice stern as she instructed, 'I think you had better come into my office.' With that she stood up and marched away.

Kitty reluctantly followed. As she walked past the group of children clustered round the television, she caught Georgie's attention. The two smiled at each other. 'Keep your pecker up, gal!' Georgie whispered harshly. And Kitty was encouraged.

'Now then, my dear.' Miss Davis sat behind her desk and Kitty sat before it. 'Explain yourself. I really thought you would be delighted that Mr and Mrs Connor have agreed to foster you.'

Not wanting to seem ungrateful, Kitty thought carefully about her answer. She looked at Miss Davis and was momentarily distracted by the sheer volume of that great body squashed into

41

the confines of an upright chair. 'I'm sorry, Miss Davis,' she answered, 'but I don't want to be fostered out.'

Miss Davis nodded her head for what seemed an extraordinarily long time. Then she sat still, cleared her throat and, just when Kitty was sure she would speak, began nodding again. It was unnerving.

'So!' The nodding stopped and Kitty was immensely thankful. 'Are you saying you don't want to be fostered out at all ... or is it that you don't want to be fostered out to Mr and Mrs Connor in particular?' She leaned over her desk, folded her blubbery arms and stared at Kitty through her little spectacles.

Kitty had been dreading this day, and now it was here, she felt trapped. 'I'm happy where I am,' she replied. 'Please don't send me away to strangers.' It had taken many months for Kitty to get used to living in this communal situation. Now she was settled, the idea of change was frightening.

'I don't understand you, Kitty.' Miss Davis was shaking her head now. 'You've been with us for nearly two years. Surely you want to be with a proper family?'

'They're not *my* family.' Her family was dead. Though she missed her mother every minute of every day, she had got used to being without her. There could be no substitute.

Miss Davis was undeterred. 'You've met Mr and Mrs Connor three times already. You knew there was a strong possibility that they would be the ones to foster you. You said you liked them, and you know that they have a son just a year older than you. When he came with them on the visits, I really thought you got on well together.' She frowned. 'You did *like* Adam Connor, didn't you, Kitty?'

'He was all right, I suppose.' Anxious not to seem ungrateful or churlish, she didn't reveal she thought the boy a little strange. Even though he chatted to her and smiled at everything she said, he still managed to make her feel unwanted.

Obviously relieved, Miss Davis took in such a great gulp of air that her chest swelled to twice its size. 'Oh, Kitty! Just think how wonderful it would be if you could go to the family before the end of this month ... in time to celebrate your fourteenth birthday.'

'I'd rather be here, with Georgie.'

Patience was growing thin by now. 'Listen to me, my dear.' After waiting for Kitty to raise her gaze and pay full attention,

Miss Davis went on in a firm voice, 'In just a few weeks' time, on her sixteenth birthday, Georgie Rogers will be leaving this establishment herself. It seems to me that it's also the ideal time for you to make a new life as well. You know that most people prefer babies or toddlers, and that's why I'm so pleased for you, Kitty. Mr and Mrs Connor have been carefully vetted. The authorities won't keep you here when there is a perfectly suitable couple willing to foster you. This is your chance to be part of a family . . . maybe your *only* chance.' Her face softened. 'You do realise you may not have any choice in the matter?'

Kitty thought about what Georgie had told her, that she had been deliberately bad just to get back here. She didn't see herself resorting to that, but Miss Davis was wrong when she said there was no choice.

'Please . . . I don't want to go to strangers.' She felt as though she was pleading for her life.

'But *we* were all strangers when you first came here, and you've grown to like us, haven't you?'

'Yes, but I was unhappy for a long time.'

Miss Davis came round the desk. She paced up and down behind Kitty before coming to sit on the edge. The desk groaned and creaked, and Kitty thought it would end up in a heap on the floor.

'Kitty?'

'Yes, Miss Davis?'

'I hope Georgie hasn't been saying anything to make you afraid?'

Kitty held her tongue. If she let it loose it was bound to tell a lie.

'Ah! I thought as much.' Miss Davis made a mental note to speak to Georgie at the first opportunity. 'I am well aware of the disastrous fostering she experienced – although it was largely her own fault, as I'm sure she has told you.'

Again, Kitty was silent.

'You do trust me, don't you?'

Kitty thought a moment. She *had* come to trust Miss Davis, but how could she trust her now when she was trying to send her away? 'I suppose so.'

'Do you recall when you were brought before the assessment board last year?'

'Yes.' She hadn't liked that at all. Those people meant well, but they didn't know how she felt. No one did . . . except maybe Harry, and Georgie.

'I know you resented being brought before the board, but it was only for your own good. Their job is to match you with a couple they believe you will be happy with. They had to ask questions, to get to know you as best they could, so they could make the right decision concerning your future. You do understand that, don't you, Kitty?'

'Yes, I understand that.'

Miss Davis gave a sigh of relief. 'We're all here to help you, Kitty.'

'Yes, Miss Davis.' Kitty kept her gaze on the floor. She didn't want to look up, afraid to acknowledge that she might be sent away against her will.

Returning to her chair, Miss Davis maddened Kitty by drumming her fingers on the desk-top. Her head was down, and her chin buried in the fleshy folds of her neck as she peeped at Kitty over the rims of her spectacles. 'I really thought you would be as delighted as I am at this news.'

'I'm sorry. And I *do* like the Connors,' Kitty admitted. 'It's just that I don't want to live with them.'

There was a moment then, during which Kitty looked at the carpet and Miss Davis looked at her. This lovely girl had come to her frightened and lonely, having seen her own mother leap to her death then her father set fire to the house, yet even in the act of destroying himself, save his only daughter's life.

This tragic sequence of events had brought the child to this place where Miss Davis, without being drawn into an emotional trap that could only hurt her too, had cared for Kitty with as much love and attention as she could rightfully give.

Now the child had blossomed into a young woman with a dark and sensuous beauty that might even yet be her downfall. Kitty was not tall, neither was she short; she was petite and feminine, with a perfect little figure and a graciousness that caught the eye. With that rich black hair and magnificent glowing brown eyes, she stood out in a crowd.

Unsettled by the prolonged span of silence, Kitty spoke her fears. 'Will they make me go against my will?'

The woman was suddenly afraid for the child. But her answer was dictated to her by higher authorities. 'We'll have to see,' she answered warily. 'We mustn't forget you've been here almost two years now. You are still a minor, and someone has to take responsibility for you. The Connors have offered you a good home. I believe we would *all* be failing in our duty if we didn't at least give it a try... and that includes you, Kitty.'

'Can I please go now?'

'For the moment.' She waved a hand and looked away. Sometimes this job could get to you.

Days came and went and soon it was Friday. As usual, Kitty said cheerio to her schoolmates and ran the half-mile to the factory where Georgie worked. The house-rules didn't allow Kitty to make any detours from school, but if she ran really fast, she could reach the factory and be back with Georgie before anyone realised she was a few minutes late.

Her friend was watching out for her. 'I won't be long,' she called through an upper window.

Kitty sat on the low wall that fronted the factory. Here in this pleasant white-painted building, they made plastic macs, rubber diving suits, and all manner of containers. When Kitty asked Georgie how she liked working there, she answered, 'We throw things about and have a laugh, and there's a bloke who works in the cutting-room who fancies me rotten... he'd give anything to get his leg over.'

You never got a proper answer from Georgie, so Kitty took it all with a pinch of salt.

While Kitty waited, the March breeze blew a sheet of newspaper down the street. When it attached itself to her leg, she picked it up and began to read. She was still reading when Georgie crept up behind her and shouted: 'BOO!' Kitty nearly jumped out of her skin. 'You're wicked,' she laughed.

'What's that you're reading, gal?'

'It's a newspaper, and it's two months old,' Kitty told her. 'It must have blown out of one of those rubbish bins.' She pointed to a row of giant bins standing in a yard some short distance away; one of them had a lid missing. 'It's all about politics,' groaned Kitty. Pointing to one headline, she read out, 'Riots in Cairo,' and another announced, 'Jimmy Carter Sworn in as 39th President of the US'.

Peeping over Kitty's shoulder at the newspaper, Georgie was

open-mouthed at the sight of a big-breasted woman advertising bras. 'Bloody hell, gal!' she cried. 'Look at them boobs! I wouldn't want to get caught in the eye with one of them.'

They laughed all the way back, and they laughed as they went up the stairs to get washed and changed. They were still chuckling as they came down to the dining room, and light-hearted when the meal was over. However, when everyone settled down to watch television or play a game of snooker, Kitty drew Georgie to the far end of the room where they sat talking until the bell summoned them for bed.

'Have you heard anything more about the Connor family?' Georgie asked anxiously.

Kitty's spirits fell. She had tried so hard to put all that out of her mind, but there was no escaping it. 'Miss Picton told me just now,' she revealed, 'I'm to report to Miss Davis at ten o'clock in the morning.' She had butterflies in her stomach just talking about it.

Georgie was philosophical as usual. 'Don't think the worst,' she pleaded. 'Maybe she just wants to tell you the Connors don't want you after all?'

Kitty didn't argue the point, but she instinctively felt there was more to it than that. 'What about you?' she asked, deliberately changing the subject. 'Did the foreman say you can stay on permanently when you leave here?'

Georgie made a face. 'No such luck,' she groaned. Sticking her stomach out, she flared her nostrils and mimicked the foreman's gruff voice. 'It's no good you asking me for permanent work, 'cause I ain't got enough to keep me regulars going, never mind tekking on a daft bugger like you.'

Kitty shook with laughter. Last week the foreman had chased her out of the factory grounds, so she knew Georgie had portrayed him to perfection. 'I'm sorry,' she apologised, 'you really wanted that job, didn't you?'

Georgie shrugged. 'So what, gal? I'll get another. If I don't they'll keep me here, and I don't want that.'

'Would it be so awful?'

'Bloody terrible!'

'It's funny, don't you think?' Kitty thought she had come to terms with Georgie's leaving, but with every passing day it got harder.

'What's funny?'

'Well ... you and me.' Kitty wasn't sure how to put it, but in the end it came out simply. 'You don't want to stay and I don't want to go.'

'You might be glad to leave if you'd been here as long as me.'

'What will you do?' The thought of that big outside world still terrified Kitty.

Georgie, on the other hand, was thrilled. 'I'll have my own little place ... a one-bed council flat, I expect. Through the week I'll work my fingers to the bone and on a weekend I'll dance the night away and come home with a good-looking fellow on my arm. After a while I'll scrimp and save and buy myself a minibus ... a bright blue one!'

Kitty was fascinated. 'But you can't drive.'

'I'll learn.'

'Then what?'

'Then I'll run people about ... take them on outings and drive them to work. I'll be my own boss. It's what I want more than anything.'

Kitty admired her immensely. 'I'll help you,' she promised. 'When my father's money comes to me, I'll buy you the brightest minibus we can find, then you can teach me to drive as well.'

Georgie shook her head. 'Not you, Kitty gal,' she said. 'I was never a scholar, and I'm no good at anything worthwhile ... but you've got brains. You were meant for better things than driving a mini-bus.'

Kitty had only one ambition in life. 'I just want to be happy,' she said. It was enough.

Georgie looked into those dark brown eyes and saw something there that was deeply humbling; there was loneliness and pain, of a kind that even their close friendship had not altogether erased. She knew her friend's background, and understood better than anyone why Kitty wanted nothing but to be happy. 'If anyone deserves to be happy, it's you,' she said, and meant every word.

Feeling herself being dragged back into frightening memories, Kitty put on her brightest voice. 'I had two letters today.'

Georgie made a face. 'It's all right for some.' Tugging at Kitty's arm, she asked, 'Come on then ... who are they from? What do they say?'

Digging into her pocket, Kitty withdrew the letters. 'You can read them if you like,' she said, handing them over. 'I don't mind.'

Georgie groaned. 'How can you ask me to exert myself, gal? I've been working behind that bloody machine all day. My legs ache, my arms feel like lead weights and besides,' she grinned sheepishly, 'you know I'm not all that good at reading.'

'Okay, I'll tell you what they say.' Kitty knew every word off by heart. She proceeded to return the letters to her pocket.

'No.' Georgie tugged at her arm again. 'Don't *tell* me, gal.' Leaning back in the chair, she made herself comfortable and closed her eyes. 'Go on then. *Read* the buggers to me.'

Kitty opened the first one. It was from her Aunt Mildred. In a low voice she read the whole letter out:

Dear Kitty,

I'm sorry I haven't written in a while, but I know you will understand when I tell you how ill I've been. All week I was laid up with the most awful flu, and I'm still full of a cough so I'm afraid I won't be able to visit as promised.

Anyway, I thought I should write and tell you that everything is fine. As I explained in my last letter, most of the proceeds from the sale of your father's house and business are safely put away. Of course there have been some expenses, and as trustee I have had to use some of the money to get the best possible financial advice. These things are never cheap. But you mustn't worry, I'm looking after your interests.

Miss Davis has kept me informed of the situation concerning your fostering. I am also told that you seem reluctant to go. I must say I think you're being ungrateful. The family sound just the right sort of people to help you get back into society. You know I would love to have you with me. Unfortunately, it isn't possible and never will be.

I'll have to end here. I feel quite ill. I have no idea whether I'll be able to see you before you're fostered out, and I certainly won't see you afterwards. But I'll be thinking of you.

From your Aunt Mildred

'Old cow!' Georgie sat up, her eyes glittering angrily. 'Why don't you write back and tell her you don't care if she's ill? Tell her you don't bloody well care if she drops dead as long as she leaves your money behind ... what's left of it, that is.'

'Do you really think she's stealing my father's money?' Kitty herself had long suspected that might be the case.

'Stealing *your* money ... not your father's any more, is it? And all that claptrap about wanting to have you with her but it not being possible ... she's lying through her teeth. The bugger never did want you.' Suddenly aware that she was hurting Kitty, she apologised. 'Sorry, gal. My tongue will hang me one of these days.'

Kitty was under no illusions where her aunt was concerned. 'It's all right,' she murmured. 'Everything you say is true. She's been promising to see me ever since I've been in here, but in almost two years I've had only three letters from her. She's never set foot inside this place ... not once. Even when I was brought before the assessment board she sent a message saying she was too ill to attend.'

For too long now Kitty had turned a blind eye. Now, though, she took a moment to let the truth sink in. 'She could have had me with her from the start. She made excuses then and she's been making excuses ever since. At first it hurt like mad. Now it doesn't hurt so much. If she doesn't want me, there's no use pining over it, is there?'

Stretching out her arms, Georgie entreated, 'Come here, gal.'

Kitty fell into her embrace. She didn't speak. Mildred's letter was stark in her mind and she was too full for words.

Georgie spoke, though, and what she said lightened Kitty's heart. 'Who cares if the old bugger don't want you, eh?' she declared. '*I* do, so you stick with me, gal and to hell with everybody else!'

'Georgie?'

'What?'

'Do *you* think I'm being ungrateful, not wanting to go to the Connor family?' Easing herself out of Georgie's embrace, she looked her straight in the eye. 'Tell me the truth.'

'Well, if you really want the truth, I'd say you'll be sent anyway, so you might as well give it a damn good try.'

'What if I don't like it?'

'Do what I did and kick up holy hell. They'll have you on

your way before your feet touch the ground ... with your bags packed and a label stuck to your arse saying: DON'T CALL US, WE'LL CALL YOU.'

Kitty smiled at that, then she giggled, and soon the two of them were roaring with laughter. Someone at the far end of the room yelled, 'Shut your gobs! We can't hear the telly!' That only made them laugh all the more and, under orders from Mrs Austin, they were marched upstairs.

In the dormitory they fell on Kitty's bed, laughing so hard the tears spilled down their faces. 'I don't think I want a label pinned to my arse,' Kitty spluttered. Georgie was so shocked at hearing her friend use bad language she erupted into a fresh bout of giggles.

When the laughter had run its course and they were calmer, Kitty remarked, 'I expect you want to know who sent the other letter?'

'Let me guess.' Lying back on the bed, Georgie pretended to be thinking. Presently she said, 'Is it to do with money?'

'No.' Kitty was enjoying the game.

'You've won a car and you're going to swap it for a blue minibus?'

'No. But if I *had* won a car, I would let you have it, and you could swap it for whatever you wanted.' Lying on her tummy she watched Georgie's changing expressions with twinkling dark eyes. How she loved it when it was just the two of them and they could tell each other their darkest secrets.

'I know! The Connors are bribing you with a trip to Disneyworld in Florida?'

'I wouldn't go if they did ... at least not until I knew them better.'

'All right then ... that letter is from a tall good-looking sex-starved bloke, with dark smouldering eyes and shoulders like a bull elephant ... and he's looking for someone like me?'

'You're wrong ... and right.' Now Kitty was teasing.

'Ah! I'm getting warm then?' Georgie sat up. 'Go on then. Which bits are right and which bits are wrong?'

'He's tall and good-looking.' In her mind's eye Kitty could see him so clearly her heart was pounding. 'He has broad shoulders ... and dark smouldering eyes.'

'But he's not sex-starved, eh?' Georgie winked. She knew

exactly who Kitty's letter was from. 'And he's not looking for someone like me?'

'He might be. How would I know?'

'Well, gal, put it like this... why would he be looking for someone like me when he can have a raving beauty like you?'

Kitty blushed to the roots of her hair. 'Me and Harry are friends, that's all,' she protested. But her face told another tale.

'Listen, gal. I've seen the way he looks at you on visiting day, and I can tell you that is not the look of a friend.' Georgie winked cheekily. 'More the look of a lover, I'd say.'

'Oh, Georgie. You *know* Harry isn't my lover.' In her dreams he was, but she would never tell. 'Anyway, I'd need to be two years older or he'd be arrested.' She summoned the courage to mention something that had lately been on her mind. 'Does it hurt?' Blushing pink she persisted, 'You know... when a man does *that*... is it very painful?'

Georgie was visibly surprised; she was also wary. 'You're asking me, Kitty gal, and you know I'm not quite sixteen, so I shouldn't have done *it* either.'

'But you have, haven't you?' Lowering her voice to a whisper, Kitty leaned closer. 'You can tell me. I won't say anything. It's just that I'd like to know.'

Glancing up and down the room and seeing that they were still alone, Georgie admitted softly, 'All right then, yes, I have done it, but I don't know if it hurts first time because I was pissed out of my mind... it was when I ran away from the first foster home and got mixed up with this bloke. A fairground helper, he was, and ooh! You should have seen him, gal... muscles like Popeye and golden hair down to his waist. He looked like one of them Greek gods.' She took a moment to savour the memory then went on, 'Anyway, he took me to some party and we all got drunk. I woke up the next morning with my legs covered in blood and a used French letter lying on the bedroom floor . . . 'course I knew what had happened straightaway.'

'Have you seen him since?'

'Naw. The bugger were gone when I woke up, and I ain't seen hide nor hair of him since.' She giggled and lowered her voice until it was almost inaudible. 'I was scared stiff the woman of the house would come home and call the police... I was on the run, remember? There were people lying all over the place, some of 'em stark naked. I washed, dressed, and got out of there before anyone saw me.'

'So you didn't remember anything about it? I mean . . . with him?' Kitty was disappointed.

'I couldn't remember that particular time. But I can remember every single time since.'

'Tell me?'

'Well . . . there was the son of that second couple who fostered me. His name was Jack, and he had a cock like a hammer.' Her eyes rolled as she went on, 'He was twenty-two . . . a nice bloke as I recall. Trouble was, he took too much of a shine to me . . . began to think I was his own private property. In the end I threatened to tell the authorities.'

'And did you?'

'No. I just ran away.'

'What was it like . . . with him, I mean?'

'It was all right, I suppose. Same as with the one afterwards . . . their plonker pushes its way in and you get a kind of tickling feeling. Afterwards, you feel tired and excited all at the same time. It doesn't hurt, not really. Mind you, I wasn't a virgin any more, so I expect that helped.' She lay back on the bed again. 'I know a lot about men,' she confessed. 'I know how bad they can be, and I know how good they can be. I know they can hurt you if they want, and I know they can make you feel like a princess too.'

Kitty was swamped with memories of her parents. 'My dad was like that,' she said. 'Sometimes he made my mother laugh, but more often he made her cry.'

'That's what I mean, gal. And if you've any sense, you'll steer clear of men who make you cry . . . the bullies, I mean . . . the ones who only know how to use their fists.' She gave Kitty a strange look, 'Do you think Harry would ever use his fists?'

'Never!' If Kitty was certain of anything, she was certain of that.

'How do you know?'

'I just know, that's all.'

'Would you like Harry to make love to you?' Rolling sideways, Georgie looked up into Kitty's blushing face. 'Tell the truth, shame the devil,' she said mischievously. 'You love him like mad, don't you?'

It took Kitty a moment to gather her courage, but when she spoke it was with a conviction that surprised the other girl. 'If loving is wanting to be with him all the time ... if it means going to sleep thinking of him and waking up the same way ... if loving is a feeling that hurts and makes you feel lonely and happy all at the same time, then yes, Georgie, I *do* love Harry. So much it frightens me.'

Georgie's smile was knowing, yet compassionate. 'There's no doubt about it, gal, you're in love.' Her expression grew serious. 'But you shouldn't be frightened of loving someone.' Knowing the roots of Kitty's fear, she could understand. 'Look, gal ... all marriages don't end up wrong. Some last for a lifetime. If you think Harry's right for you, and if he feels the same, then you shouldn't let anything come between you. On the other hand, if you really *are* frightened and think it might all go wrong, it might be best if you ran a mile.' An old look came over her young face. ''Cause when a man and woman get together, there are no guarantees.'

'This will be the last letter I'll get from him,' she said sadly. 'He and I might long to be together one day, but I don't think it can happen. I'm going to live with strangers, and he's going to university.'

'Does he *say* it will be the last letter?'

'No.' Kitty was already hardening her heart to the inevitable. 'But don't you see, we'll be worlds apart?'

'Read the letter to me, gal. Unless it's too private?'

Kitty shook her head. 'It's all right.' While she unfolded the letter, Georgie lay down and closed her eyes. Her sense of mischief returning, she pleaded, 'I'm very sensitive, and I've been brought up proper, so you'd better miss out the naughty bits ... like the one where he wants to rip your clothes off and have his wicked way with you.'

Shaking her head, but loving Georgie all the more for her naughty sense of humour, Kitty began:

'Dearest Kitty ...'

Georgie made a loud sighing noise. 'See that? Uncontrollable passion right from the start!'

'Do you want me to read it or not?'

'Go on then.'

Kitty cleared her throat and started again. This time Georgie was silenced by the soft tremor in her voice:

Dearest Kitty,

It's been a whole month since I came to see you. I don't mind telling you, it has been the longest month of my life, and I can't wait to see you again.

I hope everything is well with you? I've been thinking about our last meeting, and all the things we talked about. I hope your Aunt Mildred has been to see you, and put your mind at rest, and I hope Georgie hasn't left yet. She's a good friend, Kitty, and I know you will miss her when she's gone.

'Nice to know I'm appreciated,' Georgie muttered.

Exasperated, Kitty warned, 'One more interruption and I'll put the letter away.'

'Sorry, gal. Go on.'

'Right . . .' Returning her attention to the letter, Kitty prepared to read.

'Go on! Go on!'

'I've lost my place now!' Scanning the lines she found the point at which she was interrupted. With a wary glance at Georgie, she carried on:-

I never realised Wales was so beautiful. This morning we went mountain-climbing. Two of the blokes got into difficulties and we had to make a detour.

We're shifting base soon. While I write this, my tent is being pulled down round my ears! I should be back home next Thursday, then it's the first train Friday to London . . . and the dreaded interview at university. Keep your fingers crossed!

Kitty paused here, her face hot with pleasure, 'Why have you stopped, gal?' Georgie demanded. Peeking out of one eye she teased, 'Ah! This is where he goes crazy to throw you on the bed, eh?'

'Don't be daft!' Curling into a little ball and hiding her face from Georgie's prying eyes, Kitty recommenced:

I hope I get a place, Kitty, because I have big plans for the future, and you shouldn't be surprised if I say they include you.

Take care of yourself. I'll see you Saturday week. Miss you.

Harry
XXX

They were both subdued by the warm tone of the letter. After a while Georgie told Kitty she was lucky to have someone like Harry; Kitty assured her she knew that already.

In fact, Harry's letters brought her a deal of comfort. She kept them close; a small bundle tied with pretty pink ribbon, never too far away that she couldn't reach out her hand and touch them. She read them over and over, until they were dog-eared and creased. After a time she didn't need to read them because every word was etched on her heart.

Kitty was summoned to the office. 'It's all arranged,' Miss Davis informed her. 'From the time you've already spent with the Connor family, we are satisfied you will fit in very well. There are just a few loose ends to be tied up before you move in with them altogether.' She saw the light go from Kitty's eyes and sensed the struggle inside her. 'I realise it will be hard at first,' she acknowledged, 'but I hope you'll soon come to see them as family. Please, Kitty, for your own sake, give it your very best.'

'I'll try hard.' She had already promised herself that much.

'I do know how difficult it will be for you,' Miss Davis had seen it all before, 'and I know you don't really want to go, but think how it would feel if no one wanted you, Kitty. Think what it would be like if you had to spend another two years in this place. You're being offered a real home.' Her voice softened. 'I don't think I need to tell you, there are children here who would give anything to be part of a real family.'

Ashamed, Kitty recalled what Georgie had said: 'You might as well give it a damn' good try, gal.' Taking a deep breath she declared, 'I'll try not to let you down.'

Relieved, Miss Davis gave her some other news; delightful news that made Kitty smile. 'I'm planning a party for you and Georgie Rogers. It isn't often we have two girls leaving more or less together. On top of that, I thought it would be a wonderful idea to celebrate both your birthdays... your fourteenth and her sixteenth. What do you think?'

A party! Kitty's heart raced. 'That would be wonderful!' All her worries momentarily forgotten, her first thought was for Harry. 'When will it be?'

'Well, it will need some organising... a slight juggling of finances, and of course you'll all have to help with the cooking.' She chewed on her lip and thought hard. 'A good day would be Saturday. The following week you and Georgie will leave here and make a fresh start in life.' She beamed widely. 'Yes. Saturday, I think.'

'Could I invite someone?' With Harry here, it would be the best party she could imagine.

Miss Davis misunderstood. 'How thoughtful of you, my dear. Yes, I'm sure the Connor family would love to come.'

'I wasn't thinking of the Connor family.'

'Oh?' She looked confused, then her big face lit up. 'Of course! Your Aunt Mildred. Why, yes, if she's well enough.' She had her doubts where that woman was concerned. 'We can ask the Connors too, I'm sure it would be nice for all of you to be together for a time.'

Frustrated, Kitty blurted it out. 'I don't want Aunt Mildred here, and I'd rather the Connors didn't come. It's a party for me and Georgie... because we're going away, and because it's our birthdays.' She was angry and frightened of what lay ahead; all her emotions were churned up. 'I was talking about *Harry*! That's who I would like at the party, and I know Georgie would like him there as well.'

'Ah!' Miss Davis cursed herself for being so insensitive. 'Of course, your friend Harry Jenkins. To be honest, I thought you and he might have outgrown each other. After all, he hasn't been to see you in quite a while.'

'He's been away. But he'll be back in time for the party.' For one awful minute Kitty thought she would refuse. 'Please, Miss Davis. Once I'm gone from here, I'll probably never see him again.'

Normally, Miss Davis would have pointed out that being fostered did not necessarily mean losing your old friends. But there was something so final in Kitty's words that she made no mention of it. Instead she told her, 'Speak to Georgie first, but as far as I'm concerned, your friend Harry will be very welcome.'

There was something here she could not quite put her finger on; a distancing of sorts; the feeling that Kitty had been made to grow up too soon. It saddened her.

All week long there was an atmosphere of excitement. 'The old bugger's had me in that kitchen all night,' Georgie moaned on Friday. 'I've made enough fairy cakes to go all the way round Blackpool Tower and back again!'

'What about me?' Kitty asked. 'I'd much rather be in the kitchen than shopping with Miss Picton.' She couldn't help but smile. 'On Wednesday she lost her purse and last night she forgot the shopping trolley . . . we were getting on the bus when two of the carrier bags split wide open and half the passengers had to help pick up the groceries. The trifles were mangled, two kids ran off with the nuts and crisps, and all the apples for the fruit salad went rolling down the road and under the wheels of a lorry.' At the time it wasn't funny, but whenever she thought about it now, Kitty burst out laughing.

It was midnight. Everyone was lying in bed chattering about the party. The balloons were already blown up and lying on the table in the games room; the food was ready and stacked safely away in the big pantry cupboard; everyone was restless with excitement, and Kitty could hardly wait for tomorrow evening.

'I haven't heard from Harry,' she told Georgie, who was seated on the edge of her bed. 'I hope he turns up.' If he didn't, the party would mean nothing at all. 'It's a pity he moved base and I couldn't get the letter direct to him.'

'You sent the letter to his house, didn't you?'

'Yes, but I've told you his father doesn't like me. If he knew the letter was from me, he wouldn't give it to Harry. He'd burn it more like.'

'Maybe . . . but his *mother* probably picked up the post. She would see he got the letter, so stop worrying.' Georgie stood up and stretched. 'Goodnight then, gal. We'd best get our beauty sleep. Tomorrow we can dance the night away . . . as long as we don't fill ourselves up with them bloody fairy cakes!' As she went to her own bed the cries of other girls could be heard all along the dormitory: 'Bugger you, Rogers!' 'Piss off out of it!' There were shouts and screams as Georgie tweaked their toes and flung their blankets all over the floor, and Kitty couldn't stop laughing.

'Get to bed, you idiot!' she yelled.

Georgie turned, made a V sign, and threw herself on to her bed where she lay reading the juicy bits in a magazine until a fight broke out halfway down the room and she took it on herself to bang two heads together. Dorothy Picton came in and gave everyone a good ticking off. Before she went she turned out all the lights and dared anyone to switch them on again. After that everyone was soon asleep and the air was filled with gentle snoring.

The night wore on and morning lit the sky outside. Kitty hadn't slept much. She was thinking of Harry. There were things she had to say to him. There were other things she could not say to him, and all of it so important she could think of nothing else.

When morning came and she was sitting opposite Georgie at the breakfast table, all the problems that had kept her awake now seemed to Kitty as clear as the day. Harry would understand. If he didn't, then he would have to hurt as much as she did, and there was nothing she could do about that.

'You're quiet, gal.' Georgie had been watching her. 'I know what you're thinking.'

'No, you don't.' Kitty's heart was always lighter whenever Georgie embarked on one of her little games. This time, however, she didn't want Georgie to guess what was on her mind, or she might talk her out of it.

'You're thinking ... how long will it take Georgie Rogers to get rich.'

Kitty shook her head. 'I expect you'll be rich long before me.'

'You're thinking we might not see each other again?'

'I couldn't bear to think that.'

Georgie regarded her for a long minute before she leaned over the table and said in a softer voice, 'I know what's eating you, gal, but you mustn't worry. He'll be here, I know he will.'

Kitty's brown eyes smiled. 'Will you be all right in that flat?'

''Course I will! Goldington Road is in a good area of Bedford, ain't it? And it's not as if I'll be on my own, is it? There's a girl in the flat upstairs, and an old couple behind me. The Social Services are finding me some decent furniture, I'll have my own front door key, I've got a job, and I don't have to answer to anyone.'

'You will stay out of trouble, won't you?'

'I can't promise that, gal.' She winked. 'I'm only kidding. Do you realise this flat will be the first real home I've known . . . apart from being here? I can even take a bloke back if I fancy him. I can stay out or come home, and shut the door if I want to watch telly without all this lot spoiling it with their chatter.' She waved a hand to encompass the other girls at the table. 'So don't you worry your head about me, gal. I'm old and ugly enough to look after myself.' Breaking off a piece of toast, she nibbled at it thoughtfully. 'It's *you* I'm worried about,' she declared.

Kitty didn't want Georgie worrying about her, not when she had enough problems of her own to cope with. 'I'll be all right,' she lied. Without Georgie she would be incredibly lonely. And what she must tell Harry was already causing her a great deal of heartache.

That morning, Kitty and Georgie made their way to Bedford market. They visited every stall and tried on every hat; they teased each other and laughed a lot, and finally made their way back. 'Wait till your Harry sees you in that new dress,' Georgie said. 'You'll knock his eyes out.'

Kitty glowed. 'I can't wait for tonight,' she confessed. 'It's been ages since I saw him.' She thought about Harry, about what he might think of her new outfit, about what he might think of *her*. 'I wonder if he's changed?' she mused aloud.

Georgie laughed. 'How can he have changed?' she demanded, 'People don't change in just a few weeks.'

'*I* have!'

Georgie stared at her, at the petite figure that was now that of a young woman, at the rich bouncy dark hair, and those lovely brown eyes. 'You've grown more beautiful,' she confirmed with some embarrassment.

Kitty was disappointed. 'I didn't mean that,' she said. 'I meant I've changed *inside*.'

'I know what you meant,' Georgie confessed. 'And I know how different you are.'

Kitty climbed on the bus and waited for Georgie to sit near

the window. She sat beside her, quietly mulling over what her friend said. 'Am I really that different?'

Georgie would not be drawn. 'Just "different", that's all.'

Grateful for that much at least, Kitty didn't press her. Instead she wondered how her character had grown and matured. Certainly, there were times when she felt like a stranger to herself. Other times she was that small helpless child who had seen such terrible things they could scar her for life. Kitty was determined that would not happen to her. Yet she could never be sure, never be free.

These past weeks, though, she had felt like a totally different person from the one who had walked along that railway platform with her mother. It wasn't just the years between, nor was it the experiences she had endured since. It went much deeper than that. She had found something within her that craved its own freedom. For the very first time she felt responsible for her own actions. Rightly or wrongly, she could now make limited choices. Soon she would be a woman, out in the world, hopefully a stronger, wiser person. But that was still some time off. Until then she must be led by others. Worse, she had to trust them. That was the hardest thing of all.

During the remainder of the journey, neither girl said much that mattered. They chatted about the party, and made quiet observations about the other passengers, and soon they were walking up the drive to the big house. 'Will you let Harry do it tonight?' Georgie whispered. 'If you want to sneak off somewhere private, I'll cover for you.'

Kitty had to smile. 'If only it was that simple.'

Something in her voice made Georgie think. 'Don't let yourself get hurt, gal,' she said. 'In this life you have to take what you want.'

'I know.'

'You want Harry, don't you?'

'Not if it means *he's* the one who gets hurt.'

Georgie was quiet for a while. As they were coming into the house, she told Kitty in a soft voice, 'I know why I love you . . . it's 'cause you're special, that's why. You care what happens to others. Me, I'm a selfish bugger. I take what I want and to hell with everyone else.' Her voice broke and a tear glistened in her eyes. 'Oh, gal . . . I'd give anything to be more like you.'

She broke away and ran into the lounge, whooping and hollering and showing everyone what she'd bought at the market.

Kitty felt deeply humbled. She had been allowed to glimpse just a tiny bit of the real Georgie, and knew she would love her forever.

At five minutes to seven, everyone else was making their way downstairs. Kitty was impatient. 'Hurry up, Georgie. I want to be there when he arrives.'

'Sit still, bugger you!' She wafted the hairdryer over Kitty's hair. 'I'm almost finished.'

Kitty groaned. 'I wish I'd never let you near my hair. It feels all wrong.'

'That's because I've styled it in a different way. It suits you too.'

Kitty looked in the mirror. 'It is nice,' she admitted, 'but it's not really me, is it?' Her long dark hair was parted in the centre and tied in the nape of her neck by means of a colourful scrunchie.

'Won't hurt to change your image, gal.' Georgie admired her handiwork. 'Makes you look older ... more mature,' she observed. '*You* might not like it, but Harry will.'

When Kitty came downstairs, Harry was standing in the doorway, his dark eyes searching the room for her. Softly, she called his name. He looked at her and his smile was wonderful. He didn't speak and neither did she. Instead they stood facing each other for what seemed an age; he thinking how lovely she was, and Kitty praying she would find the courage needed to see her through these next few hours.

Blushing beneath his dark brooding gaze, she felt compelled to break the spell. 'You look good, Harry.' He had always made her feel tiny, but now he physically towered above her. He was broader in the shoulder, tanned and healthy, and there was a warm intimate look in his eyes that revealed far more than words could.

Placing his hands on her shoulders, he murmured, 'You look good too, Kitty ... lovelier than ever. More grown-up somehow.' Wearing a straight red dress with a high hem and tiny waist, she looked stunning. He ached for her, wanting to kiss her, to hold her close and tell her how much he had missed her. During these past weeks and right up to the moment he walked into the room, he had planned to confess what was in his heart, tell her he would wait for her . . . that he would be patient until she was of an age when the two of them could be together. All of that he meant to say, but now, when she was standing before him, her slim body just an arm's reach away and her expressive brown eyes gazing up at him, touching his very soul, he was lost as always.

Taking a deep breath he swallowed the hard lump in his throat. She did that to him, made him breathless and nervous, unsure of himself, unsure of her.

Quieting the turmoil inside him, he asked, 'What have you done to yourself, Kitty?' Reaching out, he caressed her long dark hair; as it tangled about his fingers, frissons of pleasure rippled through him. 'A new style?' His voice was low and calm. Smiling now, he spoke with the same honesty that had sustained their long friendship. 'It isn't really you . . . too harsh, I think.'

Kitty laughed softly. 'Be careful what you say. You just might be taking your life into your hands.'

His smile deepened. 'Would you want me to lie?'

She shook her head. 'No. We've never lied to each other.' That was something she would always cherish.

'Are you going to let a fellow die of thirst?' He glanced towards the buffet table, and all the goodies there. His eyes lit up mischievously. 'You'll have to tell me which cakes you baked, so I can avoid them.'

Kitty chuckled. 'Look here! I was only nine when I made those doughnuts. Nobody asked you to come into our garden and help yourself.'

'It's a wonder I'm here to tell the tale!' His laugh was infectious. 'Even the dog refused them.'

'Well, you'll be all right here . . . and I can safely recommend the fairy cakes. Georgie made them, and she's a first-class cook.'

Harry ate two of Georgie's cakes and congratulated her. 'Best I've ever tasted,' he admitted.

Georgie was thrilled. 'Not bad, eh? But I promise you, I won't be making cakes for a living.'

'Oh? And what *will* you be doing?'

'I'll be driving a minibus . . . a bright blue one.' With that she made her excuses, whispering in Kitty's ear as she went, 'He's too bloody handsome, gal. If I were you, I'd take him some-where safe. Every pair of female eyes in this room has got him tagged.'

Kitty's thoughtful gaze followed Georgie to the far side of the room. She watched her go to the hi-fi and turn up the volume; Miss Davis turned it down, and when she wasn't look-ing, Georgie turned it up again. Within minutes everyone was dancing, and Miss Davis hadn't the heart to interfere.

Chuckling at Georgie's antics, Harry and Kitty stood by the door. The other girls paired off with their partners. Each inmate had been allowed to invite one outsider, and the party was all the merrier because of it. The music slowed to an intimate melody. 'Are you never going to ask me to dance?' Harry teased. Taking Kitty in his arms, he danced her to the centre of the floor where they gave themselves up to the music.

From the perimeter, the observant Miss Davis gave brisk instructions to her helpers, 'Keep a sharp eye out. If you see anyone getting the slightest bit romantic, march them into the kitchen. Dorothy would welcome a few more hands to help with the washing-up.'

It was almost an hour later when Kitty got the chance to be alone with Harry. After a skirmish at the buffet table had spilled a quantity of food, Miss Davis organised a clean-up campaign.

'Would you like to see the dormitory?' Kitty had things to say and they were not for others' ears.

Harry was pleased but surprised. 'Now *you're* taking your life into your own hands,' he warned.

Every step they mounted, Kitty expected someone to call out and stop them, but the chaos downstairs meant they could sneak away unnoticed.

'I need to talk with you,' Kitty said, so they sat side by side on her bed and she took a moment to gather her wits. How should she start? What could she say? Could she make him understand her reasons for what she was about to do? Only an hour ago she'd had it all straight in her mind. Now it was all mixed up, and her courage was already weakening.

Sensing her dilemma, he took her hand in his. 'Whatever it is, you know you can tell me,' he said gently. 'You're still worried about being fostered out, aren't you?'

Kitty's every nerve-ending was thrilled by the touch of his

hand. Realising she might never again feel his skin against hers, or be so close to him as she was right now, she hated to spoil it. For one exquisite minute she let pleasure wash through her.

He spoke then, tender and loving as he told her, 'You're not alone, Kitty. If I could do anything to change your circumstances, you know I would.'

'It's all right. I've got used to being here, and I'm growing into the idea of being fostered.'

'You shouldn't be going to strangers, not when you have an aunt who is perfectly capable of taking you in.' It was a sore point with him. 'Have you heard from her?'

'Yes, I've heard from her.' Kitty could understand his anger, because it echoed her own. 'But even if she offered to take me, I would have to refuse.'

'Why?' He was not too surprised though.

'Because we wouldn't get on,' she said. What she *thought* was, Because I can't forgive her!

They talked of Mildred and her strange behaviour; they discussed Harry's recent mountaineering expedition, and his successful university interview. He outlined his ambition of being a financial consultant one day. They talked of mundane matters, laughed and chatted about this and that, indulging in small talk, meaningless exchanges, when all the while each had something far more important to confess, a special thing that was hard to bring out into the open; something that didn't really need saying, but that throbbed beneath the surface like another heartbeat.

Disturbed and excited by his nearness, Kitty began hurriedly explaining about the dormitory and how each person had their own small area and no one ever interfered with other people's belongings. Harry put a gentle finger to her lips. 'I don't really want to know all that,' he murmured, 'I want to know about *you*. I want to know that you won't come to any harm, that you like the Connors, and that you meant what you said about coming to terms with everything. I need to know that you have a happier heart, Kitty, or I can't rest.'

Holding her hand as though he would never let it go, he smiled at her with his dark brooding eyes. 'You know what I'm saying, don't you, Kitty?' He was saying he loved her. He was saying he wanted to hear that she loved him. More than that, he hoped she might make a mention of the future . . . of *their* future. 'What do you want from life, Kitty? Beyond this place, and the Connors, what then?'

She knew well enough what he was saying, and she was afraid. The wrong word from her and his whole future could be ruined. What right had she to ask him to wait for her? He was a young man on the threshold of going to university, ambitious and with a wonderful career ahead of him. She could not, would not, hold him back. Suppressing her deeper feelings, she said in a matter-of-fact voice, 'I don't want you worrying about me because I'll be fine. I'm fourteen soon, and the time will fly. When I'm sixteen, my life will be my own. It's too early to think about the future. I'll just take each day as it comes.' Her flippancy belied the awful anxiety she felt. The thought of being out there in the world, without her every move being controlled, was both frightening and exhilarating.

'Then what will you do ... when you're sixteen and free to live your own life?' He waited hopefully for her answer.

Kitty shrugged her shoulders. 'I'm not sure. All I know is, I have a lot to forget before I can be altogether free.' She could talk to Harry, tell him most things that were in her heart. 'Everyone here, Miss Davis and the others, they try but they don't really understand. No one does, except maybe Georgie. I have to forget all that happened, you see, but my parents ... the train ... that awful fire ... it's still too real. Sometimes I think it will never go away.'

'It will.' He had to promise her that. 'In time, you'll be able to think about it and it won't hurt any more.' Sliding his arm round her shoulders, he drew her close, courage swelling inside him. 'I love you, Kitty,' he murmured. 'Not like the way I loved you when we were kids.' Looking down into those wonderful brown eyes he was moved to confess, 'Like a man. *That's* how I love you now.'

'I know,' she whispered, 'but it's too soon.' This was what she had been afraid of. His love for her, her love for him ... and all it meant. She raised her face to his, her mouth half-open, her soft eyes betraying all the emotions she had prayed to conceal.

When his mouth came down on hers the pleasure was almost unbearable; the tip of his tongue touched hers and she was drowning in the need for him. His strong arms folded round her as they sank together into the softness of the bedclothes. His kisses were wonderful, strong and passionate, urgent as her need for him; his long fingers found their way to her breast, toying delightfully with her small taut nipple and creating all manner of desires in her.

Her mind was saying: No. Tell him the truth! Tell him it's all wrong. Tell him you need more time, that you're not ready. Say you don't want him. Ask him to go away and never come back!

Her heart told a different story. Don't deny the love you feel for him. Harry is the best thing in your life. For as long as you have him and his love, you will never need anyone else.

Kitty's senses were reeling. She felt warm and safe in his arms; his gentle voice murmured in her ear and it seemed so natural that they should be together.

Suddenly in the distance they heard Miss Davis's voice: 'Kitty Marsh, are you in there?' It was like the crack of a whip. Before the irate woman strode the full length of the room, Harry had composed himself enough to scramble off the bed and open a drawer which he pretended to be peering into; Kitty too was suitably subdued and standing next to him, her heart beating like a wild thing. 'Miss Davis!' Feigning horror, she gasped, 'You gave me a fright!'

Miss Davis stood for a minute, her sharp eyes noticing that they seemed very guilty. 'What's going on here?' she demanded in a stern voice.

Closing the drawer, Harry stepped forward. 'It was noisy downstairs and we needed to talk,' he confessed. 'I'm sorry if I've broken any rules.'

Kitty said it was her fault because she was the one who had suggested the dormitory. 'We had a great deal to talk about,' she said. 'Please don't be angry.'

The woman's heart softened. There was a time when she too had been young, though she had never been as lovely as Kitty. 'It's my fault as much as anyone's. I should have made sure the upper rooms were locked. Now go downstairs where I can keep an eye on you.'

As she escorted them down, Miss Davis would have thrown a fit if she'd realised what was going on behind her back. Indulging in a bit of hanky-panky herself, Georgie crept out from under her bed, 'Bloody hell! That was a close shave. It's like

66

bleedin' Trafalgar Square in 'ere!' Grinning at her nervous companion, a sickly-looking youth with pimples, she giggled, 'Back to business, lover boy. Hope the fright ain't shrunk your manhood?' then she dragged him on top of the nearest bed and helped him off with his trousers.

The party was almost over. Harry had been deep in thought for the past half-hour and Kitty was even more determined to tell him what she should have told him upstairs, before she let her heart rule her head.

'Better say your goodbyes now.' Miss Davis began herding the younger ones together. 'Time to clear up.' Everyone groaned but knew better than to argue.

In serious mood, Harry suggested, 'Walk me to the door, before she claps eyes on us and drags you away.'

Outside the breeze cut sharp. Harry took off his jacket and wrapped it round her shoulders. 'I'm sorry about what happened earlier,' he apologised. 'I took advantage.' There was more to it than that. Shocked, and ashamed of his own actions, he knew it was time to let Kitty go at her own pace.

Kitty didn't hold him to blame. She'd wanted him as much as he'd wanted her. The whole incident had only confirmed her opinion that theirs was a dangerous relationship, one in which Harry was bound to make sacrifices she could not ask of him.

All evening Kitty had put off telling him of her decision, deeply reluctant to bring an end to what had been the only light in her life. Now more than ever she knew what must be done. She never wanted to hurt him, but he could only be hurt all the more by her clinging on. Better for her to make that one awful sacrifice and let him go. But her courage was failing fast. It was now or never.

'Harry, there's something I have to tell you.' Knowing this would be the hardest thing she would ever have to do, she went on quickly, 'It's about you and me.' The words tumbled one over the other. 'If it hadn't been for you, I don't know what I would have done ... but I ...' She looked away from him, searching for the right words. 'Oh, Harry! How can I say what has to be said?'

He stopped her mouth with a kiss. 'Do you love me, Kitty?'

'You know I do.' She was weakening.

'Don't say anything else, sweetheart,' he pleaded. 'I know what's on your mind, and I can't blame you. You're angry with me, and you have every right.' His dark eyes flashed with anger. 'Up there just now, I ought to have known better. I want you, I can't deny that, and I love you so much it hurts. But that's no excuse. I'll be eighteen this year. I should know right from wrong, and it was not only wrong but selfish of me to force myself on you.' When he saw she was about to interrupt, he took hold of her hands and pressed them to his chest. 'Let me finish, Kitty. You'll never know how hard it is for me to say this but it must be said. Am I asking too much of you? Am I causing you pain when instead I should be helping you through what must be a nightmare?'

In the cool of the evening, Kitty could see his breath fanning out in the night air; she could feel it on her face. Looking into his face, she realised with a little shock how very handsome he was. Thick black hair tumbled over his forehead as he bent to speak with her; strong chiselled features and dark smouldering eyes met hers. Even when they were small children she had always loved him, as a friend she'd thought, a confidant, the brother she'd never had. Now she was made to wonder. Even then, without realising, had she loved him the way she did now?

'You could never cause me pain,' she whispered.

Her words made him smile. 'But I have,' he said. 'And I never wanted that. All I've ever wanted was for us to be together when the time comes, to plan ahead together and wait patiently for the day when I can make you my wife. But that's what *I* want. I've never asked what *you* want, and that's why I'm being selfish. And now I'm afraid. The truth is, sweetheart, I can't trust myself with you. You saw that tonight.'

Stroking her face with long sensuous fingers, he gazed at her with a tenderness that melted her heart. 'I know you need time,' he murmured, 'time to get over all the things that have happened, time to see clearly ahead . . . to think about your future. No one else can do that for you, Kitty. No one else has the right. I understand all of that, and I only want what is best for you. I'll abide by whatever you decide.' He took a deep breath. 'What I need to know is this . . . have I spoiled everything between us? Should I walk away now, and never see you again?'

Kitty hesitated. He could not know what he was asking. This

was her opportunity. She might never be free from the past, but at least she could set Harry free. With her heart in her mouth she answered him, and the words choked her. 'It might be better that way, Harry.' A thickness rose in her throat, and hot scalding tears. She stifled them. He must not see she was lying.

His dark pained eyes lingered a moment on her face, then he raised his gaze to the grey shifting sky, his thoughts in turmoil. At length he bent to kiss her, 'Out of the two of us you're the stronger,' he murmured. A long agonising moment to drink on her beauty, then, 'Goodbye, Kitty.' When she simply lowered her gaze and stared at the ground, he walked away. How he turned from her, he would never know. But when he did, he left a part of himself behind.

Fighting the urge to run after him, Kitty told herself she must be cruel to be kind. 'Goodbye, Harry,' she whispered. 'Don't forget me.'

Out of the darkness came a soft reproachful voice – Georgie's. 'You're a fool, Kitty Marsh,' she said. 'No one will ever love you like he does.'

It was the last thing Kitty wanted to hear. When she turned the tears were raining down her face. 'Do you think I don't know that?' she cried. With a sob she fell into Georgie's arms and cried till her tears ran dry.

CHAPTER FIVE

It was Monday morning. Kitty was seated cross-legged on her bed. Beside her lay two white envelopes, one addressed to her Aunt Mildred, the other to Harry.

In the bright morning light, her gaze fell on the letters. Reaching out she picked up Harry's and held it to her lips. She could still feel his kisses on her mouth, still feel his warm strong arms about her. Since the party, she had questioned herself over and over. Should she send the letter, or should she tear it up? Was it right to leave things as they were? Or, like Georgie said, wouldn't it be better at least to keep in touch with him rather than cut him out of her life altogether? Kitty had agonised, gone without sleep and prayed that she had done the right thing for both of them. She and Georgie had talked about it, argued and pondered. In the end Kitty decided that whichever way she turned, she would be doing wrong. There was an emptiness in her heart that nothing could fill, and now she was going away. Soon strangers would be here to collect her, and she was afraid. Only the thought of Harry kept her strong.

A sound at the door made her look up. It was Georgie. 'They're here, gal,' she said. 'Miss Davis has them in her office . . . they're drinking coffee, would you believe? Here we are, about to be thrown to the wolves, and all they can do is drink bloody coffee!' She flung herself on the bed with such force that Kitty bounced up into the air.

She had tried so hard not to show her feelings. Now, with Georgie beside her, and their parting so close, the words tumbled out. 'I'm frightened, Georgie. I wish I didn't have to go. I wish we weren't leaving, you and me.'

'Hey!' Georgie gave her a playful push. 'You speak for yourself, my girl! I'm sorry to be leaving you behind, but we've

71

already said we'll keep in touch, so it ain't as if we'll never see each other again, is it? But I'm glad to be getting my own place at last. To tell the truth, I can't wait to get my arse out of here!' She gave a little whoop of joy. 'My own front door key, eh? And what about you? A proper family of your very own, and from what you tell me . . . a bedroom big enough to entertain a dozen blokes at a time!'

Kitty couldn't help but laugh. 'What would I want with a dozen blokes?' Instinctively she glanced at Harry's letter.

'Ah!' Georgie caught sight of the name and address on the envelope. 'You did write it after all?'

'I don't know if I'll post it though.' Once it was out of her hands it would be too late.

'What have you told him?'

'That I'm sorry we parted the way we did, and that I was wrong to think it would be better if we never saw each other again. I've asked him to write, and given him the address of where I'm going.'

'Did you tell him how you feel? I mean . . . how you *really* feel about him? Did you say you wanted the same things he did . . . that you need him to wait for you, and there is nothing more in all the world you want, other than to be with him? Did you tell him that?'

Kitty lowered her gaze. 'No, I didn't say those things.'

'Why not?'

'Because it would be asking too much of him, and I won't do that.'

'It's what he wants.'

'It's what he *thinks* he wants.' Kitty shook her head. 'Harry is good and kind. He's always looked after me . . . when I was small, when I was growing up, while I've been in here. He was the one I ran to when my parents were fighting . . . the one who came here to see me when even my own aunt couldn't be bothered.' She looked at his name on the envelope and wondered what he was doing at that moment. Was he thinking of her? Was he thanking his lucky stars that he had been let off the hook? Or was he waiting for the postman . . . watching for this letter?

'Send it, gal,' Georgie urged. 'You ain't got nobody else except me, and I'm as much use as a fart in the wind.'

Kitty laughed out loud. 'What am I going to do without you, eh?'

Georgie took stock of her. 'Oh, you'll manage well enough,' she said. 'It's me that will miss *you*.' There was something very secret about her smile. 'To be honest, gal, I don't know if I could have survived tragedy the way you have. But, you see, you're a lion at heart, while I'm a coward. That's the difference between us.'

Kitty took hold of her hand. 'You're never a coward,' she said firmly. 'And I really will miss you . . . at the breakfast table; in the dormitory; meeting you from the factory. I'll miss the tales you tell about your workplace, and I'll miss your terrible laugh, and the way you torment Miss Picton, and oh . . . everything about you!' She had to stop there because the words wouldn't come out any more.

Georgie looked at her for what seemed an age before saying in a soft voice, 'You'll miss Harry much more, gal. It will be a long, lonely road without him.'

Kitty knew the truth of that. But there was no answer, so she gave none. Instead she put on a bright voice and a brighter smile and suggested, 'We'd best make our way down. Miss Davis will be sending up the heavy brigade.'

Georgie laughed 'What! Miss Picton? A good breeze would knock her over.'

It took only a minute for them to empty their cupboards and fill a duffel-bag each with the few things they owned. At the door they took one last look. 'Seems funny though, don't it? Georgie muttered. 'I'm glad to be going, but this has been the only real home I've known.'

'I won't miss this place,' Kitty admitted. She put her arm round Georgie and hugged her close. 'But, whatever you say, I'll miss *you*, like nothing on earth.' All those times when Kitty was alone and afraid, Georgie had made her laugh through the tears. Now she was alone and afraid again, being entrusted to strangers and made to start all over. Only this time it was worse. And this time she didn't have Harry either.

As they came down the stairs, Kitty saw them waiting in the hall: the familiar bulky form of Miss Davis, Dorothy Picton nervously fluttering in the background, and the Connors, a smart, well-dressed couple in their late-thirties, all smiling at her as she descended the stairway. 'Cor, bloody hell, gal, they don't look short of a bob or two, gal' Georgie muttered, 'I reckon you've fallen on your feet there.'

Kitty regarded her new family through Georgie's eyes. Patricia Connor was small and thin, with fair hair and brilliant blue eyes; her husband Raymond was a big man with broad straight shoulders, small dark eyes and thin brown hair scraped back from a high expanse of forehead. A quiet man by nature, his gestures and eyes spoke volumes. Kitty preferred him to his wife, but: 'They're good people,' she told Georgie. To Kitty that was more important than if they had 'a bob or two'. 'Though I don't care much for their son.'

Adam Connor was about the same age as Harry, but they couldn't be more different, she thought. He had always treated her well and made her welcome on home visits, but there was something about him she didn't like. Something devious.

Georgie was the first to leave. 'I'm sure no one would mind if you wanted a minute to say your goodbyes.' Miss Davis glanced first at Kitty, then at the Connors. 'These young women have been inseparable,' she explained with a motherly smile.

Dorothy Picton took the Connors upstairs to show them the dormitory, and Miss Davis gave George a little pep talk. 'Good luck to you,' she said. 'But remember to stay out of trouble!' She gave her a wry little smile. 'I know what a temper you've got.'

'You ain't a bad old cow,' Georgie told her, and the big woman went away to have a little weep. It was always painful when she lost one of her brood.

They were alone now. 'Take care of yourself,' Kitty told Georgie. 'We must never lose touch.'

Throwing wide her arms, Georgie grabbed hold of her. 'Come here, you bugger!' she said, and the two of them hugged and cried, but soon they were laughing, and the future seemed rosy.

'You've got my address, gal,' Georgie reminded her. 'I want plenty of letters, mind . . . full of every little detail.' She gave a cheeky wink. 'And don't miss anything out . . . especially not the raunchy bits.'

Kitty said she would write often, but she didn't know about the 'raunchy' bits.

'You never know your luck gal,' Georgie laughed, and Kitty thought she might have to invent something 'raunchy', just to keep her happy.

'Don't forget to ask the Connors if you can come and see my place.'

'I'm sure they couldn't keep me away,' Kitty answered. 'I'm counting on us being able to spend some time together, even if it's only to go round Bedford market on a Saturday.' So far, though, the Connors had given no hint that she would be able to continue the relationship. If anything they seemed to avoid the subject of Georgie altogether. It was something Kitty meant to take up with them as soon as she was settled.

Georgie was more abrupt. 'I wouldn't count on them saying yes, gal,' she advised. 'The Connor woman doesn't like me. It's plain as the nose on your face, she thinks I'm dirt under her foot.'

Kitty argued, 'How can you tell that? She's only clapped eyes on you twice . . . once when she first came to see me, and just now. You can't form an opinion just like that.' All the same, deep down she knew Georgie was right. Patricia Connor disapproved of her.

'It's my own fault,' George confessed with a chuckle. 'It were bad enough the two of us sliding down the banisters when she first saw me, but what really turned her off was when I said I'd got a splinter stuck up me arse!'

Kitty laughed at the memory. 'You only told the truth,' she said.

'Too right! And if it hadn't been for you fishing it out, that bloody splinter might have been stuck there to this day.'

When the moment came for them to say goodbye, the others had returned and Georgie was in a quiet mood. Kitty felt as though a great weight was pressing down inside her, and when her friend embraced her, she whispered, 'I love you, Georgie.'

'I love you too, gal,' came the chirpy reply. 'Don't forget now . . . you've already proved that things ain't so bad you can't rise above 'em. Keep in touch. And, remember – all the sexy bits!'

When her friend went through the door, Kitty admired the way she was still smiling and making jokes. She was shocked when Georgie turned round to wave and the morning sunlight caught the glint of tears falling down her face. In that moment, Kitty knew she had caught yet another glimpse of the real Georgie; the one she kept hidden from the world; the one that was much like Kitty herself. And she vowed to be there whenever Georgie needed her, just as Harry had been there whenever she needed him.

'Do you want me to post these for you?' Miss Davis had seen the two letters in Kitty's hand.

She thought a moment before handing one over. 'This one if you could, please.' She tore the second into shreds. 'This can go in the bin.' Against all her better instincts she decided not to contact Harry.

'Goodbye then. Be happy, Kitty. We'll be keeping in touch, as you know.'

'Goodbye, Miss Davis, and thanks for everything.' As she followed the Connors out of the door and into their Jaguar, both Patricia and her husband showered her with affection. The woman laughed and chatted and squeezed her lovingly, while her husband said very little but smiled encouragingly. One look from him said more than his wife could in a dozen sentences.

Settled in the cream leather seat, Kitty looked back. Miss Davis and the others were standing on the doorstep, waving and smiling. 'You can't know how much we've always longed for a daughter of our very own,' Kitty heard Patricia Connor say. 'We'll do everything we can to make you happy.'

The journey was slow. 'Monday morning traffic is a nightmare,' Patricia moaned. 'Still, we'll soon have you home and safe. I've planned a special family dinner for tonight . . . Adam is so excited at having a sister . . . we didn't want to foster a baby, we're too old for that now . . . we wanted someone your age . . . a young woman in the making . . . someone we could talk to sensibly . . . someone we could mould and influence, if you know what I mean?'

She went on and on, until her husband told her to be quiet because he couldn't concentrate on the road. She sulked a little, but the peace was soothing and Kitty gave silent thanks. Still, she liked them a lot, and that was a good start.

Kitty sat in the corner of the big car, anxious about her destination. With thoughts of Georgie and Harry flooding her mind, she turned her gaze out of the window and watched the changing countryside. As they drove through the pretty village of Ridgmont, with its lovely old church, she could see herself walking down the aisle of that ancient place, dressed in a long white dress and carrying a bouquet of small white roses and blue lavender.

In the past, whenever she'd entertained girlish dreams of being a bride, Kitty had always seen it that way. Every detail was etched on her soul: the church with its beautiful stained-glass window above the altar, the bouquet, the fairytale wedding gown with its sweetheart neckline and trailing veil. Every little detail, as though she had seen it in real life, as though she was cradling a premonition. One day, it said, this will all come true. It was hard to believe that now.

When she first dared to dream, she did not know the identity of the young man waiting at the altar; sometimes she would tell her friend Harry about it, and he would merely smile and say, 'Whoever he is, he's a very lucky bloke.' And Kitty would wonder about the young man. Who was he? Where and when would they meet? *Now she knew*! In her latest dreams, the young man had turned to her as she approached and his face was loving and familiar. It was Harry, tall and handsome, his dark eyes smiling at her, and she wondered why she had not seen it right from the start. Only now none of it mattered, because Harry was gone. She had no wish to be married to anyone else. This was why she was afraid for the future, afraid of being alone, afraid of being old some day, and having no one to love. It was a desperate prospect and one she pushed from her mind.

On the way out of the village stood the most delightful cottage, a long rambling place with leaded light windows and a low wall fronting the road. Kitty smiled, her heart filled with memories of Harry. She couldn't help but imagine how wonderful it would be for them to be together in such a darling place. 'Stop torturing yourself,' she murmured, and quickly concentrated her mind on other matters. Her thoughts turned to Adam Connor. He was a strange young man. Suddenly she felt apprehensive in a different way. She still couldn't quite decide what it was about him that made her cringe inside, but there *was* something. Something quietly unsettling.

As they came down the hill into Ampthill, the sun was beginning to shine and the world didn't look quite so grey. At the bottom the car turned left, through a narrow street and out into the open road. 'Home at last,' Patricia Connor said, half turning with a smile. 'A cup of tea and a little chat, then we're off to Bedford.'

Mr Connor gave her a curious glance. 'You might give Kitty a chance to settle in first!'

'Don't be silly, Raymond. I'm sure she would rather go round the shops and choose her new clothes. She certainly can't be comfortable with the awful things she's wearing.' Twisting in her seat she regarded Kitty with narrowed eyes, scrutinising the straight dark skirt, blue V-necked jumper and long mackintosh. 'That's right, isn't it, dear? You're not at all happy with those shabby clothes? You want to choose your new wardrobe as soon as possible, I should think?'

Kitty felt uncomfortable, like piggy in the middle. Hoping it wasn't a taste of things to come, she answered, 'Whatever you think best.'

That seemed to satisfy the woman for she turned and said to her husband, 'There! What did I tell you? Anyway, there's no need for you to come with us. You can go back to the office if you like . . . sell some more houses to pay for Kitty's clothes.' He made no reply to that, but gave her a long look. It was enough to silence her, at least until they got inside the house.

It was huge, a rambling white building with panoramic windows, beautifully manicured lawns and a long winding drive leading to the double garage. The inside was immaculate; almost like a showhouse on one of Mr Connor's new estates. The lounge fronted the entire length of the house, but furnished with cream leather furniture and pale plush carpets, it seemed cold and unwelcoming, not a place for living in, more a place for entertaining, Kitty thought.

The whole house was decorated to the same theme, with deep pile carpets, long floral curtains with tasselled tie-backs and swags draped above. There were three bathrooms, five bedrooms, and a beautiful galleried landing that could have been mistaken for an airport runway. 'I do like plenty of space,' Patricia cooed as she showed Kitty to her room.

This turned out to be a suite; an impossibly spacious bedroom with fitted wardrobes across one wall, a huge four poster standing in pride of place in the centre of the room, whitewood dressing-table and wardrobe, each exquisitely inlaid with golden scrolls. There was a huge vase filled with early roses standing on a small table by the window, and another on the dressing-table. The bathroom was all chrome and glass, and the sitting-room was like being in a fish bowl, with its huge windows and trailing plants. 'This is your own private room,' Patricia said grandly, 'where you can bring your friends.' She looked at Kitty, and her face was one big smile. 'Do you like it?'

'You've gone to a lot of trouble.' In truth, Kitty hated it.

Delighted, Patricia twirled on the spot, both skinny arms stretched wide as she encompassed the rooms in one extravagant gesture. 'It's all new,' she sighed. 'Carpets, curtains, everything. I even had it redecorated right through, though of course we had the entire house decorated only last year.' Chuckling, she confided, 'Extravagant, I suppose, especially when this room has never really been used by anyone.' She sighed noisily. 'Raymond and I had a little argument about it, but I won in the end. I always do.'

'I'm sure it would have been fine the way it was.' The knowledge that she had already caused at least two arguments between man and wife, made Kitty even more uncomfortable.

'Nonsense! The room was all wrong. Like I said, I wanted it to be a suitable place for you to bring your friends back to.'

'It's very generous. Thank you,' Kitty replied, while wondering, Why do I want all this space? And what friends is she talking about? 'Can I bring Georgie here?' she dared to ask.

Patricia's smile fell away. 'I don't think so,' she answered sweetly. 'I believe that young woman is a very bad influence on you.'

'Then I won't be bringing *anyone* here.'

'Oh dear! I do hope you aren't going to be difficult.'

Kitty hadn't wanted to appear difficult, though she had no intention of giving up on Georgie. Maybe it was *Mr* Connor she should be talking to. 'I don't want to seem difficult, Mrs Connor,' she apologised. 'I'm sorry if I gave that impression.' All the same, one way or another she meant to keep up her relationship with Georgie, and to hell with the consequences!

The little woman drew in a long slow breath and let it out in a weary sigh. 'Please! Don't call me Mrs Connor,' she pleaded. 'From now on, I'll be your mother. Can't you call me that? *Can't* you bring yourself to call me Mother? It would give me so much pleasure.'

Kitty thought she was asking too much and told her so. 'I will only ever have one mother, and she's gone,' she said in a flat voice. 'But, if you like, I could call you Patricia?'

'How disappointing.' She gave her best 'little girl' smile. 'You will be able to call me Mother later on though, won't you?'

'I can't promise.'

Patricia pretended not to hear. Striding to the wardrobes, she threw open the doors. 'We're going to try and fill these today,' she said. 'You're so very pretty, and I want you to look lovely and have nice things. I want people to come here and say, "Oh, Patricia, isn't she beautiful!" ' She smiled secretly. 'Every woman likes to have an attractive daughter. It kind of makes *her* feel attractive too, don't you think?'

Kitty couldn't think *what* to think, except that she was already beginning to regret coming here to live. But she kept that to herself.

Half an hour later, Raymond Connor returned to his estate agent's office, while his wife drove her own little car into Bedford. 'We'll do some shopping, then have lunch in Beale's.' Patricia gabbled all the way into Bedford. 'Then we'll explore Debenham's and after that seek out the very best shoe shops.' She chattered so much she went through two sets of red lights and almost ran into an old woman standing on the corner of the market square. 'People will get in the way,' she complained, patting her short fair hair in the mirror. 'It really is irritating.'

Bedford town was teeming with people. It took half an hour and three heated arguments to park the car in a side street. It didn't seem to matter to Patricia that there was a huge sign saying RESIDENTS' PARKING ONLY or that she ran over a child's football and sent him indoors sobbing his heart out. Nor did it ruffle her feathers when the child's irate mother threatened to call the police. 'Don't be so bloody stupid!' Patricia retorted.

With that she marched down the street, doing battle with half the residents and with her reluctant protégé in hot pursuit. Kitty remained shamed and red-faced until they arrived at the first shop, after which she was ushered in and out of changing rooms so fast she was too dizzy to think straight.

Dissatisfied with everything Kitty tried on, Patricia led the way down Midland Road and on to the High Street. 'We'll do this in an organised manner,' she announced. 'Start at the top of the High Street and work back. Beale's is situated halfway so we'll be ready for lunch by the time we get there.' When Kitty explained she had really liked a certain cheesecloth dress, Patricia was horrified. 'Makes you look like a hippy!' she said. She couldn't know how, in that moment, Kitty would have given anything to join a commune and tramp the roads.

Kitty had never been so exhausted. Whisked in and out of every shop in every street, her feet ached and her head was pounding. By the time they got back to Beale's, the two of them were loaded down with shopping bags, every loathsome item chosen by Patricia. 'I don't need all this,' Kitty protested. 'Besides, it's costing you a small fortune.'

'Not me, dear,' Patricia argued. 'It's costing *Raymond* a small fortune.' Falling into a nearby chair, she dumped the shopping bags on the floor and her handbag on the table. Scanning the counter with hungry eyes, she told Kitty, 'I'll have a pot of tea . . . not too strong . . . and a light salad, with perhaps a piece of that delightful-looking bacon flan.' She groaned and stretched out her legs beneath the table. 'It's good to sit down,' she said. When Kitty didn't move quickly enough, she urged, 'Hurry up, dear. Put your bags down. Go and get what I've ordered, and have whatever you want for yourself. Quickly now! There'll be a queue a mile long any minute.'

She tutted the whole time Kitty was arranging the bags, and moaned when two elderly women got to the counter first. 'Don't forget,' she called out impatiently, 'tea not too strong.' When other diners glanced up, she gave them one of her frosty looks.

Loaded down with a heavy tray, Kitty put Patricia's food before her, then settled down to enjoy her doughnut and coffee. With every sip and every bite she was treated to a barrage of advice about how too much coffee was bad for your health, and how doughnuts were full of harmful sugar, and how Patricia would have to teach her healthy eating. She talked of shops they had visited and remarked on the clothes they had bought, and Kitty sipped her coffee and ate her doughnut, and shut her ears to the shrill monologue that had other diners leaving in droves. 'I know I talk too much,' Patricia apologised, 'but you can't know how excited I am at having you with me. And when I get excited, my tongue has a habit of running away with me.'

'No need to apologise for that.' Kitty felt a pang of conscience, though she couldn't help thinking it might be a blessed relief if Patricia's tongue really would run away with her.

It was almost six o'clock by the time the car nosed its way up the drive. 'Home at last!' Patricia said, and Kitty sighed with relief.

As the shopping was unloaded, Patricia checked every bag. While she went ahead, Kitty was left to carry most of the enormous number of bags and bits. 'Hurry up, dear!' Patricia called, leaving her to stagger beneath the burden. 'There'll be two hungry men home soon.'

She was right about one thing. At precisely six-thirty, Raymond came through the door with a smile on his face, and it was still there after Patricia explained, 'You'll have to wait for your meal. We didn't get back until late, so it will be at least another hour before the dinner's on the table.' Exasperated, she glanced at the clock. 'I don't know where the time's gone. I hate it when I'm late with dinner, and I've planned a special one tonight, just for Kitty.' She gave her a half-smile. 'That's why I wanted the plumpest, freshest chicken the butcher could find.' She chuckled. 'You remember how annoyed he got when I kept sending him backwards and forwards until he found one I could accept?'

Kitty would remember the incident for a long time to come. By the time Patricia was finished, the poor man was breathless, red in the face, and so agitated he gave her an extra ten-pound note in her change. When Kitty discreetly pointed it out to Patricia, she retorted, 'That will compensate me for the time he wasted!' There were a few more minutes wasted when Patricia dropped the chicken on the pavement while trying to stuff her ill-gotten gains into her purse. 'Damn and bugger it!' she'd cried, blushing from her neck to her hairline when a passing clergyman gave her a scathing look.

Sensing one of his wife's awkward moods in the offing, Raymond suggested hopefully, 'I'm sure Kitty wouldn't mind if we postponed the special dinner until tomorrow night?'

Kitty thought that was a wonderful idea and said so. The thought of sitting at the same table as Adam Connor brought her out in goose-bumps.

'Nonsense!' Patricia used her favourite word and the matter was settled. 'We shall have our special dinner, and we shall sit at the table as a family. The dinner will be ready in an hour.' Anticipating her husband's protest, she told him, 'And if eating late gives you indigestion, you'll just have to suffer.'

'I wasn't going to say that,' he protested. 'Though you do have a point. You know how eating late affects me.'

'If you weren't going to say that, what *were* you going to say?' Before he could answer, she turned to Kitty. 'Honestly! I've yet to meet the man who can suffer with dignity.'

Kitty bit her lip. Watching these two was like watching a tennis match . . . left, right . . . his turn, her turn.

Now it was his turn, and he was looking straight at Kitty. 'I have something for you. It's in the car. I think you should go and fetch it.' He looked like a cat with the cream.

When he winked at his wife, she gave a little cry. 'So *that's* why you were late!' Nudging Kitty she urged, 'Go on, dear. It's your birthday present. We couldn't give it to you earlier. You'll see why. Go on, dear. GO ON!'

Intrigued, Kitty went outside. The car was on the drive. She glanced behind her and there stood Patricia and her husband. 'Go on!' called Patricia. 'Open the door, dear.'

Kitty didn't care much for all this intrigue. Peering inside the car, she could see nothing that looked remotely like a birthday present. With the exception of a big cardboard box on the back seat, there was nothing in the car at all. She opened the door and looked inside. There was nothing on the floor, and nothing inside the glove compartment. Then, as she turned away, she heard it. The smallest whimper, coming from the box. Gingerly she opened it up and there was the loveliest, tiniest bundle of fluff. 'A puppy!' All her young life she had wanted a puppy. Her mother had promised her one: 'When you're old enough to look after it.' But the day never arrived. Until now.

With gentle hands she hugged the puppy to her; it was a cocker spaniel, black and white mottled, and with ears that swept the floor. 'Oh, you're beautiful!' she murmured, nuzzling her face into the silky softness of its coat. When after a moment she came to the doorstep where the Connors were waiting, Kitty kissed them both. 'It's the best birthday present I've ever had,' she said. 'How did you know I longed for a puppy of my own?'

Raymond knew exactly how she felt, because he had never had a daughter of his own before and now he had. 'Miss Davis told us,' he explained. 'She told us how you confided it to her.'

Patricia gave him a sour look. 'Oh, but she didn't really betray your confidence,' she said. 'We asked her what you would like for your birthday, and mentioned that we were thinking of getting you a puppy, and she told us it would be wonderful because that was what you had always wanted.' Ruffling the puppy's coat, she went on, 'All the bitches were already sold, so this is a he. He was too young to be collected in time for your birthday, but I'm sure he was worth waiting for, wasn't he?'

Kitty thanked them again. 'I won't have any trouble choosing him a name,' she said. 'I'm going to call him Jasper.' Her voice fell to a whisper as she told the puppy, 'Harry's dog was called Jasper, and he lived to a ripe old age.'

Both Patricia and her husband thought Jasper was a good name. 'I'm sure Adam will like it too,' Patricia said. Raymond reminded her that it wouldn't matter whether Adam liked the name or not: 'Because the puppy belongs to Kitty, and she can call him whatever she likes.'

'You two make friends with the creature,' Patricia said haughtily, 'I have dinner to get ready.' When Kitty offered to help, she told her, 'If I was in need of help, dear, I would have asked.'

It was almost eight o'clock when Adam arrived home. Frantic with worry, Patricia ran to him as he came through the door. 'Wherever have you been?' she pleaded. 'I've been out of my mind!'

Patricia's son was her pride and joy. Tall and broad-shouldered, with thick blond hair and staring blue eyes, he had a forbidding manner about him. 'Stop fussing, Mother,' he told her. His voice was thick and low, and oddly disturbing. 'You've obviously forgotten, I told you I planned to play squash after classes.'

'No, you didn't! You said nothing to me about playing squash, or being late.' Plucking at his jacket, she demanded, 'Adam! Are you listening to me?'

He shook her off and glanced round the room. When he saw Kitty sitting on the rug, he was momentarily taken aback; he smiled, ready to exchange words with her, until he saw she was playing with the puppy. His face stiffened with anger. 'What's that thing doing here?' he asked his mother.

Kitty answered. 'This is Jasper,' she said boldly. 'He's my birthday present . . . from your parents.'

Adam looked at her for a long awkward moment, then took a deep breath that made his chest swell. When he let it out it was in a rush as he demanded of his mother, 'How come you would never let *me* have a dog?'

'Get washed, Adam. We're having a special dinner tonight . . . to welcome Kitty into the family.'

He addressed himself to Kitty. 'You must be feeling pleased with yourself? A puppy and a special dinner. My! My! We are honoured, aren't we?'

Kitty said nothing, but knew instinctively he didn't like her. When he continued to look at her with hostile eyes, she stared him out. Her boldness only seemed to antagonise him further, though he tried not to show it.

Dropping his leather bag on the floor, he strode across the room and stood before her. 'I really ought to be jealous of you,' he murmured. 'I mean . . . there was a time when I had my mother's love all to myself.' His smile widened unpleasantly.

Patricia almost ran across the room. 'Isn't it lovely to have her here with us?' she pleaded. 'We've been shopping . . . getting Kitty the things she needs to make a good impression.'

'Oh?' Keeping his eyes on Kitty, he said, 'She's had you traipsing all over town, has she? Poor you.' He laughed softly. 'But then, it's only right that you should be punished, for stealing my limelight.'

Kitty reasoned that if she and this spoilt young man were to live under the same roof they had better get off on the right foot. 'I hoped we might be friends,' she told him sincerely.

His eyes became so wide she was afraid they might fall out. 'Shame on you, Kitty,' he chided, wagging a finger within an inch of her face. 'Here am I, longing to be friends, and you can't even see it.' His expression hardened. 'Mother will tell you how much I've been looking forward to your coming to stay.' Turning to Patricia he demanded, 'Isn't that right, Mother? Haven't I been looking forward to having Kitty here?'

85

Patricia laughed, but her voice was shaky as she made an effort to reassure Kitty, 'I'm counting on you two becoming friends.'

Kitty couldn't help but notice how Patricia's mood had darkened since the arrival of her son. In fact, he seemed to have cast a shadow over the whole house.

Picking up his bag, the young man brushed past the two women. 'I suppose Father is hiding somewhere?'

'Don't be silly. Your father is working in his study.' Obviously embarrassed in front of Kitty, she declared impatiently, 'Dinner will be on the table in ten minutes. You'll see him then.'

'I expect it's spoiled. You know how I hate warmed-up meals.'

'It won't be spoiled.'

'It doesn't matter because I don't want it anyway. I've already eaten.'

'What are you saying?' Patricia was horrified. 'Are you telling me you won't be down for dinner?'

'That's precisely what I'm telling you. Now please, Mother. Go away.' Turning to Kitty, he said, 'I like your name ... Kitty. Is it short for something?'

'I was christened Katherine.' She disliked him immensely, and as far as was possible meant to keep out of his way.

'Hmh.' He considered for a moment. 'Then, I think we should try to be friends ... for Mother's sake at least. What do you think, Kitty?' He seemed to be making a mockery of her name.

'That's really up to you,' she replied coldly. She had seen the way he bullied his mother, and she noticed the fear in Patricia's eyes. 'Yes. I'd say that was up to you, Adam,' she repeated. 'If we're to be friends, you might just have to mind your manners.'

His blue eyes froze. 'Enjoy your dinner,' he said. As he strode away, the puppy chased after him. There was a scuffle, then a shrill yelp as Jasper went skidding across the floor. 'Oh dear!' Adam's smile was cunning. 'It might be best if you kept the thing away from me. I'm known for my clumsiness.'

Two days later the puppy was found lying lifeless in the garden. The vet said it had been poisoned. Kitty was heartbroken. As for Adam, he could hardly conceal his delight.

CHAPTER SIX

'He sounds a real swine.'

Accepting a glass of lemonade from Georgie, Kitty curled her long legs beneath her and made herself comfortable on the settee. All the furniture in Georgie's flat had seen better days. Situated on the ground floor of a big house on Goldington Road, it was surprisingly large, with one bedroom, a spacious bathroom, and an old-fashioned kitchen with a walk-in pantry.

'You've got this place looking really nice,' Kitty told her friend. There was a vase of flowers on the window-ledge, a bowl of fruit on the table, and the window in the lounge had a new pair of frilly curtains. 'I'm so glad everything's turning out right for you, Georgie.' Glancing round the room, Kitty saw how little things had been added since her last visit, like the television and the pretty pink lamp on the coffee table. 'It looks like they've given you that pay rise you were after?'

'Never mind about that,' Georgie told her. 'It's *you* I want to know about. Or am I being told to mind my own business?'

Kitty was sorry if she had given that impression. 'I've never kept anything from you,' she answered. 'If I didn't have you to come and talk to, I think I'd go completely mad.'

'Sorry, gal. As always, my tongue ran away with me.' She sipped at her lemonade and gave Kitty a long scrutinising look. 'You're too thin, gal, and there's dark rings under your eyes, like you ain't sleeping. It's this bloke, ain't it? This bloody Adam.'

Kitty hated loading her troubles onto Georgie, but there was no one else, not since Harry. In answer to her question she confided. 'I think Patricia's afraid of him.'

'What! A mother afraid of her own son?' A deep frown creased Georgie's face. 'Pity she didn't drown the bastard at birth!'

'She loves him.' Too much, thought Kitty. And all she got in return was humiliation and hatred. In fact Adam Connor fed on his mother's love . . . fed and grew into the monster he was.

'Then she wants her head examined.'

'These past weeks, since he's been away on an archaeological dig, she's been different, more relaxed, laughing with Raymond instead of always arguing.' The house had been brighter, and Kitty had felt less tense. But all that was about to change. 'He's back tomorrow, and already Patricia's on edge. This morning she flew at Raymond for no reason. There was a hell of a row before he went to the office. God knows what she'd do if she knew I was here.' The thought made Kitty smile. 'Happen she'd throw me out.'

'Fat lot of good that would do. The authorities would hound you down and have you back with Miss Davis before you could say Jack Robinson.' Something in Kitty's expression made her ask quietly, 'That's not what you really want is it, gal . . . to be sent back to the home?'

As always Kitty said what was in her heart. 'I won't deny there are times when I'd give anything to have things the way they were . . . you and me, the home, Miss Davis . . . everything.'

So sad and serious were the words Kitty uttered, Georgie was made to come and sit beside her. 'Don't say that, gal,' she pleaded, 'I'm so proud of you. I've never said this before, but you've been a real example to me. At the home I used to laugh and joke and pretend that none of it mattered, when it did. You were the only person to see through me . . . the only real friend I've ever had.'

'You were my friend too. More than a friend. More like a sister.'

'We're friends *now*, ain't we?'

'Forever!'

'And that feels good, don't it?'

'Feels wonderful.'

'So it's only natural I want to help you through your troubles, gal. Like you've always helped me through mine.'

'Did I do that?' Kitty hoped so. But she could never be certain.

'Oh, you did! At the home, when I were down in the dumps, you cheered me up. And when I first came here, feeling like a lost soul, who was it wrote to me every single day? And who was it missed school just to come and visit, eh? What! Time and again I might have done away with myself if it hadn't been for you.'

'I'm glad I helped.'

'Now it's my turn, gal. Don't let the buggers get the better of you, eh? It ain't like you to let your troubles get you down.'

Kitty gave a small laugh. 'I expect I'm just feeling sorry for myself.'

Georgie shook her head. 'Not you, gal. The plain truth is, you're not happy at the Connors' place.'

Kitty was already regretting having told Georgie her worries. 'I'll deal with it.'

'Are you sure, gal? This Adam sounds a nasty bugger. Can you better him?'

'One way or another.'

'So Patricia doesn't know you've come to see me?'

'No. She thinks I'm at the library.'

'Let her think it then. No use making more trouble for yourself. Have you heard from your Aunt Mildred?'

'Not a word.'

'Old cow!'

'It doesn't bother me any more.'

'Do you reckon she's looking after your money?'

'Don't know. Don't care.'

'You should have her checked out, or one day you might find yourself penniless.'

'That's what Harry said.'

'And he was right. You still miss him, don't you, gal?'

'More than ever.' More than anyone would ever know.

'Get in touch with him then.'

'I can't do that.' Not that she hadn't thought about it. Not that she hadn't taken up pen and paper umpteen times, only to discard them when she realised how she and Harry could never amount to anything. 'He's better off without me.'

'*He* can't think that, or he wouldn't have written to you via Miss Davis . . . four times, no less.'

Kitty fell silent, thinking of the letters Harry had written; in them he had begged her to get in touch with him. She never had.

'I can't understand you, gal. He's a good-looking bloke with future prospects. You love him ... miss him like crazy ... and still you're letting him go!'

'I'm letting Harry go *because* I love him.' Kitty believed the pain would ease with the passing of time, but it had been almost two months now and still the thought of him was like a knife in her heart. 'You know he'll have a better chance without me. Apart from all the other reasons, I'm too young ... we're *both* too young.'

'Not too young to fall in love,' Georgie argued. 'Not too young to know your own mind. Why must you be so hard on yourself?'

'Because I don't want to be hard on *him*. Oh, Georgie, we've been through all this before. Nothing's changed, not for me. Harry's got a place at university, and a brilliant future ... a chance to make a good life for himself. Can you imagine what it would be like if he had me hanging on his coat-tails ... a girl not yet fifteen ... someone his father resents? I have no idea what my future holds. I can't know where I'm going, or even what tomorrow might hold, but he can start to plan his future now. It's clear and simple for him. Unless he has me to consider as well. He has years of study ahead of him, exams, pressure from all directions. With me in tow all of that could be spoiled, his father might disown him. Even if we were together, what would that do to our relationship? He'd end up hating me for ruining his life.'

'Harry loves you too much for that.'

'And I love him. That's why I won't even risk it.'

'You're a stubborn bugger.'

'But I'm right, aren't I? You know what I'm doing is right?'

Hesitating only for a moment, Georgie confessed, 'I don't know, gal. All I know is you're making a sacrifice I would never make.'

The silence was fraught. Georgie continued to stare at Kitty, shaking her head and envying her strong character. Unaware of Georgie's attention, Kitty let Harry come into her heart, for the briefest moment, a moment too long. The more they talked of Harry, the closer he seemed. And the closer he seemed, the more she hurt. 'The social worker came to see me the other day,' she said presently.

Suspecting the reason for Kitty's deliberately changing the

subject, Georgie didn't press it any further. 'Social, eh? They won't leave me alone either. Still, I expect it's their job to keep tags on us.' Taking a cigarette out of her bag, she lit it up and drew hard on it. Peering at Kitty over the smoke, she asked in a softer voice, 'This social worker, what'd she have to say? Did you tell her about the arguments, and the way that bloody Adam torments you?'

Kitty shook her head. 'No. What would be the point?'

'Well, for a start, she'd have you away from there.'

'And put me where?' Kitty answered her own question. 'Back in the home?' That was the last thing she wanted.

'Just now you said there were times when you wouldn't mind being back there?'

'Only if *you* were there. You're not, so I'm probably better off where I am.' Kitty gave a wry little laugh. 'Adam Connor might be the very devil, but it's a case of "Better the devil you know".'

'I suppose you're right. All families have their ups and downs, and you should know. All the same, gal, if he makes your life a misery, kick him in the balls.'

'You haven't seen the size of him.' The idea of cocking her leg high enough to do what Georgie said was enough to bring a smile to Kitty's face.

'The bigger they are, they harder they fall.' Georgie giggled. 'I don't suppose you've ever caught sight of him in the nuddy?'

'What? Do you want me to have nightmares?' Kitty laughed.

'Shame. I ain't seen a good-size plonker since I had a quick do with the boilerman at the factory.' Rolling her eyes she went on, 'Cor! I'm telling you, gal, I've never seen a man get so excited. We got together in the machine room during the lunch break . . . he had me up against the wall behind the machines. I had my arms tight round his neck and my legs spread so far apart I could hardly keep my balance. I thought any minute he'd push me right through the bleedin' wall!' She smiled and chuckled, then roared with laughter. 'Mind you, if we *had* gone through, the gals in the sewing room next-door would have got a right eyeful . . . two scared buggers with frightened eyes, a couple of bare arses and a cock like a broom handle. Christ! It don't bear thinking about.'

Kitty laughed out loud. 'You're mad as a hatter,' she said.

'One of these days you'll get found out, and they'll give you your cards, *then* what will you do?'

'Gawd knows!'

Though she had to laugh, Kitty couldn't help but feel anxious. 'Be careful,' she said. But she knew that Georgie would do exactly what she wanted, and bother the consequences.

'Never mind about me, gal. I'm my own boss now,' Georgie reminded her. 'It's *you* I'm worried about.'

'No need. I'm fine.' Getting up from the settee, Kitty took her cup into the kitchen. 'I'd best be off, or she'll send out a search party for me.'

'You ain't asked about ... *him*.'

Kitty was taken aback by Georgie's changed mood. She sounded worried, and that wasn't like her. Even as she waited for Kitty's response, she looked anxious. 'You don't like him, do you, gal?' Georgie insisted.

'It's not that. The last time I mentioned him, you nearly bit my head off.'

'That was because you said he was wrong for me. You know how I hate being told what's good or bad for me.'

'I know. But I wouldn't be much of a friend if I didn't look out for you. All the same, I'm sorry if I hurt you.'

'I expect you still think he's bad for me?'

'Has he changed?'

'No.'

'Got a job?'

'Not that I know of.'

'Is he still dossing here?'

'When he feels like it.'

'Then he *is* bad for you.'

'What if I told you I love the idle bugger?'

'Is it ... serious?'

'If you mean would I kill for him, the answer is no. If you mean would I have his kid, or go with him on one of his burgling expeditions, the answer has to be yes.'

'Oh, Georgie!' The one and only time Kitty had seen Georgie's new 'friend' had been enough to tell her he was a bad lot. 'Don't let him use you.'

'Like I said before ... none of your business, gal.' A hardness appeared on her face. 'I told you, we all have choices to make.

You chose to let Harry go so you wouldn't hurt him, and in spite of everything I have to admire you for that. As for me, well, I've chosen a bad bugger there's no denying it. He's a liar and a cheat and I know for a fact he has other women.' She smiled uneasily. 'He even brought the bloody pox home to me, sod him! Oh, it's all right now, but he got the length of my tongue I can tell you!'

'You deserve better.' In a strange way Kitty could understand how Georgie felt. Being alone was a terrible thing and sometimes any companion was better than none at all. 'Will he ever change?'

Georgie smiled and shook her head. 'Shouldn't think so. He's been in and out of jail more times than I've had my leg over. Trouble is, I'm not sure how he really feels about me. He never tells me what he's up to . . . just comes and goes when it suits him. A quick fumble under the sheets, or on the kitchen floor, or wherever he takes the urge, and wham, bam, he's off again.' She clicked her fingers in the air. 'Truth be told he don't care *that* much for me. But he's all I've got, kid . . . good or bad, it don't matter.'

Kitty was momentarily stunned. 'Does he make you happy?' she murmured.

'I suppose he does . . . yeah. And you're right, Mac *is* a bad bugger, but in a way I count myself lucky to have him.'

'No, Georgie.' Kitty's soft voice contained love and frustration. 'It's Mac who's lucky to have you.'

There was little else to be said, and it was time for Kitty to go. 'I'll write in the week,' she promised.

'You'd better!'

Georgie walked her friend to the door, flung it open, and there stood the very man they'd been talking about. Slightly taller than Kitty, slim and wiry with small bright eyes and a bush of ginger hair, he put Kitty in mind of a fox. 'Jaysus Mary and Joseph! You frightened the bloody life outta me,' he exclaimed with a strong Irish accent. 'Sure, I were just about to let meself in.' His hand was raised ready to insert the key in the lock.

'And what makes you think I *want* you in here?' Taking hold of him by the coat collar, Georgie dragged him inside. 'What are you so nervous about anyway?' she demanded, winking at

93

Kitty. 'Coppers after you, are they?'

'Give over!' A smile crinkled his foxy features. 'What would the coppers want with a law-abiding fella like meself?' He glanced at Kitty. 'Has she been blackening my character now? Aw, you shouldn't listen to a thing she says. Sure, I'm never as bad as she makes me out to be.'

Kitty noticed the long black bag he carried, and the jagged tear in his leather jacket. Though she knew he would get Georgie into trouble one day, she realised why her friend was drawn to him because, in spite of her fears for Georgie, she herself had taken an instinctive liking to this cheeky fellow. 'Georgie wouldn't dream of blackening your character,' she said with a grin.

He looked from her to Georgie and back again, and saw the mischief between them. 'Sure you're a wicked pair,' he said. 'As for this one . . .' He flung his arm round Georgie's shoulders. 'I ought to take off me belt and leather your bare arse.' Leaning towards her, he whispered loudly, 'Matter of fact, it might be fun. What do you think?'

Laughing, she shrugged him off. 'I think you're a horny bastard.' She sniffed at his coat and wrinkled her nose. 'Gawd! You stink o' bleedin' fish! You ain't laying a hand on me till you've soaked in the bath for a good hour.'

'Ain't got an hour to spare, darlin'.' Drawing his mouth into a tight little line, he frowned hard. 'I've half an hour before I'm on me way, an' I can think of better ways to spend it than taking a bath.' The suggestion was unmistakable. And it took the light out of Georgie's eyes.

'You've never got time for me, have you, eh?' Punching him with each word, she demanded, 'Well, you can have your choice. Either you stay, at least till the morning . . . or you go right now.'

He didn't give his answer to Georgie but instead addressed Kitty. 'She's a hard woman, don't you think?'

Kitty wanted to shake him. 'She has a right to be.'

'Oh? Two against one now, is it?' He threw his bag on to a nearby chair then took off his jacket and threw it on top. He then began rolling up his sleeves. 'I can see it's time I gave her a good slapping,' he said in a low threatening voice, his eyes turned to Georgie. 'A woman should know her place.'

She saw through him. With a hard push, she sent him flying on top of his belongings. 'Don't even try it,' she warned. 'Unless you want your balls put through the chipper?'

Kitty turned away, laughing. When Mac's voice called her name she swung round to see the pair of them embracing. 'I'll slap her later,' said Mac, wincing when he got a clip round the ear from Georgie.

'You'd better not,' Kitty warned good-naturedly. Her voice hardened when she added, 'Or you'll answer to me.'

Patricia Connor had been feeling unwell for days. Raymond's threat to call a doctor had caused a mighty row and now she was sulking. It was still only ten o'clock, but she could hardly keep her head up. 'I'm off to bed,' she told him. 'Don't make a noise when you come up.'

Raymond sighed and looked up from his newspaper. 'God only knows why you won't let me call the doctor out. If you don't want him here, let me take you in the car first thing in the morning.'

'I've already told you, I'm not seeing the doctor, so leave it be.' She grimaced with pain. 'The last thing I want is him poking about, making things worse.'

'You're a stubborn woman.' Returning his attention to the newspaper, he looked forward to an hour or so of peace before he followed her up the stairs.

Kitty was finishing off some homework before she too would make her way to bed. 'Do you want me to go in the other room?' she enquired, knowing how he liked his privacy. As she looked at him now, she saw a man driven by his work, nagged by his wife, ignored by his arrogant son, and one way or another, always under pressure.

His face was wreathed in smiles when he looked up. 'That's very thoughtful of you, Kitty, but there's no need. In fact it's comforting to have you close by. Unlike the rest of the family, you make no demands on me.'

'I'm almost finished ... just a short essay to do, then I'll be out of your way.'

When he merely nodded, she bent her head to her work and within twenty minutes it was done. 'That's it,' she murmured, gathering her things and preparing to leave.

'Don't go just yet.' Folding his newspaper, he leaned back in the chair and gestured for her to come and sit opposite. 'We never seem to have time for each other,' he declared sadly. 'I feel I badly neglect you, and I never wanted that.'

Taking her folder with her, Kitty crossed the room and sat in the big armchair directly opposite him. 'It's all right,' she said. 'I know how busy you are.'

She couldn't deny he was neglecting her because he was. In fact there were times when she felt she had outstayed her welcome in this house; Patricia grew more and more impatient with her, and where Adam had once tried to disguise his hostility in front of his parents, now he blatantly humiliated and taunted her in full view of his mother.

'Are you happy, Kitty?'

The question was so unexpected, she had to think awhile before answering. Always at the back of her mind was the possibility that she might be sent back to the home and, without Georgie, it would be unbearable. It was on the tip of her tongue to lie, but she thought better of it. She didn't wish to hurt Raymond, but there was little to be gained from lying. 'No,' she said presently, 'I'm not altogether happy.'

It was his turn to think. After a few minutes he remarked quietly, 'Sometimes I wonder if we did you a great disservice in bringing you here.'

This was the first time he had said anything to her that was really meaningful. 'You've nothing to reproach yourself with,' she assured him. 'You've treated me well, and I have a real family at last. I have no right to be resentful.' But she *was* resentful; because she had lost her own family; because she'd sent Harry away; because Georgie was in Bedford and here she was, miles away in Ampthill, with strangers who didn't want her.

'Tell me the truth, Kitty.' His sad brown eyes gazed at her with the trust of a dog. 'What do you think of my son?'

'I don't like him.'

'Hmh!' He nodded his head, eyes tightly closed and his huge fists clenched together in one hard knuckly ball. 'Has he ever hurt you?'

'No.'

'But you would tell me if he did?'

'I think so.'

'I would want you to.' He made a strange sound in the back of his throat. 'Because if he did hurt you, I would have to punish him. I'm afraid I've allowed him to get away with too much.'

Kitty didn't answer. There was something odd about Raymond's manner, as though he had been drinking.

'My wife treats you well though, doesn't she?'

'Yes.'

'That's good. She has her faults, but she means well. It's just a pity she lets her son dictate to her. One day I really must do something about that.' Leaning back in his chair, he slowly ran both hands over his head, as though wiping something burdensome from it. 'Life is a funny thing,' he muttered. 'Much like the desk at my office. You think you have it all organised, then in blows an evil wind and scatters everything about.' He stared across at her and there was a desolate look about him. 'I make a great deal of money. Did you know that, Kitty?'

His strange manner made her uneasy. Impatient to leave for the relative privacy of her own room, she gave the shortest answer possible. 'I thought you must, because of the house and everything.'

'I gather your father was a successful businessman?'

Though she didn't know why, Kitty resented his talking of her father. She could not bring herself to answer, so merely nodded.

'Oh, I'm sorry, Kitty.' He seemed genuinely repentant. 'That was insensitive of me!'

'It's all right.' And it was. She stood up. 'I really am tired.'

He appeared not to have heard her. 'What do you think of my wife?'

'She's been very kind to me. You both have.'

'Not Adam though, eh?'

'I understand why he resents me.'

'So do I, Kitty. Oh! So do I.' He grinned, but his eyes remained hard. 'Have you any secrets, Kitty? Any *dark* secrets you would be afraid for people to find out?'

'I don't know what you mean.' Harry was her only secret. She could never discuss him with anyone but Georgie, and even then there were things she kept back. Things that belonged only to her and Harry.

'What I mean is . . . we *all* have secrets, Kitty. Things we never

97

tell ... things we *daren't* tell.' Again he wiped his hands over his head, then stared at the ceiling with sad frightened eyes.

Fearing he was ill, Kitty offered, 'Is there anything I can do for you before I go to bed? Would you like me to make you a drink?'

'Can you change the past, Kitty?'

'No.' Of, if only she could!

'Can you give a man back his pride?' Before she could think about that, he answered it for himself. 'No, of course you can't.' He looked at her. 'You've blossomed, Kitty ... become a real beauty.' Drumming his fingers on the chair arm, he went on, 'There are plenty of beautiful women willing to sell themselves to a man who has money and position. Scavengers most of them. Beautiful on the outside, ugly on the inside. But you'll never be like that, Kitty, because you're different. You're beautiful by nature. That's why I was drawn to you, and that's why I want you to be happy here with us.' He eyed her curiously. 'But you're not, are you, Kitty? You're *not*, and that makes me sad.'

'I'm sure I will be, in time.'

He smiled enigmatically. 'Until then you'll be living a lie, like we all do.' He held out his hand as though he would take hold of her. When she made no response he let his arm drop heavily to his side. 'If you found something out ... something about me ... would you tell tales, Kitty?'

'I hope not.' She felt as though she was being dragged out of her depth. 'It's late,' she said, glancing at the clock. 'I really am very tired.'

'Then you had best get to your bed.' As she turned he said, 'I hope the day never comes when you have to be ashamed of anything. Shame can destroy a person.'

Another time she might have said goodnight. Another time she might even have cheered him with a small peck on the cheek. But not tonight. Tonight she felt threatened as never before.

Two days later, Patricia was rushed to hospital. Appendicitis, they said. In fact it was peritonitis and she was very ill. After the operation it was decided she would have to stay in hospital for at least a week. Raymond was beside himself. 'If anything happened to you,' he told her, 'I wouldn't want to live.' And there was no doubting his sincerity.

Adam took it all with his usual complacency. 'She'll be all right,' he predicted. 'She's tough as old boots.'

At home it was unbearable. In the evenings Raymond moped or paced the lounge, and Adam hid in his bedroom playing heavy rock tapes at top volume.

Kitty's offer to keep the house clean and cook the evening meal was graciously refused by Raymond. 'We'll all do our bit,' he announced, but after a day of inexpertly prepared meals, unmade beds and Adam's constant carping, he recruited the services of a very serious-faced domestic. Miss Lacey arrived eight o'clock in the morning and departed an hour after the evening meal was finished.

Kitty went to school and came home and went to bed and got up, and every evening she went to the hospital with Raymond, and sat by the bed while he cooed and fussed over his 'darling wife'.

One day ran into another. Kitty felt totally isolated, and almost crazy. That first evening she wrote and told Georgie the news, but her anxiety was only heightened when she received a reply.

Dear Kitty,

What rotten luck! Bad as Patricia is, she is at least another woman in the house. I'm sure Raymond is almost out of his mind and won't have time for anyone else. Keep out of the other one's way though. I don't trust the bastard!

I'd ask you to come over here so we can have a laugh and a chat, but Mac's asked me to go away for a few days. How can I refuse? I'll admit I'm worried about his reasons for wanting to get away in such a hurry, but that's Mac, ain't it? (Wouldn't surprise me if he's been up to his old tricks again. I expect half the police force are after the bugger.)

Anyway, I've cleared it with the landlord and everything, and I'm off! Mac's picking me up in ten minutes . . . a 'borrowed car' he says. I've no idea where he's taking me, and to be honest I don't care. I mean to enjoy it, and there's nothing to hurry back for . . . especially as I've lost my job for being late twice in a row.

Don't look like I'll be getting that blue mini-bus for a

while yet, eh? But Mac says he means to buy it for me one day. Trouble is, how many years will he have to serve in one of Her Majesty's prisons to pay for it? I've told him it's not worth that much. I'd rather have the bugger where I can keep an eye on him,

Luv you, kid. Keep your pecker up,

Georgie

XXX

'Oh, Georgie, make sure you keep out of trouble,' Kitty whispered. But she couldn't help feeling there was a catastrophe in the offing.

The first sign of it came from an unexpected quarter. It was the early hours of the morning. Patricia had been in hospital three days. Both Adam and his father had gone out for the evening; Adam with his mates and Raymond to a business dinner. Left to her own devices, Kitty enjoyed the luxury of a late-night film. When it was over she bathed and went to bed, and after a long day was soon fast asleep.

When she awoke she wasn't certain what it was that had disturbed her, until she heard the sound again, a voice, and something else, like the awful sound your finger-nails make when scraped along a blackboard.

She sat up in bed. There *was* someone downstairs. 'Could be Adam,' she mused aloud. Yes, that was it. Adam had come in and was having a snack in the kitchen.

Going out on to the landing she looked towards his room. The door was wide open. There was no sign of him there. About to return to her warm bed, she heard the sound again, only this time there were *two* voices. 'Adam's got himself a girlfriend,' she whispered with a smile. 'With a bit of luck she might teach him to be more civil.'

Curiosity crept over her. 'Wonder what she's like?' Unable to resist, she made her way quietly down the stairs.

She was right. The sounds were coming from the kitchen. Gingerly, she inched open the door. At first she couldn't see anything, so she edged it open a bit further. The kitchen light was out but the moonlight was stronger now, filtering in through the window and lighting the shadows.

It had been suddenly quiet, but now frantic groans and squeals of ecstasy reverberated round the room.

Closer, she bent her head to see round the door, dark eyes smiling and curious at first but widening with horror and fascination as they alighted on the couple inside.

They were so near she could almost touch them. The woman was young ... twenty-one, twenty-two? Very attractive, with long blonde hair and a figure that most women would die for. Spreadeagled on a chair, she had her legs wide open and her arms clawing at the man's bare back; for a while he knelt with his head between her legs and his long pink tongue flicking back and forth, driving her into a frenzy. Now she had him by the hair and was dragging him up, kissing him on the mouth, licking his face and biting his ears, her whole body arching towards him as he thrust his erect penis into her. They were like mad things, eating each other, stark naked, rivers of sweat running from one to the other, cries mingling as they climaxed. When they crumpled in a heap to the floor they were screaming like wild animals.

Kitty couldn't understand her own feelings. She felt she should be ashamed, but she wasn't. She had never seen anything like it before and felt both repelled and excited. Then, a wave of disgust swamped her. When she first saw him, she couldn't believe it. It wasn't Adam. It was his father! *Now* she understood. 'We *all* have secrets', he'd said. This was his 'secret' ... and now it was hers. She wanted no part of it.

She turned to hurry away, and fell right into Adam's arms.

She would have cried out but his hand clamped over her mouth and his drunken face leered down at her. He too had been watching. 'I never thought the old man had it in him,' he whispered. 'But I can't say I blame him. Mother isn't the prettiest thing in the world. I imagine she must be boring in bed.' There was a fierce pride in his eyes. 'Nice to see Father enjoying himself though ... after all, we men have to keep women in their places.' He laughed softly. 'Fancy that though ... the old bastard having it away with a woman half his age!' He was seeing his father in a different light. 'Maybe he'll teach *me* a trick or two, eh?'

Kicking out, she caught him hard on the shin. When he still held her tight, she sank her teeth into the soft flesh of his hand, deeper and deeper, until the blood trickled over his fist.

Enraged, he shook her like a rag doll. 'Bitch!' Squeezing his fingers round her face, he murmured, 'If you know what's best you'll listen to what I'm telling you. Keep this little episode to yourself. After all, what Mother doesn't know won't hurt her, and it would be too inconvenient if my parents split up. When I'm gone they can do what the hell they like, but I'm not ready for all that just yet. So keep your mouth shut, or I might have to think of a way to soil your good reputation.'

Keeping his hand over her mouth, he dragged her to the foot of the stairs. 'Get to bed,' he warned, releasing her. 'And, remember ... not a word about what you just witnessed. If Mother ever has to know, *I'll* be the one to tell her ... when it serves my purpose and not before.'

Kitty held her head high. Staring at him with contempt, she spoke in a low harsh voice. 'You needn't worry about me. Unlike you, I don't want to cause trouble between them. What they do is no concern of mine.'

'And that's all you need to remember.' Spitefully flicking her under the chin, he returned to the front door and made a big fuss about entering; he sang out loud, stumbled all over the place and sent the coat-stand flying, slammed the front door and called at the top of his voice, 'I'm home!' Then he staggered across the hallway and followed Kitty up the stairs. She walked slowly, antagonising him and enjoying the experience.

At the top she went one way and he the other. Once in his room he collapsed on the bed, laughed until he cried, and fell into a drunken stupor that would keep him unconscious until late the following day.

Downstairs, Raymond thanked his lucky stars he had not been caught. Having hurriedly dressed, he showed his woman out then went into the lounge where he sat until the dawn, his head in his hands and a great burden of shame weighing him down. After a time he stood before Patricia's photograph. 'I won't cheat you again,' he vowed, but it was an empty promise. One he had made time and again, and broken time and again. But, like Adam, he believed that what she didn't know couldn't hurt her.

He was wrong.

It was Friday evening when Raymond collected Patricia from the hospital. She ran her eyes over every artefact in the lounge.

'Finger marks!' she moaned. 'And dust everywhere! I thought you said that woman was taking good care of my home?' The look she gave her husband would have floored a lesser man.

Raymond followed her gaze. 'Looks all right to me.' His awful guilt was like a tightness in his chest. Patricia could say and do anything, and he would not reproach her.

Though she thought everything shone brightly and there were neither finger marks nor dust in sight, Kitty offered to go round with a duster. 'It won't take me long.'

Patricia wouldn't hear of it. 'I'll speak to that woman in the morning. She's here for another week, so she can go over everything with a fine toothcomb.'

That was exactly what she did. The woman smiled and nodded and did as she was told, just as Raymond had asked her to do. Patricia dogged her every footstep, and for a whole week, made that poor woman's life unbearable. Kitty felt for her, but there was little she could do.

On the following Friday afternoon, she took her fat wage and went. Kitty stayed, and wished she too could just walk away. But she couldn't. She was a prisoner here, like it or not.

One evening while Kitty and Patricia prepared the evening meal, Raymond hid in his study. Adam played loud music from his bedroom and irritated everyone. 'Still, he's not really harming anyone, is he?' Patricia sighed. 'I dare say in a few years when he's out in the wide world, I'll wish he was here, playing his music and all.' She dreaded the day.

Kitty made no comment. If she had, it would have been to say Patricia should be wishing he would go tomorrow and never come back.

Soon the table was laid ready. The aroma of crackly pork roast, baked potatoes and green cabbage filled the kitchen; there was a luscious sherry trifle to follow, and after Kitty had filled the pretty floral jug with pouring cream, she was told, 'You can go and change, and tell the others dinner will be on the table in five minutes.' Patricia was in charge again, and in her element.

While Kitty was upstairs, Adam took the opportunity to have a quiet word with his mother. 'I didn't want to worry you before,' he said, 'but I think you should know Kitty was very difficult while you were in hospital.' Sitting on the stool by the breakfast bar, he sipped a glass of water, watching her with sly eyes.

Patricia could not hide her disappointment. Wiping her hands on a tea-towel, she came to sit beside him. 'What do you mean, "difficult"?'

'Spiteful.' Leaning down, he rolled back his sock and let her see the yellowing bruise on his shin. '*That's* what I mean, Mother.' Gingerly touching it he winced, though the discomfort had long gone.

'Are you telling me *Kitty* did that?'

He nodded. 'I was trying to pass her on the stairs, and she just lashed out.'

Patricia would never doubt her son's word. 'Why would she do such a thing?'

Shrugging his shoulders, he answered. 'Who knows? Perhaps she was missing you. Perhaps she has a nasty streak we don't know about yet. Then again, maybe she just felt like kicking me. After all, Mother . . . it's no secret she doesn't like me, is it?'

'Did you tell your father?'

'No. He was worried about you. I didn't want to add to his troubles.'

She hugged him. 'You're such a thoughtful young man.' She said, delighting him. 'But you really should have told your father. He could have dealt with it there and then. Kitty has to learn she cannot behave like that. I won't have it!'

'I hope you're not going to cause a fuss?' He appeared suitably reluctant.

Patting him lovingly on the back, she said, 'You leave that to me. Now go and get washed. Dinner's ready.'

The atmosphere round the dinner table was fraught. Adam pretended he was intent on enjoying the meal when really he was secretly hoping Kitty was about to get her comeuppance; Raymond was still overwhelmed with guilt, wondering how he could face his wife after what he had done; and like every evening since the shock of seeing Raymond and that woman writhing together in the kitchen, Kitty was afraid to look him in the eye. Patricia constantly glanced from one to the other, making them afraid she could look into their minds and see what they were thinking.

They were into the sherry trifle when Patricia addressed Kitty in a solemn voice. 'Adam tells me you two have been fighting. Is that right, Kitty?'

She gulped. What had Adam told his mother? Had he betrayed his father? No! If he had, Patricia would be at Raymond's throat. So what had he told her? And why?

Before she could answer, Adam piped up, 'We weren't exactly fighting, Mother. In fact, when Kitty caught me on the shin it might well have been an accident. After all, I was running up the stairs two at a time.'

Patricia gave him a loving smile. 'It's very commendable of you to explain it away like that, sweetheart,' she declared, 'but I was asking Kitty for *her* explanation.' Turning to her once more, she urged, 'Is that what happened, Kitty? Was it an accident? I do hope so. I would hate to think you kicked Adam on purpose, dear.'

Aware that all eyes were on here, including Raymond's, she looked across the table to meet Adam's cunning gaze. She couldn't help wondering why he had done this. What did he hope to gain? She saw no real reason why he should have told Patricia that she'd kicked him. Unless it was a bit of mischief, just to make her feel uncomfortable. If that was the case, then he had certainly succeeded. Just for the briefest moment Kitty was tempted to tell Patricia the truth . . . that they had seen her husband with a woman . . . that Adam had threatened her . . . that she had kicked him because he was holding her against her will, with his hand across her mouth so she couldn't call out. All of that flashed through her mind. But when she looked at Raymond, at his sad eyes and bent shoulders, she couldn't do it. 'He's right,' she confirmed. 'It was an accident. Adam was running up the stairs and as I turned at the top he tripped over my leg.' God forgive her for lying.

'That's all right then.' Patricia beamed from ear to ear. 'I was sure you would not have done it on purpose.' All the same the seed had been sown, and she couldn't help but wonder whether Adam was covering up for Kitty. It gave her a deal to think about.

For the first time throughout dinner, Raymond spoke out. Addressing Adam, he asked, 'When *was* this?'

Grinning, Adam rammed another spoonful of trifle into his mouth. For what seemed an age he kept his father waiting, before answering with a devious smile, 'Last Friday . . . I came in late. Kitty was in the hallway.' He grinned at her. 'I think she came down to investigate a noise or something . . . isn't that so?'

Kitty hated him so much she wanted to kill him. 'It was nothing,' she said. 'Nothing at all.'

Adam laughed. 'There you are, Father.' Seeing how the colour had drained from Raymond's face, he remarked, 'Kitty says it was nothing. So you needn't worry.' His voice fell almost to a whisper as he said meaningfully, 'If you know what I mean?'

After that, Patricia chatted on but Raymond was broodingly silent. The next day he arranged to take Patricia out to dinner. 'I owe it to you,' he said, and she agreed.

It was eight o'clock when they left. 'We should be back before midnight,' Patricia told Kitty. 'Don't make a mess in the house, and don't annoy Adam.' With that she gave Kitty a very odd look. 'You do have a way of getting under his skin.'

Kitty watched through the window as they got into the car; Raymond in a black dinner-suit and silk waistcoat, and Patricia done up like a film star in a long white gown and silver wrap with matching shoes. In a frustrating way Kitty both pitied and envied her.

All evening long, she kept out of Adam's way. If she heard him in the lounge she sat in the kitchen. If he came into the kitchen she went out through the other door into the hallway and up the stairs to her room. Once she thought she heard him outside her bedroom door; there had been the unmistakable sound of his footsteps coming up the stairs, then along the landing towards her room. The footsteps stopped, lingered, then went away again in the same direction. 'Come in here and I'll scream blue murder,' Kitty swore under her breath. She knew however, that no amount of screaming would bring the neighbours. They were too far away.

After a while it grew quiet, the television set was switched off downstairs, and when she recognised Adam's familiar footsteps going along the landing, she waited for the sound of his bedroom door closing.

When she was sure he must be asleep, she collected her nightgown and toiletries. On tiptoe she went to her bathroom and ran a bath full of piping hot water. Soon she was immersed in the frothy perfumed water, thinking about Harry and wonder-

106

ing what he was doing. When that became too painful she began softly to sing, her voice uplifted in a Buddy Holly song. Closing her eyes, she let the warm waters lap over her. This was sheer luxury. In the home, you had to wait your turn for the bathroom and sometimes you were lucky if you got a bath at all. More often than not it was a quick run under the shower, with a chorus of voices calling you to: 'Get a move on!'

Bathed and sleepy, Kitty returned to her bedroom. Here she sat before the mirror, brushing her thick dark hair and dreaming of Harry. Afterwards she took a moment to examine herself. 'You're thinner,' she told the face staring back at her. 'And there are shadows under your eyes.' She felt much older than her years. Nightmares still haunted her; vivid pictures of her mother leaping in front of the train . . . the train-driver's wild horrified eyes . . . and her father . . . the house burning around him, that weird smile . . . his mouth moving, speaking yet not speaking . . . what was he saying? What made them do such terrible things? The pictures never went away, nor the questions, nor the consequences which she alone had to live with now.

And, oh how she missed them. Missed her mother's beautiful smile and missed her father's black moods. Missed Harry. 'Harry.' The name fell from her lips and her heart ached all the more. 'Harry.' Just a word, a name, but everything to her. Yet in her sadness Kitty was glad for him, glad that he had the freedom she would never have again. 'One day you'll realise I did it for you,' she murmured. The thought gave her a rush of pleasure.

Climbing into bed, she enjoyed the silence. After the hustle and bustle of the home it was a wondrous thing, so quiet she could almost hear her own heart beating. Tiredness crept up on her. She fought it for a while, until the long lashes closed over her dark eyes and she gave herself up to it. She waited for the dreams to start. She knew they would.

It seemed no time at all before she was awake again, a raging thirst on her. She lay there a while, her face turned to the window. The curtains were half open and, apart from a halo of moonlight, the night was black. She wondered if the Connors had returned.

107

Out of bed, she peered through the window into the darkness. The light over the garage doors showed they were still open. 'Not back yet,' she muttered. A quick glance at the bedside clock told her it was almost eleven-thirty. Her thirst was intense.

Putting on her robe she went softly out of the room and down to the kitchen. She didn't put the hallway light on in case it woke Adam. Instead she felt her way along the banister, only putting a light on when she was inside the kitchen with the door closed behind her. 'Don't want that big ox down here,' she whispered. Looking up to the ceiling she pulled a face. 'Let him sleep. Let him die. Who cares?' She realised then how devastated Patricia would be if anything happened to her precious son, and was mortified.

It took only minutes to heat some milk. When it was cooler she poured it into a glass and sat at the big table, slowly relishing it, letting the smooth liquid trickle down her throat. 'That's better,' she murmured. The house was so quiet. Her thoughts turned to Georgie. Where was she now? What was she up to? Kitty prayed she would stay out of trouble.

She didn't hear him come in. Creeping up on her, he gripped her throat from behind, like a falcon might do when it swoops on a rabbit. She couldn't move, couldn't speak. 'You were wise not to tell,' he murmured hoarsely. 'Do you know how much I loathe your being here, in this house, at my table?' He squeezed his fingers and the pain was excruciating. 'I want you out, and I'll do *anything!*'

Kitty put up her hands and tried desperately to pull him away. The more she tugged, the tighter his grip became. He peered into her face, forcing her head up and back. His eyes were wild, burning with hatred. In that moment she believed he would kill her.

'I've always liked your name though.' And he laughed. 'Kitty ... kitten. Suits you.' Reaching over her, he poured a saucer of milk. Taking the saucer in one hand and still holding her in a vice-like grip, he jerked her from the stool and threw her to her knees. Putting the saucer in front of her he urged in an insane voice, 'Lap it up, kitten!' Pressing her down, he forced her face into the milk. When she closed her mouth and turned her head, he knelt on her back, pushing her down until she had no choice but to let the milk flow over her nose and mouth. 'Lap it up!' he ordered. Again and again he pressed her down, until she realised he would only let her go if she did as she was told.

Choking on every mouthful, she lapped it up. When it was all gone, he released her and fell about laughing. 'That was worth watching,' he cried, pointing at her with a trembling finger.

Catching her breath, Kitty leaped at him. With a strength she didn't know she had, she wrestled him to the floor and punched at him with clenched fists. His nose burst open like a fountain when she grabbed the flex of the toaster and pulled it down on his head. When her rage was satisfied, she ran up the stairs to her bedroom and locked the door. She could hear his laughter and it turned her heart over. For a full hour she stood behind the door with a paperweight in her fist. He didn't follow her. He had other plans.

When his parents arrived home, Adam was waiting, bloodied and broken. 'She did this,' he said. 'She's gone mad.'

Raymond believed there was more to it than that, Patricia was beside herself, and Kitty was brought to account for what she had done. She could have told the truth. She could have said it was Adam who'd attacked *her*. She might have revealed how it all really began last Friday, when Raymond was entertaining his lover. But he silently pleaded with his eyes and she could not bring herself to betray him.

Early on Sunday morning, Kitty was returned to the home in disgrace. Miss Davis gave her a lecture, saying how fortunate she was that charges of assault had not been brought against her. She remarked on the charity of the Connor family, and sent her away to think about what she had done. When Kitty went out of the room, Miss Davis opened the official ledger. She was angry and confused, reluctant to believe Kitty was capable of what they had described. But in her job you must never allow your heart to rule your head. The entry was made: 'KITTY MARSH. Must be watched. A danger to others.'

Later everyone attended church. Kitty was made to stand at the back. She looked up at the crucifix with tears in her eyes. '*You* know the truth,' she whispered. Just now, it was all that mattered.

Georgie was coming to the end of her journey. 'All right! All right! You don't have to push.' Clutching her belongings, she stumbled out of the van and into the yard. There was fencing all around, with tall iron gates to keep intruders out and the inmates in.

The officer in charge of the new arrivals sighed. Georgie was only two years older than her own wayward daughter. She had only just discovered the girl was into drugs, and thieving, and mixing with a bad lot. Nothing she said or did made any difference. Now, after too many sleepless nights, her work was suffering. She was touchy, short-tempered, and couldn't bring herself to confide in her colleagues. They wouldn't understand. They had husbands while she had no one, and now she was at the end of her tether. Georgie only reminded her how easy it would be for her daughter to end up being put in a borstal institution, like this one at Aylesbury.

'I'm not pushing,' she said, doing her best to be patient. 'If you moved a bit quicker we could all get on with what we have to do.' In fact, during the journey from Bedford court, she had taken a liking to Georgie. 'Do as you're told in here,' she advised in a whisper as they walked into the reception area. 'And you'll come to no harm.'

'And if I don't do as I'm told?' Impatient with everyone and angry with herself for getting involved in a burglary, Georgie was already missing Mac. He had been on the run for two days before the police finally caught him. Now he too was on his way to prison.

A burly warden stared up from her desk. She asked the usual questions and entered the replies meticulously in a ledger. Then she snapped it shut and escorted Georgie into the inner cubicles. There stood another officer, tall and elegant in her uniform but with a hard resigned look on her face that came from years of dealing with offenders. Acknowledging the other officer with a nod of the head, she then looked at Georgie. 'Strip off.' She had a surprisingly soft voice.

Looking from one to the other, Georgie drew away. 'Not bloody likely!' she cried. '*I'm* not stripping.' She gave a little nervous chuckle. 'Not for you lot anyway.'

The voice remained gentle but the threat was harsh. 'You either do it yourself, or I'm afraid we'll have to do it for you.'

'Like hell!'

It took only two minutes for the wardens to strip her. Another ten minutes to examine her all over, and another five minutes to run her under the shower. After that she was issued with a clean set of clothes and given a sheet containing the rules of the institution. 'You're here to do as you're told,' she was informed. Then she was marched into the office, where it was explained how she would be put to work for the duration of her two-year sentence. 'We're not monsters here,' she was told. 'Behave yourself, work hard, and we'll get along just fine.'

Georgie remained sullen and silent. She thought about Kitty, and felt ashamed at having gone away and lost touch. 'When can I have pen and paper?' she demanded.

'When you've earned it,' she was told. The interview was ended and she was sent on her way to learn a new set of rules. 'Serves you right, Georgie gal!' she muttered. 'You never learn.'

She looked forward to writing to Mac, and to Kitty. It had been many months since Kitty had gone to live with the Connors, and no doubt she was doing fine.

One thing was for certain: that bugger Mac might let her rot here but not Kitty. She would never turn her back on an old friend.

CHAPTER SEVEN

Miss Davis looked tired. Returning to work after three weeks away due to illness, she still felt in need of a month in the sun. 'You don't realise how fortunate you are, Kitty,' she said. 'You're young. You have your health and strength, and the looks to carry you far.' She remained at her desk, Kitty standing before her. 'You could be a model,' she said with a warm smile.

In these past months Kitty had grown into one of the loveliest creatures she had ever seen. With her long dark hair and magnificent dark eyes, she was captivating. More than that, unlike so many other young madams who had crossed the threshold in and out of this establishment, Kitty possessed no big ideas about herself, no airs or graces; indeed she seemed at times to be totally oblivious of her own beauty. That was one of the reasons Miss Davis had come to love her. The other was Kitty's warm and generous nature.

'I'm too short.'

Taken by surprise, Miss Davis shook herself alert. 'Sorry, dear. What did you say?'

Kitty smiled. She was used to Miss Davis's mind wandering off. She supposed it was the illness or creeping old age. 'You said I could be a model,' she reminded her. 'Even if I wanted to, which I don't, I couldn't because I'm too short.'

Miss Davis shook her head. 'Not "short", my dear. The word is petite. You are petite.' In fact Kitty was like a little doll, small and shapely. She was also big-hearted and had the kind of personality that brightened a room whenever she walked in. Suddenly Miss Davis found herself regretting the great hulk she was. Unmarried and glad to be so, she'd never envied those who had tied the knot especially when she had to deal with the likes of the Connors, who had lied through their teeth about

113

the incident concerning Kitty and their obnoxious son. Kitty had never revealed the truth but it was painfully obvious what had happened there. It was also obvious that theirs was a very unhappy marriage. As for Kitty's Aunt Mildred, who only lately had begun to write to her niece, she too was having marital problems.

'I'm glad your aunt has written to you, Kitty. I'm really sorry she's been so ill.'

Kitty found it easy to talk to Miss Davis. She was a kind understanding soul who genuinely loved the children in her care. 'There was something else in the letter,' she confessed. 'Aunt Mildred wants me to visit her. I thought I might go on Saturday, if that's all right?' She didn't reveal there was a certain under-current in Mildred's letter that had made her uneasy.

Miss Davis couldn't hide her delight. 'Why, that's wonderful, Kitty!' Struggling out of her chair she came round to put her hands on Kitty's shoulders. 'It's not August yet, so you still have five weeks of the summer holidays left. Maybe she has some-thing planned ... a family outing or a treat? You can't know how pleased I am that she wants to see you. It's long been a thorn in my side that your father's sister turned her back on you.' Her old eyes were moist. 'Do you think she wants you to live with them?' If she did it wouldn't be before time.

Kitty had a long memory. She recalled the argument between her father and Mildred soon after her mother's funeral. She remembered the things her aunt had said ... how she would not look after Kitty, and how the girl was not her responsibility. In her mind Kitty relived the talk Mildred had given her while she sat desolate on the stairs. 'I can't have you,' she'd said. 'I have enough problems of my own.' Loath to hold grudges she had always given Mildred the benefit of the doubt, but after all this time her heart still ached when she remembered how her aunt had abandoned her to a children's home. She could never do what Mildred had done. However difficult the circumstances, she could never have rejected her own brother's child.

'You have no idea what your aunt wants?'

'She didn't say ... only that it was important.'

'Hmh!' Miss Davis knew the house and business had been sold a long time back. 'Perhaps it's to do with your father's properties?'

'I don't know.' Money was never uppermost in Kitty's mind. She left Mildred to take care of all that.

'Sit down, child.' Miss Davis waited for Kitty to be seated. Easing her own large frame down again, she bit her lip and wondered how she might put Kitty on her guard without alarming her. 'Would you like someone to come with you on Saturday?'

'That's very kind, but no.' Kitty hated to be treated like a child. 'I'd rather go on my own.' She saw a flicker of anxiety in the woman's face. 'Why? Is there something wrong?'

Miss Davis rolled her eyes and laughed a little. 'Of course not! It's just that you haven't seen your aunt in a long while. I thought you might like some company, that's all.' She couldn't voice her suspicions, but felt it only right to warn Kitty. 'I'm here to help and advise if you need me . . . I mean, if your aunt asks you to agree to anything.'

In fact she was echoing Kitty's own thoughts. 'I won't do anything at all without talking to you first.' Georgie had already said she thought Mildred was robbing Kitty blind.

Miss Davis gave a sigh of relief. 'That's good.' Afraid she might have planted a germ of suspicion in Kitty's mind, she exclaimed, 'But, I'm not saying she would ask you to do anything untoward.'

Kitty reassured her, 'I know that.'

Suddenly the smile slid from Miss Davis's face. 'I have something to tell you, Kitty. It is hard but must be said. *Two* things in fact.'

Kitty had that same awful feeling in the pit of her stomach that she had had when Harry walked away. 'Concerning me?' she asked apprehensively.

'Concerning us both.'

'Is it to do with my being fostered out?' The last couple who had spoken with her seemed very keen. Kitty had been fearing they might apply for custody. 'Can't I stay here until I'm sixteen?'

'You know it doesn't work like that, Kitty. We are duty bound to find you a suitable set of foster parents, and a secure family home. It's a good policy, even though things do tend to go wrong occasionally.' She pulled a wry little face. 'You seem to have been particularly unlucky so far.' Her instincts told her the

115

present couple were not suitable for Kitty, but their credentials were perfect and nothing had been uncovered to discredit their application. She told Kitty as much. 'They do seem able to give you a good home,' she said. 'But it may not come to that.' Her eyes crinkled into a smile as she said more cheerily, 'Who knows? Your Aunt Mildred may be about to offer you a home with her.'

'I doubt that.' Even if she did, Kitty still had few inclinations to live with her; though if it meant avoiding being fostered out again, she might be tempted. 'When will I know if I'm to be fostered out?'

'The decision will be made very soon.' More than anyone Miss Davis knew how Kitty had been shifted from pillar to post, and her heart went out to her. 'You've had some very bad experiences, Kitty,' she acknowledged. 'That's why this time the couple are being put under the microscope.'

Kitty merely nodded. Since being returned by the Connors, she had been to two other sets of foster parents, and each time the consequences had been disastrous. First there was the middle-aged family who already had three children of their own; they saw Kitty as their own personal contribution to society and treated her as a piece of propaganda rather than a person. After she refused to be paraded before everyone at a fund-raising garden party, Kitty was smartly returned to the home. 'Ungrateful!' they said. And Miss Davis equally smartly showed them the door. The second couple had no children. Rousing Kitty from her bed between the hours of four and six every morning, they knelt in her room, wailing and moaning, renouncing the devil and all his evils. The same ritual was enacted all day Sunday and most evenings to midnight. Exhausted and disillusioned, Kitty was returned to the home at her own request.

'You said there were *two* things you had to tell me?' She was holding her breath. Could anything be worse than being fostered out again?

'It's to do with me, Kitty.' As though recharging herself, Miss Davis drew in a great gulp of air. It came out in a rush with the words, 'I've decided to retire.'

Kitty could hardly believe her ears. 'But you're not old enough!' First Georgie gone, now Miss Davis. It didn't bear thinking about.

Miss Davis laughed out loud. 'Bless you for that, dear,' she said. 'And you are right of course. I might not *look* ready for the knacker's yard, but I certainly feel it. I'm four years away from retirement age, but I'm worn out and that's the plain truth.' Worn out from years of worrying about others, worn out from years of fighting authority on her children's behalf, worn out by the increasing burden of administration, the long trying days and sleepless nights.

'I still don't know what I'll do with myself,' she admitted, 'but I need to re-evaluate my life. This last long illness told me that.' It told her she was growing older. It told her she had no real quality of life, and that time was running out. 'It took a lot of heart-searching before I finally decided,' she confessed in a quiet voice. 'Now that I have, I won't change my mind.'

'It won't be the same without you.' Kitty couldn't get to grips with it. 'I'll miss you.'

The words were inadequate. She would miss her more than she could ever say. This big kind soul had been father, mother and friend to her. She had been there from the very start, and each time the fostering had gone wrong. She was there when Harry left her life, and there when Georgie went. In Kitty's ever-changing world, Miss Davis was the one constant figure, and she had come to love her. 'I don't want you to go,' she murmured, and even as the words left her lips she regretted them. How could she begrudge this woman her rest? How could she make her feel guilty. 'No, I don't mean that,' she quickly added, and the words caught in her throat.

Miss Davis understood. 'Of course you mean it, Kitty,' she said softly. 'I don't mind. I understand how you feel. That's why I wanted you to be the first to know. I owe you that much.'

'Will you ever come back here?'

A sad shake of the head. 'No.' One word, but it carried a world of convictions.

'What will you do?'

'For the first few weeks, I mean to put my feet up and take things easy. After that, I mean to go north, to Blackburn where I come from. I have a few relatives I haven't seen in a long time.' Chuckling, she confessed, 'It wouldn't surprise me if they showed me the door. Oh, I've written, we've kept in touch, but somehow we've never sat face to face in all these years.'

117

She sighed, momentarily closing her eyes and seeing it all in her mind: the Palais near Accrington where she used to dance as a teenager, and the wonderful old buildings round King George's Hall where she and a sweetheart met every Friday night. He didn't last long though, not after he tried to get her knickers off in the back seat of the Odeon.

Opening her eyes, she sighed with pleasure. 'Oh, Kitty, it will be good to see the old town again.' A flicker of disappointment crossed her face, 'But it's all changed now, I understand. Once upon a time everybody knew everybody down our street... children played on the cobbles and women chatted while they white-stoned their front steps. The houses are posher now, with bay windows and net curtains, and everyone has inside lavatories.' She laughed out loud. 'By! I remember the times when we had to queue up at the bottom of the yard, waiting for our turn to use the loo.' Even that was a precious memory. 'My old aunt tells me they've pulled down acres of the old terraced housing and built a new shopping arcade since I was last there. St Peter's church is still the same though, and the cathedral... and Corporation Park with its lake and acres of magnificent gardens.' There was happiness in her face as she went on, 'One beautiful summer's day, Kitty, when my wanderings are over, I shall sit on the bench at the top of the park, and look over the whole of Blackburn, and all around me will be the smell of blossom and the sound of children playing.' Her eyes lit up at the thought. 'Oh! It's a lovely place, Kitty.'

'It sounds wonderful.' Kitty had visions of church spires and people who sat outside on sunny afternoons, and a lake filled with white birds and surrounded by swaying willows. 'I'd like to see Blackburn one day.' She was thinking of a house of her own, and a husband, and children. She was thinking of Harry. And her heart was sore.

Miss Davis was thinking too; about wasted time and the few years she might have left. 'Some time ago my mother left me a nice little nest egg,' she explained. 'I've been too busy to spend it, but I mean to spend it now.' Her eyes lit up. 'I've always wanted to travel... to visit far-off places I've only ever seen on the Alan Whicker programmes.' Suddenly her mind was made up. 'Yes! That's what I'll do, Kitty... travel to the corners of the earth where I've never been.'

'Will I ever see you again?' Lately she could hardly recall her mother's face. Kitty didn't want her parting with Miss Davis to be so final.

'Well, I won't be leaving for a month. After that, we'll see.' She wondered if it would be harder to keep in touch with her past than to turn her back on it and start a new life without hindrance. But, no. Kitty would never be a hindrance. 'We'll talk about it later, dear.' Rising from the chair was her sign that the little chat was over. There was one thing though. 'I'm sorry your request to visit Georgie was turned down, but I hope you understand why?'

Kitty had been bitterly disappointed by that decision. 'No, I don't,' she answered honestly. 'I can't see how it would be harmful for me to visit her. It wasn't harmful to me when we were living here, under the same roof.'

Miss Davis tried to see it from Kitty's point of view, but still had to admit, 'Georgie has always been a law unto herself. You're right of course ... she did not influence you in a bad way, but, perhaps that was because you were strong enough to resist.' She smiled at Kitty then. 'In fact, to a certain extent I believe it was you who influenced her, and for the better.'

'Well then?'

She shook her head slowly from side to side, a look of determination on her face. 'No, Kitty. You can't visit her at the borstal. The decision was made above my head and, to be honest, I'm fully in agreement. First, Aylesbury is too far, and second, and most importantly as far as I'm concerned, you should never set foot inside a borstal ... not even to visit.'

Kitty was so looking forward to seeing Georgie again. 'Why can't she be on her best behaviour?' she groaned. 'You know she's had her sentence extended again. If she keeps on like that, she'll never get out!'

'I'm afraid she's her own worst enemy.' Miss Davis had actually attended court when Georgie was brought to answer charges for fighting in the laundry room at the borstal. It wasn't the first time and, unless Georgie saw the error of her ways, it wouldn't be the last. 'This is something she has to deal with in her own way,' she advised Kitty. 'She's fortunate to have a loyal friend in you.'

'I can't seem to help her though, can I?'

'Don't think like that, Kitty. You are the most stable influence in her life. You've helped her more than you realise. If it hadn't been for you . . . your letters and loyalty, I honestly believe she would have gone from bad to worse. In a place like that you need a friend to believe in you.'

All that evening Kitty busied herself. She made entries in her diary, all about the conversation between herself and Miss Davis. She flattened Mildred's letter inside the pages, and returned the diary to the back of her bedside cupboard. After that she went downstairs and chatted to some of the girls; one in particular by the name of Margaret, a young girl who was here because of a court order and her parents' constant neglect of her. 'I miss my mum,' she told Kitty.

'So do I,' Kitty told her gently, 'but it won't be long before you're home again.' In a way she envied the girl because there would come a day when she would be with her mother again. It gave her cause for thought, and what she thought was this. Too much had happened for her to go back. It was the future she must think of now, not the past.

Her own thoughts came as a shock to her. She had travelled a long painful road before realising her parents were gone for good; that Mildred had much to be ashamed of; that Harry would never leave her, not while her heart beat warmly and her dreams were filled with memories of him. 'Come and sit beside me,' she told the girl. And while she told her a story of princes and thieves, Kitty was put in mind of herself as a five year old when her own mother used to tell her the very same stories.

While she told the tales her eyes filled with tears. She didn't realise the child had fallen asleep beside her until the little body slumped sideways and would have fallen off the chair if Kitty hadn't caught her. Gently, she took the tired bundle upstairs where she undressed her and tucked her in her bed. 'Goodnight, sleep tight,' she said, planting a soft kiss on the sleeping face. 'It won't hurt you to go to bed without being washed . . . just this once.'

Dorothy Picton agreed. 'Let her sleep,' she said. 'The poor little mite's been fretting ever since she arrived.' Thanking Kitty for her help, she sat by the child's bed for a while, leaving Kitty to return downstairs.

It was ten o'clock when the film finished. 'Goodnight,' Kitty called out. There was a chorus of 'Goodnight' in return, as she went up the stairs two at a time. Tomorrow was Saturday and she was to see Mildred. The thought spurred her on.

She got into her nightgown and, after a quick wash, cleaned her teeth and climbed into her bed. Sleep didn't come easy. Kitty was too full of excitement. She thought of tomorrow, of Mildred, and Georgie, and Harry ... 'Harry.' His name was on her lips as always, and she felt so close to him it was as though she could reach out and he would be there. 'If you want him, he *will* be there,' she whispered in the darkness. She did want him, more than anything else in the world, but she would never let him know that. The reasons she sent him away still held good ... their ages ... his future. She had nothing to offer him, and so she would go on pretending. For Harry's sake.

Kitty turned this way and that as the nightmare gathered pace. Scenes flickered through her dreams like an old film ... her mother jumping to oblivion ... her father ... the burning house. Miss Davis was leaving now. Kitty was all alone. But then Harry was there, his arms open to comfort her, his dark eyes brimming with love. 'Come on, sweetheart,' he was saying, his voice soft and coaxing. 'I won't let anything hurt you.'

Kitty woke then, rivers of sweat running down her back, scalding tears running down her face. It took a while to realise it had only been a dream. But, no, it wasn't. It was true ... all true. And she wondered how long the past would haunt her before she found a measure of peace.

The following morning Kitty made an extra special effort to look her best. When she came downstairs her dark hair shone like freshly made chocolate, her face was fresh and glowing, and apart from the faintest dark shadows under her eyes, showed no sign of the previous night's traumas; she had on her prettiest dress, a swinging calf-length style in vivid blue. The wide belt accentuated her waspish waist and the V-neckline was perfect for showing off the string of amber beads.

'You look like you're off somewhere special?' Dorothy Picton was enjoying a cup of tea before the early morning rush.

'I'm seeing Mildred today,' Kitty replied, her brown eyes shining.

Miss Davis wished her well. 'Mind what I said, though,' she warned. 'If your aunt wants you to sign anything, it might be wise to speak with someone first.'

Kitty assured her she would sign nothing: 'Without speaking to you first.'

'Cheerio then, and give my regards to your aunt.'

Since handing in her notice, she felt as though she had been given a new lease of life. There was no doubt she would miss this place and everyone in it, but if she didn't go now, she was convinced she would die across her desk, or running up the stairs when one of the children screamed out in a nightmare . . . the way Kitty used to, she thought sadly. She had lost count of the times Kitty had cried out in her sleep when she first came here. Thank God that was a thing of the past. Or was it? Miss Davis looked at her, and wondered. Were the nightmares still plaguing her? In her lonely heart was she still crying? She prayed not.

The bus was packed with early-morning shoppers all going into Bedford market. 'Is this anybody's?' Without waiting for an answer, a tall fair-haired lad threw himself into the seat beside Kitty. Shabbily dressed in faded leather jacket and torn jeans, he emitted a smell that put Kitty in mind of the time she and Harry used to clean out her pet rabbit's hutch; other passengers wrinkled their noses as the odour wafted towards them.

For most of the half-hour journey, he kept slyly glancing at her, occasionally winking when she was compelled to lift her gaze and look him in the eye. When he pressed his leg against hers it was the last straw. 'Excuse me!' she said, springing out of her seat and pushing by him.

'Where d'you think *you're* going?' He gawped up at her. 'There's no stop here, and there ain't no other seats left neither.' He grinned, and her temper rose. Locating his toes, she ground the ball of her foot down hard.

'JESUS!' Grimacing in pain, he hopped along the seat. 'You've got bloody big flippers for a little 'un!' he groaned, rolling his eyes and clutching his foot.

'Oh, I am sorry,' Kitty apologised. But she wasn't. She was only sorry she hadn't done it ten minutes ago.

A little old lady beckoned her over. 'There's room next to me,' she croaked, shifting along the bench seat and squashing everyone. When Kitty squeezed in beside her, she chuckled wickedly. 'I've been watching that mucky young fella,' she remarked, gesturing with a nod of the head towards the fair-haired man, 'and I reckon you did right.' Her gnarled hand patted Kitty's knee. 'I reckon he got what he deserved.'

Kitty hadn't realised she'd been under surveillance. 'I didn't know anyone was looking.' Her face blushed a gentle pink.

'Oh, I see everything. That's why I ride on the bus, to watch the goings-on.' Leaning forward she spoke in a whisper. 'Last week I saw two grown men kissing each other!' she exclaimed excitedly. 'And yesterday I nearly got caught up in a fight when the conductor threw a drunken woman off the bus.' She hugged herself with delight. 'If you want to see the world, buy a ticket for a bus-ride,' she suggested. 'It's better than sitting at home.'

Kitty laughed heartily. 'I see what you mean.'

When the fair-haired young man turned round to stare at them, the old woman glared back. 'You should be ashamed!' she called out. As he ducked down in his seat, she addressed Kitty indignantly. 'The randy bugger!' she said. 'He stinks an' all. Shouldn't think he's had a wash in weeks.' Folding her arms over her podgy stomach, she went on, in a voice that was loud and clear and which made Kitty want to hide under her seat, 'No woman's safe any more, not even on a bus-ride. It did my old heart good to see the way you trod on his foot like that.' She grinned wide enough to show pink gums as she addressed the other passengers who were revelling in the uproar. 'Serves him right for making advances where they're not wanted! Did you see the look on his face, though? By! He'll be hobbling for a month if not more!'

Now the centre of attention, the young man got out of his seat and scurried down the aisle, scowling at the old biddy as he passed by. As he stood on the platform waiting for an opportune moment to escape, she ranted on mercilessly.

Wishing he'd never got out of bed that morning, the young man waited for the bus to reach the next corner, then, as it slowed to negotiate the turn, jumped to the pavement. When it went past he grimaced at the old woman and made a very improper gesture with his fingers.

'No respect!' she grumbled, shaking her head at Kitty. 'No respect at all!'

Plucking a tangle of knitting out of her bag the old dear settled down to finish a pair of lemon bootees. 'Got a grandchild on the way,' she told Kitty proudly.

'Congratulations. Is it your first?'

'No. Got three, I have. One girl, two boys. The boys are my elder daughter's . . . lovely husband she's got, and a nice house with a big garden.' An expression of disgust crossed her features. 'It's my younger daughter who's got the little girl . . . two years old she is, with the other due in a fortnight. She weren't so fortunate in her choice of husband, I'm sorry to say.' Flicking a thumb over her shoulder in the direction where the young man had jumped off the bus, she added with a snort, 'You've just met the father, so you'll know what I mean. It isn't the first time he's tried to pick up other girls, though I must say you're the youngest as far as I know.' Her tongue clicked, and her needles clicked faster as she warned grimly, 'Just wait till I tell our Doreen what he's been up to! He'll get the length of her tongue and no mistake!' She chatted on and on.

Kitty was speechless.

From the station, Kitty walked the half mile through the shopping arcade and along Midland Road; she crossed by the statue of John Bunyan, through the flower gardens and straight across, on to Park Road where her Aunt Mildred lived. In contrast to the noisy bus-ride, the quiet leisurely walk gave her time to think. She was suddenly nervous. It had been years since she had seen her aunt, and now she wasn't sure how to talk with her any more.

The sun was shining and there was a cooling breeze as she walked up the pleasant, tree-lined road. The houses on Park Road were solid and grand, relics of Victorian times when families were large and a horse and carriage might stand on the drive. Mildred had inherited the house from her parents, while her brother, Kitty's father, had been left the business.

Like the business, the house had been in need of modernisation. Mildred and her husband had worked hard on it in the early years, spending a small fortune and every spare minute renovating, and soon their smart abode became the blueprint for every other house in Park Road.

Kitty stood outside for what seemed an age; far enough away

not to be seen, but near enough to smell the roses in the garden. Above her the birds trilled out a merry song, and down the road there was an argument in progress, voices raised in anger and children crying. Disturbing sounds, carrying her back.

After a while, she plucked up enough courage to venture closer. She had come this far, so she might as well get it over with, she thought. As she approached the main door, the curtains moved and suddenly her name was being called out.

'Kitty!'

It was Mildred. She had seen Kitty through the window and was running down the path to greet her. 'Oh, I'm so glad you came. I didn't think you would.' Laughing and crying at the same time, she threw her arms round Kitty and held her close.

Kitty was shocked. Mildred had always been a smart tidy woman, with short neat hair and an air of self-confidence. This woman was nothing like that; she was nervous and untidy, with straggly unwashed hair. There was an unkempt, neglected look about her that shook Kitty to the core. 'Are you ill?' It was the first thought that came to mind. Now, when Mildred held herself away, Kitty was amazed to see the tears swimming in her eyes.

Her aunt glanced about nervously. 'You'd best come inside,' she urged. 'We don't want the neighbours talking.'

As Mildred propelled her indoors, Kitty couldn't help but smile to herself. Worried what the neighbours might say? That was more like it. Perhaps she hadn't changed so much after all.

Kitty was wrong. The inside of the house told a sad tale of neglect. In the sitting room, the curtains were half closed, shutting out the bright daylight and throwing the room into gloom; the carpet was littered with cups and plates and overflowing ash trays. Every chair was littered with clothes, haphazardly flung over arms and backs, some folded, some not, but all in need of a good wash – as was Mildred herself. Beside the settee a number of wine bottles lay scattered. Most of them were empty, others spilled their contents over the carpet, creating long meandering stains. 'I haven't had time to tidy the place,' her aunt excused herself.

'It's all right,' Kitty assured her. 'I can help.'

She caught a small glimpse of the old Mildred as her aunt set her face and argued, 'You'll do no such thing! I've never in my life asked a guest to tidy up.' Rushing round, she did her best to make the place look respectable, but it was too long neglected and she gave up in despair, falling on to the settee. 'I'm no use,' she groaned. 'No use at all!' She was sobbing now, head in hands, shaking like a soul in torment.

Kitty sat beside her. 'Let me help,' she pleaded. 'I *want* to help.' All of a sudden it didn't matter that Mildred had turned her back on her when she was in need. What mattered was that her aunt was in trouble. She seemed ill ... desperate. And Kitty didn't know what to do for the best.

Mildred startled her by laughing out loud. '*You* want to help *me*?' She stared at Kitty in disbelief. 'The years in that place must have softened your brain! Have you forgotten what I did to you? Have you forgotten how I left you to the wolves? Don't you know what I've been doing all this time? Pretending I was ill and couldn't come to visit. Scheming and lying ... anything so I didn't have to take responsibility for you. Have you forgotten all that, Kitty Marsh? HAVE YOU?' There was rage in her voice, but somehow Kitty knew it was not directed at her.

'All that's in the past now,' she said firmly. 'You sent for me, I'm here now, so what is it you want?' There was anger in her own voice. Mildred couldn't be more wrong. Kitty had *not* forgotten. She never would.

'Have you been desperately unhappy, Kitty?'

'I've learned to survive.'

'What about Harry?'

'What about him?' Even the mention of his name brought a pang of loneliness.

'You and he were always together as children. His mother cared for you too. I expect they visit you often?'

'Mrs Jenkins was kind to me, yes.' At first, she thought, only at first. 'Harry's gone away to study. He means to make something of his life.' She had given him that much at least.

'I expect you get lots of letters from him?'

'He has more important things to do than write letters to me.' She had ignored the letters he had written, destroying his hopes and her own as well. 'I don't suppose I'll ever see him again.'

'You astonish me. I always imagined you two would ...'

'Well, you were wrong.' Kitty couldn't let her finish that sentence. It would be too painful.

126

'I did a dreadful, unforgivable thing when I let them put you in an institution.'

Kitty found herself thinking of Miss Davis and instantly defended her. 'It's a good job there are places like that, and people willing to take on the responsibility.' Then the thoughts she was trying so desperately to suppress spilled out in a harsh accusation. 'Especially when there's no one else.'

Mildred peered at her through misty eyes. 'You hate me, don't you?' She shivered visibly, as though someone had walked over her grave.

It took a moment for Kitty to answer. When she did it was in a soft, firm voice. 'No, Aunt. I don't hate you.' She had suffered feelings of bitterness at first. But over the years her emotions had changed, and now seeing Mildred like this seemed to settle the score between them. 'Why did you send for me?' She had her suspicions, but wanted her aunt to speak out.

Mildred too, had been surprised on seeing Kitty. She had half expected to meet the same young girl who had been taken into care. Now though she was faced with a young woman, a beautiful creature with a mind of her own. Discreetly she studied her niece: the slender graceful figure, the shapely legs and mature presence, the big nutmeg brown eyes, small straight nose and full sensuous mouth, the way her thick dark hair framed that lovely face, and above all else, the quiet strength that radiated from her. Her maturity was a shock to Mildred, and for a moment she was distracted.

'Your uncle's gone, you know,' she said, her head dropping as Kitty stared at her in astonishment. 'He's taken the kids . . . said he wouldn't leave them with a drunkard.' Looking up she pleaded, 'Why would he do that? I'd never hurt my kids. I'd cut off my right arm first.' Digging beneath the settee cushion, she withdrew a bottle of gin. With shaking fingers she undid the top and took a long drink. Afterwards she let the bottle rest in her lap and dropped her head to her chest, staring at the carpet while rocking herself backwards and forwards, oblivious to Kitty's presence.

Kitty watched her for a minute. Never having come across a situation like this before, she wanted to do and say the right thing. But the one question that now burned in her mind was '*Are* you a drunkard?'

Mildred stopped rocking, but kept her face averted and her eyes on the carpet. 'I think so,' she answered. Then she looked up, slowly raised her arm and with a jerk of her wrist, sent the half-filled bottle flying across the room; it shattered against the wall and showered its contents over the bureau.

Kitty got the impression that she was expected to clear up the mess. Instead she remained seated, her eyes firmly focused on Mildred's face. 'Did that solve anything?'

'No!' came the surly answer.

'What *will*?'

'Nothing. It's too late for all that.'

'Why did you send for me?'

'I wish I hadn't now.' Mildred still couldn't look her in the eye.

Kitty sensed the game she was playing. 'I'd better go then.'

'That's right. Bugger off!'

Rising from the settee, Kitty crossed the room without a backward glance. She sensed she would not get as far as the door before Mildred called her back. And she was right.

'Don't go yet, Kitty . . . please.'

She turned but made no further effort to move. 'Why shouldn't I go? You just said you wished you hadn't sent for me.'

'I didn't mean that.'

'What *did* you mean?'

'Please, Kitty. I have to talk to you.' Mildred's voice shook.

She returned, but this time she sat a short distance away.

Mildred fidgeted nervously. 'I can't blame him for taking the kids.' She lowered her gaze. 'Sometimes, when I've been drinking, I'm not responsible for my own actions.'

'Can't you get help?'

'It's not as easy as that. It isn't just the drinking. That's only half the problem. It all started when your uncle lost his first job . . . remember I told you that the last time I saw you?'

Kitty nodded. God! The times she had thought about that. But it didn't matter now. The hurt had passed.

Mildred continued, 'He soon got another job . . . better paid, with a company car and all the perks. We should have been happy then, but things were never the same between us.' She was wringing her hands, sweating profusely. 'There was another woman ... I started drinking. We fought about this and that and the kids sided with him. Oh, I don't blame them ... I was hell to live with.'

'Will he come back?'

'I hoped he would, but I know now I was just fooling myself.' She made a bitter sound, somewhere between a laugh and a sob. 'Now, he wants to bleed me dry ... see me in the gutter!' Clambering out of her seat, she went to the bureau; it was wet and sticky with gin. Impatiently wiping away the spilled liquid, she winced when a fragment of glass sliced into the palm of her hand. Ignoring the trickle of blood she opened the bureau and took out a long white envelope. 'He's washed his hands of me,' she muttered. Tossing the envelope at Kitty she told her, 'There's your answer. See for yourself.'

The letter was from a solicitor, a formal notice that Mildred's husband was filing for divorce.

Kitty read it with a solemn face. Afterwards she laid the letter on the coffee table. 'He might change his mind?' she suggested hopefully, though in truth she realised the hopelessness of Mildred's situation.

'He won't.' She had no illusions. 'He's set up home with that slut!'

'Is she a slut?'

''Course she's a bloody slut! She stole another woman's husband, didn't she?'

'Sounds to me like he didn't need much persuasion.'

'That's spiteful.'

'What about the children?'

Mildred stared at Kitty, and there was a world of regret in her eyes. 'He wants custody of them ... and to "negotiate our joint assets". As for the children, they've turned their backs on me. Edward has a job and a flat of his own. He doesn't visit ... says I'm an embarrassment. The other two have always been their daddy's little darlings.' She gave a hard laugh. 'Poetic justice you might say. I turned my back on you, and my kids turned their backs on me. I expect you're thinking I've got what I deserve?'

'I wouldn't wish that on you.'

Mildred was shocked into silence. She had seen something in Kitty that made her mortally ashamed. Returning to the settee, she stared into space. 'I really am sorry for what I did,' she confessed. 'It wasn't all for selfish reasons. I hoped it would shake your father out of his grief... make him live up to his responsibilities.'

'I understand that now.'

'And do you forgive me?' Her gaze was intense as she waited for Kitty's response.

It was not an easy question, and for Kitty there was no easy answer. Though she truly believed that Mildred had been punished enough, there was still a deal of resentment in her heart. There was also a fervent wish to make peace. 'I'm here, aren't I?'

Mildred visibly sighed with relief. 'You don't know how grateful I am for that,' she said. 'I honestly didn't think you'd come.'

'Why did you send for me?'

'To confess.' She put up her hand, as though to stem any further questions. 'This is very hard for me.' She turned away and stared into the empty firegrate, her hands folded on her lap. They were trembling uncontrollably. A moment to gather her courage before the words came out in a rush. 'The money from your father's house... the business...' She turned to look at Kitty, and the tears were running down her face. 'It's all gone, Kitty.' Her voice broke on a sob. 'God forgive me!'

Kitty had half expected something like this. Harry's earlier warning returned to mind, and she felt numb. 'Is there nothing left?' Her voice was flat, emotionless.

'I've signed papers, taken the money out bit by bit until now there's nothing left.' Mildred continued to stare at Kitty, her face contorted with pain and her eyes red from crying. Her whole body was shaking. 'I'll make it up to you somehow,' she promised. 'My solicitor says Len has the right to half of everything. I might have to sell this house. I don't care about that any more, but when the house is sold, I'll give you what I can... it won't be enough to right the wrong. Nothing ever will.'

'I don't want a penny of your money.' There was an unnatural hardness to Kitty's voice. 'You're right. Nothing can ever excuse what you did, but making yourself destitute isn't the answer either. I don't want that on my conscience.' She rose to leave. 'If that's all, I'll be on my way.' It had been a mistake coming here, she knew that now.

'Don't go, Kitty.' Mildred was blocking her path to the door, 'Please! There's no one else you see . . . only you.'

She braced herself. 'I'm sorry, Aunt, I have to go now.'

'And you'll never come here again, will you?' Her voice rose hysterically. 'You're like the rest of them . . . none of you want me.' Waving her arms frantically she bawled, 'GO ON THEN! Leave me here to rot. I don't suppose you'll mind having *that* on your conscience!'

Kitty's temper snapped. 'Why should I care what happens to you? You never cared about me. You made your excuses and left me to the authorities. You stole my father's money and now you expect me to pick up the pieces?' It was too much. 'Look at yourself! Look in the mirror and you'll see why your life is falling apart. You're a mess! That's not my fault. So why should I have you on my conscience?'

Mildred couldn't let her leave. If Kitty walked out of that door now, she would end it all. Summoning the small amount of dignity she had left, she squared her shoulders and looked her in the eye. Sighing from deep down, she pleaded with her eyes as she said softly, 'Because you're family . . . and you're all I have left in the world.'

Her softly spoken words jolted Kitty out of the rage that was swelling inside her. She looked at Mildred and saw a pathetic thing, wretched and haggard, her bloodshot eyes swimming with unshed tears and her breath smelling of booze; she saw a creature close to destruction, and suddenly her own mother was in her mind . . . that beautiful lady in a red two-piece, with a world of sadness in her eyes. She saw the same sadness in Mildred's face now. 'I can't stay,' she muttered. 'Please, Aunt, don't ask that of me.' How could she stay? Why should she be responsible for a woman who had treated her the way Mildred had treated her? How could she face her every day, living in this pig-sty and letting herself be drawn into a situation that was not of her making? With steely determination she brushed past her aunt and hurried to the front door.

Before she could open it, Mildred was on her. 'DON'T LEAVE ME!' she cried, just as Kitty had cried for her when she was taken from the court to the children's home.

Struggling to shake her off, Kitty was appalled when Mildred fell to the floor and there, on her knees, grabbed hold of her hem, clinging like a drowning man to a life raft. 'I'm frightened,' she sobbed, 'There's no one else I can turn to.'

Kitty's heart felt like stone. 'You know how *I* felt then! You know what it's like to be thrown aside... to feel alone in a world filled with strangers.'

Mildred lowered her gaze. 'I know what I've done,' she whispered. 'I only wish I could turn the clock back.'

'Well, you can't!' A kind of hatred overwhelmed Kitty then. With a clenched fish she thumped the door and shattered the glass panel. She ran, out of the door and down the street, her mind in a whirl and her heart black with rage. Mildred had tapped something deep inside her, some awful festering resentment that she had long suppressed. But it was released now, surfacing with a vengeance as she sped blindly down the street, fighting the urge to go back and strangle her aunt with her bare hands.

Behind her, she could hear Mildred calling out. Kitty didn't listen. She didn't stop. She ran and ran, until somewhere between the bus station and Mildred's house, she slumped against a wall and burst into sobs. 'Are you all right, dear?' an old woman asked as she passed by. When Kitty nodded, the old soul went away, occasionally looking back and shaking her head.

It took a while before Kitty was composed. Wandering into the John Bunyan gardens she sat on a bench and watched the traffic go by. She became mesmerised by the traffic lights... green, amber, red, amber, green. Her eyes followed the sequence, while her mind played tricks. A young man ran for his bus, tall and athletic with dark wayward hair. She saw him from behind and for one moment thought she knew him. 'HARRY! HARRY... WAIT!' her voice rang out.

He turned. It wasn't Harry. And she was devastated.

She sat a while longer. A woman walked by with her young daughter. Kitty was put in mind of herself and her mother. Her brown eyes grew softer, she almost smiled. Her rage was over, but the loneliness was overwhelming.

Kitty knew what she must do. It would not be easy, but she would not forgive herself if she did not try. Getting up from the bench, she made her way back towards Park Road. With each step her heart grew quieter and, as she neared her aunt's house, she felt older somehow, as though she had finally left her childhood behind. She could hear her own steps echoing against the pavement, slow and measured.

The front door was wide open. Kitty went through to the lounge and there was Mildred, sitting cross-legged on the floor with a bottle of gin raised to her mouth. When she saw Kitty, her eyes opened wide and slowly the bottle was lowered. Her face melted into a sad smile and she took a deep breath, held it for what seemed an age, before exhaling, seeming to shrink like a deflated balloon. 'You came back,' she whispered, her head lolling to one side as she looked up. 'Oh, Kitty! You came back.' She began crying.

Kitty knelt beside her. 'I had to.'

'Thank you.' That was all. It was enough.

Closing her fingers round the gin bottle, Kitty asked gently, 'Do you really need this?'

Tears flowed down her aunt's face. She couldn't speak. Instead she moved her head slowly from side to side.

As Kitty removed the bottle, Mildred threw her arms round her. 'I'll look after you,' she promised. 'As God's my witness.'

Holding her at arm's length, Kitty regarded her through misty eyes. 'We'll look after each other,' she said, and her smile was the smile of a woman at peace with herself.

On their knees they clung to each other, and laughed, and cried, and thanked the good Lord for bringing them together. It was a wonderful thing.

CHAPTER EIGHT

Miss Davis was both delighted and intrigued. 'Whatever do you mean, Kitty?' she enquired. 'Either your aunt is going to take responsibility for you, or she is not. Which is it?'

Kitty was in a dilemma. 'It isn't as straightforward as that,' she said lamely. The fear uppermost in her mind was that the authorities would not allow Mildred to foster her; after all she hadn't even been able to take care of *herself*, let alone be a responsible guardian for her niece.

Miss Davis pointed to the chair before her desk. 'It seems to me you have a problem,' she told Kitty kindly. 'I think you had better sit down so we can thrash it out.'

Kitty did as she was told. Then she sat in the chair for a whole two minutes before she could reveal what was on her mind. Meanwhile, Miss Davis sat and waited, patient as ever, her eyes never leaving the girl's troubled face.

Realising there was only one way to tackle it, and that was head on, Kitty took a deep invigorating breath before speaking out. 'My aunt has asked me to move in with her...' Seeing how the older woman's face lit up she quickly went on, 'I've said yes. But...' She bit her lip, her brown eyes troubled as she recalled her visit. Finding her aunt drunk and unkempt, with the house in a sadly neglected state, had been a shock she still hadn't come to terms with.

Kitty had toyed with the idea of hiding the truth but, knowing how any keen social worker would worm out the true situation, she decided to have it all out in the open and hope for the best. 'There *is* a "problem",' she admitted. 'Or rather there was.'

'Go on, Kitty.' The voice was encouraging. Miss Davis had already guessed the cause of her anxiety. 'I gather the problem lies with your aunt. Am I right?'

135

Kitty nodded.

'Is it to do with your father's money? The house and business?'

'Not really.'

'What then?'

'I want you to know that I don't care about my father's money . . . not the house nor the business.' Rightly or wrongly she still blamed him for her mother's death. 'But . . . my aunt has used all the money anyway.'

'*Spent* it, you mean?' Miss Davis was sitting bolt upright now. This was a potentially disturbing situation.

Kitty saw the official expression on her face and was quick to assure her, 'It's all right. I know where the money went. We talked it through and it's all right. Honest.' She didn't say it was largely squandered on booze and 'drying out' clinics, together with huge legal fees to fend off a greedy husband. 'There's nothing for you to be concerned about.'

'I see.' The last thing Miss Davis wanted was to interrogate Kitty. 'But there is something you are concerned about?'

Kitty had to choose the right words or spoil her chances of going to live with Mildred. 'I'm just frightened that the authorities might not let me live with her.' Fear betrayed itself in her voice. 'I'm worried they might still send me to foster parents.'

Miss Davis regarded her curiously. 'You must know we would rather send you to a relative than to an outside foster home.' She saw Kitty fiddling with her fingers, and knew of old that this was a sign of nervousness. 'Kitty! The years might have made me a bit slower, a bit deafer, and a bit more cantankerous but I am not so senile I can't tell when something is wrong.'

Kitty began to relax. 'It isn't wrong exactly. Well, not now it isn't.' Already the situation was beginning to rectify itself.

'What is it then? Ever since yesterday when you returned from your aunt's house – after a very long visit, I might add – you have skilfully avoided me. No, don't deny it.'

'I wasn't about to,' Kitty protested. 'I was avoiding you for a reason, and now I'm ready to tell you.'

'And I'm still listening.'

Kitty knew she could trust this woman, and so she told her everything. How she had found Mildred drunk and tearful, begging her to stay. How her uncle had left, taking the children and threatening to make Mildred sell the house so he could have half and set up home with his new woman. 'She's had so many troubles, you see,' Kitty explained with feeling. 'It's no wonder she'd given up.'

'I can't imagine she's had any more troubles than you, Kitty. And *you* never gave up.'

'I had people to help me. I had Georgie and you ... and Harry.' He more than anyone had helped her through. 'Aunt Mildred has no one.'

'She had you, Kitty.'

'No. I was just another burden.'

'And now?'

'Now we understand each other.'

'Are you sure you want to live with her?'

'At first, when she asked me to live with her, I said no. Then I thought about it and realised it would be for the best. She's all the family I have, and she really wants me with her.'

'What about the drinking? You know we can't allow you to live with her if that continues.'

'It won't. She's promised me. We spent ages cleaning up the house yesterday. She's happier already. She said the drink was a means of forgetting, a kind of crutch, that's all. She won't want it if I'm allowed to move in. You see, she'll have someone to talk to. She doesn't need the drink any more. *I'll* be her friend instead.'

Miss Davis was torn two ways. On the one hand she could sympathise with Kitty and her aunt. On the other it was her duty to protect the girl from others ... from herself if need be.

Kitty saw the doubt. 'Please, Miss Davis,' she pleaded. 'I don't want to be with strangers any more. I just want to be with my aunt ... my family.'

There was a long poignant moment while Miss Davis pondered the matter, then in a crisp voice that bespoke her authority, she told Kitty, 'All right. Leave it with me for now. I'll see what I can do.'

Kitty was thrilled. 'I knew you'd be on my side,' she whispered. 'How will I ever thank you?' Her heart was beating nineteen to the dozen. To get out of the institution ... to be free, responsible for her own actions. It was too much to hope for ... too good to be true.

Fearing she might have given the wrong impression, and knowing how strict the board was in matters like these, Miss Davis cautioned her, 'Don't get your hopes up. I said I would do what I could. In view of what you've told me ... the drinking and everything ... well, I can't promise.'

'But you *will* do your best?' Kitty's heart skipped a beat.

'You know I will. But your aunt will be thoroughly vetted. The slightest indication that she might be a bad influence, or that she is not capable of looking after you ...' Regarding Kitty with serious eyes she asked, 'You do know what I'm saying?'

Kitty knew, and she was trusting Miss Davis as never before. If she was not allowed to go to her aunt, she would not go with that foster couple either. Last night she had lain awake until the early hours, thinking long and hard about her life. Now that she and Mildred had settled their differences, she was already beginning to look forward to moving out of here and into Park Road. If the authorities forbade it, then she would take the only other option – and that was to run away, somewhere where they could never find her.

Miss Davis saw the determination in Kitty's expression. Suspecting the reason for it, she pleaded, 'Don't do anything you might regret. I've promised to do all I can. I hope you know me well enough to realise I won't go back on my word.'

When Kitty had gone, she made arrangements to visit Mildred, to find out for herself whether the woman had Kitty's welfare at heart. After all, she had shown very little affection for the girl up until now.

The next two weeks flew by. Kitty's prospective foster parents were informed of the situation. Obviously disappointed, they reluctantly agreed to await the outcome before deciding whether to abandon the idea of fostering, or wait for another teenager. It seemed they had their sights set on a young adult, rather than a helpless baby; there were several toddlers available for fostering but they were not interested. Miss Davis had her suspicions and reported them to her superior. The couple were interviewed again and were deemed to be suitable. The matter was left to rest there for the time being.

When the board convened, Miss Davis spoke out for Kitty. 'I believe it will be in her best interests to go to her aunt,' she declared.

The committee members examined the report on Mildred. Initially they had harboured doubts, but several interviews and many visits later, they were satisfied. It was agreed that Kitty should go to her aunt, with their blessing.

Kitty was over the moon. 'I'm not staying on at school,' she told Miss Davis. 'When I'm sixteen, I want to get a good job. I want to earn enough money to travel.'

Miss Davis laughed. 'You've obviously thought about it, so I won't try and dissuade you . . . although you should think carefully about leaving school, Kitty. You have a good head on your shoulders, and there are many opportunities for a girl with your talents.'

Kitty was adamant. 'If I'm so talented, then I should be able to make my way in the world, with or without paper qualifications.'

'I don't believe I've ever met anyone so strong-minded!' Miss Davis exclaimed. She took Kitty into her embrace. 'Take care of yourself, my girl,' she said, her eyes glinting suspiciously.

'I will,' Kitty promised. 'And please don't worry about me.'

Later, when all was arranged and Kitty was ready to leave with the social worker, Miss Davis wished her well. 'And what do you intend to do with all this money you mean to earn?' she asked with a twinkle in her eye. She was in no doubt at all that Kitty would make an impression on the world.

She thought for a minute before wondering aloud, 'Wouldn't it be wonderful if I could help Georgie to get that blue minibus she's always wanted?'

Miss Davis had to smile. 'That would be nice,' she said. What she *thought* was: Be careful, Kitty. Georgie might be a good friend, but she could also be a long-term liability! She was on the brink of saying it aloud, but knew it would make no difference. Kitty was a loyal creature. When first she came to the home, Georgie had taken Kitty under her wing. Now it was the other way round, and, as far as Miss Davis was concerned, Kitty had got the raw end of the deal.

CHAPTER NINE

Harry shivered as he went into the shower; soon though the water was sprinkling down, warm and soothing to his aching back. That morning he had helped his father clear two dying elm trees from the back garden. The day before, a rotten branch had fallen and smashed the fence down.

Turning this way then that, he worked the flat of his hands all over his tanned shoulders, letting the soap run between his thighs and washing the soft skin there; he turned again, leaned his head back to wet his thick dark hair, shampooed it, lathered and rubbed it, rinsed it and turned once more to swill away the remnants of soap. Clean and dripping, he stepped out into a steamy room.

Grabbing the towel he wiped his face, rubbing his hair dry as he went into the bedroom. The reflection in the mirror showed him to be a grown man, well endowed, with hard flat stomach, broad shoulders and long, strong muscular legs. He had grown taller, filled out in all the right places.

As he combed his hair before the mirror, the dark eyes shone with vitality – and something else, a quiet sadness that had grown since he and Kitty parted. His gaze fell on her photograph; it had been taken with his new camera while Kitty climbed the tree in their garden and posed cheekily on an overhanging branch. He had been anxious that she might fall and in his haste had taken the picture to one side. It only made it the more endearing.

He picked up the photograph. Kitty's face smiled up at him. He smiled back and all the old memories overwhelmed him. 'Will you ever want me again?' he murmured. 'Will you ever love me the way I love you, Kitty Marsh?' There was a tinge of anger in his voice. He had come to realise why she had sent him away but would not press her. 'It has to be your decision, Kitty,' he murmured. 'You know how I feel.' Lonely, that was how he felt.

Never a day passed when he didn't ache for her, didn't want her beside him, didn't long to hear her laugh, or see her smile, or hear her voice. In his mind and heart all of those things stayed alive, but it wasn't the same. Not like the real thing. 'I hope you're getting on well with your new family,' he told her softly. How he envied them, having Kitty there every day, her beauty and quietness filling a room, bringing their own special pleasure.

'I understand why you can't find a place in your life for me now,' he acknowledged. 'But one day maybe things will change. I hope so, Kitty. God willing.'

Kissing the photograph, he replaced it on the dresser. Taking a pair of blue cords and a polo-necked jumper from the wardrobe, he quickly dressed, ran his hands through his drying hair and went down the stairs two at a time. 'Something smells good!' he called out as he came into the kitchen.

Linda Jenkins was alone there. 'Your father and sister have already had their breakfast,' she said. 'When you've had yours, he wants to see you.' Inclining her head towards the door she explained, 'He's in the other room.' There was a look on her face that told him he was in for a lecture.

Helping himself to toast, he poured out a mug of tea and sat himself at the table. 'I suppose he means to rant on and on again?' The idea of going through it all once more was deeply trying.

'I'm sorry, son, but your father will have his say, whether you like it or not.' Linda sighed, dished out his eggs and bacon then sat down with her own beans on toast. 'I've already told him it's too late now. What's done is done, and there's no use crying over it. But he won't listen.'

'That's because he's a stubborn old sod.'

'Hey! Not so much of the "old", my lad! That paints me with the same brush.'

'But we've been through it time and again. Why can't he see it's what I want?'

'Because he still hasn't realised that you're a grown man now, capable of making your own decisions.' She gave him a weary look. 'To tell you the truth, son, he still harps on about Kitty Marsh.' She lowered her gaze, scooped up a pile of beans on the end of her fork and rammed them into her mouth.

Anger rose in him. 'What do you mean? What about Kitty?'

She took her time answering, hoping he would calm down. 'You know what he's like,' she said presently, wiping her mouth with a paper napkin. 'Your father never did like you associating with the Marshes. He thinks you and the girl got too close, and if I'm honest so do I.' She raised her head defiantly. 'You have to admit, son, it wasn't very wise. Not when everyone knew they were a troubled family.'

His dark eyes flashed angrily. 'And the things that happened ... losing her mother and father in that way ... the business ... Mildred ... Dad's being laid off. You think it was all Kitty's fault?'

She laughed nervously. 'No! No! Of course I'm not saying that.'

'You're saying I ought to have seen it all coming ... that I should have deserted Kitty when she needed me?'

'I'm not saying any such thing, only ...' she hesitated, uncomfortable beneath that fierce gaze. 'Well, you did rather get caught up in it all, didn't you?'

'So, you're saying it was wrong to befriend Kitty? You're saying I should have turned my back on her? You and Father have decided that I made a wrong decision because I didn't know my own mind.'

Pushing his plate away, he stood up. 'And if I didn't know my own mind *then*, I can't possibly know what I'm doing *now*, is that it?

'I'm not sure *what* your father believes. But, to be honest, son, you are making a rash decision. One that could affect your whole future.'

'So! When it comes down to it, you're as bad as each other.' Raising his eyes to the ceiling, he gave a deep sigh. 'I really thought you would understand. I'm not a kid any more. I've changed. My priorities have changed, can't you see that?'

'You're growing away from me. I never wanted that.'

'I don't want that either, but it's *you* who's driving a wedge between us. You and him.'

'Finish your breakfast.'

'I've lost my appetite.'

'Your father's waiting.'

Squaring his shoulders, Harry strode across the room. 'I'd best get it over with then, while I'm in the right mood.'

Ron Jenkins had grown bitter, and it showed in his face. Hard of feature and lined beyond his years, he rarely smiled. 'Took your time, didn't you?' Pointing to a chair he demanded, 'Sit down. I don't want a stiff neck staring up at you.'

'Then don't stare up at me.' Choosing to ignore his father's invitation, Harry remained standing.

'And don't you be so bloody cheeky, or I'll take my belt to you!'

'It's a bit late for that, Father.' Taking a deep breath, he said, 'You wanted to talk to me?'

His father didn't look up. Instead he kept his gaze averted. 'I want you to change your mind about going to business college. I want you to ring the university and tell them you've decided to accept the place you were offered there.'

'I've already accepted the business course.'

'Turn it down then!'

'I won't do that, Father.' Harry's resolve was evident.

'Damn and bugger it!' Springing out of the chair, Ron rounded on his son. 'How could you do it? All the teachers you've ever had all said the same thing: "Mr. Jenkins, your son is a brilliant mathematician ... he'll make his fortune in the world of finance." ' Groaning, he stretched out his hands and gripped Harry's shoulders. 'You could work in the city ... buying and selling ... making millions. It's all I've dreamed of, son.'

'That's *your* dream, Dad. Not mine.' There had been a time when he believed all of that might be glamorous; when he listened to his father. Somehow, though, he had come to believe there were more important things in life.

'So you're throwing it all away for a bloody business course?' Ron shook his head in disbelief. 'Oh, I see now!' His eyes glittered. 'It's her, isn't it? It's that bloody Kitty Marsh!'

'Kitty has nothing to do with it. How could she? I haven't seen her in months.'

'But that's just it! You can't get her out of your mind, can you? She's gone off to a new life, and you're throwing yours away because you can't be part of hers. That's it! I'm right, aren't I?'

Harry was shocked. Rage built inside him, exploding into words. 'You're right when you say I can't get Kitty out of my mind. And you're right when you claim I want to be part of her life. But as for my throwing away my own, you couldn't be further from the truth. I want to make good, and I want to *do* good wherever I can. But it has to be *my* choice! *You* work in the city if you want to. *You* buy and sell and wheel and deal. *You* be the millionaire. Just allow me to live my life the way I see fit.'

'It *is* her! She's talked you into this. Kitty Marsh places no value on money or property... she proved it by letting that bloody woman rob her blind. It is her that's changed your mind, isn't it? ISN'T IT?' Ron raised his fist as though to strike.

Harry stood his ground. 'Hit me if it'll make you feel better,' he said coldly. Slowly his father lowered his fist, and Harry went on, 'I think we'd best clear the air about a few things before I leave. Firstly, Kitty has nothing whatsoever to do with my decision. I won't deny she has no craving for material things, and I'll admit it's only my gut instinct, but Mildred has a lot to answer for... she's robbed Kitty blind, and the rumours are enough for me. But Kitty would never stoop to Mildred's level.

Eyeball to eyeball with his father, he suddenly realised he was not intimidated by him. It was a good feeling. 'Unlike you, Dad, Kitty is not vindictive. I trust her judgment better than I trust yours.' This was no time for holding back. It was a time for honesty. 'Mildred will never be happy with what she'd done. One day, she'll realise the depths to which she sank, and she'll suffer for it... she'll punish herself far more than Kitty or the courts could ever do. Kitty knows that, and now so do I.'

He paused, letting the words sink in. 'Money isn't everything, Dad. What counts in the end is what you do with your life. And, yes, there's nothing more I'd like than to share my life with Kitty. I know we're still far too young and I know only too well she's turned her back on me. In spite of that, I still haven't given up on us. I can wait if I have to. Time is on my side.'

Harry's passionate outpouring had silenced his father who looked at him now through envious eyes. 'You've got guts, I'll say that.'

Harry's manner softened. 'So you understand what I'm saying?'

'I don't want to understand.' Ron felt like an old, old man. 'Are you still set on defying me?'

'If that's how you're determined to see it.'

'Then I can't give you my blessing.'

In little more than a whisper, Harry said, 'I'm sorry if I've let you down, Dad. But I wouldn't be happy doing what you want. I'll be leaving first thing in the morning. I'd go with a happier heart if you could see me off.'

The other man's face was set hard. He was unrelenting. 'I've said my piece. We can't agree, so you'd best be off.' With that he crossed the room, opened the door and waited for Harry to leave. Afterwards he slammed the door shut and slumped in the chair, to think about what his son had said. 'It's that Marsh girl,' he murmured. 'She's come between us, just like I always said she would.'

The following morning Harry rose early. He ate heartily at the breakfast table, and told his mother, 'I'll miss you.'

For the last few minutes Linda Jenkins had been quietly watching her son, thinking what a handsome young man he was; with those dark sincere eyes and strong splendid figure, he would draw any woman's attention. She couldn't help but feel he had wasted too much of his youth on Kitty Marsh.

Since the two of them were small they had spent so much time together, there was little left for other friendships. Secretly she hoped he would meet a girl at college, a girl unhindered by problems, a girl with a normal family who might welcome Harry into their hearts and look on him as their own son. Now of course she held the same opinion as her husband where Kitty was concerned. What she wanted for her only son was a stable relationship, one where he would never be called on to make too many sacrifices; a marriage where the children would have two sets of grandparents, and the strength of family unity all around. He could never have that with Kitty. She was alone, an orphan, a burden who could only place a greater burden on any man she married. Linda prayed that man would not be her son. Yet, in her heart, she knew how much Harry loved Kitty. She had long realised the passion and fierce loyalty between those two, but she had believed it would pass, that it was just a childish thing.

146

But it had not passed. Over the years it had only grown stronger. The ties between those two young people were still there. Deep, binding ties, a wonderful sense of belonging that made her envious made her realise what she had missed. A great surge of guilt overwhelmed her when she found herself wishing Kitty Marsh had never been born.

At the sound of Harry's voice she looked up, mentally shaking herself and putting on a bright smile. 'It isn't *me* you will miss,' she gently chided, 'it's my cooked breakfast.'

He grinned. 'It's you I'll miss,' he assured her. 'I know you feel the same way Dad does about Kitty, but you never ram it down my throat the way he does. You give me space to breathe, and I'm grateful for that.'

'I still hope you can forget her and get on with your own life.' She disguised the emotion in her voice by giving a little cough. 'I'm your mother. It's only natural I want the very best for you.' She went on softly, 'Life is cruel, son. Make one single mistake and you'll spend the rest of your days paying for it.'

'What mistake? Are we talking about Kitty?' His dark eyes glittered angrily. 'Because if we are, you might as well know – I mean to marry Kitty when she's old enough . . . if she'll have me.'

His dark striking looks carried her back over the years, tearing at her heart and filling her with shame. She tried to shut out the memories but they persisted, bringing other images of another young man: the landlord of the first house she and Ron had rented when they were first married. He too was tall and dark, with rich wayward hair and smiling eyes that set your heart racing; he had a warm strong nature she had never known in anyone else since . . . except in her son, Harry.

She wondered, as she had wondered many times since, about the one occasion when that young landlord had taken her into his arms and right there on the sitting-room floor made love to her. It had been one brief, exciting episode in an otherwise uneventful marriage. Sometimes she wondered if her husband guessed that Harry was not his son. Maybe that was why he was so unloving. But how could he know? If he suspected he would surely have confronted her before now? With every day that passed her secret grew harder to live with. It was one that must never be told, least of all to Harry. She would have

147

to live with it until the day they laid her to rest. In Harry she saw his real father, and wanted the world for him. *In Kitty Marsh she saw her own punishment.*

The time came for him to leave. Linda had packed a flask and sandwiches for the long train journey to Lancaster. 'It'll save you a small fortune,' she told Harry, ramming them in his rucksack. 'You'll need every penny you can get. Stretching your grant won't be easy, and with your dad not earning like he used to, we won't be able to help.'

Harry hugged her. 'You've done enough for me.' If only his parents could accept his love for Kitty, he would feel so much better. He glanced round anxiously. There was still no sign of his father. 'Dad isn't coming to see me off, is he?'

Linda shook her head.

'I'm not sure what he's more angry about . . . opting out of university, or still wanting Kitty.' He frowned, 'I thought Sarah was coming home last night?'

'You know her. Here one minute, gone the next. She might as well move in permanently with that new friend of hers!'

He hardly ever saw her these days. 'Sarah has more freedom than I ever did.'

Linda chose not answer. 'You'd best get off, son, or you'll miss that train.'

Right up to the moment of departure, Harry looked for his father. There was no sign of him. Low-spirited, he strapped his rucksack to his back and began his way down the path. 'Ring me when you get there, son,' Linda called. He promised he would. She watched him out of sight and remained on the step, thinking. She was alone now. Alone with a man she no longer loved. It was a sobering prospect.

From behind the net curtains, Ron saw Harry leave. Then he sat in his chair and took out a packet of cigarettes. Lighting one up, he lapsed into deep thought. After a while he took a long drag on the cigarette, let the smoke trickle out through his half-open lips and muttered bitterly, 'I'm sorry you couldn't see things my way, Harry. But then why should you? After all, you're not my son.'

The tears trickled down his face as he realised what a coward he'd been all these years. From the first minute Linda uncovered the face of her newly born son, he'd known the baby did not belong to him. The infant's hair was too dark, his limbs were too long, and later, when those black eyes smiled up at him, his suspicions were confirmed. But it was already too late. In those early days his love for Linda overrode everything else. Besides, even before he could crawl, Harry had wormed his way into Ron's heart. And when, over the years he had not given Linda a child, Ron came to realise that Harry was all they had, all that kept them together, 'But you've left us now, Harry boy,' he said, walking to the window and looking out, 'Your sister will be next, I suppose.' Sarah had grown distant, and selfish too. In truth she had never been much of a daughter. He sighed from deep within. 'Where do we go from here . . . me and your cheating mother?' There was no anger in him, no revenge or guilt. There was just a feeling of immense relief, and a crippling sense of uselessness.

It was chilly on the platform. Beyond the enclosed station the sun shone brightly and the day promised to be glorious. But here, where Harry stood, the air was cold, mischievously gusting through the tunnel and lingering where the sun could not penetrate. He toyed with the idea of putting on his sweater; he even got it out of the rucksack, but then he reasoned it was only a few minutes before the train arrived. It would probably be packed and hot, with hardly a window opened, and he would only have to take the sweater off again. He dismissed the idea and, after a struggle, stuffed the sweater back into the rucksack, wondering why it was that things never went back the same?

While he waited, his glance was drawn to the end of the platform. This was where Kitty's mother was said to have jumped. This was where Kitty too might well have lost her life. Suddenly she loomed large in his thoughts. If she had died that day, his life would have had little meaning. The thought made him tremble inside. Even though she was out of reach just now, she was alive, thank God. He stared at the fatal place a moment longer before looking away.

Kitty remained at the forefront of his thoughts. He wondered if she was happy with her new family. He hoped so. He hoped she was already regretting her decision to end their relationship. He hoped she was already planning to get in touch with him. He hoped she loved him still . . . he hoped the years would pass quickly . . . he hoped . . . Dear God! He wanted her so much, wanted to see her . . . to touch her.

'Hope it's on time.' The young woman's voice startled him. She was tall and slim, with bright eyes and well-groomed hair; dressed in old jeans and a loose-fitting blouse that fluttered in the breeze. Through the flimsy material he could see the outline of her breasts. 'It's bloody cold on this platform!' She remarked with a shiver.

'Like the North Pole,' he laughed. She had a look of independence he thought, and maybe a little arrogance. There was a severity about her eyes that detracted from her smile.

Pointing to his rucksack, she said, 'You wouldn't have a sweater in there, would you?' In fact she had watched him take it out and put it back again. She shivered again for good measure.

'As a matter of fact, I have.' Looking down, he saw the goosebumps on her arms. 'Would you like to borrow it?' he offered.

'Why not? As we're going on the same train.'

'Where are you heading?' Taking the sweater out of the rucksack, he gave it to her. He would have given far more, if only it were Kitty here with him.

Putting on the sweater, she hugged herself. 'Smells good,' she said. 'Girlfriend wash it, did she?'

He laughed and shook his head.

Brazenly eyeing him up and down, she asked, 'Where are you headed?'

Taken aback by her boldness, he took a minute to answer. 'Lancaster College.'

Laughing out loud, she revealed jubilantly, 'That's funny. So am I!'

'Oh?' Somehow he wasn't surprised.

He smiled. 'It's a small world.'

She laughed again. 'Same train, same college.' Hugging his sweater to herself, she remarked with delight, 'Thrown together by the wicked hand of Fate.' Looking up at him with calculating eyes, she asked, 'What do you think?'

'I think we'd best get on this train.' It was bearing down fast.

In a few minutes they were boarding. 'Hot and stuffy in here,' he remarked. The train was packed and the windows shut tight.

Excusing himself, he leaned over to open the nearest one. 'Is that all right?' he asked a rather fat and irritable man.

The man was about to open his mouth when his companion, a plump kind-faced woman, replied, 'That's fine, young man. Thank you.' The man scowled at her, and she smiled sweetly in return. Harry imagined the man must rule the roost at home.

'What's your name?' his own companion asked, throwing her rucksack on to the parcel shelf. 'Mine's Susan, and I don't like it shortened to Sue, so be warned.'

Holding out his hand, he answered in a friendly voice, 'Harry. Pleased to meet you.'

She didn't let go of his hand straightaway. Instead she held on, her eyes devouring him. 'Harry, eh? That's a good strong name . . . suits you.'

When at last she was sitting opposite, still wearing his sweater in spite of the clammy atmosphere, Harry wondered if she meant to chatter all the way to Lancaster.

Much to his relief she didn't chatter at all. Instead she read a magazine, flicked through a newspaper, and finally started on a novel. She seemed to busy herself throughout the journey when all the time she was slyly peeking at him, at his long legs and handsome face, at the way his thick hair fell over his ears and tumbled across his forehead. And what she was thinking was, Wonder what he's like in bed? And she made up her mind to find out at the first opportunity.

PART THREE

1980

Losers

CHAPTER TEN

Kitty was eating her toast when the postman slipped the mail through the letter-box. 'I'll get it!' she yelled excitedly. Leaping out of her chair she was down the hallway and at the front door before Mildred could open her mouth.

There was a card from Paris, showing the Eiffel Tower; it was from Miss Davis, who according to the short note was 'thoroughly enjoying the coach tour', and 'in two minds about the proposed trip to a night club to see some rather well-endowed women kicking their legs up in the air'.

Kitty was still laughing when she returned to the table. When Mildred read the card she laughed even louder. 'Looks like she's seeing another side of human nature,' she said. Kitty agreed, and they both envied her a little.

The only other correspondence was a small white envelope stained with tomato sauce. 'No need to ask who that's from,' Mildred observed with a grin.

As soon as Kitty saw the childish scrawl she knew it was from Georgie. Tearing open the envelope she scanned the one-page letter with eager eyes. Smiling as she realised it contained hopeful news.

Mildred finished her breakfast, waiting patiently while Kitty returned to the table. Engrossed in the letter, she propped it against the teapot, reading it over again while she nibbled at her toast.

'Well, are you going to tell me what she says?' Mildred enquired adding with a little grin, 'Or is it too private?'

''Course it isn't,' she chuckled, wiping her hands on a paper napkin.

'She hasn't been up to her old tricks again, has she? Hasn't got into trouble with the authorities again?'

'Nope!' Kitty mischievously kept her guessing.

'What then!' Mildred was used to Kitty's delightful little ways. They made life worthwhile. She had found a new lease of life when the authorities agreed her niece could come home with her.

'I'll read it to you, shall I?'

'Go on then.'

Taking the letter in her hands, Kitty began.

Hello again,

As promised when you last visited, I'm giving you the news the solicitor gave me this morning.

I expect you're waiting to hear whether I'll be coming out soon? Well, so am I! It seems like I've been in here for a bloody eternity. I know it's my own fault! Every time they're about to let me go, I cock the bugger up!

Anyway, I've just been told the appeal board meets next week. As you know, I've been on my best behaviour since the last fight, so I'm hoping they'll kick me out.

I know I'll still have to report and all that stuff, but it won't be so bad, not after losing my freedom for so long.

I wish I wasn't so quick-tempered. The trouble is, in these places everybody wants to rule the roost. I just have to let them know who's boss!

Anyway, I must say cheerio. We've to go and queue for the slop they call breakfast, though I must admit the new cook does a tasty spotted dick. Which reminds me ... the minute I get out, I'm picking up the first fella I find. I'll give him such a thrill his hair will stand on end ... along with other things!

Right, I'm off then. See you next visiting. Till then, keep your fingers crossed, gal. At least we've got an appeal date at last. If they don't let me out for Christmas I'll break down the bloody walls!

> *Lots of love from,*
> *Yours truly,*
> *Convict 99*

Mildred laughed. 'She's as nutty as ever,' she declared, liberally sprinkling sugar on her cornflakes.

Kitty lapsed into thought. Georgie's letter had brought a smile to her face, but it had also unsettled her. There was something underlying her remarks, and Kitty was concerned. 'Georgie's desperate,' she remarked thoughtfully. 'I'm worried about her.'

'Desperate?' Mildred glanced up in surprise. 'What makes you say that? She sounds bright and chirpy enough to me.'

Kitty was convinced. 'You don't know her like I do. She might want me to believe everything's all right, but it isn't. I can read between the lines. Georgie's had enough. She wants out of that place, and if the appeal is unsuccessful, who knows *what* she'll do?'

Seeing the anxiety in Kitty's lovely face, Mildred reasoned, 'It's no good thinking the worst. Anyway, if Georgie has been on her best behaviour, they're bound to take all that into account.'

'I hope so.' There had been two previous attempts to have Georgie released and each time she had blotted her copy book. 'As long as she doesn't lose her temper and start a fight before the hearing.' Knowing Georgie, it was very possible.

'Oh, I'm sure she has more sense.'

Kitty's thoughts had already moved on. 'If they *do* release her, I don't suppose she could stay here until she gets on her feet?' Seeing the horror on Mildred's face, Kitty was quick to reassure her. 'I'm sorry. You've had enough problems. Georgie would only be another.'

After giving the idea some thought, Mildred asked worriedly, 'If I said no, would you move out and find a place where you and Georgie could share?' The thought of Kitty leaving haunted her. Her niece had been her salvation; her strength. She still was.

'Why do you ask?' In fact Kitty had toyed with that very idea, but was well aware how vulnerable her aunt was.

'Because I know what good friends you and Georgie are.'

'*We're* good friends too, aren't we, you and me?' She decided it might be better if, for now at least, she avoided the issue of Georgie's possible homecoming.

Mildred's smile said it all. 'I hope we're the very best of friends,' she answered. 'I can never thank you enough for what you've done, Kitty . . . forgiving me . . . coming here to stay. You've turned my life around. I lost one family and gained another in you. I have a job, my self-respect, and I have you.'

Reaching across the table, she touched the back of Kitty's hand. 'I don't deserve you. After what I did to you, it's a wonder you didn't want to tear out my throat.'

Kitty's mind returned to the day she had run from here; run from herself, from the despair inside her. 'There *was* a moment,' she admitted. On that day when Mildred clung to her, drunk and demanding, trying to explain away the awful things she had done, pleading for pity and tearing at Kitty's heart, there had been one shocking moment when, if she had not wrenched herself away, she might have done her aunt harm.

'It's best forgotten,' she replied now. 'We all make mistakes.'

There was a brief silence, during which Mildred considered how close she had come to ruining her life. Kitty would never know how truly grateful she was.

In the momentary lull, Kitty contemplated the future. As always, Harry figured large in her mind. Deep in her heart she still saw herself in that wonderful wedding gown; saw the church as plain as if she had known it all her life when in fact she had never set foot inside such a quaint little place. Beside her stood Harry . . . handsome as ever.

She ached for him. Where was he right now? she wondered. In two weeks' time it would be Christmas. Colleges and universities would soon be closed for the holidays. Harry would be footloose and fancy free. The thought hurt, though she tried not to let it cloud her image of him . . . of his tall lithe figure and easy stride, his dark tumbling hair and brooding eyes. Footloose and fancy-free . . . What was he planning for the holidays? Without her. Her heart grew heavy. She made herself think rationally, made herself feel good for him. Pride surged through her. He was making something of his life, and that was wonderful.

But what about now? Right now? This very moment in time? Was he on his way home to Woburn Sands? Did he have a student friend striding along beside him? No doubt his parents would make the student welcome. No doubt his father would be delighted; he always had such ambitions for his son.

A thought occurred to her . . . perhaps he wasn't coming home for Christmas! Perhaps his studies had taken him on a trip abroad? Now she imagined him on a plane or a train, being whisked away to foreign parts . . . globe-trotting. Pride mingled with sadness. He felt so far away, yet so near she could feel his presence.

She had let him go to carve out a career without her holding him back. One day she hoped he might see that. One day, in the future, they might find each other again. With all her heart, she hoped so. But if one day it was too late, if one day he found someone new and forgot all about her, if that day ever came, she had only herself to blame.

'I was afraid the authorities would say no to my having you here.' Mildred's quiet voice intruded on Kitty's thoughts. 'If it hadn't been for you, helping me clean out this place and making me respectable, giving me the confidence to face them – well, I'm certain they would have turned me down and sent you to the foster parents.'

'That was a lifetime ago.' At least it seemed that way to Kitty.

Mildred shook her head. 'When you walked through that door with your few belongings I never dreamed you'd be allowed to stay. Not that you would really want to.' She frowned, obviously agitated as she pleated the edge of the tablecloth. 'I've never done right by you.' Mildred had so many regrets.

Smiling, Kitty put her at ease. 'Like I said . . . a lifetime ago.'

Mildred regarded her with pride. 'Look at you now though . . . a woman any man would die for.' Certainly Kitty had blossomed. Slim and pert, with the same elfin face and shining brown eyes, long dark hair loose to her shoulders and a smile to dazzle even the darkest day, she was exquisite. 'In a little over three months you'll be eighteen,' Mildred reckoned.

'Time flies,' Kitty mused aloud. In fact these many months had sped by so swiftly it was frightening.

Mildred was suddenly pacing the room. 'I'll always be ashamed I didn't come to your fourteenth birthday party,' she insisted. 'And we couldn't afford a party for your sixteenth. But we can afford one now.' Excited she spun round. 'How about if I put on a party for your birthday next March?' Once the idea took hold she wouldn't let it go. 'Oh Kitty! It would be wonderful! The biggest party this house has ever seen!'

She stared at Kitty with eager eyes. 'It's time we had a party. Time we celebrated. I'm finally and permanently shut of a two-timing husband. I'm satisfied the kids are all right without their mother, and for the time being at least, I've managed to fend off my ex-husband's greedy idea that I should sell this house.' The fight was still ongoing, but with Kitty's support, Mildred had been as stubborn as he was. 'What do you think, Kitty?

Shall we have a party on your birthday?'

Kitty wasn't keen, but she didn't want to dash Mildred's spirit. 'Whatever makes you happy,' she agreed.

'But you don't like the idea?' Mildred's smile fell.

'I'm not too sure about it,' Kitty confessed. 'But if you want a party, we'll have a party.' Right now it was the last thing she wanted. She remembered the other party. Harry had been there.

Mildred sensed there was something troubling Kitty. 'All right,' she said, 'you don't have to decide now. There's plenty of time. We'll leave it till the New Year. See how you feel then?'

Kitty was grateful. 'Let's enjoy Christmas first. After that, I promise I'll think about it.'

'Fair enough.' Mildred knew better than to insist. Experience had shown Kitty had a mind of her own.

She glanced at the clock. 'I'd best get ready. I don't want to keep Jack waiting.'

'I'm sure he wouldn't mind.'

'You're right,' Kitty admitted. 'Jack Harpur is the most patient man I've ever met... too accommodating by half. He should be more assertive.' More like Harry, she thought. But then, Jack was Jack and Harry was Harry, and they were as different as chalk from cheese.

Realising Kitty had again lapsed into deep thought, Mildred wondered, 'Do you ever think about that *other* young man? On the odd occasion when I visited your mother, I seemed to recall you and the boy were close friends.'

Kitty was astonished her aunt should remember, especially when she herself had made a point of never mentioning his name. When she answered, her smile gave nothing away. 'You mean Harry Jenkins?'

'That's right. His mother was a great friend of ...' Mildred bit her tongue. It didn't seem right to mention Lucinda.

'It's all right,' Kitty assured her. 'As you say, Mrs Jenkins was a friend of my mother's. And Harry ... well, I haven't heard from him in ages.' She didn't admit that was of her own choosing. That was something between her and Harry, a private thing ... like the way they felt about each other.

'People grow up. They change, and all too easily forget old friends.' Mildred sounded resentful.

'Sometimes that's the best way,' Kitty suggested. Leaning on her elbows she took a precious moment to let herself indulge in old memories. Sometimes it was good to let the past wash over you.

'Harry Jenkins was a handsome young man as I recall.'

'You recall right.'

'Water under the bridge, eh?'

'Something like that.' Nothing at all like that, Kitty thought. But she couldn't bring herself to talk about Harry, not with her aunt. Not with anyone.

'What time is Jack collecting you?'

Kitty's brown eyes swept the clock. It was quarter to nine. 'In about an hour.'

'Hardly ideal weather for trying out a boat.' Mildred peered out of the window. The sky was dark and ominous. 'Wouldn't surprise me if it rained cats and dogs all day.'

Kitty laughed. 'Then we'll find out whether it leaks.'

'And you might end up in the sea as well.'

'In that case, I'm sure Jack will decide against buying the boat.' Still chuckling, she got out of her seat and began clearing the breakfast things. 'I'll wash, you wipe.'

'You'll do no such thing.' Mildred quickly gathered the crockery. 'You do more than your share as it is. Anyway, I'm on afternoon shift, so I've time to spare.' She paused to smile at Kitty. 'Whoever would have thought I'd end up as supervisor in a sweet factory?'

'You like it though, don't you?' Kitty too had been astonished when Mildred saw the advert and decided to go for it. Since starting at Metrix, she had gone from strength to strength. Now she had vitality in her step, had regained her trim figure, and though she had a few grey hairs, was a neat, attractive woman of not quite fifty.

'I love my job,' she replied. 'Now you'd better hurry, or he'll be here and you won't be ready.' She paused and looked up. 'Kitty?'

'What?' She was on her way out of the door.

'Is it serious ... with Jack, I mean?'

Kitty thought a minute. She liked Jack. Since the first day she had started as invoice clerk in his father's boat and chandlery business, Jack had been a real friend. But she didn't love him. How could she? 'It's not serious on my part,' she said. It was on his. She knew that, and it bothered her. 'Why do you ask?'

'Because I'm nosy,' Mildred laughed. 'And because I've seen the way he looks at you.'

'Don't worry. He knows the score.'

'And what's that?'

'He knows I don't feel the same way ... never could.'

'Jack Harpur is a good man. He's also a good catch ... with a share in his father's boat business, two cars, and a cottage in West Bay!'

'I didn't realise I'd told you so much about him.'

'Ah! You see what I mean? He's on your mind without your even realising it. It's only a matter of time before he grows on you.'

Kitty smiled. 'I see. Trying to marry me off before I'm even seventeen?'

Mildred was shocked. 'What a thing to say!'

'Well, for your information I have no immediate plans to get married.' No plans at all in fact. For the moment she was content to let life carry her along where it fancied.

'*You* may not have plans to marry, but what about your boss?'

Kitty had no answer to that. She merely dismissed the subject with a cheeky wink before departing to get ready for her date.

A short time later a silver Jaguar drew up outside the house and a young man stepped out. 'He's here!' Kitty had been watching through the window. 'See you later,' she called.

'Good luck!' Mildred heard the door slam. 'Stay on your guard, Kitty,' she murmured, waving through the window as they drove away. 'He might be wealthy, but he's also very lonely. From what you've told me he usually gets what he wants, and as far as I can see he idolises the ground you walk on.' She turned from the window. 'Wealthy, lonely and besotted with you. He wants you but you're not sure whether you want him. Someone is bound to get hurt.'

Shaking her head she returned to her housework. 'I'd say there was a dangerous situation brewing.'

Mildred didn't know how right she was.

The long drive to Elsworth took them along the busy A34, then through pretty little villages where the traffic slowed and the scenery was breathtakingly beautiful.

Kitty loved travelling. 'It was good of you to bring me along,' she said. 'Though I expect my work will pile high while I'm gone, and the phone won't stop ringing.'

'Dad can answer the phone. It won't hurt him to stay out of the yard for a day and sit behind a desk. It might make him realise how hard you have to work.' Smiling, Jack glanced at her. 'Who knows? He might even be persuaded to give you a pay-rise.'

'I've just had a pay-rise.' Laughing she remarked, 'Though I wouldn't say no to another if he insisted.'

They both knew it was unlikely. Ted Harpur was a generous employer, but he stuck rigidly by his rules. He had four men and two women on his payroll, and any pay-rise was given on the last day in November, or not at all.

Settling back in her seat, Kitty quietly regarded her companion. Jack Harpur was twenty-eight years old; she only knew that because his father had mentioned it when Kitty was first recruited. He was enthusiastic, hard-working and generous to a fault. An only child, he had been showered with both love and material things, though as a man, and junior partner in his father's firm, he earned everything he owned.

Kitty had detected only one small, puzzling flaw in his character. There were times when Jack seemed unsure of himself, anxious and almost desperate to please. It was an odd thing, especially as his parents doted on him. It was inconceivable that he should have any money worries, and he was happy in his work – so much so that he worked all hours God sent and, while he had enjoyed many light-hearted liaisons with members of the opposite sex, had never embarked on a serious relationship, let alone considered marriage.

Peeping at him now, Kitty couldn't help but recall her aunt's well-meaning teasing. And she was right of course. Jack had got his sights set on her, even though she had made it plain she was neither old enough nor ready for a serious encounter with anyone. Not even Harry. She wondered what it was about her that had made Jack interested. Somehow she didn't believe he was after a one night stand.

Like so many times before, she couldn't help but compare him with Harry. Where Harry was dark-eyed, Jack had eyes as blue as the sky. Harry was tall and muscular. Jack was of medium height and square-set. His hair was bleached by the sun, and he had the lightest sprinkling of freckles on his forehead.

Where Harry was quiet and assertive, Jack talked a lot, impressing his customers with his vast knowledge of boats; he knew every make afloat and had learned the technical details off by heart. He revelled in passing on this information.

Kitty knew very little about boats; her job at the chandlery kept her well and truly in the office, where she made out the invoices and appeased the customers when they rang up to query delivery dates and the like. She did have a smattering of knowledge though, such as the back of the boat was the 'stern' and the front was the 'bow' – or 'fore' and 'aft' as the sailors said. She knew the bedrooms were called 'cabins' and had learned a little jargon concerning the parts that were fitted from the boatyard, like the radar that guided them, or the sounding equipment that might detect submerged debris and thereby avert a collision. The window of her office looked out over the yard, and from here she could see the men at work, cleaning, stripping and refurbishing engines and boats. Ted Harpur chose his workers carefully. They were skilled and industrious, and widely respected in the boat trade.

The Harpur yard was one of the busiest around, making more money and selling more boats than any other locally. Jack and his father dealt in used and new boats, and travelled far and wide if there was a bargain to be had. They were trusted by buyer and seller alike. Kitty recalled one man in particular, who waited months for the right boat to be found for him. When Jack located one berthed in Malta, he and his father flew out there and sailed it home. It was bought for six thousand pounds, sold to the man for ten. He then paid another two thousand pounds to have it completely refitted. When he sailed it away it looked like new. Jack and his father had made a healthy four thousand profit on the sale and a further five hundred pounds on the refitting. 'Everyone's satisfied,' Jack told Kitty. 'That's what you call good business.'

'What kind of boat are you hoping to buy today?' she asked as he pulled up at traffic lights.

'A Sealine cruiser,' he answered. 'Apparently the owner has just remarried and his wife doesn't like sailing. The boat has been in dock ever since.'

'Have you a buyer for it?'

Surprised, he turned to her. 'Listen to you,' he chuckled delightedly. 'You're already talking like a chandler's wife.'

Embarrassed, she turned her attention to their surroundings. They were driving along a narrow lane, with high grass banks and trees that spread their branches over the hedge. Ahead the willows had formed an arch over the road. 'It looks just like a tunnel,' Kitty remarked. 'Isn't it beautiful!'

His hand reached out to touch hers. 'I wouldn't know,' he murmured. 'I'm too busy looking at something else that's beautiful.'

She blushed and he loved her all the more. 'I might have to move you out of your job, Kitty,' he confessed.

She was horrified. She had visions of being sacked. 'What do you mean?' Anxiety showed on her face.

'I'm a wealthy man, with a certain image to maintain.' Though he spoke with the hint of a smile, there was a serious expression in his eyes. 'It goes without saying that a man in my position would not want his wife working in a dreary office.'

'I'm not your wife.' Now she realised what he was getting at. She also realised she had been foolish to agree to come on this trip.

'I'm asking you to marry me, Kitty.' His hand was still clutching hers and his blue eyes were intent on her face. 'What do you say? Will you make me very happy and name a date?'

'I can't.'

'Why not?' He was persistent.

'Personal reasons,' she said impatiently. 'I don't want to talk about it.' It was because of Harry, of course, but that was none of Jack's business.

He laughed. 'It can't be another man! I don't allow you enough time to have a social life.'

'Like I said ... I don't want to talk about it.'

'Later then?' He was like a dog with a bone.

Searching for an answer that would not hurt him too much, Kitty was relived when they turned on to a main road and he was forced to divert both his hand and his attention from her. Yet she knew this was not over. She had witnessed his dogged determination when negotiating a deal. Jack was not a man to give up lightly.

It was midday when they arrived in the picturesque village of

Elsworth. 'We'll do the deal,' he told her as they pulled into the Tanner boatyard. 'Later, maybe we can take in the sights.' He winked at her. 'I'm in no hurry to get back.'

All eyes turned their way as he parked the streamlined Jaguar. 'A car like this speaks for you,' he said as he locked the doors. 'It reflects success . . . tells people you're a man who can't afford to waste time.' He was immensely proud of his car – and his status.

As they walked up the steps to the office, Kitty was enchanted. The boatyard was situated off the River Hamble in a natural lagoon formed by an extravagant curve where the river meandered. Its perimeter was lined with blossoming shrubs set in neat rows that rose and fell like the pattern on the edge of a pie-crust.

Inside the lagoon there were many sailing vessels: boats with their sails rolled high, streamlined cruisers with flybridges atop and spacious sundecks beneath, and moored all around in the water were a number of smaller boats, rubber dinghies and wooden-hulled vessels of the older kind. Beneath a clear blue sky and brilliant sunshine, it made a very pretty picture.

There was a wonderful sense of peace here, a certain timelessness. Kitty had felt the same atmosphere at the boatyard. It was a deeply pleasing, soothing sensation.

The vessel Jack hoped to buy was a fifty-foot cruiser; with every conceivable extra already fitted. It had four well-equipped cabins, two fore and two aft, and was outfitted with the best that money could buy. The yard manager took them over it, extolling its virtues and going into great detail about the equipment that had cost the owner a small fortune.

Jack was impressed. 'It's a good boat,' he told the yard manager. 'I think we might be able to come to a deal . . . depending of course on whether the price is acceptable to me.'

'I'm afraid I can't agree a price without the owner's being present,' the manager explained. 'But there's nothing to stop you from making an offer. If you give us a minute when he arrives, I'll put the offer to him.'

Jack did not like dealing with middle men. 'I'd prefer to put it to him myself,' he said. 'What time will he be here?'

With a sour expression, the manager answered in a flat hard voice, 'I have been authorised to act on his behalf, but if that's the way you want it, I suppose I've no objection.' Glancing towards the yard's entrance his frown and his temper worsened. 'Christ knows where he's got to! He should have been here an hour since.' Still hoping for a good commission, he gave a little smile. 'We'll have to be patient. I'm sure he's on his way.'

'I still have other boats to see, you understand?' Jack lied. In fact he had not come across a boat of this quality in a long time, and was thrilled by its superb condition. He desperately wanted the vessel, but was experienced enough not to show the extent of his enthusiasm.

The manager could see a sale slipping away. 'I'm sure it will be worth your while to wait,' he pointed out. 'Especially as there are two more prospective buyers coming out this afternoon.' He was playing Jack at his own game. The owner wanted a certain price and he himself was duty bound to make a respectable profit. In Jack he saw a shrewd businessman and knew from experience he would have to handle things very carefully, if he was to land this particular fish.

Jack was not deterred. 'I know the advert said he was asking a hundred and fifty thousand, but he must know he'll have to come down,' Jack said. 'Have you any ideas what price he'll settle for?'

'No idea at all, sir.' The manager prided himself on his ability to lie while looking a man straight in the eye. It was a talent that came from years of trading.

Jack knew he was lying. 'Box in my corner and I could make it worth your while?'

The manager did a quick mental calculation. The owner had already ordered a new boat through this yard, and no doubt all the extras would come through here too. The owner was a prime customer, rolling in money. When this deal was done, at whatever price, he himself was sure to be paid a handsome commission. He shook his head. 'Best if you talk with the owner yourself,' he answered smugly.

Kitty had witnessed the whole thing. It put her in mind of two boxers circling each other in the ring, testing the other's strength. She had seen Jack perform like this many times. He was skilled at it, tried and tested, filled with quiet confidence. However good the other fellow was, she knew Jack would come off best in the end. He always did.

While Jack and the manager sauntered about the boat discussing this and that, Kitty wandered at will. She had never set foot on a boat this size before. Going from one cabin to the other, she ran her hand over the highly polished brass railings, lovingly stroked the thick quilted eiderdowns, and sat in the big swivel-chair at the helm. 'Head for the Caribbean, my good man!' she grandly instructed an imaginary captain, then crumpled up laughingly, glanced furtively about and hoping she hadn't been overheard.

An hour later Jack came to find her. 'There's a problem,' he explained. 'The owner was supposed to meet us here, but there's just been a phone call to say he's been delayed.'

Kitty knew there was more to it than that. She could tell by the look on his face. If Jack was anything, he was honest. 'Delayed? For how long?'

'He can't get here until tomorrow.'

'What does that mean exactly?' She knew it could mean one of two things.

Jack began to spell them out. 'We can either leave here now, and I'll have to make other arrangements to meet the owner and clinch the deal . . .'

Kitty concluded for him. 'Or we stay overnight somewhere, and you clinch the deal in the morning?'

'That's it, I'm afraid.' He looked really dismayed. 'I'm leaving the choice to you, Kitty. Whatever you say is all right by me.'

She saw the disappointment on his face. She saw how frustrated he was at not having secured a deal, and quickly realised she had little option. If she insisted on going back and he lost the deal, she would only blame herself. 'Now that we're here, we'd better stay,' she said, putting the smile back on his face. 'You'd be impossible to work with if the owner sold that boat to somebody else.'

He couldn't hide his delight. 'Thanks, Kitty! You've made the right decision.' He beamed from ear to ear. 'That's the businesswoman coming out in you.' Pecking her on the cheek, he returned to the manager's office at a nonchalant pace; aware that the man was watching, Jack didn't want to seem overanxious. 'I have two other boats to see hereabouts,' he said, 'so we might as well stay over.'

'Suit yourself.' The manager had been worried that he had

lost the sale. Now he believed he had all but clinched it.

Jack chuckled as he climbed into the car beside Kitty. 'She's as good as mine!' he exclaimed. 'And isn't she a beauty?' Studying the cruiser through the open car window, he mused aloud, 'I've a good mind to have her done out in my own colours and keep her.'

Kitty made no comment. Instead she gazed at the boat and imagined herself lying on the sun-deck, basking in the sunshine under a turquoise Mediterranean sky.

Having admired the vessel, Jack turned his attention to Kitty, secretly admiring the fine cut of her profile, the rich spill of dark hair and the long, long lashes that fringed her expressive brown eyes. He had always thought her incredibly lovely. He thought so now, and his need for her was tenfold. 'Be my wife,' he urged, 'and I'll take you anywhere in the world you want to go.' He glanced at the vessel once more. 'I'll even name her after you. Think of it... the *Kitty Harpur* has a good ring to it, don't you think?'

'Do you really want to know what I think?'

'Of course.'

'I think we should find somewhere to stay. I want a shower and I want feeding.' They hadn't stopped on the way and she was famished.

Jack eased the car out of the park and on to the lane. 'It's all in hand,' he revealed. 'Apparently there's a quaint old inn about a mile away. According to the manager of this yard, we should get a first-class meal and excellent hospitality there.'

'Sounds like his brother owns it,' she quipped. It sounded ideal though; a long shower, then a satisfying meal in pleasant company. As long as he didn't push the question of marriage.

Elsworth itself was a page right out of history. There were tiny thatched cottages with leaded light windows, hanging baskets drooping with myriads of blossoms, old-fashioned shops with big bow windows and bulls' eye panes. The people were warm and friendly, and as they did a little shopping... nightclothes for themselves, a present for Mildred, and a new pipe for Jack's father... Kitty felt happy at heart. Jack was a handsome man and a charming companion who knew how to please a lady.

The inn was everything she'd imagined: brass jugs and copper pans hanging from old oak beams, an enormous inglenook fireplace festooned with attractive displays of dried flowers and old pewter. The waiter who served their meal was a mountain of a man, with red bushy hair and mutton-chop whiskers. 'Straight out of Dickens,' she whispered. Curious, Jack looked up; the fellow in question glared at him, and after that Kitty kept her observations to herself.

She enjoyed the meal. It was a splendid affair, cooked to perfection and served with a smile. Beef chasseur and whole small vegetables for Jack, chicken and rice for Kitty, followed by fruit salad and cream.

With the main course Jack ordered a carafe of wine, which he poured liberally, and when that was gone, he ordered two brandy liqueurs and a pot of coffee. 'Did you phone your aunt?' he asked.

'I did.' Kitty smiled at the thought of what her aunt had said. 'She warned me against you . . . said you might be trying to lure me into bed.'

He gazed at her lovingly. 'Is that what *you* think?'

'I'm not sure.' She sipped at her coffee. 'What *should* I think, Jack?' She felt naughty. '*Are* you trying to seduce me?'

'I'd be a fool if I wasn't.' His hand slipped across the table to caress hers. 'But to tell you the truth, I wouldn't want it to be that way.'

'Oh?' She made no effort to remove his hand from hers. In an odd way it was comforting. 'What way would you want it to be then?'

He took another sip of liqueur and it was a moment before he answered. During that time he stroked her fingers, then raised them to his mouth and touched them with the tip of his tongue. All the time he avoided her gaze, as though mentally preparing himself. Presently, he looked at her and his eyes were filled with love. 'You never gave me an answer,' he accused softly. 'I asked you to be my wife, and you never gave me an answer.'

Kitty felt light-headed. 'I think I've had too much wine,' she said, astonished when her voice rose in a giggle. 'Maybe my aunt's right after all, and you mean to have your wicked way with me.'

'Kitty! Didn't you hear what I said?'

'I heard.' She'd heard him the first time too. The answer was still the same. 'I've already told you . . . I can't marry you.'

'Of course you can.' There was a look on his face she had never seen before, and a certain tone to his voice that made her think of Miss Davis. 'I won't take no for an answer,' he insisted.

Kitty was angry that he should dismiss her answer as though it was not important. 'I'm afraid you'll *have* to take no for an answer,' she told him firmly. 'I can't . . . *won't* . . . marry you, so you might as well give up on the idea.'

'I love you.' There was a world of sincerity in his face.

'What about the others?'

He looked shocked. 'What others?'

Kitty smiled patiently. 'The one who rang for you every day when I first came to work in the office, and the long-legged beauty who was your constant companion after you ditched the first one. It's none of my business, I know, but how many were there before that? Did you love them all?' Her aim was to play down the 'love' he claimed to feel for her; to make him realise he could have his pick of women, so why should he want her?

'They meant nothing . . . companions, that's all. Oh, I don't deny I've painted the town, and yes, I've had my share of women.' A look of disgust crossed his face. 'But those relationships were never meant to be permanent.' His voice fell to a whisper. 'Haven't you noticed how lonely I am lately? There are no women in my life now . . . no one I want to be with . . . just you, Kitty. It's you I want . . . you I love . . . you I need for my wife. I have never proposed to any other woman, and I never will. I *love* you.' Leaning forward, he softly murmured in her ear, tenderly kissing her face, 'Let yourself love me, Kitty. Let me take care of you.'

Deep down she knew he really did love her. And if she had never known Harry, she might even have been drawn to Jack as a partner. It was a frightening thought. 'Don't ask me again,' she warned, 'or I might have to find another job.'

Now it was his turn to be frightened. 'All right, Kitty, I won't ask you again,' he vowed. 'But I want a promise from you in return.'

'What kind of promise?'

'That you'll think about what I've asked.' When he saw she was about to protest, he assured her, 'The way I feel won't change. But I'm hoping your answer will. I'm hoping you'll decide that being married to me wouldn't be so bad after all. I'm hoping you'll realise there are no rules that say both partners should love each other to make a successful marriage. I love you enough for both of us. Consider that, Kitty. It's all I'm asking.'

There was little she could say that would convince him that her mind was already made up. How could she marry him when she didn't love him? How could she spend her whole life with a man who would only ever be second best to her? What about children? What about the way her life would change? He lived in a social whirl . . . spent money like water. His friends were wealthy, elegant people, versed in the ways of the world, while she was a young and ordinary working girl who preferred tea to wine, and had never worn a designer outfit in her whole life. However hard Jack tried to convince her, she would still be out of her depth. A round peg in a square hole.

'Don't say anything now.' His voice interrupted her thoughts. 'Just remember . . . I love you with all my heart. I know something of what you've suffered in your life, and I swear before God, I will never let anything or anyone hurt you ever again.'

Before she could respond, he summoned the waiter. 'What time is breakfast?'

'First serving at eight, sir.'

'Thank you.' He slipped the man a five-pound note.

'That was a bit extravagant,' Kitty declared as they made their way up the broad stairway.

'Money was made to go round,' he answered. 'The poor chap probably only earns as much as that in two hours.'

Kitty laughed. 'I don't earn much more than that myself,' she teased.

Outside her door he put out his arms and pinned her there. 'As my wife you would never have to work again,' he reminded her. 'You might consider that too.'

'Goodnight, Jack.' He was a persistent sod!

He gazed at her longingly, his pale eyes appearing stunningly blue in the overhead light. Without a word he bent his head and kissed her full on the mouth. It was a tender kiss, loving and suggestive without being forceful. Against her better judgment she gave herself up to it.

Later, when she was lying in bed, it occurred to Kitty that she had really enjoyed that kiss. 'Silly bugger, Kitty Marsh!' she chided herself. 'Now he'll think you're warming to the idea of marriage.' Something else occurred to her then, and she had to chuckle. 'You're a bit free with the bad language tonight an' all, my girl!' She pulled a wry little face and turned over. 'Must be the wine,' she muttered. 'It's all your fault, Harry Jenkins. If it wasn't for you, Jack might be a good catch. As it is, I can only love one man at a time.'

Harry was her man, she thought, and it was for Harry she was saving herself. 'Maybe it's time I found you, my love,' she whispered. 'Maybe Georgie was right all along, and I should never have let you go in the first place.' Now, as she closed her eyes she could see him. Her heart soared, and her determination strengthened. Harry's mother would tell her where to find him. With that thought in mind she fell into a deep, deep sleep.

In the early hours Jack came to her. Having secured a pass key from the man to whom he had given five pounds, he let himself in. For a long time he sat on the chair beside her bed, just gazing at her sleeping face. 'I want you so much,' he whispered. 'I've never loved anyone like I love you.'

The minutes passed. The sound of the bedside clock ticked the night away, and still he made no move. Her arms spread out across the pillow, her dark hair spilling across the pillow and her face turned towards him. 'You're very beautiful,' he told her softly.

Beneath his robe he was naked. Slowly he took it off and laid it on the back of the chair. Then he slid into bed beside her.

In her dreams Kitty was lying with Harry. She could feel his skin, soft and warm against hers. His kisses were gentle, his arms strong about her. When he penetrated her she yielded to him, wanting him, hungry for his love. Oh, she had waited so long, and now he was here. Drained and contented, she lay quiet in his arms. Tomorrow they would talk. Tomorrow they would make plans.

In the morning she awoke, turned her head on the pillow and saw him there; he was smiling at her, blue eyes brimming with love. 'I had to see you,' he said, holding out his arm for her to lie against his chest. 'I knew you wanted me too.'

Kitty stared at him in disbelief. Then she got out of bed, went into the bathroom and locked the door. When she came back to the bedroom, he was gone. Slumping before the dressing-table she examined her image in the mirror. 'You fool!' she groaned. 'What have you done? Oh, Kitty, what have you done?'

It was nine o'clock when she went downstairs. 'Just coffee please,' she told the waiter. 'Oh, and have you seen Mr Harpur?'

'He went out an hour ago, miss. I'm to tell you he's gone to the boatyard and should be back before ten thirty.'

Kitty thanked him. Then she took her coffee into the lounge and tried unsuccessfully to read the morning papers. 'Damn him!' she muttered, slamming the paper down. 'Damn him! Damn him!'

When he returned, excited and thrilled because he had secured a deal on the boat, she rounded on him. 'Did you have it all planned?' she demanded. 'Was it all arranged beforehand... you and this "owner" who was so conveniently delayed?'

The expression on his face told her the truth. 'If you think that, then there's nothing else for me to say. I'll take you home. If you feel you should find another job, I won't try to stop you.'

In the car they sat in silence; Kitty bitterly regretting what had happened, and Jack regretting only that she didn't feel the way he did. 'I'm sorry,' he apologised. 'I had no right to come into your room.' He was devastated, believing that one mistake could take her from him forever.

Kitty remained silent, cursing herself, cursing him, wishing it hadn't happened but accepting it had. Wishing there was a way to turn back the clock, but knowing of old that there was no way she could do that.

The traffic was heavier than usual. The journey seemed to drag on forever. She glanced sideways at Jack's face, a miserable, unhappy face. She had not spoken a word to him in two hours and knew how he must be suffering. Serves you right, she thought. She was angry, with him and herself, then she felt guilty. When she closed her eyes she saw Harry's face. What now? she asked herself. What now?

CHAPTER ELEVEN

Kitty stood by the kitchen window, arms folded, brown eyes turned to the star-filled sky. 'I don't know what to do about Jack,' she murmured. 'He just won't give up.'

Mildred was seated at the kitchen table, her hands clasping a mug of cocoa and her eyes resting on Kitty's troubled face. 'Come and sit here,' she said. 'I've made you a mug of cocoa . . . drink it while it's still hot.' Like Kitty, she had been unable to sleep.

Coming to the table, Kitty took up her mug, then put it down again. Leaning forward she ran her hands through her tousled dark hair, dropped her head and closed her eyes. 'He's driving me crazy,' she groaned. 'I can't sleep, and I can't work. It's been worse since his father went to America . . . everywhere I turn, Jack's watching me.'

He was there when she answered the phone, smiling at her from the doorway; he was there when she looked up from the filing cabinet; he was there the minute she arrived and when she left. 'I've been seriously thinking about looking for another job.' Raising her head, she looked at Mildred. 'I don't want to,' she admitted. 'But what choice have I got?'

'You know what Jack's problem is, don't you?'

Kitty was amused to see Mildred actually smiling. 'Me!' she declared, now smiling herself. '*I'm* Jack's problem, that's what you're going to say, isn't it?'

'I don't have to now. You've said it yourself. Of course you're his problem! If you think he's driving you crazy, what do you think you're doing to *him*? He sees you every day, yet you might as well be at the other end of the world. You won't talk things through with him. You won't let him take you out, and you return all the little gifts he sends. The poor sod's head over

175

heels in love with you, and you still can't make up your mind what to do about him.'

Kitty laughed, and the tension was broken. 'You're wrong,' she chuckled. 'I *do* know what to do about him.' Clenching both fists she shook them in the air. 'I'm going to strangle him!' she said through clenched teeth. 'If I look up once more to see him gawping at me, I swear to God I'll do away with him!'

'I thought you liked him?'

'That's just it. I do have a soft spot for Jack,' she admitted. 'If only he'd give me time to get my thoughts together.' But secretly she knew all the time in the world wouldn't make any difference. Her heart belonged to Harry.

'You don't love him, that's the root of the problem?'

'You could say that.' Kitty's brown eyes softened. 'I do like Jack,' she confessed thoughtfully. 'And I know he would take care of me like I've never been taken care of before.'

'But you're afraid?'

'No. Not afraid exactly.'

'What then?' Mildred saw shyness creep into Kitty's face and started to wonder. 'You haven't been keeping secrets from me, have you?'

Kitty was startled. 'Like what?' Harry was her secret and would stay that way until she was sure he still wanted her. The time was soon. Very soon. Until then she thought it best not to talk about her hopes.

Mildred sensed something about Kitty's mood. 'Oh, nothing,' she muttered. 'I just wondered if there might be another man, that was all.' Saving Kitty the trouble of answering, she went on in a quieter voice, 'That night when you and Jack . . . you know?'

'When he came to my room at the hotel?'

'Well, yes.' Mildred looked a little uncomfortable. 'You don't regret confiding in me, do you, Kitty?'

Kitty's face melted into a warm encouraging smile. 'Who else should I confide in?' she asked gently.

'Did he . . . force himself on you?'

Kitty shook her head. 'It wasn't like that,' she answered truthfully.

Mildred took a sip of her cocoa. 'I'm sorry,' she said. 'I'm sure you would have told me if he had.' She didn't ask any more questions. Instead she finished her cocoa, took her cup to the sink and rinsed it, then she made for her bed with the parting remark, 'All the same, it's a pity you can't bring yourself to love him. You could do worse than mary a man like Jack Harpur.'. Lately she had come to realise she was leaning on Kitty too much.

Kitty remained downstairs until the dawn crept over the rooftops. She was too restless to sleep, and too tired not to. She thought about Jack, and Mildred's remark, and murmured to the sky, 'She's right. Jack would make a wonderful husband. He's kind and generous, and when he loves, he's really dedicated.' But she couldn't convince herself. 'He's not for me. I could never give him the affection he deserves.' Suddenly she felt adrift, cut loose from everything that mattered. The loneliness was overwhelming. But then she thought of Harry. Somewhere out there, he might be thinking of her. It was a warming thought.

A moment later she turned out the light, closed the kitchen door and went to bed.

The following day was Saturday. Feeling as if she'd spent a night on the tiles, Kitty got out of bed. After a few minutes yawning and stretching, and rubbing the sleep from her eyes, she threw open the curtains. At first she couldn't believe what she was seeing . . . the trees, the lawn and even the tiny round knobs on the gate posts were covered in a thick carpet of white. 'It's been snowing!' There was a childish excitement in her face as she pressed her nose to the cold windowpane, her shining eyes big with wonder as they viewed the world outside. Fluffy flakes splashed on to the glass, sliding down to make starry patterns in front of her nose. 'Oh, I hope it snows till Christmas,' she said wistfully. The year had gone so quickly. Her childhood had long gone; now her youth had gone.

She refused to let thoughts of the past mar her joy. 'MILDRED!' Her voice rang out, frightening a robin who was hopping through the snow, 'Mildred . . . it's snowing!'

Running along the corridor, she called to her aunt: 'Get up! Look out of the window . . . it's snowing!'

Thinking the house must be on fire, Mildred sprang out of bed and flung open her bedroom door. 'Whatever's going on?' she cried, bleary-eyed and looking like the wrong end of a mop.

177

Laughing, Kitty swung her round. 'It'll snow till Christmas,' she promised. 'You'll see! It'll snow till Christmas!' Propelling Mildred through the bedroom she snatched open the curtains. 'See that? The skies are full of it.'

Mildred was happy when Kitty was happy, but in truth she hated the snow. She loathed the cold weather, and couldn't wait for the summer. 'You'll be asking me to make snowmen with you next!' she exclaimed with horror.

Kitty laughed and swung her round again.

Shivering at the very sight of the snow, Mildred drew away. 'I'm off back to my bed,' she declared. 'You can go out and freeze your hands off if you like, but I'm not setting foot out of this house until Monday morning. By that time the snow will have gone, I hope.' Disgruntled, she got into bed and threw the duvet over her head. 'Shut the door on your way out,' she called in a muffled voice.

'If you're that tired, you won't want me to fetch you a cup of tea?' Kitty teased. Before Mildred could answer she ran out and pulled the door to, holding on tight so it couldn't be opened from the other side.

It was only a few seconds before Mildred was tugging at the other side. 'You bugger!' she yelled. 'Let go of this door!'

'Why? I thought you were so tired you wanted to spend the day in bed?' Kitty knew how her aunt coveted her morning cuppa. Neither hell nor high water, not even a heavy snowfall, would keep her from it.

There was a short silence. Then, 'All right . . . put the kettle on. I'll be down in a minute.'

Kitty went about her duties singing. After a few minutes seated at the breakfast table with Mildred, who carped and moaned that at her age she needed a good night's sleep, Kitty washed the breakfast cups, ran a hoover round the house, and polished every surface in sight, singing all the while and thrilled at the prospect of seeing Georgie. 'She's back before the board on Monday,' she reminded Mildred. 'I hope they release her this time.'

Mildred had lost patience with Georgie. 'She would have been released long ago, if only she'd learned how to curb her temper.' She sighed. 'Who am I to talk anyway?' she asked. 'I've done exactly the same with that greedy ex-husband of mine. Now he's after my blood.' Reaching behind her, she plucked a brown envelope from the dresser. With a shrug she threw it across the table. 'It came yesterday.'

Concerned, Kitty opened it and drew out the letter. As she read her expression changed from curiosity to anger, then to anxiety. 'It says here you have to sell the house and contents.' She was so shocked she fell into a chair. 'He can't *really* make you sell this house, can he?'

Pointing to the letter, Mildred explained, 'As you see, that letter is from his solicitor. They don't usually issue those instructions unless they've done their homework.'

'But it's *your* house!' Kitty was certain her aunt had the right to refuse. 'It was left to you by your parents. It was he who cleared off. It was he who set up home with another woman. And even then you haven't shirked your responsibilities because, since you started work, you've done your bit to support the children. Doesn't that count for anything?'

'It seems not. He says it's not enough. He wants his share of everything . . . including this house.' Mildred sighed wearily. 'I'm tired of fighting,' she said. Clenching her fists together, she banged them on the table. 'Damn the man! I'm beginning to think it might be better if I do sell the bloody house, just to get him off my back once and for all.'

Kitty was appalled. 'Is that what you want?'

''Course it isn't! As you said, this house was left me by my parents. It's where I was born. It's where I grew up . . . where I got married from.' She grinned. 'That was a mistake if ever there was one.'

Coming round the table, Kitty bent down to hug her. 'Don't let them take it from you,' she urged gently. 'There has to be another way. Perhaps you could get a mortgage to give him his share?'

'I've thought of that, but I'm not too keen. It would be a millstone round my neck.' Touching her hand against Kitty's she apologised. 'It's not your problem. I shouldn't have told you.'

'Oh?' Kitty was disappointed. 'I thought we'd agreed to look after each other?'

Mildred gave her a look of love. 'You're a blessing to me,' she said. 'Now get off and see that wayward friend of yours. Tell her what I said. If she'd learned how to curb her temper, she'd have been out of there long ago.'

A few minutes later, Kitty was hurrying down the path, kicking the snow beneath her feet and thinking what a wrench it would be for her aunt to part with this lovely old house.

Watching from the window, Mildred was thinking the same. When Kitty turned to wave, she waved back. 'I wish I had your strength,' she said under her breath.

Surprisingly, the bus was on time. In fact, if Kitty had been just one minute late she might have missed it. 'I thought the weather would hold you up,' she told the conductor as she clambered onto the platform.

'Did you now?' He was only two months away from retirement. Completely bald beneath his cap, he had a long narrow face with thin arched eyebrows and lips you could slice a loaf with. His hands trembled as he rolled out the ticket, and when he smiled, as he did now, his false teeth played a merry tune against his gums. 'Off to the borstal again?' Taking off his cap he scratched his pink head. 'I should have thought she'd been out it by now.'

Kitty crossed her fingers and winked. 'Next week ... if all goes well,' she whispered. She had confided in this old man some time back, on an empty bus when returning from a visit to Georgie. It was the first time her friend had had hopes of being released, and the first time she had had her hopes dashed. Kitty had been softly crying when the conductor sat beside her, and she'd told him everything. Since then he had taken a keen interest in what he believed was a strange relationship between his 'respectable' passenger, and a convict who couldn't stay out of trouble, even in jail.

After paying her fare and thanking him for his concern, Kitty made her way down the aisle. Other passengers marked her out of the corner of their eyes; they had overheard the remarks made by the conductor and were curious. More than that, they were drawn by Kitty's dark beauty. In her long boots, calf-length coat and black beret, she made a striking figure. Her smiling brown eyes shone from her face and her long dark hair made a striking contrast with the cream-coloured collar of her overcoat.

When she sat down, taking off her beret to shake the snow from it, she smiled at one young woman, who made a sour face and quickly looked away. Must have got out of bed the wrong side this morning, Kitty thought, pulling the beret back over her thick wild hair. After that she concentrated on the journey ahead. If she was to be let out on Monday, Georgie would need all kinds of help. To that end, Kitty had been to a local letting office, where she'd acquired a list of rented properties for Georgie to glance through.

Taking the list from her bag, Kitty perused it for most of the journey. There was one place in particular she hoped Georgie might like. It was a one-bedroom, ground-floor flat, in a street not too far from Mildred's house. 'You'll like this one,' Kitty whispered hopefully. Marking the place with a pencil, she noted, 'The rent's reasonable too.'

Georgie was all smiles when Kitty showed her the list, 'You're a good mate,' she said. 'But I don't want to tempt Fate by looking at it. Put it back in your bag. If they let me out on Monday, the two of us can go and inspect the place. If it's good enough for a lady like meself, then I'll be glad to take it.' Her face broke into a grin. 'I'm glad you're here,' she said. 'Give us a fag, and I'll tell you me life story.'

'I don't know if I could stand it,' laughed Kitty, 'but I'll give you a fag anyway.' Taking out a packet of Players, she deliberately held them at arm's length. 'Have you stayed out of trouble since I saw you?'

'I haven't punched anybody's face if that's what you mean.' Stretching her arm out as far as she could, Georgie still couldn't reach the cigarettes. 'Aw, come on, gal! Have a heart!' she pleaded.

Kitty narrowed her eyes. 'Will you keep out of trouble until Monday?'

'I'll try me best.'

Unimpressed, Kitty returned the cigarettes to her bag, 'Not good enough,' she declared.

Georgie was frantic. 'All right! All right! I ain't been in no trouble, and I ain't got no intention of spoiling me chances before Monday. Cor, bleedin' hell, gal!' she cried indignantly. 'Anybody would think I were allus fighting!'

Kitty's eyes opened wide as she said with disbelief, 'Now why would anybody think that?'

Groaning, Georgie dropped her head to the table and folded her arms over it. From the depths of her soul came a pitiful wail, 'Give us a fag, for pity's sake!' When Kitty put the packet into her hand, she looked up, an elfin grin spreading from ear to ear. 'You're a good 'un,' she said. 'What are you? A bloody good 'un!' Taking a cigarette out of the packet, she put it between her lips and waited for Kitty to hand over a box of matches. She lit the cigarette and slid the packet into her pocket. Making smoke-rings, she settled back in her chair and eyed Kitty with some apprehension. 'Are you all right, gal?' she asked.

'Never better.' Kitty didn't reveal she had been sleeping badly.

'You're a bleedin' liar, Kitty Marsh.'

Kitty's smile broadened. 'Is that any way to treat someone who's come out in the snow and travelled on a crowded bus to bring you a packet of fags?'

Georgie laughed. 'You bugger! You won't put me off like that.' Pulling her chair closer to the table, she said in a softer voice, 'You ain't fooling me, gal. I know summat's up.' Suspicion dawned. 'It's that bleedin' aunt of yours, ain't it?' Clicking her fingers she exclaimed, 'I knew it! What's she been up to now, eh? Stolen the fillings out of your teeth, has she?'

'That's not fair, Georgie. Mildred has nothing to do with it. Besides, she has her own troubles at the minute.'

'So what's wrong with you then?' Drawing on her cigarette again, Georgie blew the smoke out through her nose. 'It's a man, ain't it?' Her face fell. 'Men are allus trouble.'

'You're never far wrong, are you?' Kitty hadn't told Georgie about Jack. She wondered if she ought to.

'You can tell me, gal,' her friend assured her. Her eyes scanned Kitty's face. 'It isn't Harry Jenkins, is it? He hasn't tracked you down and asked you to marry him?'

'No, it isn't Harry,' Kitty revealed. 'You know that I sent him away.'

'I said you were crazy then, and I haven't changed my mind . . . Harry was good for you. I told you no man would ever love you like he did, and they never will.'

Kitty couldn't speak for a minute. She was thinking of Harry, and her heart was heavy.

'If it isn't Harry, who is it?' Georgie wouldn't let it drop now. 'I know it's a bloke, so you might as well own up, gal.'

'Wait until you come out, then we'll talk about it.' Kitty

thought it best not to say any more. 'You've enough on your mind at the minute.'

Georgie was adamant. 'Bugger that, gal!' She even nipped her cigarette out in the ashtray. 'If you don't tell me, I'll be going mad wondering. Come on, out with it.'

Kitty knew there would be no peace until she'd told her. 'It's my boss. He's asked me to marry him.'

Georgie was speechless, mouth wide open and eyes like saucers. Suddenly she was laughing, then she was deadly serious. 'How can you marry him when it's Harry you love?'

'That's just it, I can't.' Kitty couldn't get Harry out of her mind. 'In fact, I've been thinking of finding Harry and asking if he still feels the same way about me.'

''Course he does, gal.'

'I don't think so. I think he's forgotten all about me.' It hurt to think that, but it was a very real possibility.

Georgie was already on another track. 'This boss of yours? Rich is he?'

'Rich enough, I suppose.'

'Does he really love you?'

'Yes, I think he does. He *says* he does.'

'How does he treat you?'

Kitty smiled. 'Like I'm made of china. He's generous and kind, always wanting to please.'

'Sounds like a dog!'

'Jack's all right, but he won't take no for an answer.'

'Have you slept with him?' Georgie was nothing if not bold.

Kitty confided everything; about how they had gone to look at a cruiser he wanted to buy, and how they had to stay overnight at a hotel. She told how Jack came into her room and they made love. And when it was told, she felt much better.

'What was it like?' Georgie's eyes glittered. 'Was he any good?'

Kitty blushed. 'He was gentle.'

Georgie groaned. 'That don't sound very exciting, gal!' She saw Kitty was getting agitated and decided to change the subject. 'If he's kind and gentle like you say, and if he's rich enough to keep you in comfort for the rest of your life, maybe you *should* marry him.'

'Maybe.' Kitty was shocked by her own answer. If she was

beginning to lose hope, there would be little point to anything.

Georgie knew she was thinking of that first and only love. 'When do you mean to talk to Harry?'

Kitty brightened. 'I thought I'd invite him to my eighteenth birthday party.' In fact the more she thought about it, the more she saw it as the perfect opportunity to find out whether he still wanted her.

Georgie thought it was a brilliant idea. 'I'm invited too, ain't I? That bleedin' aunt of yours won't shut the door in me face?'

'You don't have to worry. Mildred wouldn't do that. All you need to worry about is curbing that temper of yours, at least until Monday.'

'I ain't worried about that, gal, 'cause one way or another, I'm getting out of here.'

'What's that supposed to mean?' Kitty had no illusions where Georgie was concerned.

Georgie's expression gave nothing away. She lit her cigarette again, took a long drag of it, and with each word emitted smoke in little spurts. 'I miss my fella,' she said evasively. 'The bugger's been out these past months and only visited once. I'm sure he's got another woman.' Her eyes sparked. 'She'd better watch out, because if I get me hands on her she'll know it!' Suddenly her mood changed and she was chuckling. 'It's like I said, gal, men are trouble.'

After that they reminisced about Miss Davis. 'I had another card from her,' Kitty said. 'She's staying in Blackburn for a while, then she's off to the Canary Isles for Christmas.'

Georgie remarked, 'It's all right for some, ain't it!' and they both recalled how kind Miss Davis had been to them.

They talked again of Jack, and Georgie said she wished some rich bloke would whisk *her* off on a cruiser. 'That'd show my bloody fella where to get off!' she grumbled. Harry was mentioned several times. So was Kitty's eighteenth birthday party. Georgie promised she would be there come hell or high water, and when she had finished her fourth cigarette, it was time to say goodbye. 'I'm lucky to have you,' she told Kitty. 'You got the bad end of the bargain when you got me for a friend.'

'I don't want to hear that kind of talk,' Kitty told her.

They held each other for a time before parting. As usual, it was a bitter experience. 'The next time I see you it will be outside these walls,' Georgie promised. But Kitty didn't hold her breath. She had heard it all before.

Before Kitty's eighteenth birthday, two things happened. Two disturbing events that were destined to turn her world upside down.

All weekend, she had Georgie on her mind; so much so that she rang Jack at his home and asked for Monday off. Considerate as ever, he offered to take her to Aylesbury, but Kitty gratefully refused. 'I'd like to be there on my own,' she explained. 'If she isn't released, they might let me see her, and if she is released, I want to be waiting when she walks out of the gates.' The idea of helping Georgie shape a new life was thrilling. 'We've already agreed to see a flat in Wentworth Street,' she explained. 'And there'll be so much to arrange . . . furniture, clothes and such.'

Jack understood. 'If there's anything I can do, you've only to ask,' he said. 'Meanwhile, I expect the two of you will be off round the town and I won't catch a glimpse of you for a week.' He knew how fiercely loyal to Georgie she was.

'Let's hope she's released first,' Kitty reminded him.

In fact Georgie *was* released. But it wasn't Kitty she went off with. After a long wait in the biting cold, Kitty was delighted when the prison gates opened and Georgie ran out, laughing and squealing. They were excitedly making plans when suddenly a small familiar figure rounded the corner and came towards them. 'Well, I'm buggered!' Georgie screamed. 'It's Mac! IT'S MAC COME TO FETCH ME!' While Kitty looked on, she ran into his arms. There was a lot of laughter and some intimate talk, during which Kitty stood quietly by. She couldn't help feeling apprehensive. Mac had caused Georgie a great deal of heartache in the past. Would it really be so different this time? she wondered.

After an emotional reunion with her 'fella', Georgie took Kitty aside. 'I was wrong, gal. He ain't got another woman. The bugger's been away trying to get a job and a place for us to stay. He didn't want me to know until everything was all right, a surprise like. Well, he's managed to get a job on the bins in Weymouth, and a caravan not too far from the seaside.' Flinging her arms round Kitty, she laughed for joy. 'He loves me, gal,' she said in a broken happy voice. 'It ain't like the bugger's whisking me off on some luxury cruiser, but a caravan by the seaside will do for now.' Georgie seemed like a new person. Gone was the sour set of her mouth and the bitterness from her eyes. She was deliriously, wonderfully happy.

'Take care of yourself,' Kitty pleaded. Hiding her true feelings, she wished Mac and Georgie well. 'You've got my address,' she told her friend. 'Don't forget to keep in touch.'

She watched Georgie walk away, her arm linked with the Irishman's and the two of them chatting and giggling like two year olds. 'God keep her safe,' Kitty murmured. Then she turned and headed for the bus stop, a forlorn and lonely figure. It seemed everyone she ever loved went out of her life all too quickly.

Mildred was not surprised. 'You put too much trust in that young woman,' she declared angrily. 'What kind of friend is she to go off like that? Couldn't she have spent a day or two with you first?'

'She's in love,' Kitty replied. 'What with being let out of prison, and then Mac's turning up like that, it's not surprising she wanted to be with him.' In fact she was bitterly disappointed. 'Anyway, I doubt whether she would have stayed here. She's got it into her head that you don't like her.'

'I'm a bit wary of her, that's all.' Mildred didn't look up. She didn't explain further, just toyed with the sugar bowl, knocking her spoon against its side time and again.

'What's the matter with you this morning?' It was plain to Kitty that her aunt was in a foul mood. She had slammed and banged about since first setting foot in the kitchen, and now she had spilled the sugar bowl over and left a white sticky trail along the tablecloth.

'I had a bad night, that's all.' Getting out of her chair, Mildred set about cleaning up the mess. While she did so she glanced at Kitty, saying, 'I'm sorry. I've got too many things on my mind, I suppose.'

'Do you want to talk about it?'

'Better not,' she answered, leaving Kitty even more bewildered. With that she rushed out of the room. A short time later the two of them went their separate ways, Mildred to the factory, and Kitty to the boatyard.

Jack had left a note on Kitty's desk, together with the largest box of chocolates she had ever seen. The note explained he had gone downriver with a prospective buyer, but would be back in time for lunch, and that he had taken the liberty of booking a table for lunch at the Berni Inn. 'I won't take no for an answer,' he wrote, 'I know you've been starving yourself lately.'

After suffering Mildred's strange mood at breakfast that morning, and what with Georgie gone, Kitty felt in need of a little cossetting. By the time Jack returned, she was looking forward to lunch with him. 'Did you make a sale?' When he walked in the door he had a look on his face like the cat that got the cream.

'Nope.' Coming to the desk, he dared to put his arm round her waist.

Pulling away, she remarked with amusement, 'For a man who hasn't made a sale, you're looking very pleased with yourself.' As a matter of fact he was looking remarkably handsome in dark cord trousers and a navy pullover that brought out the blue in his eyes.

'If I'm looking pleased, it's because you're still here. That means you haven't made the usual excuse to leave before I get back. That means you're having lunch with me, and that makes me very happy.'

'And the sale?' She knew he must be worried, because there hadn't been a sale these past two months.

'There's always another day and another buyer,' he said nonchalantly. 'There's only one Kitty Marsh.'

The inn was crowded as usual. It seemed every man and his woman made their way here on that winter's afternoon. Kitty thought it a lovely place, with its old souvenirs of sailing days gone by, mastheads and ships' wheels, plaited anchor ropes and brass bells, all decorating the dining room and the bar beyond. At the entrance was a quaint little bridge, beneath which a long pool meandered and huge goldfish lazed away their days. 'It must be lovely to own a place like this,' Kitty murmured as they were shown to their table.

'Is that what you really want?' Jack asked. 'To own a place like this?'

She shook her head. 'No. To tell the truth I don't know *what* I want.' She wanted Harry, but what if he didn't want her?

She didn't eat much. She was too concerned about Georgie

to eat. 'Are you going to tell me what happened?' Jack's voice disturbed her. The touch of his hand on hers was even more disturbing.

'What makes you think anything's happened?'

'Because if everything had gone as planned, you wouldn't have come to work this morning.' In a lower voice he went on, 'I take it Georgie wasn't released from prison yesterday?'

'Then you take it wrong.'

'Oh!' He looked suitably penitent. 'Where is she then?'

'She's gone.' Saying it made it seem final somehow.

Just then the wine waiter brought their order, and before the conversation could continue, the first course was served. 'You said your friend was gone?' Jack appeared confused. 'Gone where?'

'Her boyfriend, Mac, turned up at the gates. Apparently he's got a caravan and a job in Weymouth. He's taken her there.'

'I see. And how do you feel about that?'

Kitty took a sip of her wine. In truth she didn't know how she felt about that. Replacing the glass on the table, she replied, 'If Georgie's happy, then I'm happy.'

'But you're not, are you?' He longed to hold her, to protect her. When she shut him out it was frustrating.

'I just wonder if he's good for her, that's all.'

Now it was Jack's turn to mull things over. He had spent most of the morning at the helm of a boat and that whetted a man's appetite. The soup was thick and hot, and outside the wind was biting. Picking up his spoon, he took a healthy mouthful of soup, and broke off a chunk of bread while secretly regarding Kitty's lovely face. It was a troubled face, one that smiled too easily when the heart beneath was broken. 'This man . . . Mac . . . does she love him?'

Kitty had been deep in thought. 'I'm sorry, Jack? What did you say?'

'I asked if Georgie loves this man she's gone off with?'

That made Kitty smile. 'Blindly,' she answered. 'That's how she loves him.'

'That's how I love you, Kitty.'

'Please, Jack. Not now.'

'I want you all the time.'

'I know.'

'Do you resent that? Do you resent me?'

'No.'

'But you don't love me in the same way?'

Kitty's dark eyes flashed angrily. 'Is that why you brought me out? If so, I'd like to leave right now.'

He put up his hands. 'Sorry,' he said, shamefaced. 'I know I shouldn't corner you like this. It's just that I can't look at you without wanting you.'

'Then *don't* look at me.'

His answer was an enigmatic smile.

Kitty had a small appetite at the best of times. Today she was hungry but couldn't force the food down. Finally she gave up. 'Jack?'

He looked up, dabbing at the corners of his mouth with the napkin. 'You are still talking to me then?'

She wasn't quite certain whether she should put the question, but asked it anyway. 'Is the business in trouble?'

His smile evaporated. Glancing around the crowded room, he appeared nervous. 'What makes you say that?'

'It's just that there have been no sales for the past two months. We've bought more boats in, but nothing's going out. On top of that, the accountant seems always to be asking for you, and you seem always to be avoiding him.'

'It's easy enough to explain, Kitty. You know what accountants are like. They chase you over the slightest thing, then charge you a fortune for the privilege. He can wait. But if it worries you so much, make an appointment for me to see him next week. As for buying boats in and not selling, well, you know yourself the boat trade in general is in the doldrums. People want to offload but most boatyards aren't buying. That's where we come in, to snap up the boats at a fraction of their value.'

'But it must be eating away at your capital? Surely that can't be wise?' She had learned a lot about the business and saw the need for caution.

It was true things were slow, but he knew from past experience it would all come right. 'When demand picks up, we'll make a killing.'

Kitty wasn't convinced. 'Is it true your father's leaving the business?'

'He feels now is the time to retire, that's all.'

'Are you angry I asked?' From the look on his face it was obvious she had touched a raw nerve.

Sliding a hand over hers he said softly, 'My business is your business, Kitty. I'm flattered you take such an interest.'

After that he seemed to have lost his appetite. Clicking his fingers, he summoned the waiter and paid the bill. In no time at all they were seated in the car and making their way along the river bank. When they reached the old-fashioned iron bridge, he pulled in beneath a large overhanging willow tree. Leaving the engine running, he flicked it out of gear and pulled on the handbrake.

'Why have we stopped here?' Kitty was surprised. The way he'd rushed her out of the restaurant, she'd believed he must have an urgent appointment.

'I can take you straight back if you're in a hurry?' Turning to her, he seemed like a little boy lost.

Kitty smiled at him. If he loved her the way she loved Harry, it was easy to understand how he felt. 'It's all right,' she told him, 'I'm in no hurry.' In no hurry to get back to the office. In no hurry to deal with the pile of invoices that waited on her desk. In fact she was in no hurry to leave this beautiful place, with its quiet waters and graceful swans, and long swaying branches that touched the water's edge. It was soothing somehow, a place where she could think – of Mildred, and Harry, and now Georgie. What was going on? Why was her life falling apart again?

In a tender voice, he apologised. 'I'm sorry about Georgie. I know how you'll miss her.'

'As long as she's happy, that's all that matters.' It wasn't though. What mattered was whether Mac would take advantage of her again, whether he would lead her back into bad ways, into burglary like before, and consequently back into prison. If that happened, Kitty knew it would drive Georgie to desperation.

Looking at the scenery, Kitty's mind grew quiet. 'It's so lovely here,' she whispered. There was still a smattering of snow lying on the top of the river bank. It made a pattern like the icing on a cake. Along the river four men in a boat were practising their stroke; the coxswain's voice rang out strong and clear, urging them on. In their thick jumpers and woolly hats they made a colourful sight.

Suddenly she was aware that Jack was gazing at her. She turned and just for that moment a rush of warmth came over her heart. He was lonely too. Compassion showed in her face. He leaned forward, his mouth seeking hers. When he kissed her, she did not pull away. Instead she pressed towards him, wanting the closeness of his love, needing to be needed.

The kiss lasted for what seemed an eternity. Just once she opened her eyes and saw the ecstasy on his face. His face became Harry's face, and she knew she was cheating. 'We'd better go,' she murmured, her lips close to his, moving against his mouth as she spoke. To be so near, so deeply loved, was a good feeling.

As they drove back to the office, Jack didn't say anything and neither did she. Now and again he would turn, and glance, and smile, and she would do the same. There was a new feeling between them, a kind of bond. He was delighted. She was troubled. Only time would tell.

That night Mildred was full of apologies. Though she seemed more like her old self, Kitty suspected she had something very serious on her mind, something more than the letter from the solicitor. Something Kitty believed had to do with her. 'Have I done anything to upset you?' she asked anxiously.

'You've never done that to me,' Mildred answered with a pang of conscience.

'Are you sure there's nothing on your mind? Nothing I can help with? Am I paying you enough board? I can pay more if you need the money? I have savings. They're yours if you want them.'

'Oh, Kitty!' Mildred sighed, then smiled. 'You pay more than enough, and no, I do not want your savings, but thank you all the same.' Switching off the television, which had been on in the background, she swung round in the chair, looking at Kitty and saying in a very firm voice, 'All right. I can't hide anything from you for long, so I might as well admit. Yes, I do have something on my mind, and yes, it is giving me a few bad nights. That's why I've been so short-tempered lately, and I'm sorry. I don't have the right to take it out on you.'

'Is it to do with this house?'

'Sort of.'

'It's that solicitor's letter, isn't it? I knew it would play on your mind.' Kitty felt so helpless.

'The letter just got me thinking, that's all.' Beyond that, Mildred would not be drawn. But the air was clearer and they were able to talk more easily.

'Did you have a good day at work?' Kitty wondered whether it was something there that could account for Mildred's problem.

'Busy as usual,' Mildred replied, getting up to make her way to the kitchen. 'I fancy a sandwich. Do you want one?'

'What kind?' Having eaten hardly anything at lunch and only cheese on toast for tea, Kitty was famished.

'I'm having cheese. But there's some of that ham left, and a tin of sardines. I could do them on toast if you want?'

'I'll have the same as you, thanks.' Getting out of her chair, she went to the kitchen too. 'I'll make us a drink,' she offered.

As they worked the conversation continued, with Kitty relating how she and Jack had gone out for lunch.

'Oh? I thought you intended to keep him at arm's length?' But Mildred wasn't too surprised.

'He turned up just when I was feeling low.'

'About Georgie?'

'I suppose.'

Something in Kitty's voice made Mildred turn and look at her. 'Are you falling in love with Jack Harpur?'

Kitty gave a small laugh. 'Afraid not,' she said. But she couldn't be certain.

'Pity.' Shaking her head, Mildred returned to her sandwich-making.

Kitty was curious. 'Why do you say that?'

'Because he would make a good husband, that's why.' She turned again, the knife in her hand, a knob of butter stuck to it. When she wagged the knife at Kitty the butter fell off. 'And because it's time you had someone to look after you . . . someone like Jack Harpur, a man who idolises the ground you walk on.'

Astonished at Mildred's outburst, Kitty almost scalded herself. Carefully replacing the kettle, she accused, 'If I didn't know better, I'd say you were trying to marry me off.'

'No such thing!' Her aunt appeared offended. But Kitty was right. 'Marry her off' was exactly what she wanted to do. It would give Kitty the new life she deserved, and would solve another problem too, Mildred's problem. One that she had kept secret these past months. One that would not go away. Nor did she want it to.

Kitty carried the tray into the lounge. Setting it down on the coffee table, she poured the tea into china mugs and handed one to her aunt. 'You're right anyway,' she admitted, 'Jack would probably make a good husband.'

'But not for you?'

'I don't think so.' Kitty seemed to remember having this very same conversation before. 'His father's leaving for America.'

'Lucky him. The sun shines brighter there.'

'I've an idea the business isn't doing too well, but Jack says it's fine, and that he'll make rich pickings when demand for boats picks up.'

'There you are then. It's a bit slow at the factory too, although we still hear of small businesses starting up all over the place.' Mildred took a healthy bite of her cheese sandwich. She switched on the television news. There was fresh evidence regarding the shooting of John Lennon in New York on 8 December; a short film showing President Reagan doing a walk-about; and a profile of the murderer dubbed 'The Yorkshire Ripper'. 'They must catch that bastard soon!' Mildred said. Kitty agreed, and as always her heart went out to the victims and their relatives.

After washing up the supper things, Kitty had a long lazy bath and an early night. She could hear her aunt downstairs long after the hallway clock had struck midnight. 'It's that ex-husband of hers,' she muttered under the bedclothes. Somehow she could never imagine Jack wanting to throw his wife out on the streets. She didn't like to admit it, even to herself, but Jack Harpur was growing on her. Not in the exciting passionate way Harry had. More in a comfortable, pleasing kind of way. 'Sounds like an old slipper,' she chuckled. Funny, though, that was exactly the way she did see him.

Jack was out of the office all next day. 'Gone to look at a new crane,' his message read. 'I'll call you at home tonight.'

All day she kept her head bent to her work. At five it was done; the files were in order, every invoice entered and paid, and she even found time to make half a dozen overdue phone calls, mostly regarding late delivery of equipment for the yard. 'See what I get through when you're not around?' she murmured, looking at the neat desk and thinking of Jack.

On her way home she got off the bus outside Peacock's auction yard; they were selling Christmas trees. After a flurry of bidding, she managed to acquire a six-footer with long thick branches and a perfectly shaped peak. 'The fairy's arse will fit nicely on top' the porter crudely remarked. He arranged delivery for that night, and charged her a pound. 'Don't get nowt for nowt these days,' he grunted.

His eyes were so small behind mounds of pink flesh that Kitty couldn't tell whether he was looking at her or at the woman standing beside her. In any event he was licking his lips as if he could make a meal of someone. Paying her pound, she said thank you and hurried away. At first she felt a little unnerved by the incident, but once she got outside, had to smother the laughter. 'He's right,' she giggled. 'The fairy's arse *will* fit nicely on top.'

Kitty's next stop was the shop at the bottom of Park Road. Like most privately owned corner shops, it stayed open until all hours. 'Tree decorations?' the man asked. 'I've got a really good selection this year.' He pointed her in the right direction and half an hour later she emerged with a small apple-box filled to the brim with tinsel, coloured glass balls, and four packets of assorted balloons.

Though in a much brighter mood than she had been the day before, Mildred wasn't really keen to hang Christmas decorations, but Kitty persevered until she was obliged to help, and soon the house was dripping with Christmas pretties.

When the tree arrived forty minutes after Kitty, that too was dressed, and soon there was a cheery Christmas atmosphere all over the house. 'It won't be too long before we have to start thinking about your party,' Mildred remarked, climbing down the stepladder and looking decidedly precarious. 'I shall have to replace this old thing before someone gets hurt,' she remarked. Then she said something that got Kitty wondering. 'Mind you, it's hardly worth it now.' When she saw Kitty regarding her with a curious expression, she blushed with guilt and turned away, leaving Kitty feeling shut out again.

If that small remark had disturbed Kitty, it was nothing to what her aunt said a short time later when the two of them were blowing up the remaining balloons. 'Remember what I said yesterday ... about there still being new businesses starting up?' Patting a bright blue balloon, Mildred watched it float on to the carpet, her gaze briefly flickering to Kitty as she waited for an answer.

Deep in the throes of inflating another balloon, Kitty gasped, 'I remember.'

'Well, we've been looking for a new haulier to carry our goods nationwide ... the other one put his charges up again and the boss told him where to get off. Anyway, the office put out an advert and the response was just amazing.'

'I'm not surprised. Contracts are hard to find these days. We have the devil of a job shipping the boats across the country. It costs the earth.'

'Are you listening to me?' Mildred swung round, impatient to impart her news. 'You'll never guess who got the contract!' Her eyes crinkled into a smile and it was all she could do to sit still.

Returning Mildred's smile, Kitty played along. 'I haven't the faintest idea,' she confessed. 'So you'd better tell me, then we can get on with blowing up the rest of these balloons.'

'It was an old friend of yours ... Harry Jenkins.' Unaware of the devastating effect her revelation was having on Kitty, she turned her attention to the task in hand. 'I had a long chat with him. Apparently he changed his mind about going to university ... His father wasn't very pleased, but he should be, because Harry's done quite well for himself. He has a thriving haulage business now ... two juggernauts and another in the pipeline now he's secured the Metrix contract.'

Choosing another balloon, she went on, 'He's made a handsome young man, quietly spoken and easy to talk to.' She gave a deep sigh. 'If I was twenty years younger, I could fancy him myself.' She dreamed a while, then dealt another innocent blow to the already shocked Kitty. 'I knew you wouldn't mind, so I've asked him to your birthday party. He was delighted, said he hadn't seen you in a long time ... said how he would look

195

forward to it.' She chose a red balloon, which she began stretching this way and that, easing the fabric so it might expand more easily. 'He got married six months back . . . someone he met at college. Of course I asked him to bring her. I knew you would want me to. That's all right, isn't it dear?' When she looked up, Kitty was gone. 'While you're in the kitchen, pop the kettle on,' Mildred called out. 'After all this blowing and puffing, I could do with a drink.'

In the kitchen Kitty stood with her back to the wall, tears flowing down her face, her brown eyes glazed with sadness. 'Oh, Harry! What have I done?' she whispered. 'You needed me, and I sent you away . . . straight into someone else's arms.' Her eyes closed and she could see him, tall and straight, his strong shoulders bronzed by the sun, dark eyes smiling at her, turning her heart over the way they always did. Now they would never again smile at her in that special way.

That night was the longest of her life. She fell asleep well after midnight and woke up before daylight broke the sky. She paced her room and sat by the window, lay on top of the bed, and all she could think of was what she had lost. 'My own fault,' she kept whispering. 'I should never have let you go.' The tears fell on her pillow and dried there. Nothing eased the heartache. Nothing could bring him back. Harry was gone, and she was the loser.

CHAPTER TWELVE

'To hell with you and the bloody contract!' Susan's face was red with rage. 'The last time I had a holiday was our honeymoon six months ago. Since then you've buried yourself in your work ... half the time you're out after contracts and the other half you're either up to your neck in paperwork or driving the lorries yourself. Why don't you hire another driver? Why can't you pay somebody to come in and help? There must be any number of people in Blackburn who would welcome a nice little job like that. Christ almighty! Anybody would think you had to do the whole bloody lot yourself!'

Used to her vicious tirades, Harry stood with his back to the fire, hands thrust into his pockets and long legs apart. His dark eyes smouldered as he waited for her to finish. When at last she threw herself into a chair, glowering at him from beneath drawn eyebrows, he waited a moment for her to calm down, then in a low controlled voice, said, 'How do you think I built this business up? Through sheer hard work, that's how. By doing most of the graft myself ... admin, driving, carrying the goods on my back, packing, loading and accounting for everything that was carried in my name. If a tyre needed changing, I was the only one there to do it ... crouching in the pouring rain, wondering what the hell I was doing there or what it was all for.' Thoughts of Kitty still clouded his mind. 'I had dreams and I worked hard to see them come true. Now I have a business to be proud of, but it's only the beginning. I mean to build an empire, and if I have to do it with my own two hands, then that's the way it will be.'

'You promised to take me abroad in the spring ... Cyprus, you said.'

'We'll go to Cyprus,' he confirmed. 'Have I ever gone back on a promise?'

197

'No. You always keep your word.' Now she was smiling, enticing, her lips pouting for a kiss as she stretched her legs out, her short skirt riding up to show her slim thighs. 'Do you want me, Harry? Do you want your wicked way with me?'

He didn't answer. Her solution to every crisis was sex, not love. He had already learned to his cost that she didn't know *how* to love.

She was up against him now, opening his shirt and rubbing her breasts against his broad chest. Reaching up, she twined the short dark hairs over her fingers. 'I love the feel of your chest,' she murmured. 'It's hard ... like him.' Her fingers dropped to the zip on his trousers. When she tried to undo it, he clamped his hand over hers. 'No!' It was just a word, one quiet word, but it was enough to inflame her.

'What the hell's wrong with you!' Snatching away, she eyed him with hostility. 'You haven't got another woman, have you?'

His smile infuriated her further. 'Talk sense, Susan,' he chided. 'When would I get the time?' Again his mind was filled with the warmth of Kitty. For her he would make all the time in the world.

She didn't like his answer. 'Are you saying you *would* have another woman, if you'd got the time?' A flicker of fear crossed her pretty face.

Stretching to his full height, he groaned. 'At any rate, I thought you wanted to spend Christmas in style?'

'I do! It's all booked, isn't it?' Anger flared. 'You told me the hotel was booked. It is, isn't it?'

He nodded. 'Are you packed?'

'Not yet.'

'What in God's name have you been doing all day?' She hadn't been cleaning the house, that was painfully obvious. There was a pile of dirty dishes in the sink, a basket filled with dirty clothes beside the washing-machine, cigarette ash all over the fireside rug, and several magazines littered across the armchair.

Turning on the charm she answered, 'I've been to the hairdresser's, had my nails manicured, done a bit of shopping.' Rolling her eyes she moaned, 'You wouldn't believe how much they charge for a facial!' Twirling round on the spot she invited,

'It's worth it though, don't you think? Wouldn't you say I look beautiful?'

He regarded her for a moment. Certainly she was a very attractive woman, tall and slim, very feminine, her long brown hair swept up in a mass of curls. He suddenly felt guilty. Whenever he looked at Susan he couldn't help but compare her with Kitty. He was doing that now, substituting every feature, every movement, seeing Kitty's small petite figure, her rich dark hair and expressive eyes that glowed with the colours of autumn leaves. Punishing himself again. Always punishing himself. 'I'm sorry,' he apologised, running his hand along her arm. 'You'd best get packed if we're to be in Manchester before dinner.'

She clung to him then, not knowing exactly why he had apologised. Not knowing he looked at her and saw the woman he would always love. 'It's me who should be saying sorry,' she admitted grudgingly. 'It can't be nice to come home to a tip, and no meal after a hard day's work, but you see I've been out all day. When I got back I was dog tired.'

'No matter. We can have a meal at the hotel.'

'I've arranged for the cleaner to come in while we're away,' she said placatingly. Stroking the contours of his face with her fingers, she looked up at him, at the strong classic lines of his features, at his wonderful dark tumbling hair and brooding eyes. He was her man. She had wasted her time at college while he had made good. Harry Jenkins had been a difficult man to snare. She'd be a fool to let him go.

'While you're packing, I'll check the yard ... make certain everything's secure.'

Once outside, he made straight for the Tautliner; a magnificent juggernaut, painted in blue and cream like the others. It had been his very first wagon, bought with a hefty bank-loan against a contract he'd secured and money he'd earned and saved. He'd found he had a natural instinct for business. Young as he was, he might have gone out and enjoyed himself, frittered away his years. Instead, he'd put his head down and worked like a bloody slave, rarely going out, hardly mixing, just work, work, work. Then, and afterwards, driven by one single ambition: so that when Kitty contacted him, he would have a good life to offer her. Instead, it was Susan who was enjoying the fruits of his endeavours; Susan who wore his ring on her finger; Susan who was there when Kitty was not. She had been his saviour in the beginning. In the end she was his punishment.

He sat behind the steering wheel, huge and round, cold and hard to the touch, not very pleasing to the eye, yet capable of manoeuvring the long snaking monster behind, guiding it through meandering roads, up hill and down dale, as though it was light as a feather when in fact it weighed upwards of thirty-eight tonnes.

'You've done me proud,' he murmured, gripping the wheel and surveying the dashboard – these days the controls of an HGV resembled the inside of a cockpit. 'I shan't part with you in a hurry,' he promised. He had a soft spot for this vehicle. In the early days it had been his constant companion, a loyal trusted friend. Now it had a new driver, one Harry had chosen for his character rather than his skill; though that was every bit as important when handling a sizeable beast such as this.

After locking the lorry, he checked the others, then the goods bay and the yard in general. Everything was secure. Finally he checked the tall gates, shaking the heavy padlock and thrusting home the bolts. The snow had gone, but the wind was cutting. 'Roll on the spring,' he muttered, pushing his way back to the house. The thought of seeing Kitty again would keep him going until then.

Susan was ready. Dressed in long white boots and a cream fur-lined coat, she could have been a model. 'I suppose you'd rather stay at home than spend Christmas in a hotel,' she sneered as they left the house.

'You're right, I would,' he admitted. Stowing the suitcases in the boot, he shut the lid and got into the car beside her. 'Instead of making a journey to a strange hotel on a dark freezing night like this, I'd much rather spend Christmas at home, yes, with a tree and trimmings, and a log fire burning in the grate.' And Kitty curled up beside me, he wished. God! How he regretted letting her turn him away. But then, what choice did he have? No man had the right to force himself on a woman if she didn't want him.

Now Kitty was lost to him. Now it was too late. He had made his bed with Susan and would have to lie on it. After only a few weeks of marriage he had come to realise he had made the biggest mistake of his life in marrying the student he had met on a train, once, a lifetime ago. That student had been pretty, bright and wonderful company. This wife was greedy, petulant, wanting only glamour, travel and parties, while he wanted a family, a proper homelife. And Kitty. When she turned him away he really believed it would be just a matter of time before she contacted him; before his mother would pass on a message from her. But there was none. No letter to say how much she longed to see him again. After a time he came to see she had shut him out of her life forever. When he was at his lowest, Susan was there, sweet, enticing, a bright happy distraction, helping him pass the time, helping him through, but never helping him to forget. He could never forget. Now he was invited to Kitty's eighteenth birthday party, and his soul was torn in so many ways. Eighteen! Was it as long ago as that? Though he was still a young man, he felt very very old. Without Kitty, the light had gone out of his life.

'God! There you go again . . . off in a world of your own. It's like talking to a bloody zombie.' Susan's shrill voice pierced the air, startling him out of his thoughts.

'Sorry. I was just thinking.' It seemed he was always apologising to her these days. Guilt, he supposed. Guilt and a desperate need to be alone with his thoughts.

Not an easy woman to pacify, Susan shrieked at him, pounding her fist on the dashboard with every word. 'You're *always* thinking! Or working, or wishing for something you can never have!'

For one awful minute he suspected she might have read his thoughts. 'What do you mean?' he asked quietly. 'Wishing for something I can never have?'

'I don't *know* what I mean exactly.' Calmer now, she racked her brains. 'It's just that sometimes you seem to be miles away . . . or *wishing* you were.'

'You're very perceptive,' he answered. 'I won't deny there are times when I'd like to be miles away.' At least he could be honest about that.

She didn't care too much for that answer. 'You never told me that.'

'I don't have to tell you everything.'

'Do you wish you were miles away from . . . me?'

'Sometimes.' He smiled, but it was a mirthless expression.

'Bastard!'

'So you keep telling me.'

'I don't mean to be spiteful. It's just that there's nothing much for me to do. You know I get bored easily.'

'Get a job. Help me in the office if you like.' He knew what her answer would be though, and he was right.

'Why should I?' She was sulking now. 'Why should I work like a skivvy? We don't need the money.'

He spun the wheel to turn the corner of the High Street, his attention momentarily taken up with the road and the increased volume of traffic. 'Nobody's asking you to work like a skivvy,' he told her. 'And you're right. We don't need the money.'

'Then why the hell are you asking me to work?'

He sighed. Susan could be the most difficult woman on God's earth. 'You just said you were easily bored . . . "Nothing much for me to do", that's what you said, wasn't it?'

'Yes, but it doesn't mean I want to *work!*' She spat out the word as though it was bitter on her tongue. 'I wouldn't mind sitting at your desk . . . answering the phone for you.'

'I'll get you a desk of your own, if you like. Matter of fact, it might not be a bad idea.'

'It's a terrible idea.' Would she never learn to keep her mouth shut? 'You'll want me typing next, breaking my finger-nails, and after it's cost a small fortune to get them perfect.' In the half-light she lifted her hands to admire them. 'Perhaps I can do something less strenuous? Yes, I'll think about it.'

Glancing at her, he had to smile. She was nothing like he'd thought she might be.

Having said more than enough she remained silent for the rest of the journey, dozing in her seat, turning fretfully and swearing beneath her breath when a stray dog made him slam on his brakes, sliding her forward in the seat.

When they drew up outside the hotel she sat up, cooing with admiration. 'There! I told you it was a perfect place to spend Christmas,' she declared. Clambering out of the car, she hurried towards the foyer, cursing like a trooper when the heel of her boot caught in a grating but smiling sweetly when a tall white-haired gentleman rushed forward to release it. 'No harm done,' he said with a wink. She blushed and walked on, glancing back, to see if her elderly admirer was still looking: smiling broadly when she saw that he was.

Busy getting the cases out of the boot, Harry had seen the whole thing. He shook his head and smiled. There was no one like Susan for putting on a show when she had a mind to.

It took only a few minutes to register. 'We have a wonderful Christmas programme planned,' said the desk clerk.

'Right now I'll settle for a good hot meal.' Not having eaten for the better part of the day, Harry's stomach was rumbling.

'Whenever you're ready, sir. Dinner is being served now, up until nine-thirty. We have a comprehensive menu ... carvery if you prefer, or à la carte. We try to cater for everyone.'

'I'm sure you do,' Harry replied.

'I'll ring for a porter, sir.' He still had his hand on the bell when Harry took the cases, and his wife, and got into the lift. 'A man used to looking after himself,' the clerk muttered.

'You want me?' The porter came out of nowhere, a tiny fellow with thin hair and huge feet.

'No.' The clerk had never taken to this new porter.

'You rang the bell. There ain't nobody here.' Glancing round, he saw the foyer was empty, the dining room full. 'So what do you want?'

The clerk leaned over his desk. In a stiff polite voice he said, 'I want you to piss off!'

The porter shrugged his shoulders. 'Fair enough,' he said. 'I'll piss off then.' And as he went he put two fingers behind him infuriating the clerk by making a very distinctive V-sign.

When, half an hour later, Harry and his wife entered the dining room, all eyes filled with admiration. Wearing tailored grey trousers and a fitted black jacket Harry attracted the women with his dark dashing looks. Susan knew she looked good in the new green silk blouse and straight cream skirt that showed off her legs to perfection. 'Charming couple,' said one man to his wife; she didn't answer, her lustful eyes following Harry's every move. Two young waitresses stood in the far corner. 'Now *he* could do whatever he liked to me any time he liked,' crooned the older one. The younger one giggled and sighed, and wondered if she would ever have a husband as handsome as that.

An hour later they left the dining room and made their way upstairs. Susan wouldn't let it be. 'You promised we'd go abroad in the spring, end of March you said. Now you've been invited to this bloody party, it won't spoil our plans, will it?'

'No reason why it should. Anyway, the holiday's already booked and partly paid for. I haven't got money to throw away.'

'What if I don't want to go?'

'What . . . on holiday?' He knew what she was getting at, but didn't feel in the mood for her petty little games.

'The party! What if I don't want to go? I won't know anyone from Adam.'

'You don't have to come if you don't want to.' He knew she would. He knew her love for parties.

'Do you want me to come?' Again, that sense of insecurity that had first attracted him to her.

He felt like a louse. 'Yes,' he answered. 'Of course I want you to come.'

'This Kitty Marsh. Who is she, Harry?'

He was in the bathroom when the question was put. He lingered there for as long as it took him to compose his face. Coming into the bedroom, he said, 'A girl I grew up with.' A girl I saw blossom from child to woman, he thought. A girl I fell in love with. A girl I would have been proud to call my wife.

Susan watched him come to bed, naked and magnificent. Harry never slept with clothes on. She liked that. 'What's she like, this Kitty?'

Realising he must be on his guard, he took a deep breath to calm himself. 'She's had a hard life,' he said. 'Her parents died within a short time of each other. After that she was put in a children's home and offered out for fostering.'

There was something about his manner, something about the way he slid into bed and quickly turned out the light, that made her feel uneasy. 'Poor little sod!' she exclaimed, slithering close beside him. 'But what I meant was . . . what is she like? You know . . . is she pretty? Quick-tempered? Is she friendly? What does she do for a living?' Roving her hand over the hardness of his stomach, she purred in his ear, 'Does Kitty Marsh have a boyfriend?'

His heart died inside him, her words echoing against his brain, driving him mad. 'Does Kitty Marsh have a boyfriend?' Her Aunt Mildred had said something to that effect . . . 'Kitty has a strong admirer in the boss of her firm,' she had told him. 'Jack

Harpur would marry her tomorrow if she said yes. I think it's only a matter of time before they tie the knot.' Only a matter of time before they tie the knot! He wanted to scream, to strangle someone with his bare hands.

'Love me, Harry,' Susan's soft persuasive voice whispered in his ear. She was touching him, stroking him. He felt himself growing hard. Hard with anger. Hard with desire. Suddenly he was on her and she was writhing beneath him, groaning with ecstasy as he pushed into her, again and again, driven by an insatiable need, a need no other woman but Kitty could fill.

CHAPTER THIRTEEN

'You look younger every day!' Kitty regarded her aunt's slim figure and sparkling eyes, and was glad that at last Mildred seemed to have completely shaken off her depression. 'Come on, what's the secret?' she asked mischievously.

For the briefest moment Mildred looked worried, then she smiled and put on her coat. 'Don't know what you're talking about,' she lied.

'There *is* something,' Kitty insisted. 'Since Christmas I've seen a real change in you.' The two of them were standing in the hall, Mildred looking in the mirror while she tied her silk scarf round her neck, and Kitty watching her every move. 'If I didn't know better I'd say you were in love,' she teased. In the back of her mind she was certain her aunt had a man hidden away, though she couldn't understand why it should be kept a secret.

These past few days Kitty herself had been living a lie. The prospect of seeing Harry in just a short time was too exciting. The knowledge that he was married overwhelming. She hadn't been able to sleep, had gone right off her food, and her work was suffering because she couldn't get him out of her mind. More than once Jack had commented that she seemed to be 'miles away'.

'What do you mean?' Mildred queried. 'What makes you think I'm in love?' As she turned, her expression was incredulous. 'A woman of my age?' She arranged the scarf neatly about her neck and put on her gloves, the faintest blush tinting her cheekbones.

Reaching up to take her long coat from the peg, Kitty wisely made no remark. Instead she put it on, threw her long woollen scarf round her neck and slid on her black leather gloves. 'Hmh!' she muttered as they went out of the door. 'Love doesn't have

207

any respect for age. Sixteen or sixty, makes no difference.' Closing the door behind her, she shivered. 'Will this rain never stop?' It had been pouring all night, and now it was softly drizzling, the sky was grey and heavy with clouds and there was a damp chill in the air. 'A fine day for a party!' Kitty remarked as she strode briskly down the street. 'Wouldn't surprise me if no one came.'

'Oh, they'll come,' Mildred declared. 'They'd better! We've prepared enough food to feed an army.'

Kitty's mood darkened. 'I wish I hadn't agreed to this party,' she admitted. 'I don't know any of your workmates. Georgie won't be there, and neither will Miss Davis.'

'It's a pity she couldn't come.' Mildred made no mention of Georgie. 'Still, if her sister's ill, you couldn't really expect her to accept the invitation.' Glancing at Kitty, she wondered why there was such sadness in her face. 'It's your eighteenth birthday, Kitty. It wouldn't be right not to celebrate it.'

She paused to look in Richard's shop window; there was a stylish blue dress in the display. 'I suppose not,' she murmured. 'All the same, I wish I hadn't agreed to it now.'

Mildred found herself looking at the dress too, although it was too young for her, too pretty and daring. 'Honestly, Kitty, I don't understand you. Most young women love parties. I know you would have liked Georgie to come, but to tell you the truth, I'm not surprised she didn't answer your last letter. In fact it wouldn't surprise me if she wasn't back in prison somewhere!'

Strolling on towards the main shopping arcade, Kitty had to admit, 'It wouldn't surprise me either. That fella of hers is bad news . . . always was.' Even with Mildred around, and Jack forever standing at her shoulder, there were times when Kitty felt so alone it was like a physical pain in her heart. 'I wouldn't have minded if Georgie didn't want to come to the party, but I wish she'd replied to my letter. I worry when I don't hear from her.' She couldn't help feeling her friend was in some kind of trouble. Until she knew for certain, she wouldn't be able to rest.

'You're surely not thinking of going all the way to Liverpool after her?'

'If I have to. But I'll write again and give her a chance to answer before I make my mind up.' The last letter she'd had from Georgie was too bright, too cheerful, and too full of nothing that mattered. 'It's funny she never mentioned why she and Mac moved from Weymouth.'

'I thought you and Jack had plans for next weekend?'

'*Jack* had plans,' Kitty corrected. 'He wants me to spend a weekend in London with him, go to a show, see the sights, that kind of thing. A "birthday treat" he says.'

'Very nice too.'

'I haven't agreed yet.'

Slowing her steps, Mildred linked her arm through Kitty's. 'You've been on edge this last week,' she remarked softly. 'Is it because of Jack? Is he bullying you again?' She sighed. 'I don't know why you don't just say yes and put the poor bugger out of his misery.'

'He doesn't give me time to think, that's why. Everywhere I turn he's there. He's keeping to his promise not to ask me to marry him, but he might as well ask, because it's in his eyes every time he looks at me.' She gave a little laugh. 'I'm beginning to think he wants to drive me crazy, or wear me out so I won't have the strength to argue when he carries me down the aisle.'

'Oh? So you're expecting him to carry you down the aisle?' Mildred could hardly hide her relief.

Sensing anxiety in her aunt's comment, Kitty answered, 'There you go again, trying to marry me off. Jack's got you on his side, has he?'

Mildred realised her mistake. 'Sorry.' Squeezing Kitty's arm by way of apology, she admitted, 'I shouldn't poke my nose in.'

'No, you shouldn't,' Kitty gently chided. 'I've got enough problems at the minute without you trying to organise my life as well. I need you on *my* side, not on Jack's.' Reaching into her coat pocket, she took out the shopping list and quickly ran her eyes down it. 'We need another four bottles of plonk, some niblets, and at least two packets of paper napkins.' Pointing to Woolworth's, she suggested, 'We can get the napkins there.'

'And the niblets from Marks and Spencers,' Mildred declared, turning right towards the stores. 'As for the plonk, we'll have to shop around. Oh, and we mustn't forget the cake. I want to have a look at it before they deliver.'

As they rushed round the shops, buying this and that and spending more than they had planned, Kitty was glad the talk of Jack and marriage had been put on hold. She knew it would raise its ugly head again. But for now at least, she was safe. A little voice in the back of her mind kept saying, 'Harry's out of your reach now. He's got a wife, so why shouldn't you marry Jack? Be safe, be mollycoddled. Make him happy at least, because there's no use dreaming any more.'

It was a funny thing though. Dreams have a life of their own, and when you have cherished them for as long as Kitty had, they will not die easily.

It was almost midday when the two of them ran from a sudden downpour, into the nearest café. 'Two milky coffees and a cheese sandwich,' Kitty told the woman behind the counter; a busy homely body, with sharp blue eyes and spectacles perched on the end of her little nose.

'Is that a cheese sandwich for one or a cheese sandwich for two?' she asked with a grin.

Turning to Mildred who was arranging their many shopping bags on the floor beside their table, Kitty asked, 'Are you sure you want nothing to eat?'

Mildred nodded. Taking off her coat, she gently shook the rain from it, then sat down, more than once glancing at her watch, fidgeting and nervous, as though she might be late for an appointment.

Bringing the tray, Kitty set the drinks and plate on to the table before sliding the tray into the slot beneath. 'Is there something we've forgotten?' she asked, her brows knitted in a frown as she took off her own coat and almost fell into her seat. 'I saw you looking at your watch just now. You seemed anxious, as though you were in a hurry to get away.' Mildred had been like that a lot lately. Sometimes in the evening she would pace the floor, like a wild cat in a cage waiting to get out.

Taking a grateful sip of her coffee, Mildred waited a moment before revealing in a soft, almost childish voice, 'Well ... there is something I'd quite like to do before I go back to the house. You don't have to come with me though. I'll be fine.' A rising blush suffused her face. 'You don't mind do you, Kitty?' Knowing what she planned to do made it difficult for her to look her niece in the eye.

Kitty was puzzled. 'Of course I don't mind,' she said with an encouraging smile. 'Go ahead and do what you've got to do. Anyway, there's more than enough to keep me busy until you get home.'

'That's just it. I don't want you getting everything ready on your own. It doesn't seem right.'

Kitty sighed impatiently. 'Whose party is it anyway? Look, you've done more than your fair share already, and besides it'll do me good to get stuck in.' She giggled. 'It might even take my mind off Jack and his puppy-dog eyes.'

'You're sure?' Mildred was still anxious. 'I won't be gone long, I promise.'

'You be gone as long as you want.' There were times when Kitty felt like the adult and Mildred acted like an eighteen year old. 'Honestly! Anyone would think you have to answer to me for your every move.'

They finished and went their separate ways. 'Tell them to be careful with the cake,' Mildred pleaded before she rushed off. 'Tell them it's to go on the dresser. It'll be safer there until we arrange the buffet table.'

'Stop worrying, I'll see to it.' Kitty promised. A twinkle came into her eyes as she ordered with a smile, 'You'd best get going. After all, you don't want to keep him waiting.'

An expression of horror crossed Mildred's face, then guilt, then a quizzical look and a smile that said, 'You don't know. You *can't* know.' Then she was gone, leaving Kitty with handfuls of shopping bags and an intriguing little mystery. 'What if you *have* got a fellow?' she muttered as she made her way home. 'Good luck to you, that's what I say. You don't need to concern yourself about what I think. After all, what does it matter?'

But it *did* matter. Before the night was over, Kitty would discover how Mildred's plans were about to alter all their lives.

Emptying the bags on to the kitchen table, Kitty left them where they fell. 'Tea first,' she sighed. 'A minute to get my breath, then we'll see.' She took off her wet things, went upstairs and rubbed her damp hair with a towel before combing it; she rinsed her face, took off her stockings, put on her flatties and returned downstairs to the kitchen. Here she made herself a mug of tea and took it into the lounge where she sat with her feet up for

211

a while. 'That's wonderful!' she sighed. Kicking off her shoes, she wriggled her toes. It had been a hectic shopping spree. It was good to be home, in front of a cheery fire.

Leaning back in her chair, she relaxed, enjoying the quiet moment of her own company. 'Oh, Jack! Jack! Why can't you take no for an answer?' she sighed, 'It's not that I don't like you, because I do. But if you keep on following me round like a lovesick calf, you'll only force me to look elsewhere for a job.' She had to laugh though, and did. 'Men and sex!' she muttered. 'You can't separate one from the other.'

Taking another sip of her tea, she let her thoughts raise everything that had happened in her life. It wasn't often she allowed that to happen. These days she had learned to shut her memories out. It was less painful that way. Today, however, she had a feeling that things were about to come to a head. There were things going on that she couldn't quite fathom. Irritating, disturbing things, *little* things that played on her mind and frayed her nerves: Mildred and her little secret; Georgie moving from Weymouth to Liverpool, saying less than nothing in the one or two letters from there, and then not answering Kitty's letters at all.

The feeling of unease was so strong that she was forced to get up from the chair and walk about the room, cup in hand, head down, a sensation in her heart as if a lump of lead had just been planted there.

Her sense of peace dissipated, she put her cup on the mantelpiece and, leaning forward on her hands, she stared into the burning coals. The heat from the fire warmed her face, making her sleepy. She hadn't slept last night, nor the night before. She hadn't slept in many a long night. She wondered if she would ever have a good night's sleep again. She doubted it. 'Damn you, Harry!' she exclaimed.

Throwing herself into the chair, she groaned. 'NO! It's not your fault. It's mine! *My* fault! *My* decision! *My* loss!' Closing her eyes, she leaned back in the chair. For what seemed an age she sat there, filled with regrets, angry, empty inside, desperately trying to shut out the teeming images. It was an impossible task. The images were flesh and blood, living and breathing, making her want to laugh, making her want to cry; images of herself and Harry as they were . . . as they could have been.

212

The tears rose. She choked them back. So many times she had stifled them, hardened herself against them, but the regrets never really went away. 'You fool, Kitty! YOU BLOODY FOOL!' She took a deep, deep breath, calming herself, loving him so much she could hardly breathe. 'Oh, Harry . . .' Her voice rose and fell in a whisper, like a long drawn-out sigh that lifted her heart before dashing it again. Opening her eyes, she leaned forward in the chair, her brown eyes dull with pain, her head drooped as though she carried a great crippling weight on her shoulders.

Getting up, she paced the floor once more. After a while she went into the hallway and looked out of the window, watching for Mildred, mesmerised by the new fall of rain. It came down in sheets, silvery dark against a bleak grim sky. Small swirling puddles settled on the path, black and threatening, swilling over the edges on to the lawn, turning green to brown.

Restless, she walked to the other side of the hallway to where Mildred's small crucifix hung. She spoke to the figure imprisoned there, 'If You know everything,' she whispered, 'You must know how unhappy I really am.' Fear rippled through her. She had to gather every ounce of her courage to admit her love for Harry. 'If You know what I think, and what I feel . . . You must know how sorry I am that I sent him away. I can never love anyone but him. You know that too.' She didn't realise that when she sent Harry away, but she realised it now. And it was a heavy burden to bear all alone.

Strangely she had derived a deal of comfort out of her little conversation with the Lord. 'Jack would think I was mad,' she smiled. But she didn't care. Jack could think what he liked.

'Soon, Harry will be standing here in this house, in this room!' The knowledge was thrilling, yet daunting. 'How should I greet them, Harry and his wife?' She didn't want him to see she still cared for him. She wouldn't embarrass him like that, or herself. No doubt he had forgotten all those wonderful moments they'd had as children – moments she still cherished and would cherish forever. 'Be happy for him,' she told herself. 'Don't let them see you're bothered. Make Harry and his wife welcome. Show them how good a host you are.' Of course! Smile and be damned, isn't that what they said? It was the only way.

Suddenly she was stronger, more at ease with herself,

213

confident to the point of arrogance. 'Hurry up, Mildred,' she cried, staring out of the window again. 'We've a lot to do before the guests arrive.'

And that was how she would treat Harry and his wife. As guests, just like the others. 'When he smiles at you, smile back. Congratulate him on getting married. Make friends with the lucky young woman. It's your eighteenth birthday, Kitty Marsh, you should be making merry.' Spinning round, she fell into the chair with such force that she sent her skirt up above her head. 'Laugh as though you hadn't a care in the world,' she told herself.

She laughed now, but it was a hollow sound. 'Atta girl!' she cried, stealing one of Georgie's phrases. 'Don't let the buggers get you down!'

Startled by the insistent sound of the phone ringing, she leaped up and grabbed the receiver, 'Hello.' She felt dizzy, as though she'd been at the wine.

Jack's voice answered. 'Is that you, Kitty?'

'Who else would it be?'

'Sorry. It didn't sound like you, that's all. You sound breathless, as though you've been running.'

'You don't sound too bright yourself. Is there a problem?' For weeks now she had suspected there was, but Jack was not a man to discuss his personal affairs.

'No problem, sweetheart.' His voice brightened. 'Just checking that everything's all right for tonight?'

'Everything is perfect.' If only it was. But then nothing in life was ever perfect.

'Got everything you need then?' He was back to his old self. 'You've only to ask.'

'Thank you all the same.' Why was he so insistent? So determined to make her reliant on him?

'I rang earlier, but there was no reply.'

'That's because there was no one in.'

'Where were you?'

There it was again, that certain tone of voice, like a father scalding a naughty child. 'Does it matter?'

'It does to me.' Now he was that hurt little boy again.

'Mildred and I did a bit of last-minute shopping.'

'Oh.'

'Jack?'

'Yes?'

'Are you sure there isn't a problem?' She eased herself into the nearest chair. 'You sound a bit down.'

'Tired, I expect. I've been helping to scrape that old hulk ... you know, the one we bought for a song. I'm certain it'll make us a small fortune when it's varnished and refitted.'

'Considering the time and effort you've put into it, I hope so.' She suddenly remembered something. 'There was a note on my desk asking me to prepare Ben's wages, holiday pay, week in hand, all his dues in fact.' Ben had been with the firm since the early days. 'Can I ask why he's been laid off?'

'Because he's past his best.'

He was lying and Kitty knew it. 'He's a good man. Works hard, knows his job. And he's honest.'

'I'm well aware of that.' Before she could say anything else, he pointed out bluntly, 'The men are *my* business, Kitty. I hire and fire who I like. But it's good to know you take such an interest in the company. Ben is one issue. You're another.'

'You're saying he's dispensable and I'm not?' She liked old Ben.

'I'm just saying I could never afford to fire you. Unless, of course, you agreed to marry me?' There was a short silence while she could imagine him smiling on the other end of the line.

When he realised she was not rising to the bait, he spoke again. 'Look forward to seeing you later, sweetheart. Make yourself beautiful. Love you.'

The phone went dead. 'Why do I let you get away with it?' she demanded, glaring at the receiver. 'Talking to me as though we have a close relationship going.' Mind you, she deserved it. Hadn't she let him into her bed? Hadn't they made love? Wouldn't any man think he had the right to be intimate after that? Well, of course he would! She was a fool for thinking otherwise.

In the first few weeks after that night, Kitty had been desperately worried she might be pregnant. As time passed and she discovered her fears were groundless, she sent up a prayer of thanks.

After a while, though, she began to worry about something

215

else. *Why* wasn't she pregnant? *Why* hadn't it happened? Surely it was unnatural? A man and woman, deep in the throes of lovemaking, with no protection? She *should* be pregnant! Oh, she was thankful, there were no two ways about that. But it played on her mind all the same, and the more she thought about it, the more she wondered. There remained only two possibilities. Either Jack was infertile, or she was. OR SHE WAS! But how could that be? How could any woman be infertile when she wanted children as much as Kitty wanted them? It had always been her dream; she and Harry, married, with any number of children.

She and Harry. Though the bitterness ran through her, she had to laugh. Without Harry the dream was already broken. Without children? Dear God! She mentally shook herself. It didn't even bear thinking about.

Mildred returned two hours later. 'I'm sorry it took so long.' Breathless and excited, she rushed into the kitchen. Her cheeks were cherry red and there was an aura about her that put Kitty in mind of Georgie whenever Mac was around. 'Is there a brew going?' she asked. Ripping off her coat and shoes, she dropped into the chair with a loud sigh. 'My feet are throbbing, and I've a backache like a coalman on his first day!' Lolling back in the chair, she let her arms fall over the side. 'There isn't a sandwich going as well, is there?' she enquired with a grin. 'I'm starving, but it's my own fault. I should have had one when you offered before.'

'You look like you've been through a stampede,' Kitty remarked, at the same time bustling about to produce a hot drink and a chunky ham sandwich.

'I think everybody must have waited until you'd gone to come out of their hidey-holes.' Gratefully accepting the food put before her, Mildred explained, 'The shops were full to bursting. Honest to God, I thought I'd never get out alive.'

'I thought we'd already got everything we needed?' Something new about Mildred made her curious, and a little scared.

She pointed to the bags she had deposited on the kitchen table. 'I thought we might need more sandwich fillers,' she lied. 'Oh, and I bought two dozen fairy cakes and a trifle!' She didn't buy them, they'd been given to her, but she wasn't ready to tell

Kitty. Not yet. Later she would *have* to tell her, but first there was the party. She didn't want to spoil Kitty's big day.

Unpacking the goods, Kitty remarked, 'I could have made a trifle. You know it's my speciality.' Miss Davis had shown her how to make the most succulent sherry trifle. 'You said we had enough with the gâteau and flan, so I didn't bother.'

'I was wrong.' Mildred had done wrong before where Kitty was concerned. She had disowned her, stolen from her, and now, oh now! She was plagued with guilt at what she was about to do next.

'Are you all right?' Kitty sensed the despair that washed over her aunt. For the briefest moment it transferred itself to her.

Gulping down the last dregs of her cup and leaving the sandwich half-eaten, Mildred stood up. 'A good long bath will revive me,' she said. 'But first, we ought to rearrange the furniture in the lounge.'

'I've already done that.' It had been a laborious but enjoyable task. 'I've also laid the dining table with the white cloth you put out.'

Mildred didn't seem at all surprised. 'Crockery? Cutlery?'

'All out.' Kitty was proud of the way she had used the time while her aunt was out. 'You'll find the fire banked up and the drinks set out ... bottles to the left, glasses to the right as you instructed. All we need do now is lay the kitchen table with the food, ready for taking in at the given time.'

Now Mildred was surprised, and a little disappointed. 'I'm sorry, Kitty,' she said. 'I should have been here to help. It is your birthday after all.'

Clearing away the cup and plate, Kitty shrugged her shoulders. 'All the more reason for me to get stuck in.'

And for the rest of the time they had left before guests started arriving, that was exactly what she did, and Mildred as well.

By seven the food was all set out: triangular sandwiches plump with all manner of fillings; miniature sausage rolls on sticks; individual juicy pork pies; two enormous quiches made by Mildred, one of bacon and cheese, the other a wonderful blend of chicken and vegetables topped with shaped tomatoes. There were numerous wicker platters filled with niblets: crisps, nuts and tiny coloured biscuits. Apart from the trifle, the desserts were also ready sliced: a mountainous Black Forest gâteau, and a huge strawberry flan finished with a pattern of red cherries.

Preparations complete, the two of them fled upstairs; Mildred to her room, and Kitty first to her bedroom where she collected her toiletries and robe, then to the bathroom, where she stripped off and luxuriated in a hot foamy bath.

Mildred was the first to emerge from upstairs, smart as ever in a blue blouse and dark pleated skirt. In an odd way she looked like a schoolgirl on her first date, flushed and excited, constantly fidgeting, not knowing what to do next, and watching the door as though at any minute she expected a knight in shining armour to come galloping through.

Upstairs, Kitty got ready. Fresh out of the bath, she dried her hair and swept a comb through it. Soon it was bouncy and gleaming. Desperate to look her best when Harry and his wife arrived, she went through her wardrobe again and again. Finally she chose the dress she'd bought with her first week's wages. An elegant creation in black and red, she had got it home, decided it was not really her after all, and hung it in the back of her wardrobe, where it had stayed ever since. 'Wonder if it still fits?' she mused aloud, holding it to herself in front of the long mirror.

She decided she would wear it, then she wouldn't, then she would, then she wouldn't. Twice she returned it to the wardrobe, before getting it out again and laying it over the bed. 'It's certainly lovely,' she whispered. And it was.

The most expensive garment she had ever bought before or since, the dress was slim-fitting, long to the calf, where it kicked out with a flirty hem of black, and just the teeniest tease of red lace showing beneath. The waist hugged like a second skin. The narrow shoulder-straps showed off her throat and shoulders to perfection, and when at last she put it on, having the devil of a job to do up the zip which went almost the whole length of the dress, Kitty was astonished with the result. 'You look like a film star!' she gasped. The dress made her taller somehow, slimmer, and more sophisticated. She felt good. In fact she felt *deliciously* good! 'Sexy, that's what it is,' she giggled, turning round and round before the mirror. 'Sexy but elegant. You did right to blow half your wages on it,' she decided. But wrong to hide such a fabulous dress away. Still, it wasn't as though she had been to any parties, and this was certainly a party dress.

'Made for tonight,' she said, and couldn't wait to see Harry's eyes when he caught sight of her in it.

Some short time later she walked into the lounge and stood at the door, patiently waiting for Mildred to look away from the window where she had been this last half hour. 'What do you think?' she asked, doing a twirl.

Her aunt's eyes widened. Her face softened and for a minute Kitty thought she was going to cry. 'Oh, Kitty!' She moved her head slowly from side to side as though in disbelief. When she spoke, her voice was low and tearful. 'It's beautiful. *You're* beautiful.' Her gaze travelled from the top of Kitty's shining dark hair to the tip of her black patent shoes.

Kitty stood there, not knowing what to do. Mildred's reaction had surprised her. There was a sadness about it that touched her own heart.

Smiling encouragingly, Mildred opened her arms and Kitty went to her. For a while the two of them held on to each other, gently rocking back and forth, reliving memories both good and bad; Kitty wishing her mother was here to see her, and Mildred wishing she could lessen the shock which she would soon have to administer. 'When you came to me you were just a girl,' she murmured. 'Now look at you.' Holding her niece at arm's length, she admired her again. 'Kitty Marsh, you're a sight for sore eyes!' she laughed with delight. Kitty laughed too, and the bad memories were gone.

The day was being swallowed by twilight when the first guests arrived. Mildred introduced everyone. 'This is my niece, Kitty,' she told two middle-aged couples with broad smiles, greying hair and stunningly white dentures. 'You've heard me talk about her many times.' She looked on proudly while Kitty shook hands with each and every one. They were good people, friendly and open. She felt comfortable with them, though her attention was momentarily distracted by the long curly ginger hairs up the nose of the bigger man, and when she shook hands with his wife, a horrifying vision in floating lace and tulle, she was almost welded to her by the sweat on the other woman's palm.

'You didn't say how lovely she was!' the woman complained loudly to Mildred, then smiled widely at Kitty until her teeth nearly fell out, after which she clamped her mouth shut and

Mildred couldn't get a word out of her.

As they walked away, her husband could be heard saying in a harsh whisper, 'Bloody gnashers! When will you do as I ask and see the dentist?'

Whereupon she answered in the sweetest voice, 'Look, dear . . . isn't it time you attended to your own problems and trimmed those disgusting hairs in your nose?' Afraid someone might have overhead their sarcastic exchange, she turned round to smile serenely before helping herself to a gin and tonic.

Guests arrived thick and fast after that. There was the young receptionist from Mildred's firm, a pretty-eyed creature, with horn-rimmed spectacles too large for her tiny face and her dark hair tied back in a bun. Kitty thought she would look so much more attractive with her hair down, and spent half an hour wondering whether she might suggest it to her. She decided against it when Mildred explained how she herself had put the very same suggestion to the young lady in question, to be greeted with a flood of tears.

'It's a wig, you see,' Mildred explained in a whisper. 'Apparently she had a scalp condition when she was fourteen and lost all her own hair.' Kitty was filled with compassion.

Most of the guests were Mildred's workmates. In addition there was the cheeky milkman who'd invited himself after Kitty explained what the extra milk was for. There was Mrs Lewis from the corner shop, and the young couple who had recently bought a cruiser from Jack Harpur and made friends with Kitty in the process – a motley crew who appeared to gel together very well. 'They're a nice bunch,' Mildred said, and Kitty agreed.

Mingling with the guests, changing the records on the turntable, making certain every glass was topped up and every plate overflowing with food, she had hardly a moment to breathe. Now and again she would glance at the door. 'Where is he?' she muttered, putting a smoochy record on so the couples could dance. 'Why isn't he here?' Through every minute, every song, every time someone called her name and gave her a party kiss, she was thinking of Harry. She tried not to think of his wife. Soon enough she would see Mrs Harry Jenkins in the flesh. Until then she only had thoughts of him.

'Are you expecting someone else?' Kitty discovered she was not the only one watching the door. Mildred had hovered nearby, fluttering about, her eyes glued in that direction every time Kitty looked up.

When Kitty came up behind her to ask who she was looking for, Mildred nearly dropped the tray she was carrying. 'You gave me a start!' she cried, the tray trembling in her hands as she tried to steady herself.

Swamped with guilt, she clutched Kitty's arm and gave her the best answer she could under the circumstances. 'I'm expecting Mr Sibley.' Her seemingly innocent smile gave nothing away. 'He's a very nice gentleman from work. I told you I'd invited him, didn't I?'

Kitty's face broke into a cheeky little grin. 'Shame on you!' she teased. 'You never said a word, and well you know it.'

'I meant to. I thought I had.'

'You're blushing again.'

'Give over, Kitty!' As she swung her gaze to the open door, Mildred gave a little gasp. 'Eddie!' The tall, distinguished-looking gentleman came further into the room. At once his eyes met Mildred's and the two of them rushed to greet each other; Mildred obviously relieved that she didn't have to lie any more to Kitty.

'I'd like you to meet my niece,' she told him, drawing him across the room to where Kitty stood waiting.

'Ah!' When he glanced down on Mildred with warm caring eyes, she blushed to the roots of her hair. 'So *this* is your niece?' He turned his smile on Kitty, and she felt he was a likeable genuine type, and obviously smitten with Mildred. Kitty wondered whether he was married. Certainly he would be a good catch, she thought. Aged about forty, tall and distinguished, he had a ready smile and a firm handshake. 'Pleased to meet you, Kitty,' he said, and she couldn't help but notice how proud Mildred seemed whenever she glanced at him. It was food for thought. Was this her aunt's little secret? Had she found herself a man? Kitty wondered.

As they walked away it was obvious to Kitty that these two were more than just work colleagues or even good friends. There was a certain intimacy between them, a quiet mellowing of spirits, that told quite a different story. Another thought struck Kitty. Eddie Sibley must have been given a key to this house. How else had he been able to let himself in?

Suddenly everything seemed to fit into place... Mildred's recent furtive behaviour; the glow in her cheeks, and a shyness which Kitty had not noticed before. And what about the times when Mildred had stayed late at work... coming home at all hours with stars in her eyes, mooning about like a lovesick girl? Yes. It all began to make sense now.

Kitty did not begrudge her any of it. In spite of her own deep loneliness, she was glad for Mildred.

In between her hostess duties, Kitty couldn't help watch the two of them, so lost in each other, so right together. Even so, somewhere in her deeper self, she felt a rush of anxiety. There was no reason for it, no explanation that she could see. It was just a cold feeling, a sense of insecurity that quickly passed when she saw them laughing together. Her heart filled with pleasure at the sight of it. She had not seen Mildred so happy in ages.

It was almost nine when the doorbell rang. Kitty was in the throes of changing a record, convinced that Harry was not coming after all, wishing the party was over and hoping everyone would soon go home so she could think straight.

Mildred let them in just as the music struck up a haunting Roy Orbison song that tugged at the heart-strings. Curious but not daring to hope, Kitty turned round and looked straight into Harry's dark smiling eyes. For a moment the song enveloped them, then he smiled and stepped forward, his arms extended in greeting. 'Hello, Kitty.' His voice was soft and low, invading her heart and making it soar.

Ever since Mildred had told her Harry was coming to the party, Kitty had carefully rehearsed what she would say to him. Every word was imprinted on her brain. 'Hello, Harry,' she would say in a cool voice. 'It's lovely to see you again.' She would keep her distance, not let him touch her for too long, or look at her too deeply with those wonderful dark eyes. 'I understand you didn't go to university?' she would comment with some surprise. 'What did you do? How have you come to own a haulage firm? What made you move to the north? Did you know Miss Davis has a sister in Blackburn? I don't suppose you've seen her?'

It was all going to be very friendly, very aloof, but welcoming. She would congratulate him on becoming his own boss. She would then ask about his parents, and smile sweetly at the woman he had chosen in preference to herself. She would say all the right things, be the perfect hostess, and not for one minute would she let him see the pain she carried behind her warm smile.

Now, though, her smile was too telling, too soft, giving too much away. The right words would not come. She was tongue-tied. As his arms closed about her, she shuddered with pleasure, afraid he might feel her heart beating against his own. 'It's good to see you, Harry,' she murmured, longing to kiss him, aching to hold him just one minute longer.

For one delirious moment she closed her eyes. When she opened them again it was to look straight into the face of a young woman whose hard blue eyes stared at her with some hostility and a little amusement. 'This is Susan,' Harry said, drawing her forward. 'I suppose your aunt mentioned I was married?'

'Yes, she did.' Kitty stretched out her hand in greeting, inviting the other woman to make friends. 'I'm so pleased you could come,' she said. But she wasn't pleased. She was jealous.

'Harry dragged me here,' replied Susan, chin high, looking down her pretty nose. Gazing round the room, she shrugged her shoulders. 'If I'd known it was to be an ordinary party, I doubt if I'd have come at all.'

Kitty was certain she heard Harry groan, but keeping her gaze fixed on the other woman, enquired in a sweet voice, 'What kind of party did you expect?'

'I had an idea it might be more glamorous.'

'I'm sorry if you've travelled a long way only to be disappointed.'

'No matter. We're here now.' Susan smiled at Harry, who chose not to smile back. 'So! You two were at school together?'

Harry's gaze fell on Kitty's face. 'More than that,' he answered quietly, and it was just as well he didn't see his wife's expression.

Hiding her despair at seeing them together, Kitty's eyes went to the wedding ring on Susan's slim white finger. A rush of envy surged through her. She thrust it away, forcing herself to answer brightly, 'All that was a long time ago.'

'Harry hasn't forgotten,' came the sarcastic reply.

Kitty wisely ignored the implication, asking, 'I hope he's given you a good account of me?'

Susan's eyes flashed angrily. 'As a matter of fact I was beginning to wonder if there was something I hadn't been told,' she said icily. 'You see, he never even mentioned you, until just recently. I don't suppose he would have mentioned you then, if we hadn't been invited to your party.'

'Harry always was a deep one,' Kitty replied. 'I owe him a great deal.' She owed him her sanity. She owed him a return for the loyalty he had shown her when there was no one else. Above all else she owed it to him not to give his wife any reason to suspect there was ever anything more than friendship between them.

Susan gave a brisk nod. 'It seems he's got a lot to tell me then,' she retorted. 'Exactly how long have you known Harry?'

'It seems like all my life,' Kitty answered truthfully. She could feel the young woman's hostility towards her. Determined not to cross swords, she asked, 'Would you like to use my bedroom to freshen up?'

'Do I look as if I need freshening up?'

It was obvious to Kitty that Harry's wife was spoiling for an argument. Aware that he intended to intervene, she quickly replied, 'I'm sorry. It's just that you've come a long way. Would you like a drink then? Something to eat perhaps?'

She kept her gaze focused on that insolent, unbearably attractive face. But it wasn't easy when her thoughts and senses were alive with him. Out of the corner of her eye she was too aware of his nearness, too disturbed by his presence; that tall familiar figure, handsome and strong as ever, honed by his labours, made confident by his success. But then Harry was always confident. Harry was always going to do well. Wasn't that why she'd sent him away?

'I think I would like a drink, yes.' Susan's voice was softer now, deliberately friendly. 'Could you take my coat?' Turning her back on Harry she waited for him to whip the coat from her shoulders. She lifted her face for a kiss but he pretended not to notice, making sure no one else noticed either. Always the gentleman, but raging inside because of her behaviour, he would get no pleasure out of humiliating Susan in public. Besides, she was doing that all by herself.

As Kitty turned away to take the coat, Susan called out, 'I will freshen up after all. You're right. The journey was tiresome, and I do feel a little jaded.' In truth she wanted to see more of this house, Kitty's bedroom in particular. Before the night was out she wanted to know Kitty a little better because only then could she gauge what she was really up against. There was a certain attraction between her husband and Kitty Marsh; a dangerous chemistry that made her uneasy. This party had worried her. Kitty Marsh had worried her, and now after seeing how lovely she was, how like the sort of woman Harry would have gone for if she hadn't ensnared him, Susan was determined to put as many miles between the two of them was possible; and even more determined to ensure that this was the last time he came into contact with his 'old school friend'. Harry Jenkins was hers, and Kitty Marsh could go to hell!

Kitty showed Susan to the bedroom then left her there. 'If you need anything, please ask,' she invited. 'I won't be too far away.'

Hurrying down the stairs, she wondered how Harry had come to marry such a spoilt self-centred creature. But then she realised how he must love her, and after all, Susan was a very beautiful, sophisticated woman, far more elegant and accomplished than she herself could ever be.

All the same, as she came into the lounge, thrilled to see Harry making a bee-line straight for her, she hoped her love for this man had not impaired her judgment of his wife, because much as she had tried not to let it happen, she had taken an instant dislike to the woman upstairs.

As he crossed the room towards her, Harry could not take his eyes off Kitty. She was exactly as he remembered her, and yet nothing like. She was incredibly beautiful. In that black dress with the red lace peeping through, she made his pulses race, but it was her eyes that took him back, those soft brown eyes that lit with a loveliness from within. Unlike Susan, she was warm and open in her nature. He had always loved her. He loved her still, with an intensity that frightened him.

When he reached her, she smiled up at him and his heart was wide open to her. The soft strains of a Nat King Cole song filled the air. Without a word Harry stretched out his arms and enfolded her in them, moving her round the floor, his head bent to hers as they danced together, two young sweethearts, needing each other, loving each other so very much. Theirs was a forbidden love, but it flowed between them as naturally as day flowed into night.

From the far side of the room, Mildred saw them together. She saw how closely he held her, and how wonderfully content Kitty appeared to be in his arms, and suddenly she knew. 'In love!' she muttered. 'I must have been blind.'

'What did you say?' Eddie bent his head to hear.

'Nothing,' she replied hastily. 'I was just singing with the music.' As she spoke she looked over to the door and there was Susan. She too had seen, and realised, and now the anger was all over her face. 'Excuse me a minute.' Mildred realised she must waylay that arrogant young woman, or there might be a scene. Without waiting for Eddie's response she rushed across to where Susan stood, her features set like steel as she glared at Harry and Kitty, so at home in each other's arms.

'I hope you feel refreshed?' Mildred asked, diverting Susan's attention. On the way over she had grabbed a glass of wine from the dresser. Handing it to Susan, she remarked, 'My dear, it's wonderful to hear Harry has built up his own business. Mind you, I always thought he would.' In fact she hadn't known Harry all that well; only that every time she went to see Kitty's parents, her niece would either be in Harry's house, or he would be in hers. As far as Mildred was concerned, they were just friends. It had never occurred to her how much they meant to each other.

Susan was not easily fooled, nor was she about to be side-tracked. 'Tell me about Harry?' she suggested. 'And Kitty? I understand they've known each other since schooldays?'

'That's right.' Mildred knew she had to be very careful if she was to avert a row between husband and wife. 'Went to the same school, lived not too far away from each other. Very firm friends they were. But then they went their separate ways, and as far as I know never saw each other until Harry came to my company for the haulage contract.' She sensed a cunning behind Susan's questions, 'Mind you, Harry's sister, Sarah, was never far away. Gone abroad now, I believe.'

'Never saw each other, you say?' Susan was only a little placated. 'Never wrote? Never phoned?'

Mildred shook her head. 'Not that I know of. You must understand what it's like? Children pal up at school, then grow up and away from each other. When I met Harry again after all those years, I was delighted to see how well he was doing. I thought it would be nice for the two of them to say hello again.'

Susan's gaze went to the couple who were still dancing. Her voice was small and stiff, her eyes narrowed as she observed their closeness. 'They seem delighted to meet again, don't you think?'

'Only natural,' Mildred said lightly. 'Old friends and all that. I suppose after tonight they'll go their separate ways and never make contact again.' Somehow she knew that was not true. There was something wonderful between those two. Something wonderful, *and tragic*.

The music came to an end. 'You dance like an angel,' Harry murmured. Now that he had her in his arms, he didn't want to let her go. While he was talking, the next song came on, a ballad, the kind of melody you made love to. 'Stay,' he pleaded. 'One more dance, Kitty?'

Realising they were being observed, she reluctantly suggested, 'It might be better if you asked your wife for the next dance.'

His gaze lifted. Susan smiled at him, that hard little smile he knew so well. It meant trouble, but he had learned how to handle that. 'I see what you mean,' he acknowledged bitterly. 'But I would still rather dance with you.'

Kitty laughed softly. She didn't know whether he was teasing, playing a game they used to play as children. Out of the corner of her eye she saw both Mildred and Susan coming towards them. 'The army's advancing,' she joked. She didn't feel like joking. She felt like murder!

'Really, Harry,' Susan purred, 'you're neglecting me.' Draping herself over him, she drove him backwards, stepping to the music, giving him little choice but to dance with her.

Mildred was tempted to ask questions, but Jack's timely entrance prevented that. 'You look stunning!' he gasped, drawing Kitty into an embrace.

She thought he looked handsome too. He had on a new beige suit, his fair hair was smartly cut, the grey shirt and tie brought out the colour of his ocean-blue eyes, and he carried an air of confidence that had been lacking in him these past weeks. 'Enough of that,' she said, drawing away. 'I'm hungry. What about you?'

'Famished!'

They ate and drank a little, and in between mingled with the guests. 'Aren't you going to introduce me to the handsome couple over there?' Jack asked finally.

Kitty's brown eyes followed his gaze. Harry was looking at her. Susan was talking to Mildred, no doubt quizzing her about Kitty, 'That's Harry Jenkins and his wife,' she explained. 'Harry's an old friend of mine.'

Jack's voice hardened. 'Are you sure he's not an old lover?'

'What do you mean by that?'

He returned his plate to the table. 'He hasn't taken his eyes off you, that's what I mean.'

'You don't own me, Jack. Whether Harry was my lover or not is none of your business.'

His smile told her that he hadn't believed his own suspicions. 'Sorry,' he said. But he wasn't altogether satisfied.

Mildred went to talk to her other guests, while Kitty introduced Harry and his wife. 'And this is Jack,' she explained, 'my boss.'

He slid his arm round her shoulders. 'More than that, I hope, Kitty?'

Memories of the night they had spent together rushed through Kitty's mind. When she blushed, Harry's heart fell. What exactly did Jack Harpur mean to her? he wondered.

As the evening wore on, people grew merrier and danced longer; Mildred and Eddie spent more time together, sitting in a corner whispering like two young lovers, and Susan took up more of Jack's time than was natural. It occurred to Kitty that she was trying to make her jealous. 'She's probably punishing me for dancing with you,' Harry told her. 'She plays this little game where she tries to make me jealous.' His smile betrayed his despair. 'It's my fault,' he confessed, 'I can't make her happy.'

Kitty glanced to the far side of the room, where Jack was entertaining Susan by telling her stories of his many escapades. She was laughing, her blue eyes intent on his face. 'Are you sure she's just trying to make you jealous?' Kitty asked. 'She seems to be genuinely enjoying Jack's company.'

'I hope she is,' Harry replied. He felt guilty where his wife was concerned. 'Do you and Jack intend to marry?' He had to know.

Kitty's answer was like music to his ears. 'Jack would like that. But I'm not ready.' She wondered if she ever would be.

'Kitty?'

She looked up. His dark gaze reached into her soul. She felt so much love for him it was like a physical agony inside her.

'Is there somewhere we could talk?'

Kitty couldn't look at him. What was he asking? What did he want to talk about that he couldn't say here and now? Could she trust herself if they were alone? 'Do you think we should?' Her eyes pleaded. 'What about Susan?'

He glanced across at her. 'She probably won't even notice. Like you say, she seems to be enjoying the company.'

Without another word, Kitty put down her glass and walked away, Harry discreetly following.

Coming into the kitchen, she felt the need to apologise. 'I'm sorry it's in such a mess,' she muttered. His nearness was intoxicating. She didn't know how to react or what to say. Harry had that effect on her.

They were just inside the door. Every work surface was littered with implements and crockery. 'Looks like you and your aunt have worked very hard,' he commented. They were so close her shoulder was touching his chest. He could hardly breathe.

She kept her gaze averted, not daring to turn, afraid he might see what was really in her heart. 'What did you want to say to me, Harry? What was so important that you couldn't say it in there?' Her voice was trembling, her hands were shaking, and she knew he felt the same.

'I love you, Kitty.' The softest whisper, but it touched her very soul. 'I have always loved you. You know it, don't you?'

'Don't say that,' she pleaded. 'It's been too long, Harry. You're married now. We've gone our separate ways.'

'Are you saying you don't want me?'

She lowered her gaze. How could she lie? God help her but she did want him. In spite of the fact that he was married, she wanted him to take her here and now. She needed him so much. No, Kitty! a warning voice sounded in her head. He isn't yours. You have no right!

Gently he turned her towards him. Outside the street lamp flickered, sending a soft halo of light into the room. Placing the tips of his fingers beneath her chin, he raised her face to his. 'I waited for you, Kitty. All that long time, I waited, always believing you would write, but you never did. I wrote to you though, time and again. Pouring my heart out, asking you to let me back into your life. Letters I never posted. I wanted to see you, to talk with you. In the end I realised you didn't want me back. You shut me out, Kitty. Why did you do that?'

'For your sake, not mine,' she whispered. She had been so wrong. She could see that now. But it was too late. 'I wanted you to have a good life,' she murmured. 'I would only have held you back. Then there was your family ... your father. He never liked me. It would have split your family. I was in a home, too young to make plans. You would have had to wait, and in the end it would have been you making all the sacrifices. I couldn't let you take on such a burden.' With a wistful smile she told him, 'You're successful now, with your own business. I don't think you could have achieved that if you'd had me to worry about.'

'You'll never know how wrong you were!' Catching his breath, he grabbed her hard by the shoulders, raising her to her toes, his face so close to hers she could feel his warm breath on her mouth. 'You little fool! Why didn't you say all these things before?' he groaned. 'You can't have any idea of the hell you put me through.'

'And me,' she whispered. 'It was hell for me too.' He could see her sadness, the tears trembling in her lovely eyes, and cursed the circumstances that kept them apart.

Kitty held back the tears. She didn't want him to see her crying. She had been through too much to let it swamp her now. Safe in Harry's strong arms, she wondered where it had all gone wrong. Though she resented the woman who had taken her place, it saddened her to think that Harry was discontented. 'You're not happy, are you?' she asked softly.

His dark eyes ravished her. He was angry, lost without her in his life. For a minute Kitty believed he would not answer. But then he whispered harshly, 'How could I be happy without you?'

She could find no words to comfort him. No words to right the wrong she had done. And so she looked away, and closed her eyes, and when in a minute he snatched her to him, she cried out, a small stifled gasp that mingled with his breath when

230

his mouth covered hers. 'I love you, Kitty,' he murmured. 'I could never love anyone else!' Again the anger, and such a need that it stirred a fire inside her.

With his arms holding her and his kisses burning her mouth, it was as if all the bad things had gone forever. There was just Kitty and Harry, and this great abiding love that spanned the years and wound them together forever.

Suddenly the door opened and Mildred came in, wide-eyed yet not surprised to find them together. She had seen enough during the evening to realise what was between them still. 'Your wife's waiting to leave,' she told Harry in a firm voice. Having been at the wrong end of a failed marriage she saw her own husband in him.

'Thank you,' he said, his hand sliding into Kitty's. He saw the disapproval on her face, yet could not let go of Kitty. Mildred didn't understand. No one did. 'You must think I'm a monster?'

Something in his voice, a kind of honour, made her hesitate. 'It isn't for me to say,' she answered. Glancing from him to Kitty, she could see they were deeply in love. Any fool could see that. She thought about the years since her brother had done away with himself, and her own part in shaping Kitty's life afterwards. She thought about Kitty's forgiveness, and the way that young girl had come into her own life, bringing sunshine and hope where there had been none.

Mortified with shame, her gaze softened when she looked at Kitty. 'She's gone to fetch her coat,' she said. 'You have a minute to say goodbye.' With that she went, leaving them alone, and a little ashamed.

Harry was the first to speak. 'I can't take back anything I've said,' he assured her. 'I married Susan for all the wrong reasons, but that wasn't her fault. And it wasn't yours. I had no right to come here ... forcing myself back into your life. I won't stop loving you just because we're apart.' He stroked her face, gazing at her with soft dark eyes. 'You know what I'm thinking, don't you.'

She nodded her head. Of course she knew, because wasn't she thinking the very same? He was wondering if there was a chance they might pick up where they had left off? He was hoping Susan could be told the truth ... that she and Harry loved each other, and that they longed to be together. That was what Harry was thinking. But it was wrong. 'I wish you hadn't come here,' she murmured. If she had never seen him again, she might have got over him in time. Now she never would.

He understood. 'Forgive me?'

Kitty merely nodded. He kissed her once more. 'I'm sorry, sweetheart.' She smiled at that. He had always called her 'sweetheart' because that's what they had always been.

At the sight of Harry standing alone by the door, Susan swept across the room. 'I understand you went out for a breath of air,' she remarked with a sly little grin. 'To tell you the truth I didn't even miss you. I was enjoying myself too much to notice.'

Pointing to Jack, who was now chatting with Kitty at the table, she enquired, 'Did you know he and Kitty Marsh are to be married?'

Her announcement was like a fist in his stomach. 'Married!' He stared at her. 'Are you sure?'

'Oh, yes! Some time this year by all accounts.' Having cunningly planted the seed, she held out her coat, at the same time remarking that the matter of Kitty's forthcoming marriage was of little importance to either of them. 'Let's get home, darling,' she purred, making her way to the door.

Harry drew her back. 'Don't you think it would be good manners to thank Kitty's aunt first?' It was typical of Susan to walk out without so much as a goodbye.

Making a sour face, she glanced round the room. 'I don't believe it would matter. It's not as though we'll ever see these people again, is it?' she asked pointedly. 'Besides, apart from Jack Harpur's sparkling company, it's been a tedious little party.'

Ignoring her spiteful comments, he strode away. As he approached Mildred and her gentleman friend, so did Kitty and Jack. 'Thank you for a lovely time,' he told Mildred.

'I'm pleased you were able to come,' she answered. Gone was her anger. Love was a powerful master.

Before they left, Kitty was urged to open all her presents; there was a silk scarf and a number of bottles of perfume which was strange because she never used it. Eddie and Mildred had bought her a beautiful white silk blouse.

'Goodbye, Kitty... Jack.' Harry's gaze went from Kitty to Jack and back again. 'Oh! Nearly left without giving you your birthday present,' he apologised. Reaching into his pocket, he drew out a small box wrapped in silver paper and tied with ribbon. Laying the box in her hand he said softly, 'Happy birthday.' His dark eyes enveloped her, his smile for her and no one else. He had meant to give her the present when they were alone in the kitchen, but Mildred's timely intervention had sent it right out of his head.

Susan arrived just in time to see him hand the present over. 'You sly thing,' she chided sweetly. 'And I didn't even see what you'd bought.' Jack smiled at her and she grinned like a Cheshire cat, turning on the charm and congratulating herself. If she could stir a pot of mischief she was in her element.

Kitty saw none of that. Instead she was looking at Harry, her smile warm and intimate. 'Thank you.' Turning to his wife she smiled at her, hiding the ache inside. 'Thank you both,' she said. She realised Susan was itching to see what the present was, but had no intention of opening it now. It was too private. Whatever the box contained, it was from Harry and she would cherish it. The fact that Susan had not helped in its choosing only made it the more precious.

'Goodnight then, and thank you for a lovely party.' Susan's words drifted behind her as she hurried away, inwardly seething yet cunning to the end.

Shaking Harry's hand, Jack wished him well. 'Your wife's been telling me all about how you came up from scratch,' he revealed. 'I can see you're a very ambitious man, and as far as I can tell there's no reason why you and I shouldn't be doing business in the future. Good hauliers are the very devil to find.'

Harry thanked him. 'I mean to expand my business until I have a fleet to be reckoned with,' he vowed. Then he kissed Mildred lightly on the cheek and thanked her; only the two of them knew the real reason for his gratitude. Afterwards he kissed Kitty too, a swift inadequate expression of his affections. Holding her hand a minute longer than was necessary, he told her, 'Be happy, sweetheart.' Only Mildred noticed the pain in his voice. And Kitty of course. And when he had gone, she was lonelier than ever.

'I should be seethingly jealous,' Jack commented.

'What are you talking about?' For one awful minute Kitty was afraid he had seen her and Harry emerge from the kitchen.

'Your old schoolfriend,' he explained. His voice was

233

light-hearted, but his eyes were hard and calculating. 'The way he held on to your hand, I thought he might leave his wife here and take you instead.'

Kitty's answer was dismissive. 'Harry and I belong to another time.' She turned away, walking to the table where she helped herself to a measure of gin and tonic. Raising the glass to her lips, she muttered beneath her breath, 'To us, Harry, and what might have been.' She took a sip, grimaced at the bitter taste. Replacing the glass on the tray, she began clearing the table.

'What's the matter with her?' Jack had never seen Kitty in such a pensive mood.

Mildred wondered whether to take him apart for his insensitivity. However, not wanting to fuel his suspicions, she suggested tactfully, 'I expect having Harry here has opened up old wounds ... the loss of her parents, the children's home, all of that.' Giving him a little prod she urged, 'It might help if you went and talked to her. She's probably feeling very lonely.' Because Harry's gone, she thought. But there was no need for Jack to know that.

Mortified that he might have been the cause of Kitty's quiet mood, he hurried to find her. In the kitchen she sat by the table, gazing at Harry's unopened present and mulling over the events of the night. When Jack walked in, she quickly dropped the present into the table drawer, went to the sink, ran the hot water into the bowl and feverishly began washing the dishes.

'I can be so stupid sometimes,' he said sheepishly. Grabbing a tea-towel, he waited to wipe the dishes. 'I'll go if you like?'

Putting a bowl on to the drainer, she touched his hand with soapy fingers. 'Don't be silly.'

The relief on his face was pathetic. 'You mean you don't want me to leave?'

Her wonderful smile hid an aching heart. 'And who would wipe the dishes?' she asked with a twinkle in her eye.

Encouraged by her friendliness, he caught hold of her arm. 'Kitty, I know I promised never to ask you again, but we need each other. Please, Kitty, you'd make me the happiest man on earth if only you'd be my wife.'

'Don't, Jack.' Her smile fell away and in its place there was a look of hopelessness. 'We've been through this too many times.'

'You're torturing me.'

'No, Jack. You're torturing yourself.'

'Do you find me so unattractive?'

'No. In fact you're a good-looking bloke.'

'You don't like me then?'

'That's not true and you know it.' Dropping the dish-cloth into the bowl, she wiped her hands on the tea-towel he was holding. 'It might be better if we went back into the lounge.' Without waiting for him, she left the room. It was a moment before he followed, just in time to say goodbye to Mildred's gentleman friend.

A short while after that, Jack reluctantly departed, leaving Kitty alone with her aunt. 'My feet are throbbing like mad,' Mildred moaned, flopping into the kitchen chair. 'These new shoes are sheer hell.' Bending forward she eased the shoes off her feet. 'Oh! What heaven!' she sighed, wriggling her toes. 'Honest to God, what we women go through in the name of fashion.'

Finishing off the washing-up, Kitty stacked the crockery into the cupboard. 'Are you sure you weren't wearing them to impress your new fella?' she asked mischievously.

Mildred regarded her for a minute. Aware that Kitty's life might be turned upside down by her exciting news, she was tempted to maintain her silence until tomorrow. However, she had put it off too long already. Events had moved too quickly and now she was obliged to let Kitty know exactly what had been going on. 'Sit here a minute,' she invited. 'We need to talk.' As she twisted in the chair, her sore foot collided with the table leg, causing her to grimace with pain.

'I know you're waiting to tick me off about Harry,' Kitty guessed, 'but it can wait a minute.'

Mildred was surprised. 'Who said I was going to tick you off?' she demanded.

'Why else would you want to talk? And don't forget I saw your disapproving expression when you found us together in the kitchen.' All evening, Kitty had been half expecting to be taken aside by Mildred. When she wasn't, it occurred to her that her aunt was biding her time, waiting for just such a moment as this.

Mildred was both impatient and uncomfortable. 'Whatever are you doing?' she asked, peering at Kitty who was on her knees beneath the sink-cupboard.

'Be patient.' Taking a plastic bowl from the cupboard, Kitty filled it with equal measures of cold and hot water. 'Put your feet in there,' she invited, setting the bowl on the tiles. She then brought a hand towel from the cupboard, chuckling aloud when Mildred eased her feet into the soothing water, her face a study in sheer delight as she sighed with pleasure.

Drawing up a chair, Kitty sat in front of her aunt. 'Now then. What's so important it won't wait until tomorrow?' She still supposed it was to be a lecture on hiding in the kitchen with another woman's husband. But it wasn't like that with her and Harry, was it? WAS IT? Suddenly she felt ashamed, indignant. Harry was hers and always would be! Even as the thought rippled through her mind she knew it was not the way of things. He was *not* hers. He was married to Susan, and she must accept that fact. 'It *is* to do with me and Harry, isn't it?' She didn't want to talk about him. She didn't even want to think about him. But she couldn't help herself. He was part of her existence, inside her, alive with every beat of her heart.

Gingerly lifting one foot out of the water, Mildred patted it dry with the towel. 'I can't deny I was shocked to see how strongly you and Harry felt about each other,' she confessed. Raising the other foot, she dried that also, then she draped the towel across the back of the nearest chair and slid the bowl away. Drawing the chair closer to Kitty, she crossed her bare ankles and went on in a gentle voice, 'It isn't for me to tell you what to do. And, to tell you the truth, that was not why I wanted us to talk.' She swallowed and braced herself. This was not going to be easy.

Kitty was intrigued and a little afraid. 'You look as if you're about to walk the plank,' she said, trying to lighten the situation.

'Kitty, forgive me if I'm prying into your affairs,' Mildred apologised, 'but now that you've raised the issue of you and Harry, I would be failing you again if I didn't advise you to be very careful what you do. After all, he has a wife, and I'm sure you wouldn't want to be responsible for a broken marriage?' The memories of her own were too close, too awful.

Kitty's voice was solemn. 'You needn't worry yourself,' she answered. 'Harry and I don't intend seeing each other again.' Thinking it was bad enough. Actually saying it was too final. She took a deep breath. 'If that's all, I think I'll go to bed now?' Not to sleep, she thought, but to remember those few precious moments when he held her in his arms.

She would have got out of the chair and left there and then, but Mildred put out her hand. Gripping Kitty's fingers in her own, she asked softly, 'You love him, don't you?'

Kitty couldn't look at her. 'Yes,' she whispered, 'I do love him . . . very much.'

'Yet you let him go?' Mildred had wondered about that. Suddenly she realised. 'You thought you'd be a burden, didn't you? *That* was why?' She squeezed Kitty's fingers encouragingly. 'From what I saw tonight, Harry is a man deeply in love. Unlike me, he would never have deserted you, especially if he thought you loved him. So I can only think he left because you asked him to.'

'Harry has made a good life for himself.'

'I see.' She took her hand away from Kitty's, and straightened her back. For a while she looked at her niece and her heart went out to her. But no good would come of raking over old coals. 'What about Jack?'

Kitty was taken aback. 'What about him?'

'How do you feel about being his wife?' She had good reason for asking.

Kitty had to smile. 'He doesn't give up, that's for sure. After promising he wouldn't, he asked me again tonight.' Before Mildred could voice the question she added, 'I'm afraid he went away disappointed.'

'Would it be so awful, being Mrs Jack Harpur?'

Kitty thought 'awful' was a little strong. 'It's not what I want,' she said. What she wanted was to turn the clock back, but that was like asking for the moon. She gave a little laugh, saying philosophically, 'But then, we can't always have what we want, can we?'

Mildred mused on Kitty's wry comment before advising, 'I'm sure I don't have to tell you of all people how sometimes we have to settle for what we have . . . instead of what we want.' She regarded Kitty's face, the elfin features and abundance of dark hair, the telling brown eyes with their thick dark lashes. And not for the first time she wondered what would become of this big-hearted young woman. 'About Jack . . .' She had to pursue it, because she truly believed that in the circumstances, being Jack Harpur's wife would be the best solution for Kitty. She couldn't bring herself to speculate on the way it would also salve her own conscience for the blow she was about to deliver. 'I honestly think you should consider his offer. He worships the ground you walk on, and has few vices that I can think of. Oh, I know I didn't take too kindly to him at first, but I've come to feel he would be a good husband to you, Kitty. You wouldn't go short of anything either.'

She felt there was more to Mildred's enthusiasm than she was admitting. 'Why the hurry to get me down the aisle?' Her forthright gaze met Mildred's. 'Is there something you're not telling me?'

Getting out of her chair, Mildred plodded on bare feet to the other side of the room where she stood with her back to the sink and her face turned up to the ceiling. Biting her lip, she asked, 'What do you think of Eddie?'

That was not the question Kitty had expected. It threw her for a minute. 'I liked him,' she answered. 'He seems a really nice bloke.' She smiled. 'I'd say he was smitten with you, since he hardly left your side all evening.'

Mildred's gaze softened. 'Would you be very surprised if I told you he'd asked me to marry him?'

In a minute Kitty was across the room. 'That's wonderful!' she exclaimed giving her a hug. 'You sly thing... a proposal, and you never said a word!'

Mildred had not dared to hope for such a reaction. The relief showed on her face. 'Don't you mind?'

Kitty laughed for joy. 'MIND!' She danced her aunt round the room. 'I'm thrilled for you.' Now she was firing questions. 'You said yes, I hope? When is it to be? Can I be maid of honour?' Suddenly aware of the severe look on Mildred's face, she drew away. 'What's the matter? Is there a problem?'

'Not for me, Kitty. But I'm afraid my getting married does pose a problem for you.'

'In what way?'

'Eddie wants me to live with him. But, I'm still in such a mess. My ex is abroad all the time, but he'll be back with a vengeance. I've managed to fend him off so far, as you know. But the house will have to go.'

Surprised that Mildred should ever want to sell this lovely old house, yet realising that it was her aunt's decision and no one else's, Kitty reassured her, 'If you're worrying about me, then please don't. I know how hard it's been, though you've put on a brave face through it all. Now, maybe the time is right to let go.'

Suffused with shame, Mildred told her quietly, 'I should have told you before, only I was too much of a coward. You see, I've already found a buyer. I had the estate agent here one day while you were at work. He had a couple on his list who were looking for a place like this, in this area.' Steeling herself against the astonished expression on Kitty's face, she went on hurriedly, 'I've already exchanged. I'm sorry, but we have to vacate this house two weeks from today.'

Kitty could hardly believe her ears. 'TWO WEEKS!'

'I know I should have told you,' Mildred muttered, 'Eddie kept on to me to tell you, but I couldn't bring myself to come out with it.' Her voice broke and she hung her head. 'I've always been a coward,' she croaked. 'Nobody knows that better than you.'

Kitty didn't hesitate. Taking the wretched woman in her arms, she said, 'You're no coward. Look how you got yourself together again after the break-up of your marriage. I'm happy for you, and I don't want you to worry about me. You're right, of course . . . you should have told me, given me time to adjust, time to look around for a place of my own. But it's all right. We all make mistakes.' Me more than most, she thought.

Feeling as though she'd had the stuffing knocked out of her, Kitty sat down again. 'There are always flats coming up over Bromham way. I'll ring a few agents in the morning. As for furniture, I'm sure I'll find what I need at Peacock's auction rooms.'

'Oh no!' Mildred wanted so much to make amends. 'Eddie's bungalow is lavishly furnished, and I won't need half of what I've got here. Take what you want, Kitty. I'd much rather you had it than put it out for sale.'

She loved the furniture in this house. It was old, and loved, and full of character. If she searched high and low she would never find the like. 'Are you sure?'

'You'd be doing me a great favour,' Mildred confessed. 'Please, Kitty . . . take whatever you want. I know you'll look after it.'

Kitty's brown eyes shone with pleasure. She looked at the

beautiful dresser that had been handed down through genera-
tions. 'You wouldn't sell that, would you?' she asked, knowing
how Mildred cherished it.

'Yes, I would,' Mildred lied. 'If you don't take it, it will have
to go to the auction rooms.'

'I don't believe you!' Kitty was incredulous. 'It was your
mother's and her mother's before her.'

Mildred smiled serenely. 'Kitty, you're talking about your own
grandmother . . . and great-grandmother. The dresser has been
mine for many years, and now it's yours, if you want it.'

'Thank you. I would love to have it.'

They embraced then, and it was as though they had been
travelling for a very long time, neither of them knowing which
way life would take them, meeting and parting, their paths
merging one with the other. Now they were parting for good,
each going her own separate way, and it was a sobering thought.

For a while they talked of exciting things, like where Mildred
and Eddie would be married, and where they would spend their
honeymoon; what kind of dress Kitty would wear when she was
maid of honour. They promised never to lose touch. 'It would
do my heart good to see you married and settled,' Mildred
persisted. 'I know how you would dearly love to be a mother,
to make a proper home for yourself and your family.'

'I don't know that it will ever happen,' Kitty confessed. It
had always been her dream, and now it was gone, with Harry,
and his wife, and the life they were building together. It would
be Susan who bore his children, and she would have to live
with that knowledge.

Sensing the despair in her voice, Mildred told her, 'There's
time enough yet. You're still very young.' She knew Kitty was
yearning for Harry, and feared it was a bad thing.

Later, when the two of them had gone to their bedrooms,
they both lay, too excited to sleep. Mildred wondered about the
future, filled with plans and hopes, and wishing she had met
Eddie years ago. Kitty was still awake when the dawn rose,
casting a soft and beautiful glow over her little world, a world
that was soon to disappear like the night sky. Kneeling by the
window, with her chin resting on folded hands, she was just a
little afraid of the future. 'Where do I go from here?' she asked.
She felt incredibly lonely, the kind of loneliness that she had

not felt in a very long time because now it was mingled with hopelessness. She could see the future laid out before her – a small flat overlooking a busy road, endless rows of traffic at the front, and someone else's back yard at the rear. It would be all she could afford, yet she must try to make it into a home. And even that would take money, probably more than she had in her savings account.

She began thinking about all the things she would need. Even with Mildred giving her furniture, there were all the other items, personal things that Mildred would take with her to her own new home, like cooking utensils, pictures to decorate the walls, and all the many artefacts that make an empty place a home.

The only truly beautiful thing in that flat would be her grandmother's dresser, and her only visitor would be Jack. Georgie was too far away, and too taken up with her own life. Harry had said a final goodbye, and her aunt would never again be there when she needed to talk: in the middle of the night; over the breakfast table; in the evening after a hard day at work, when Mildred would sit with her feet in a bowl and the two of them would chat about this and that, and none of it important.

Only now did Kitty realise how few friends she had made. The prospect of being alone in that flat was bleak. 'How can it be a home when there's no one there but me?' she whispered.

For one brief moment she even entertained the idea of marrying Jack. After all, he did love her. She would have security, and she had come to feel affection for him. But affection was not enough. If she were to marry Jack she would be living a lie, cheating not only herself but him, and that would not be fair.

Thrusting the idea from her mind, she climbed into bed, but there was no rest. She spent a restless hour or two, subconsciously fearful of the future, waking and sleeping, thinking and wondering, afraid of the emptiness that stretched before her. Finally she sat up, her mind in a whirl. Maybe it was time to make plans, to do something that would take her right away, open up a whole new world for her? Yes! That's what she would do. Tomorrow, she would think it all through. Tomorrow, in the light of day, she would be able to think more clearly.

With a lighter heart she fell into a deep contented sleep; not realising that so often the promises we make ourselves are destined to be broken, thin strands of hope, severed by the way in which others weave their lives, and in the way those lives touch on ours.

While Kitty slept, two letters were winging their way to her. Both disturbing. Both to shape her destiny for many years to come.

CHAPTER FOURTEEN

'But it makes sense to marry me!' Jack argued. Mildred and Eddie had gone to see the florist, leaving Jack and Kitty talking.

Jack believed he would never get a better chance of persuading Kitty to be his wife. Ever since he'd been told that she was to be turned out of her home, he had taken it on himself to be her protector and provider, if only she would let him, 'Why should you live in some poky little flat, when I can build you the house you've always wanted? We could go to Cyprus for our honeymoon ... make our way there on the cruiser if that's what you want.' His eyes lit up at the thought.

Kitty got up from her chair and stared at him. In a firm voice she explained, 'I've already given you my answer, Jack, and it's no!'

'And you still won't change your mind?'

'Please leave, Jack. I promised my aunt I would write out the place cards. The hotel needs them tomorrow, together with a seating plan.'

'I'll help you.'

'No!' Swinging round, she faced him with angry eyes. 'I'm better on my own.'

'All right.' Shrugging his shoulders, he thrust his hands in his pocket and scowled. 'If that's what you want?'

'It is.'

'But we're still on for dinner, aren't we?' As always he had driven her to the edge of her patience. 'I'm sorry,' he said. 'It's just that I can't stand the thought of you living alone. I want you with me. I want to take care of you.'

'JACK!' For all his faults she couldn't help but like him.

'All right! All right! I'm going.' And he went quickly, before he ruined what was left of their relationship.

Sighing with relief, Kitty settled down at the dining table, to write out the place cards. When that was done, she turned her hand to wrapping the present she and Jack had bought the happy couple. It was a splendid oil painting, a seascape that could grace any room. 'I'm sure they'll love this,' she muttered, sticking a silver bow on the top right-hand corner.

That done, she went upstairs and began rummaging through her wardrobe. 'Didn't realise I had things I've never even worn,' she observed with some surprise. It wasn't all that often she went to the shops, although of course, Jack was always sending her little presents ... silk scarfs, expensive jumpers and even a whole box of sheer nylons that languished on the bottom of the wardrobe unopened. 'You're too extravagant, Jack Harper,' she chided with a little smile. 'The way you spend money, it's a wonder you're not bankrupt.'

She went through the drawers, cupboards and bedside cabinets, sorting the good from the bad, the needed from the unwanted, and when it was all done, she had four carrier bags, two cardboard boxes, and a huge bundle filled with things that were hardly used and never likely to be.

After that she showered and changed, answering the telephone in between, cringing when each time it was Jack at the other end. 'You are still coming out to dinner with me, aren't you?' he pleaded in the first call. In the second he confirmed the time he would collect her; in the third, when Kitty threatened not to answer the phone again, he told her he loved her, he was sorry, and there was nothing more he wanted in the whole world than for her to be his wife. Kitty warned that if he was going to pester on that particular issue she would not come out with him. 'Hand on heart I won't,' he promised.

The fourth and final call was again from Jack, pleading with her to understand why he couldn't take her out after all. 'You know that forty-foot Birchwood I've been waiting for all day. Well, it's just arrived. It's an absolute beauty. I can't trust the driver to put it in the water, not with that crane playing up. The prospective buyer wants to try it out first thing in the morning, so I'm sorry, darling, there's nothing for it but to roll up my sleeves and put her in the water myself.' He pleaded for her to understand, promising they would enjoy their dinner out another night. 'When the boat's sold, and we'll have cause to celebrate!'

'That's all right,' Kitty assured him. In fact she was immensely grateful. With the wedding a little over a week away, there was still much to do.

Mildred collected the afternoon post as she came in. 'Here's one for you,' she said, handing Kitty a dainty white envelope.

Taking the envelope Kitty turned it over in her hands before holding it to her nose and gently sniffing. 'Perfumed,' she remarked curiously. 'Who on earth would be writing to me in a perfumed envelope?'

'You won't know if you don't open it,' Mildred chuckled. 'I don't suppose for one minute it's from Georgie?'

Kitty laughed at that. 'Not for one minute,' she confirmed. 'This perfume smells very expensive. Georgie tends to get hers from the market stall.'

While Kitty opened the envelope, Mildred attended to her many items of wedding correspondence. She had a fistful of replies to her wedding invitations, and a pile of bills that must be settled in the next week. 'I must have been mad to let Eddie rush me,' she sighed, pushing her spectacles back from the end of her nose.

Kitty took out the letter. 'Don't tell me you're beginning to regret it all?' she asked with a sly little smile.

Mildred shyly bowed her head. ''Course I don't,' she said tenderly, adjusting her spectacles. 'We were made for each other.'

Kitty smiled and returned her attention to the letter in her hand. The spidery scrawl was neatly written in the centre of the page; the edges were painted with garlands of flowers, and a sprig of blossom at each corner. Intrigued, Kitty silently read.

As she did, the colour drained from her face. Finally she dropped the letter to her lap and leaned back in the chair, her eyes closed and her hands visibly trembling.

Sensing the change of mood, her aunt looked up. Kitty's face told its own story. 'What's the matter?' she asked, laying her pile of correspondence on her knee. 'Bad news, is it?'

Gathering her dignity, Kitty put on a bright smile. 'No, it's good news really.' She handed the letter over. 'Read for yourself.'

Straightening the page, Mildred again adjusted her glasses and began to read aloud:

245

Dear Kitty,

First of all, please let me say how very much Harry and I enjoyed your party. I had heard so much about you from him, so you can imagine how delighted I was to meet you at last.

We would dearly have loved to come to your aunt's wedding, but because I haven't been feeling too well, I'm afraid we will have to decline.

However, I know how delighted you will be when I explain the reason for my not feeling too good. Harry and I are expecting our first baby, due at the end of October.

I won't mind whether it's a boy or or a girl, but Harry aches for a son, so I'll do my best to produce one for him.

I expect you know of Harry's ambition to father at least two children, so if this one is a son for Harry, who knows, maybe the next one will be a girl for me?

I have formally answered your aunt's kind invitation.

Harry sends his regards.

> *Yours affectionately,*
> *Susan*

Mildred sat very still for what seemed an age, then she gave the letter back to Kitty. Peering over her spectacles, she murmured, 'I didn't realise how much you loved him. I do now, and I'm very sorry, Kitty. I know how you must feel.'

The letter felt like a ton weight in Kitty's trembling fingers. Carefully folding it, she replaced it into the envelope. 'I'm happy for them, she said. 'Susan's right. Harry always talked about having a family, a son.' She sent her mind back over the years, to the garden they played in as children, where they swung on the apple tree, and Harry pushed her too high and wouldn't stop until she screamed. She recalled the very first kiss they had shared, and the way he had often talked of his future, his dreams and ambitions, and his intention to have a family of his own some day. 'A daughter with your lovely nature,' he said. 'And a son to run with, to play football with, a son who would look to his father for guidance. A son with your shining brown eyes, Kitty,' he had whispered, and her young heart had sung for joy.

All that was gone now. Another woman was carrying Harry's son. Another woman, with hard blue eyes, and a jealous nature. But then she had every reason to be jealous. Harry was a man among men, strong and caring, with a smile that could brighten even the greyest morning.

'Will you write back?' Mildred enquired. There was nothing she could do but just be there. Sometimes life could be so cruel. Here was Kitty who had endured so much, forgiven those who had taken from her, befriending anyone who turned to her, and yet was still denied the happiness she deserved. Then there was herself, a selfish woman who had wronged this lovely girl, driven her own family away and drowned herself in booze and self-pity. If it hadn't been for Kitty ... Oh! She daren't dwell too much on that. Especially now, when she had found Eddie, and happiness, and a whole new life. But she didn't deserve it. Time and again she had told herself that. She did not deserve it. And now Kitty was dealt another blow, a blow that must have cut deep. But Kitty would not let it get her down. She always rose above life's adversities. That was what made her so special.

'Of course I'll write,' Kitty said. 'How could I not congratulate them on their wonderful news?' Even in her despair, a tide of joy swept through her, for Harry's sake, and for that fortunate child who would have him for a father.

'You don't have to be lonely, Kitty.' It was more a heartfelt plea than a statement.

'I'm not lonely,' Kitty lied. 'I've told you before, you're not to worry about me.'

'Jack adores you. Why don't you at least think about a life with him?'

Kitty gave her a warning look. 'You're getting to be as stubborn as him. I won't contemplate a life with Jack because I don't love him. It wouldn't be fair.'

'Love isn't everything.'

Kitty didn't answer straightaway. How could Mildred say that, when for these past months she had found a whole new meaning for living? 'Would you marry Eddie if you didn't love him?' she asked simply.

Mildred's eyes flickered. Unable to look Kitty in the face, she lowered her gaze. 'I have no right to tell you how you should live.'

'Neither has Jack ... or Georgie,' Kitty said softly. 'But it doesn't stop them from trying to run my life either.'

The smile in Kitty's voice made Mildred look up. Relieved that she had been forgiven, she said, 'It's because we love you.'

'I know.' Desperate to change the subject, she observed, 'You've got a good pile of correspondence there. Anything exciting?'

Filtering through the assortment of mail, Mildred drew a letter out. 'Here's the reply from Susan Jenkins ... not coming as she said.' Quickly putting that to one side, she opened another. 'Oh, look! Miss Davis will be coming after all.' They had feared she might still be on her travels.

'That's wonderful!' Kitty declared, her face wreathed in pleasure. 'It'll be lovely seeing her again, and she's bound to have so many stories to tell.'

All in all, there were twenty-two people coming to Mildred's wedding; most of the guests who had attended Kitty's party and a number of Eddie's relatives, none of whom Kitty knew.

Mildred saved the good news until last. 'You'll be pleased to know that Georgie has answered at last, and yes, she's decided to turn up after all.' The card from her was bent at the corners, crinkled and grubby.

Kitty read it and whooped for joy. 'I'll strangle her!' she cried. 'Why hasn't she replied to my letters? Why didn't she let *me* know she was coming to the wedding, instead of just scribbling a card to you?'

Thrilled at Kitty's change of mood, Mildred laughed. 'You should know what she's like by now. I expect she's playing her usual little tricks ... wanting to keep you waiting and then surprise you at the last minute.'

Kitty agreed. 'You're right. That's exactly what she would do.' But now she would see her! Georgie was coming to the wedding after all! Oh, she couldn't wait to talk with her, to catch up on everything, to see for herself that Georgie had come to no harm.

There were tears of joy in her eyes as she told Mildred, 'I was so worried about her. After she moved from Weymouth to Liverpool, she kept shifting about, going from one address to another. Honest to God, I was at my wit's end.'

'Well, you can stop worrying now.' Taking off her spectacles, Mildred gathered the replies and took them to the bureau. 'We'll have to check the seating plan,' she said thoughtfully, tapping a pen against her teeth. 'And don't forget you've got another fitting for your dress.' She would have gone on, but Kitty lured her into the kitchen with the promise of a slice of fruit cake and a mug of tea.

For the next half-hour they sat round the kitchen table, talking mainly about Kitty's new home. 'Do you think you'll be happy there?' Mildred wanted to know.

'It's fairly spacious,' Kitty replied. 'With two bedrooms... useful in case Georgie comes to stay. It overlooks the embankment and it's closer to work. On a nice day I can *walk* to the boatyard, or even in winter if the buses aren't running.'

Mildred recognised the ploy. 'I already know all that,' she chided. 'What I asked was, will you be happy there?'

'I don't see why not.' But she did see why not. She saw she would be alone again. She saw Harry would be miles away, with Susan and their child. As for Georgie, well, even at the best of times Kitty had little idea of where that will o' the wisp might be. Would she be happy? Mildred had asked. Well, all she could do was try, and try she would. Even though her move from this house seemed to be a step back. A step back to another time, when she saw little reason for getting up in the morning.

For the rest of the evening they chatted and laughed, and Kitty suppressed the ache inside. She was glad for Mildred, glad that she had found a man to love, a man who loved her too. And Georgie was coming to the wedding! Georgie! The idea that she and her friend would soon be together again was like a ray of sunshine reaching into a dark place.

For the next few days life was hectic. Jack gave Kitty time off to help her aunt, and Mildred left work two days earlier than planned. There were numerous trips to the dressmaker's, and even more to the many shoeshops in Bedford and Cambridge, where Mildred and Kitty searched far and wide for a pair of shoes that would slide painlessly over Mildred's bunion. 'If I have to stand in that registery office for any length of time, and then stomp about afterwards at the reception, I don't want to be in agony,' She moaned. 'I expect I'll have to dance as well, and there's nothing worse than aching feet when you're being swung round the floor.'

That tickled Kitty. 'You're expecting a lot if you expect Eddie to "swing" you round the floor!' she remarked cheekily.

'There's nothing wrong with a girl living in hope!' Mildred retorted with a wink. When she bent down to fasten her boot-lace, the button on her skirt popped off and went spinning across the room. 'Too many cakes!' Mildred said indignantly, and the pair of them creased up laughing.

The list of things to do seemed endless. There were flowers to arrange, clothes to be got ready, the honeymoon details to be gone over, and so much more that Mildred was afraid they would never be ready on time. On top of that, there were numerous visits to the solicitor who was dealing with the house sale. 'The buyers seem to think they can move in on the day we get married!' Mildred complained. 'When they know very well the completion date is for the Monday after. I can't have them moving their stuff in here when you're trying to move yours out. Besides, you'll need to spend the Sunday here, so you can get the flat properly organised before you move in.' After a particularly harrowing visit to the baker, who had mis-takenly sold her cake but promised to have another ready on time, she threw herself into a chair and seemed close to tears.

'Calm down,' Kitty told her. 'If he says he'll have your cake ready, I'm sure he will. Mr Jackson has his reputation to think of, and you know how highly he values that. Everything will come out right in the end, you'll see.'

Mildred wasn't so sure, but Kitty was right. Come Friday evening, all was in order. Kitty took her out for a drink in the local pub, and they chatted until they were thrown out at closing time. 'I feel a bit merry,' Mildred giggled on the way home.

'Shame on you,' Kitty said. 'I don't reckon Eddie knows what he's letting himself in for!'

The rain started when they were halfway home, falling out of the skies as if God was emptying his bath. By the time they ran up the drive, they were like a pair of drowned rats. 'Where's the key?' Kitty hunched her shoulders while the rain pelted from the guttering and ran down her neck.

'I thought you had it!' Mildred giggled. She fell up the steps and lay flat on her back. 'I'm pissed as a post!' she said, struggling to get up.

Feeling light-headed and happy from the wine, Kitty fumbled in Mildred's pockets. When that didn't produce the key, she searched her own. The key was nowhere to be found. 'It's no good,' she decided in a fit of giggles, 'I'll have to get a ladder from the shed and try the bedroom window.'

'That's no good,' Mildred told her. 'The shed's locked and the key's inside the house.'

'I reckon I'll have to go the police station then,' Kitty suggested. Sitting on the step beside her drunken aunt, who was still flat out on her back, she couldn't help but giggle. 'Do you reckon we should ring the fire brigade?'

'Do what you like, as long as you don't ask that cow next-door for help!' Mildred chuckled. 'She'd be like a dog with two balls if she knew we were locked out.'

Kitty stared at her. 'TAILS!' she corrected. 'A dog with two TAILS ... not a dog with two balls.'

Mildred wasn't altogether convinced. 'He'd still have two balls though, wouldn't he?' she declared indignantly. 'I mean ... he wouldn't be a dog if he didn't have two balls, would he?'

'You're out of your mind,' Kitty said, stemming the tide of laughter rising up inside her. 'Get up from there. Come on.' Sliding her arms under Mildred's prostrate body, she tried unsuccessfully to sit her up. 'Get up, or you'll catch your death of cold!' she demanded.

When Mildred appeared to be trying to help herself, Kitty gave an extra hard tug. Mildred jerked backwards, Kitty fell on top of her, and they both tumbled sideways. Something gave way beneath them and Kitty couldn't believe her eyes. 'It's open!' she cried. 'The front door's open!'

'Well, I'm buggered!' Mildred shrieked, grabbing hold of Kitty. Soaked to the skin and balancing on her knees, Kitty couldn't hold her weight. The pair of them fell in a heap on the mat, and laughed until they cried.

'We're supposed to be ladies!' Kitty announced between bouts of laughter. 'I can hear Jack now ...' Mimicking his voice she said, 'Really, Kitty! This is no way for a lady to behave!'

The next-door neighbour didn't think so either. Woken by the noise she was peeking out from behind her net curtains, horrified to see two grown women rolling about, engulfed in fits of laughter. Flinging open the bedroom window, she yelled into the driving rain, 'SHOWING YOUR KNICKERS! YOU SHOULD BE ASHAMED!'

Kitty was mortified. Somehow she managed to get her aunt inside and close the door. Even harder was the effort to get her up the stairs, stripped off, dried down, put into her nightgown, and then into bed. 'I never knew you had it in you,' she chuckled as she tucked her in. Mildred, though, was sleeping like a light gone out.

The next morning was agony. 'Look at me!' Mildred wailed, staring in the kitchen mirror and putting out her mottled tongue. 'How can I get married looking like this?'

Taking her by the shoulders, Kitty led her back to the table. 'Drink this,' she said, fetching a glass of liver salts. 'And you'll feel like fighting the world.'

Sip by sip, Mildred gingerly downed the entire contents. Taking a moment to recover, she regarded Kitty with some degree of envy. 'You look disgustingly healthy.'

'I don't feel it,' Kitty confessed. In fact she felt as if she'd been put through the mincer.

After several cups of tea, they began to come alive. 'I'm going for a shower,' Kitty said. 'Then we'd best get you looking something like a bride.'

Upstairs she sat by the window, gathering her thoughts. 'A wedding for Mildred ... a baby for Harry.' She smiled wistfully. 'Congratulations, Harry,' she murmured, 'I hope you get the son you want.'

Just for the briefest moment her brown eyes grew bright with the threat of tears. 'Come on, Kitty!' she chided. 'This is not a day for tears.' Then she collected her toiletries and hurried to the bathroom. This was Mildred's day, and nothing must be allowed to spoil it.

Downstairs, Mildred collected the post. There were three congratulations cards, from people she had forgotten to ask; a red electricity bill which had already been paid; two circulars; and a long grubby brown envelope with what looked like tea stains on the top left hand corner. The postmark showed that it had been posted in Liverpool. 'It's from Georgie!' Impatiently tapping her fingers on the kitchen table, Mildred debated as to whether she should show the letter to Kitty. 'I wouldn't be at all surprised if that little minx isn't coming after all,' she muttered. 'And Kitty will be so disappointed.'

Getting up from her chair she paced the room, occasionally glancing at the grubby brown envelope and tutting with disgust. 'It would be just like her to change her mind at the last minute! That one doesn't give a damn about Kitty, or she wouldn't keep turning her life upside down.' With every word her own guilt lay heavy on her mind.

'Well, you can wait until after the wedding!' she decided, dropping the letter into the dresser drawer. 'I won't let you spoil Kitty's day, or mine!'

That done she threw the red bill and circulars into the pedal-bin, and took the congratulations cards to the lounge where she propped them up on the mantelpiece. Coming back to the kitchen, she paused to glance into the hall mirror. 'Buck up, Mildred,' she told her dishevelled image. 'It's your wedding day.'

The next few hours were frantic. When at last they saw the car arrive, it was one last look in the mirror and an undignified rush down the path. 'I'm already late,' Mildred complained.

'Bride's privilege,' Kitty said. The bemused driver smiled at her in the mirror, thinking if he was thirty years younger she wouldn't get out of this car without promising him a date.

The wedding went smoothly. Mildred looked wonderful in her pink two-piece and little feathered hat. Her feet were comfortable too, in a pair of easy-fitting beige shoes with a neat little heel and fancy braiding round the edge.

Kitty looked stunning in a calf-length cream dress with sweetheart neckline and long tapered sleeves. Her dark hair was swept up and tied with a pink ribbon to match Mildred's suit and she carried a smaller version of the bride's bouquet – a simple triangle of rose buds with a whisper of green fern.

The reception was held at a nearby conference centre, and everyone had an enjoyable time. 'I still haven't seen Georgie,' Kitty told Mildred, taking her aside.

'Don't worry,' her aunt urged. 'If she's coming by train, it's possible they're running late, and if she's travelling by car, she could well have got caught up in traffic. She'll be here.' Relieved when she saw Jack coming towards them, she gently chided, 'He's looking for you. Have you been neglecting him again?'

As Kitty turned, Jack planted a kiss on her mouth. 'You look wonderful, darling,' he cooed. 'Star of the show.'

'*Mildred*'s the star of the show,' she reminded him. Jack had the most amazing talent for saying the wrong thing.

'Point taken,' he acknowledged, walking with her to the buffet table. 'Have you been trying to avoid me?'

'What makes you think that?' In fact she hadn't.

'Because every time I turn round you're gone,' he answered peevishly. 'I suppose you're looking for *him*?'

Kitty swung round. 'Looking for who?' Her brown eyes flashed angrily. She knew very well who, he was referring.

'What's his name? Harry Jenkins? Your old sweetheart?' While he spoke his fists were clenched and there was a look of rage on his face.

'You're wrong,' she answered soberly. 'I wasn't looking for Harry. I thought I told you? His wife's expecting a baby and not feeling too good. Otherwise they would have been here.' She had tried so hard not to think about Harry, and now Jack had raised the issue, tainting it with jealousy. 'You don't like him, do you?' she asked pointedly. 'I sensed that from the first.'

Jack's quick smile covered his real feelings. 'If you like him, then so do I,' he lied. In fact he had seen the chemistry between those two and ever since had been eaten with envy. If he got the chance he would gladly cut out the heart of Harry Jenkins.

Kitty told him how she was concerned because Georgie had written to say she would be here. 'And there's no sign of her.'

'Oh, I'm sure she'll turn up,' Jack casually assured her. 'Like a bad penny.'

Time fled by and still Georgie didn't show. Now it was the hour for Mildred and her new husband to leave, and everyone was gathered outside in the thin spring sunshine, waving and laughing as the happy couple climbed into Eddie's newly acquired Ford Capri.

'Good luck!' Kitty yelled as they pulled away. 'Have a wonderful honeymoon.'

'I mean to!' Mildred called back. Then she threw her bouquet out of the window, straight into Kitty's arms.

'I think she's trying to tell us something,' Jack whispered, sliding his arm round her. And Kitty had the most awful feeling he could be right.

As he drove her back to the house, Jack had an idea. 'Why don't we call at the flat? I've got time on my hands, and I can see to those little jobs you wanted done. What was it now? Curtain poles to be fitted, and that new work-top in the kitchen? It shouldn't take more than an hour.'

'It might be a good idea,' Kitty agreed. 'If I wasn't wearing this lovely dress, and you weren't wearing a suit that must have cost the earth.' His suit was a new one, grey silk with straight-cut trousers and a narrow jacket. As always, he cut a dashing figure.

Keeping his eyes glued to the road, he reached behind him to retrieve a pile of clothes from the seat. 'Two sets of overalls,' he said with a little grin. 'One your size, one mine.'

Kitty laughed at his cheek. 'Sorry. It's a good idea, Jack, but the key to the flat is back at the house.'

'You underestimate me.' Dipping into his top pocket, he produced the key. 'Mildred gave it to me. She's worried you won't get the flat finished in time for when the furniture removers arrive at the house.'

Leaning back in the plush leather seat, Kitty shook her head. 'You're a pair of conspirators,' she said, smiling in defeat.

The flat was in a delightful spot. Overlooking Bedford river, it had a panoramic view of the whole embankment. But it was a cold unwelcoming place, with two poky bedrooms, a bathroom you could hardly turn round in, and a lounge so small that Kitty wondered if she would get two chairs in, never mind a settee as well. The kitchen was long and narrow, and smelled of damp. 'You don't have to live here,' Jack reminded her. 'All you have to do is say the word and we'll redecorate my house exactly as you want it.'

Kitty was astonished to find herself actually thinking about the prospect. 'Thank you all the same,' she decided. 'But I'll manage.' The disgruntled expression on his face made her smile.

She opened the door of the flat and the rank odour rose to greet them. 'How can you live here with that awful damp air creeping everywhere?' Jack had no intention of giving up.

'Don't worry about it.' Throwing her overalls into the bedroom, Kitty wagged a finger at him. 'You can change in the sitting room.'

'I mean it, Kitty. Why don't you take time to look for a better place?'

'Where do I stay in the meantime?'

'With me of course.'

'I thought so.' Shaking her head, she told him, 'Anyway, there aren't all that many flats for rent in Bedford. I searched far and wide for this one, and well you know it.' When it seemed he might try again, she gave him her sweetest look. 'Will you stop worrying? By the time I've finished with this place, it'll be a cosy little home.'

In her heart she knew it never could be. However hard you tried, there were some places you could never turn into a home. This miserable flat was one of those. But it was all Kitty could afford, so she was determined to do the best she could.

She had taken off her dress and petticoat and was about to put on the overalls when his touch startled her. 'Why don't you admit I'm right?' he murmured, taking her in his arms. 'You and me, two loners, aching for someone to share our lives with. What's so wrong about us being together, Kitty? What could be worse than being alone? Oh, I know I could have any woman, but I could never be sure it was me they wanted. All they could see would be my wealth ... the way of life I could offer them. I don't want that. It's *you* I love, Kitty. No one else.'

'I couldn't marry you, Jack. It wouldn't be fair.' It was hard for her to say it, but it had to be done. 'I could never love you in the way you want me to.'

His smile fell away. Now they were *both* thinking of Harry, like a steel thread that bound them together; one filled with love in her heart, the other with envy and hatred. 'Love isn't everything,' said Jack.

Kitty smiled. Mildred had said the very same. She was wrong. Jack was wrong. Love *was* everything.

He tilted her face towards him. 'Forget him,' he urged.

Kitty didn't answer. She could never forget Harry. He was engrained in her soul.

'Marry me,' Jack's soft voice murmured in her ear. 'Marry me, Kitty, and I promise ... you will learn to love me.' His

256

hands roved her body, touching her bare flesh, arousing her, arousing himself. 'I want you, Kitty,' he moaned. 'Don't turn me away. Please don't turn me away.' Strong fingers curled behind her back, undoing her bra.

Kitty was only flesh and blood, and she had been without love for so very long. Sensing her response he slid his hand down her panties, through the triangle of hair and into the soft moistness between her thighs. She could feel him hard and strong against her, and God help her, she wanted him too.

He was so gentle. With his arm around her, he eased her to the floor. Baring her breasts he tenderly kissed each one, tantalising the erect nipples with the top of his tongue. When she gasped with pleasure, his mouth covered hers. Her eyes were closed, her whole body trembling with a yearning she could no longer suppress. Tenderly parting her, he thrust himself into her body, moaning when the thrill coursed through him. 'I love you,' he whispered, over and over. 'I love you.'

He was a gentle lover, content to be with her, to be part of her, if only for a short time. While he lay with her he loved her. But it was a shallow love, an emotion that touched nothing deeper than his own selfishness. The plain truth was, Jack was in love with the idea of love. But he was genuine in that he wanted Kitty; wanted to take her for his own, to love and to cherish. He craved a permanence in his life, and the more she said no, the more he needed her.

All too soon the lovemaking was ended. Exhausted and satisfied, he lay over her, his heart racing. 'That was beautiful,' he murmured, nibbling her ear.

Kitty too felt satisfied, but it was not emotional fulfilment, more bodily gratification. This time there was no shame, only regrets. Regrets that when Jack was making love to her, she had been thinking of Harry. And, though she had enjoyed the lovemaking, she knew it was only a substitute for the real thing. It had been pleasurable, that was all. It had not engaged her heart.

This time, though, she didn't turn from him. Instead she happily joined him in work on the flat, fitting the curtain poles and sliding a work surface into place. They didn't talk of love, nor did they speak of marriage. But even as they worked, he was making plans. On the way home he seemed bolder. 'I always knew you loved me.' His hand reached out to touch hers. 'You will marry me now, won't you, Kitty?'

She told him again, 'Nothing's changed, Jack. My feelings are still the same. What happened just now, well . . .' She didn't want to hurt his feelings, but he was so persistent she had little choice. 'It doesn't mean I've decided to marry you.'

Confident that she was stringing him along, he merely smiled, pressed his foot on the accelerator and kept secretly grinning all the way to Mildred's house, 'I'll come in,' he said, clambering out of the car. When she protested that there was no need, he smiled again. 'You might want to rethink your plans.'

'Oh? And what "plans" might they be?'

'All I'm saying is, you might decide not to send your things to the flat after all. You might decide to have them sent to my place.'

It was Kitty's turn to smile. 'I don't think so,' she said. 'In fact, I'd appreciate it if you left me now. I have a great deal to do, and you'd only get under my feet.'

'Suit yourself. But the offer's there. You might as well do it now as later.'

Kitty hated his arrogance. 'Clear off, Jack!' The tone of her voice left him in no doubt that he was pushing her too far.

He shrugged his shoulders. 'Ring me if you need anything.' Still smiling, he pushed his hands into his pockets and turned away, whistling a merry, irritating tune as he went down the path.

'Haven't you forgotten something?' Kitty's voice sailed after him.

'You want me to help after all?'

'No. What I want is to feel safe at night.' Stretching out her hand, she winked at him. 'The key to the flat, please.'

Spinning it through the air, he watched her catch it. 'I forgot I'd put it in my pocket,' he lied, climbing into his car. 'Now don't forget . . . all you have to do is pick up the phone and we can arrange for your things to be brought to my house this afternoon.'

He went away jauntily while Kitty went indoors shaking her head. 'I have to hand it to you, Jack,' she muttered, 'you're as stubborn as a bloody mule!'

Back at Mildred's house, Kitty was preoccupied with thoughts of Georgie. Why hadn't she come? Was she all right? Worried and angry all at the same time, she went straight to the kitchen to make herself a well-deserved cup of tea.

No sooner had she settled at the table than the phone rang. Leaping out of the chair, she ran into the hallway, hoping against hope it might be Georgie. 'It had better not be you, Jack!' she warned.

It wasn't Jack. Nor was it Georgie. It was Mildred. 'We've stopped for a bite to eat,' she explained, 'and I just had to ring you. I've forgotten something, you see.'

Dropping her voice to a whisper, Kitty teased, 'Don't tell me! You've forgotten your knickers?'

Mildred laughed, then she was serious again. 'I've done a dreadful thing and I hope you'll forgive me. A letter came from Georgie and I hid it in the drawer. I guessed she wasn't coming after all, and didn't want you to be upset before the wedding.' In her eagerness to excuse what she'd done, her words tripped over each other. 'I'm sorry, Kitty. I really thought it was for the best.'

'It's all right.' In her deepest heart, Kitty hadn't expected Georgie to turn up at the wedding and she said that to her aunt now. 'So get on with your honeymoon.'

'Wait a minute.' The sound of money being dropped into the phone box halted their conversation, before Mildred asked, 'Read the letter, Kitty. If it's anything serious, I'll never forgive myself.'

'Which drawer did you put it in?'

'The kitchen dresser.'

'Hang on.' She put the phone down and hurried to the dresser. Retrieving the grubby brown envelope she returned to the phone, tore the envelope open and took out the letter. Straightening it with one hand she picked up the receiver with the other. 'You're right,' she confirmed, 'it is from Georgie.' Her anxious eyes scanned the message, and her hands began to shake.

'What does she say?' Mildred's voice pierced Kitty's silence. 'KITTY! WHAT DOES SHE SAY?'

Injecting a measure of humour into her voice, Kitty told her, 'You might have guessed! She and that no-good bloke of hers are back together. Georgie knew you wouldn't welcome him at you wedding, so she decided not to come herself.' Her bright voice belied the truth. 'So there you are. Now you'd better get back to that husband of yours. I'm taking care of everything at this end, so you can relax. Have a lovely time, and I'll see you when you get back.' Mildred would have gone on about Georgie and how sorry she was, but Kitty cut her short. Satisfied, Mildred said her goodbyes and hung up. 'No use spoiling your honeymoon,' Kitty murmured. Taking the letter to the kitchen she spread it out before her on the table, and began to read:

Hello, sunshine,

You're not going to be pleased with me! I can't come to your aunt's wedding after all. I shan't be sending a present either. Not when I can't even afford a loaf of bread!

I've had a few ups and downs lately, but I'll sort it out because I'm a survivor. Just like you.

Talk to you later. Take care of yourself, my beauty.

Love from Georgie

Kitty carefully folded the letter and replaced it in the envelope. There was only one line from that sad little letter that stayed with her. She whispered it now, allowing the meaning of each word to sink in: 'Not when I can't even afford a loaf of bread.' It told a story all its own; not just that Georgie was broke, and that maybe her fella might be in prison again, but something much more important. It told Kitty that Georgie desperately needed her. 'She's a proud stubborn woman,' Kitty murmured thoughtfully. 'Georgie would never have let it slip that she had no food ... unless she was crying for help. And who else would she have to turn to? For whatever reason Mac isn't there.' Kitty deduced that, not so much from what Georgie said, but from what she didn't say.

'God Almighty!' She recalled how long the letter had been hidden in that drawer. 'Precious hours wasted!'

She was angry with Mildred, then tried telling herself it wasn't her aunt's fault. For weeks now, she herself had been planning to go and see Georgie, and each time she had allowed other things to get in the way. 'Well, I'm not wasting any more time!'

she vowed. 'I'm on my way, Georgie gal. I'm on my way.'

While Kitty showered, the phone rang incessantly. When she came into her bedroom to dress and prepare for her long journey, it rang again with the same stubborn insistence. With only a towel to cover her nakedness, and shivering with cold, she impatiently snatched up the receiver. 'Kitty Marsh. Hello.'

Jack's voice made her shiver all the more. 'Just ringing to see if you need any help?'

'Not now, Jack.' She so much wanted to be on her way. Georgie needed her, and there had been enough time wasted already.

'You're sure now?'

'I'm sure.'

'Okay. You're too independent for my good, but talk to me if you need any help getting ready for the removal men.' There was a click as he put down the phone.

'Good God . . . I'd forgotten all about the removal!' She frantically dialled his number. When he answered she was full of apologies. 'I do need your help after all,' she admitted. 'Can you come round?'

He was delighted. 'Just try and keep me away! I'll be there in half an hour.'

'Half an hour,' she told herself, rushing about to get ready before he arrived. Ringing British Rail she checked the timetable and best route for trains to Liverpool. That done, she cleaned her teeth, brushed her hair, put on some make-up, and quickly dressed. 'Warm and comfortable, and easy for a train journey,' she decided. Rummaging in her wardrobe, she settled on a black polo neck jumper, and smart navy slacks. It took only a minute to slip into them, and even less to put on her dark ankle-length boots.

Grabbing a suitcase from the top of the wardrobe, she packed enough clothes and toiletries for at least two nights.

Next, she returned to the kitchen and scribbled out a short note:

Jack,
  I've had a letter from Georgie, and I'm going to see her.
I'm not sure how long I'll be away, but it will probably be
a couple of days. I hope to persuade her to come back, and

help me get settled in my new flat.

I'm sorry it's such short notice, but I didn't know myself until a little while ago.

I'd be really grateful if you could please oversee the removal? You'll find all the details, house keys, phone numbers and times, in the box on the hall table. It's all organised, so there shouldn't be any problems. If there are, I know you can take care of everything.

I'll ring you later.

Thanks,
Kitty

She put the front door key in an envelope with the note, and sealed it.

Pausing by the hall table on her way out, she checked the contents of the box, to make sure everything was there for Jack. Then she checked her handbag, counted the notes in her wallet, and made certain she had her cheque book and the train timetable.

Satisfied, she left the house, propped the envelope containing the note and key on the door knocker, and hurried away before Jack could arrive and offer to take her all the way to Liverpool.

Twenty minutes after he had phoned, Kitty was on her way down the street, dressed against the cold in her long cream-coloured overcoat, with a black woollen beret pulled at a jaunty angle over her dark hair. 'Sorry, Jack!' Catching sight of him at the bottom end of the main street, she quickly ducked into a doorway until he had passed. Running to the taxi rank, she gave her directions to the driver. 'Please hurry or I'll miss the train!'

By the time Jack had arrived at the house and read the note which Kitty had put on the knocker, she was speeding to the station. When, some time later, he burst on to the platform, red-faced and breathless, she was already settled in a compartment, speeding her way to Liverpool; and to her dearest friend, Georgie.

The thought of seeing Georgie again gave her a good feeling. At the same time she was a little afraid, because there had been an undercurrent of fear in her friend's letter.

Kitty couldn't be certain what she would find when she arrived in Liverpool. 'Hold on, gal,' she murmured in Georgie's accent. 'We'll sort it out. You've got my word on it!'

CHAPTER FIFTEEN

Kitty walked out of Liverpool station. Suddenly all her troubles seemed a million miles away. 'Mornin', luv!' A round-faced woman carrying a bairn gave her a friendly smile.

Returning her warm greeting, Kitty went in search of a taxi. There were three waiting. Hurrying to the first in line, she rummaged in her bag to check Georgie's address. 'Number four Albert Street, please,' she said, returning the slip of paper to her purse.

'Two minutes, pet,' the driver said with a grin. Putting out his fag, he took hold of her suitcase. ''Ere, gimme that.' Throwing it in the boot, he remarked cheerfully, 'Been a lovely day. Makes you feel like whistling.'

And that was just what he did, all the way down the High Street and on towards the docks, like a bird after a mate.

Kitty was fascinated by the sights and sounds of Liverpool. It was a bustling place, a piece of history. The Mersey stretched before them and the docks were like another world, a painting in the sunlight, with ships and ferries, people and traffic, alive with the same heartbeat. Kitty had never seen anything quite like it. There was a kind of magic here, a timelessness that made her feel insignificant.

The taxi driver slid his window back to ask. 'Been here before, have you?'

'No, more's the pity.' But she would come again, she was sure of that. 'Which hotel do you recommend?'

'The Albert,' he said without hesitation. 'That one's far and away the best. I know 'em all, lived here all me life,' he said proudly. Pointing to the new development on the left, he said. 'It's all changed now . . . new houses and the like. Nothing stays the same. Before that new development were built, there

265

were a maze of back streets. Everybody knew one another. They raised each other's kids . . . they went in each other's houses as if they were their own. If they had a problem, it were everybody's problem and they solved it together.' Shaking his head, he lapsed into a brief silence, reliving old memories, recalling old friends and loved ones who had gone before and whom he might never see again. 'I were born here,' he said, 'and I'll happily end my days here.'

Kitty could understand his pride. 'What is it that makes Liverpool so special?' she wanted to know.

He laughed at that. 'I suppose you could say it were the Beatles who made Liverpool famous. But it isn't just that, is it, love? Long before the Beatles were even born, Liverpool was a mighty port.' Leaning backwards he asked, 'Did you know we sent thousands of convicts from here? Poor buggers. Some of 'em guilty of no more than stealing a loaf of bread, or getting drunk and brawling on the streets. That were all it took to get sent to the other side of the world in them days. Torn from home and family to God knows what!' He shook his head in disbelief. 'Don't bear thinking about, does it, eh?'

Kitty knew what it was like to be torn from home and family. 'Life can be cruel,' she muttered.

He didn't hear her. Coming up to traffic-lights he cursed when they changed against him. 'I've never yet caught these bloody lights at green!' While they sat waiting for them to change, he told Kitty, 'When you come right down to it, miss, I reckon it's *people* who make or break a place. Doesn't matter whether it's a country village, a new town, or a big old city like Liverpool, it's always the people who make it what it is. Flesh and blood, hearts and minds, that's what really matter.'

The lights changed while he was talking. He didn't notice until a motorist behind sounded his horn and startled him. 'Up yours, mate!' he shouted, jabbing two fingers out the window as he moved off.

Seeing Kitty smiling, he grinned. 'Motorists are different,' he said sheepishly. 'It's war on the road.' Swinging the taxi to the left, he said, 'We're near Albert Street now. What number did you say, love?'

'Number four.'

Twisting slightly in his seat, he looked at her in the mirror.

'Number four, eh?' He was curious. Most of the big old houses in this area had been turned into flats. When he brought folk here they were usually looking for short-term accommodation. Somehow this passenger was different. *Was* she looking for a place or maybe searching for a friend or relative? Or was it something more complicated than that? He prided himself on being able to guess his passengers' intentions, but this one had him puzzled. She was young and friendly, and very lovely, but there was a certain sadness in her face that tugged at his heart-strings. Whatever errand she was on, he hoped it was for the best.

As it turned out, Kitty was in for a terrible shock.

The minute he turned into the street, an ambulance came screaming past. 'Jesus!' Pulling over, he let it go on. 'Somebody's in trouble,' he said, following on. 'Poor sod. I'd rather them than me. I can't stand hospitals . . . the smell and all that.'

Kitty watched the ambulance as it drew up. 'It's stopping in the street,' she remarked. In the back of her mind there was a dreadful suspicion. But no! She mustn't think things like that.

Taking a deep breath she sat back in the seat, counting the house numbers as they went at a steady pace down the street. 'Twenty-six . . . twenty-four . . . twenty-two . . .' She tapped the cab window. 'It's on this side,' she said.

'I can't say for certain, luv,' he muttered in a sombre voice, 'but I reckon that ambulance has stopped outside number four.'

Kitty felt her heart turn over. When they reached the house and she jumped out, the ambulance crew was already racing up the stairs. The neighbours were gathered on the pavement. 'Best stay where you are dear,' warned a kindly old woman with her hair in curlers. 'Them staircases is narrow, and they'll be fetching the lass down any minute. The poor thing's in a bad way, they say.' She shook her head. 'Fellas!' she said bitterly. 'It's allus over some fella or another.'

Kitty hardly dare ask. 'This lass you're talking about . . . who is she? What's her name?' While she waited for the woman to answer she silently prayed: Please don't let it be Georgie. Please don't let it be her. Fear clogged her throat, and she could hardly breathe.

'Oh, I don't live here,' the woman said, 'I live next door but two. The woman in the downstairs flat told me about it.

According to her, the lass in the next flat to hers had a real
set-to with her fella some time back. Anyway, the lass took it
bad, and locked herself in her room. Wouldn't come out for
nobody, not even the social worker.' She lowered her gaze.
''Taint right, it is, eh? Poor little bugger. 'Course, what with me
living next-door but two and keeping myself to myself, I didn't
see all that much of her. Her name is Georgie something, that's
all I know, and now they say she's done away with herself.'

When Kitty almost collapsed, the woman gave her a wary
look. 'Are you all right, dearie?' She saw Kitty's colour drain
away and cursed herself for the tongue she could never control.
'They're coming,' she cried. Gripping Kitty's arm, she tried to
draw her aside. 'Come away, pet. They'll not want us gawping.'

Breaking from her, Kitty ran across the pavement, praying as
she ran that it wasn't Georgie. All her hopes and prayers
counted for nothing when her stricken brown eyes glanced down
on that white familiar face. 'Oh, no. NO!'

'Do you know her, miss?' One of the ambulance crew caught
her as she swayed.

Dazed with fear, Kitty gasped. 'It's my friend Georgie. I have
to go with her.' Following the stretcher into the ambulance, she
sat beside her friend all the way, unable to take her stricken
gaze from the blood-soaked bandages round Georgie's wrists.
As the vehicle sped through the streets, and the initial shock
subsided, Kitty found herself filled with a terrible anger. 'Don't
you die on me, you bugger!' she said; then, in a softer voice, 'I
love you, sweetheart.' To see mischievous, wicked Georgie
trussed up in blood-stained bandages, with tubes attached to
her arms, was more than she could bear. But she *would* bear it.
And she would be strong. For Georgie's sake.

All that night Kitty kept a vigil by her friend's bedside, holding her hand, then pacing the floor, then sitting beside her again
and softly praying. Nurses came in and out, seeing to Georgie,
quietly attending to the drips and exchanging a few words with
Kitty. 'Will she be all right?' was her anxious question. Over
and over again: 'Will she be all right?'

In the morning the doctor told Kitty, 'She's lost a lot of
blood.' When Kitty asked if her friend would pull through all
right, he answered, 'We'll just have to hope that she *wants* to
pull through.' Beyond that he had few words of comfort to offer.

In the afternoon of the next day, Georgie's eyes flickered open. 'Hello, you,' Kitty said, tears flowing down her face as she took hold of Georgie's hand. Georgie appeared to be confused. She stared at Kitty, frowned, and closed her eyes again.

'She'll be fine now,' the doctor said. 'We can all breathe a sigh of relief.' He also warned that Georgie would have to talk with the hospital psychiatrist. 'It's not enough to treat the symptoms in cases like these,' he explained. 'You have to treat the *cause* . . . the reason why she did it in the first place.'

Kitty understood and appreciated that. But she had a lurking suspicion that Georgie was not the kind to discuss her problems with anyone, least of all a hospital psychiatrist.

That night, after booking a room by phone at the Albert Hotel, Kitty slept in the chair beside Georgie's bed. Her every bone was aching and stiff, when she was woken by a soft giggle. 'You'd best get in beside me, you silly sod.'

Opening her eyes, she saw Georgie leaning over the edge of the bed, arms outstretched as she tried to touch her, and the faintest of smiles on her face. Kitty got out of the chair. 'Oh! Georgie! Georgie!' With tears streaming down her face, she slid her arms round her best friend and hugged her. For the longest five minutes of her life, Kitty held her close. 'I love you,' she kept saying. 'I love you.' They clung to each other and sobbed, and Kitty gave up a silent prayer of thanks.

Later, though Kitty realised the danger was far from over. Georgie refused to talk to the doctor about her problems. 'I don't need no shrink,' she said, and so for the time being they left her alone. Kitty, however, did not. 'If you won't talk to the doctor, then you can talk to me,' she urged. 'What made you do it, Georgie? Why didn't you turn to me? You know I would do anything for you.' She would never forget how Georgie took care of her when she was frightened and alone.

Georgie looked at her for a long moment, until at last she murmured, 'I'm sorry, kid. I didn't mean to hurt you.'

Kitty stroked her hand. 'It doesn't matter about me,' she answered. 'What matters is you. I want to help if I can . . . if you'll let me?' She feared Georgie might shut her out just as she had shut out the doctor.

Smiling, Georgie shook her head. 'You can't help,' she murmured. 'No one can help.'

'You're wrong, Georgie.'

'I don't think so.'

'Was it Mac? I knew he'd left you. But he's left you before and you've got over it.' She wished to God Georgie had never met him. He had brought nothing but trouble to her.

'He ain't just left *me* this time.'

'What do you mean?'

Georgie threw back the bedclothes and pointed to her stomach. '*That's* what I mean,' she laughed. 'He's put me up the bloody pole!'

At first, Kitty didn't know what to say. It was worse than she had feared.

'It should be you and Harry having this baby,' Georgie said. 'The poor little bugger would have had a good home then. What will it have with me, eh?' Bitterness crept into her voice. 'For weeks after Mac left I was like a lost soul. There were plenty of times when I wanted to end it all, but I didn't have the courage.' She laughed cynically. 'They cut off the gas, so I couldn't even put my head in the oven. I was flat busted broke. I hadn't had a proper meal in ages, I couldn't sleep, and every morning I was bringing my heart up in the lavatory.' She paused, her eyes glazing over as she went into a kind of trance, reliving the long days and nights when she was all alone.

Kitty squeezed her hand. 'Go on,' she urged, 'I want you to tell me everything.'

'You know how it is, Kitty. You've been through it,' she said. 'The loneliness and the fear. No one to care or hold you close just when you need it. Waking at night in a sweat and wondering how it will all end.' Her mouth smiled, but her eyes remained dull and serious. 'I even thought about going on the game,' she confessed shyly. 'I still have my looks, I reckon, and this bump wasn't so big. Anyway some men prefer making love to a pregnant woman, so I could probably earn a fair living.' She sighed and bowed her head. 'In the end, though, I couldn't do it. It wouldn't feel right with Mac's baby growing inside me. The truth is, I honestly believed the kid and me would both be better off if I ended it all.'

Kitty had little sympathy with that. 'You've no right to speak for the baby,' she reminded her softly.

'I know that now.'

'I want you to come back with me.'

'What?' Georgie's eyes lit up.

'After the honeymoon Mildred and Eddie are going to live at his place. The house has been sold and I've got a little place of my own along the embankment. I want you to come and live with me, Georgie. We'll work it out together, you and me ... like we always have.' The flat wasn't really big enough for the two of them, but it would be great having Georgie around.

She, however, wasn't so enthusiastic. 'Let me think about it.'

'It's Mac, isn't it? Don't you think he's done you enough harm?'

'Maybe. But what if he comes back and finds me gone? God knows what he'd do without me.'

'He'll do what he's done before. Mac's a survivor. He'll manage. Anyway, if your suicide attempt had been successful, he *would* have come back and found you gone. He'd have had to manage then all right, wouldn't he?'

'You're angry and I can't blame you ...'

'Too right I'm angry! Do you really expect me to let you go back to that awful little bedsitter ... to let the same thing happen all over again? What if Mac never comes back?' In her heart Kitty believed they had seen the last of that little worm.

'Do you really want to help?' Georgie had problems she did not want Kitty to know about.

'Any way I can.'

'Then go home. Please.' If Kitty should find out what trouble she was really in, Georgie knew there would be no stopping her.

'I can't do that, and you know it.' Kitty was puzzled. It wasn't like Georgie to send her away. 'There's more to this business than meets the eye,' she decided. 'And I'm not going anywhere until you've told me the truth.' Folding her arms, she sat back in the chair with a determined air. 'All of it, mind.'

Realising she had little option, and knowing Kitty's stubborn nature, Georgie decided to tell the truth. 'The day before they brought me in here, the landlord gave me a week's notice, so on top of everything else I ain't got no home to go back to.' When she saw Kitty about to interrupt, she said firmly, 'It's no use your arguing I can come back and live with you because I don't want to. No offence, kid, but I have to hang about these parts. For Mac, you understand.'

'No, I don't understand,' Kitty told her. 'I think you're a fool

271

and I wouldn't be a friend if I didn't tell you so.' She felt there was something else. She saw it in Georgie's eyes, and in the way she kept clenching her fists together, as though she was deeply agitated. 'You still haven't told me everything, have you?' she said pointedly.

Georgie took a deep breath. She didn't want to involve Kitty in such a bad thing, but there was no one else, and she desperately needed advice. 'Before he ran off, Mac was in big trouble with a moneylender.' She paused, ashamed and unwilling to reveal the extent of his stupidity. Now, though, she had another reason for telling Kitty. 'It wasn't all Mac's fault. We both spent the money . . . cars, gambling and having a good time. Night after night Mac would come home from the bookies, his pockets stuffed with money, and it would be great. We took out a mortgage on a posh house near the centre. We filled it with the best furniture money could buy. Oh, Kitty, it was like every dream I ever had was coming true.' She smiled and her whole face lit up. 'He's not bad, you know. Not really.'

'What happened, Georgie?' Kitty was not interested in hearing about how wonderful Mac was.

Georgie shrugged her shoulders. 'It all started to go wrong, that's what happened,' she answered bitterly. 'Mac got drunk one night and smashed up the car. I found out later it wasn't even insured. When I tackled him about it, he flew into a rage, told me to mind my own bloody business, and if I didn't like the way things were I could get out.'

She laughed. 'But we kissed and made up. We fought like cat and dog, but we *always* kissed and made up. That was half the fun of having a row in the first place.' Her smile slipped into a deep frown. 'I'm sure you can guess the rest, kid. He got into really heavy gambling, said he was going to put things right. It just got worse. We began to lose everything . . . the furniture went a piece at a time. I begged him to stop but he wouldn't. Men started coming to the house, playing cards till all hours of the morning. They got drunk and there were terrible fights. The police warned him time and again, but he wouldn't listen. They put him away for a time.'

Her hands trembled as she went on, 'I thought . . . when he came out, if he knew about the baby . . . things would be different. But he couldn't handle it. The moneylender was on his

272

back every minute and he was going crazy.' She paused to steady herself. 'Mac did a runner. The bank snatched the house back, and the moneylenders decided to give me a rough time.' She gave a kind of snigger, her eyes wide and frightened as she told Kitty, 'Ten thousand quid! That's what they said he owed, and they didn't care whether they got it from me or him. As he was nowhere to be found, they gave me two months to clear the debt.' This time she laughed out loud. 'TEN THOUSAND QUID! I ask you? Where in God's name was I supposed to lay my hands on that kind of money?'

Kitty was appalled. 'These men. Where can I find them?'

Georgie took one look at her face and her mouth fell open in horror. 'Oh no!' She put up her hands as though to push away the very idea. 'If you're thinking of talking to them mad buggers, you'd better forget it. I'm not letting you anywhere near them. What! They'd cut your throat soon as look at you.'

No amount of persuasion on Kitty's part would make her change her mind. 'I'll deal with them,' she promised, though how she didn't know.

Kitty wisely made no more mention of it. There would be time enough to find out who had been harassing Georgie. For now, the most important thing was to get her better. 'When you're able, I want you to stay with me at a hotel,' she told her. 'If you won't come south with me, and you've been thrown out of your bedsitter, we'll have to find you a place to live.'

'I'm a bloody nuisance, ain't I?'

'Tell me something new.' Kitty's smile was mischievous. Secretly she was delighted that Georgie was beginning to sound more like her old self.

'You little cow!' Georgie chuckled. 'You're not meant to agree with me.' She could see Kitty was still waiting for an answer. 'All right then. I'll come and stay with you at a hotel, but only for a few days. To be honest, it will be good having you to talk to, though I can't promise not to bounce all my problems off you.'

'I'd be disappointed if you didn't.' She had no intention of leaving Liverpool until Georgie was well and truly settled in a new place, and wanted to be certain that the moneylenders were off her back for good. How on earth she was going to achieve that she still couldn't see. But she would do it somehow, God

273

willing. One way or another she would find them and be rid of them once and for all.

In fact it was the moneylenders who found her.

Satisfied that Georgie was sleeping, Kitty sought out the nurse. 'When she wakes, could you please tell her I'll be back first thing in the morning.' The nurse promised she would and Kitty left. She was looking forward to a good night's sleep herself. Since the day she'd arrived in Liverpool and Georgie was rushed to hospital, she had not slept more than a few hours at a time, and now it was beginning to tell on her. She felt bone weary and emotionally drained. 'Thank God I arrived in time,' she muttered as she came out of the hospital and into a dimly lit street. 'Georgie's safe and that's all that matters.' If Georgie had killed herself, part of Kitty would have gone with her.

As she rounded the corner, she heard a sound behind her. Turning, she peered along the street. In the distance she could see the brightly lit hospital building. Beyond that was darkness, and an eerie silence. She walked on, but her every sense was alert. Convinced she was being followed, she paused to look round once more.

It was then that he grabbed her, one arm round her throat, the other across her mouth preventing her from crying out. With a quick, rough movement he spun her round and slammed her against the wall. Moving his arm from her throat, he wrapped his thick fingers round her neck and pinned her fast.

'That one in the hospital . . . what's she to you?' he grunted, his big pock-marked face grinning at her. 'Your sister, is she?' Each time he spoke he jabbed at her throat, making it impossible for her to speak. She was terrified, but burning with rage that he should have caught her unawares like that, treating her as though she was dirt beneath his feet. She felt the urge to wipe that grin off his face, but he was big and powerful and she was at his mercy.

'She owes my boss a lot of money,' he whispered, leaning forward until his face was almost touching hers. 'I'm going to uncover your mouth, then I want you to tell me when he can expect his money back.' Before relaxing his hold, he warned in a sinister tone, 'Scream out and I won't think twice about breaking your pretty little neck.'

Kitty knew he meant every word. She also realised why

Georgie had been desperate enough to try and end her life. This scum, and possibly others like him, had driven her to it.

Taking a moment to recover from the shock, and rubbing her throat with the palm of her hand, she never took her eyes off his grinning face. All fear left her. Blind anger coursed through her as she thought of Georgie. 'You bastards! She nearly killed herself because of you.'

'Now that would have been a real pity, because she and her bloke had that money in good faith and we want it back. So far we haven't found the bloke, but then why should we when we still have her? You see, the boss ain't particular who pays it back, so long as it gets done.'

'How do you expect to get your money from her, when she's flat broke? Mac didn't just run out on you, he ran out on Georgie as well. You must know she's been thrown out of her bedsitter for not paying the rent? And if she can't pay her rent, what makes you think she can pay you ten thousand pounds, for God's sake? Haven't you got the sense to see you can't get blood out of a stone?'

He seemed pleased. 'You know all about it then? But you're a bit behind the times, lady. You see, it *was* ten thousand pounds. With interest it's now more like twelve, and every day the boss is made to wait, it goes up. As for getting blood out of a stone, if she can't pay in money, she'll pay in kind.'

'What's that supposed to mean?' The threat was evident.

His eyes narrowed. 'You seem like an intelligent woman. Work it out for yourself.'

'I want to speak with your boss.' Maybe he could be made to see sense.

'Sorry.' He let her go then. '*I* speak for him, and this is what he says . . . twelve thousand pounds, in cash, by Friday night.'

'Or?'

'Lending money is perfectly legal. We always get our borrowers to sign on the dotted line, so don't waste time going to the police.'

'But it was Mac's debt. You can't hold anyone else responsible for it.' Kitty was clutching at straws.

'I can see she didn't tell you everything!' He stepped back 'Twelve thousand in cash. Eight o'clock Friday night, your hotel foyer.'

Kitty was astounded. 'You mean you know where I'm staying?'

'I know everything. It's what I get paid for.' With that he strode away, disappearing into the night like a phantom.

It took a moment for Kitty to compose herself. What did he mean... 'I can see she didn't tell you everything'? First thing in the morning she would gently tackle Georgie, but she would keep this sordid little incident to herself. There was nothing to be gained from telling Georgie about it.

Back at the hotel, she carefully dropped a remark as she collected her keys from the clerk. 'The taxi driver's just been telling me how he was threatened by a moneylender,' she said casually. 'I told him he should have gone to the police.'

'Wouldn't have done any good, I'm afraid,' came the quiet reply. 'Ruthless moneylenders are a plague on any city, but they always manage to stay on the right side of the law.'

The clerk confirmed what Kitty had already been told. Disillusioned, she went to her room and sat on the bed for a long time, deep in thought, frantically wondering how she could get Georgie out of this awful mess. 'You bugger, Mac!' she sighed. 'If you were here now I'd cheerfully wring your neck.'

She had no way of laying her hands on the kind of money that was involved. There was only one person she could think of, and that was Jack. 'I'll ask Jack to lend me the money,' she decided, picking up the phone. 'He can take it back out of my salary.' She actually chuckled, 'I might still be working for him when I'm old and grey, but it'll be worth it, just to give Georgie peace of mind.' Herself too, because she couldn't go from here without knowing her friend was free of debt. Mac had left her many times before and she had coped. She would cope with that, but moneylenders were a different kind of trouble.

While she waited for Jack to answer the phone, she began talking to herself. 'Friday, eh? I don't trust him. I've got to make certain he can't threaten Georgie ever again... got to be sure...' A voice at the other end of the phone interrupted her. Relief swept through her at the sound of Jack's voice. 'Hello, Jack?'

'Kitty! I've been worried out of my mind. You didn't even tell me where you'd be staying, or how I might contact you. I've been worried sick! What made you hurry away like that? I would have taken you to see your friend, you know that. Where are you? What have you been doing? When are you coming home?' He would have gone on and on, but Kitty intervened.

'I'm sorry, Jack, but listen. I need your help.' She went on to explain everything. Keeping nothing back, she told him the whole truth, about the money Mac had borrowed, the gambling and the debts. She explained how the moneylender was within his rights to demand the debt cleared with interest, and that she suspected Georgie had signed the papers: 'Or how could they have come after her for the money?'

'Good God! What kind of people have they been mixing with? Has she talked to the police? Stay out of it, Kitty. I don't want you involved in this sort of thing.'

'Credit me with some intelligence, Jack.'

'What exactly is it you want from me?'

'Twelve thousand pounds. I'll pay you back every penny, you know that, even if it takes years.'

The silence at the other end was devastating. It seemed to last for hours, when in fact it was only a minute before his agreement made her sag with relief. 'Of course you can have the money,' he said. 'You know I can't deny you anything.'

When she needed him he was always there. It was a comforting thought. 'You'll never know how grateful I am, Jack.'

'Grateful enough to marry me?'

At first she thought it was a teasing remark, so she answered in kind, 'One day, maybe.'

'No. Not "one day", Kitty. Now. One month from Saturday.' Something about the tone of his voice and the way he seemed to wait for an answer put her on guard.

'Are you saying you'll lend me the money, but only if I marry you?' It was incredible.

'That's what I'm saying, Kitty. Except, of course, I won't be lending you the money. I couldn't ask my wife to pay back a loan, now could I?'

He was being arrogant and she hated him for it. 'I'm sorry,' she apologised, 'I had no right to involve you.'

'The money's here if you want it, Kitty. So am I. Remember, I love you.'

Stunned by what she considered to be blackmail, she put the phone down. 'I don't know who's worse, you or the moneylender,' she muttered. Now she didn't know how to help Georgie. Who else could she turn to? What about Harry? 'Harry would know what to do,' she murmured, and his name on her lips brought the warm excited feeling it always did.

She couldn't get Harry out of her mind. His business was doing well, and she knew if he had the money he would not hesitate to lend it to her. 'How can I ask him though,' she wondered aloud. 'It isn't easy building up a business, and that wife of his would probably give him hell if she thought he'd helped me.' But it wasn't just that. The thought of seeing Harry again, talking to him, having his dark eyes looking into hers, was more than she could bear. 'Don't rake over old coals,' she told herself firmly. 'Harry isn't yours any more. He never will be.' Of all the tragedy in her life, of all the loss and the loneliness, of all the fear and the pain, losing him was the one thing she could not come to terms with, and the hardest thing of all was that it had been her own fault.

Not knowing which way to turn, she let her heart dwell on Harry. How she loved him still! How she longed for him to hold her. How she envied his wife . . . lying in his strong arms at night, seeing his face over the breakfast table, exchanging the usual chit-chat a married couple might share; the laughter and secrets; holding hands; intimate little looks that no one else could perceive; the awful loneliness when they were separated, and the joy when they were together again. How she yearned for all of that. Not with Jack but with Harry. Her first and last love.

Lying on the bed, she let the memories wash over her. For a while she was happy, with Harry.

Exhausted, she fell asleep. When she woke it was pitch black in the room, and for a moment she was startled. Then she heard the rumbling of traffic outside, the wail of a police siren and the laughter from a group of people beneath her window. 'You'll soon be jumping at your own shadow,' she chided herself.

Even so, she could not altogether rid herself of the awful feeling that she was in danger; not because of Georgie or Mac, and not even because of the moneylenders. In their own way each had put her through the wringer. She was strong enough to cope with all of that. But Jack! It was Jack who had stabbed her in the heart. Jack who had put an impossible price on friendship. Jack who had shocked her to her very roots, and was demanding to own the rest of her life. That was why she felt threatened. In danger of losing the only thing she possessed: herself. She had turned to him because he was the only one who could help her, and now he wanted her very soul in exchange.

She undressed, and bathed, then put on her nightgown and went to the window where she drew back the curtains and gazed into the night. The skyline of Liverpool was an imposing sight: tall thin church-spires reaching to heaven; steep tiled roofs and towering multi-storey office blocks and flats; the old and the new mingling perfectly, making a jagged pattern across a dark cloudless sky.

'So this is Liverpool.' She smiled with a strange kind of contentment. 'You're very beautiful,' she breathed and, for a moment, wondered about all the people down there. People with worries; people filled with hatred and love; lonely people; others struggling to cope with extended families. Families. That was what life was all about. 'Isn't that what you want, Kitty? To have a family of your very own?'

She thought about her conversation with Jack. He had given her no choice. 'Would it be so bad?' she asked herself. 'You can't have Harry, and you desperately need children of your own. For all his faults, Jack will make a good father. Tell him yes, Kitty. Let him take care of you. Georgie will be out of trouble and you'll have a real home. Tell him yes. What difference does it make now?' None at all, she decided. Being married to Jack would not greatly enhance her life, it was true. But then, it would not altogether destroy it either.

However, she decided he could suffer a little for his devious ways. 'Make him wait,' she told herself. And the idea gave her a certain satisfaction.

The next morning, after a good night's sleep, Kitty came into the dining room and ordered a hearty cooked breakfast – two sausages, a slice of crispy bacon, one egg and two pieces of fried bread.

'Disgustingly delicious,' she muttered as it was set before her.

When every scrap of that was eaten, she drank two cups of coffee and left a pound for the waitress. As she walked towards the telephone in the foyer, she chuckled at the size of the breakfast she had just enjoyed. 'The prisoner ate a hearty meal,' she chuckled, trying to convince herself that it wouldn't be as bad as she feared, being Jack's 'prisoner'.

He was thrilled. 'We'll be happy, you'll see,' he cried over the phone. 'You always knew it was only a matter of time before we tied the knot.'

'Yes, round my neck,' she answered under her breath.

'I've got an important buyer coming in tomorrow, but I'll have time enough to go to the bank and make the necessary arrangements for the money. I'll see you Friday morning, darling.'

'Thank you.' Kitty's voice was cold; so was her heart.

'Take care of yourself. Remember, I love you.'

She put the phone down. 'I'll never forgive you, Jack,' she muttered harshly. But she was grateful for the money. Grateful that she could help Georgie.

There was always a price to pay in this life, Kitty thought as she made her way to the hospital. The trouble was, she seemed always to be paying.

Georgie couldn't believe her ears. 'Jack's settling the debt! Oh Kitty! You can't know what a weight you've taken off my shoulders.' She cried with relief, and after that she went from strength to strength.

The following morning, she was released into Kitty's care and a room was arranged for her at the hotel. Kitty took her out for the best meal she had ever had, and afterwards they talked until the early hours. 'How can I pay him back?' Georgie wanted to know.

'Don't worry about it,' Kitty told her. 'It isn't a loan, it's a gift.' My gift to you, she thought, and the realisation was bitter-sweet.

Georgie asked about Mildred's wedding, and Kitty gave her every detail. 'I wish I could have been there,' Georgie sighed. 'Only, well you know why I couldn't.' They were quiet for a time then she asked, 'What about Harry?'

Taken unawares, Kitty couldn't hide the love she felt for that man. 'What about him?' she asked innocently.

'Oh, come off it, Kitty Marsh!' Georgie tormented.'You know very well what I mean. You told me in your letter that your aunt had asked him to the wedding. Did he come? What did you say to each other? Is he still as handsome as ever? I want to know everything.'

In answer to her questions, Kitty told her, 'No, Harry couldn't come to the wedding but he came to my party, and yes, he's every bit as handsome as ever. We didn't get the chance to talk much. His wife wanted to leave early. It was a long drive home so they left before everyone else.'

'Long drive?' Where does Harry live?

'I thought I told you that in my letter?'

'You probably did, but you know what a memory I've got, so tell me again.'

'Blackburn. Harry and his wife live in Blackburn.'

Georgie's eyes screwed up in concentration. 'Hmm! Not too far from here then?'

'Not too far.' Though it might as well be the other end of the world, Kitty thought.

'What's his wife like? Not as pretty as you, I'll bet.'

'She's very attractive.'

'Harry doesn't love her.'

'Why do you say that?'

'How can he love her when he loves you?'

'You couldn't be more wrong, Georgie. Harry and his wife are very happy together. Susan's expecting their first baby.'

'He'll probably adore the baby 'cause he's as daft about kids as you are. But he doesn't love his wife.'

Kitty thought it was time to change the subject. 'It's late. You should be in bed,' she told her. 'You won't come back to the south with me, so we're going to be busy tomorrow. We've got to find you a decent place to live.' She ran her fingers through the newspaper cuttings on the table. 'There's all these to check out, and more besides, if none of these are suitable.'

Picking up one of the cuttings, Georgie skimmed through it. 'I've already told you, these places are too expensive, *and* they want three months' rent in advance.'

Kitty was adamant. 'And I've already told you . . . leave it to me.' Rising from her chair, she rounded the table and kissed Georgie on the cheek. 'Now get off to bed.'

When Georgie had gone to her own room, Kitty glanced once more through the cuttings. 'You're right,' she admitted, 'they are expensive, but I don't intend leaving you in some dirty old doss-house.'

Kitty slept well that night. She had come to terms with the idea of marrying Jack, and had seen Georgie blossom since learning the debt was to be paid – though Kitty made certain she didn't know Jack's terms for being so 'generous'. Georgie would likely refuse his help. Kitty had no intention of letting that happen.

Georgie wanted a great deal of waking. 'Leave me be,' she groaned when Kitty shook her awake. 'It's been ages since I've slept in such a comfortable bed.'

'Sorry, kid,' Kitty chuckled, stripping the clothes off her. 'We've a lot to do this morning. You can have a lie in tomorrow.'

Sliding out of bed, Georgie moaned and complained. She grumbled while she washed and dressed, and all the way down to the dining room. She pulled a miserable face all through breakfast, and was still complaining when they came out into the street. By the time they boarded the bus for the first address, she was in a better mood. 'Sorry, but I'm a miserable old cow first thing in the morning,' she told Kitty.

'Yes, I had noticed,' Kitty replied with a sideways grin. In fact, she remembered Georgie's impossible moods from their days in the children's home. Somehow they only made her love her all the more.

The first address was a basement flat on Viaduct Street. It was down a set of narrow dark stairs and the windows were so filthy the daylight couldn't get through. 'It's like a bleedin' prison!' declared Georgie. Kitty gave the landlord a ticking off for his misleading advert and they set off once more; this time to Maudsley Street, where the advert described: 'a very desirable second-floor flat, with all mod cons and a wonderful river view.'

As it turned out, the 'mod cons' was a bathroom shared by all six residents in the house. The 'river view' was a glimpse of the Mersey in the far distance, and a closer one of a dirty little brook that ran into the back yard and which, according to the woman in the ground-floor flat, 'Brings the rats into the yard with every downpour.'

'Jesus Christ! At this rate I'd rather sleep on a bench in the park,' Georgie said. Kitty told her to be patient and marched her off to the bus stop where they quickly boarded a number 10 and headed for the next viewing in Market Square. 'It's probably a space under one of the fruit barrers,' Georgie said, disgruntled. But Kitty could see the funny side of it all. When she smiled at the comment, Georgie smiled back, and soon they were giggling. It was so good to feel close again, to share each other's up and downs.

By the time they got off the bus at Market Square, the sun was bright and strong in a surprisingly blue sky. 'Good job it ain't pissing down!' Georgie muttered. 'Flat hunting's a bugger when it's pissing down.' A slim attractive woman going into the newsagent's gave the two of them a look of disgust.

'Such language!' she hissed, glaring at Georgie in particular.

Kitty quietly reprimanded Georgie. 'Behave yourself,' she warned. 'This might be the place we're looking for, and that woman could well turn out to be one of your neighbours. It would be a pity if you started off on the wrong foot.'

Georgie was suitably humble. 'You're right,' she admitted. 'Me mouth allus was bigger than me brain.'

Checking the address, Kitty realised it was the very newsagent's that the woman had gone into. 'Let's hope she isn't the landlady,' she remarked, leading Georgie into the shop.

Thankfully, as they went in the woman came out, giving Georgie the same shrivelling look. 'Miserable old cow!' Georgie muttered, giving a little cry when she got a good hard dig in the ribs from Kitty.

The owner of the shop was a little man with a warm homely smile. 'What can I do for you?' he enquired, pushing his rimless spectacles back on to his fat little nose. 'You're new to these parts, aren't you? I know everybody who comes in this shop, but I've never clapped eyes on you two before. Come to live round 'ere, have you?'

Kitty handed him the cutting. 'My friend here is looking for a place to live. We've come to see the flat you've advertised.'

He peered over his spectacles at Georgie. 'You're expecting, aren't you?'

'Well, ain't you the nosy bugger.' Her grin widened. 'I won't give you no trouble, matey, and neither will the young 'un if I'm living here when it arrives.'

His smile showed he had taken a liking to her. He looked at Kitty, and thought they seemed a decent pair of young women, though he had a sneaking suspicion that Georgie was likely to be trouble. 'Were you the one who was swearing just now?' he asked her. 'Mrs Jolly came in here in a right state . . . she said there was a young woman outside with a tongue like a sewer rat's.'

Georgie liked him, and she said so. 'And I've a feeling I'd like to live on this street. I think the two of us could get on all right, but I'd be a liar if I said a wrong word never passed my lips. You see, I've been a rough 'un, and I've run with rough 'uns. I'm no angel and never could be.'

Kitty was proud of her. 'She's all right,' she told the shop-keeper, 'and don't let her tell you any different.'

He looked from one to the other until his gaze rested on Kitty for a full minute. 'I reckon you're *both* all right,' he said, smiling. Reaching beneath the counter, he handed the key to Kitty. 'Through there.' He pointed to a side door. 'You'll see the stairs leading up to the living quarters. Since the missus brought her mother to live with us, we've outgrown the space up there. I've bought a house two doors down from here and to tell you the truth, I did want a man to take on the flat . . . security and all that.' He gave Georgie another long scrutinising look. 'But I reckon a woman as swears like you do, would be just as good as any man in an emergency.' He laughed out loud when Georgie promised if anyone tried to break into his shop, she'd have the whole street out in minutes.

'Why, it's lovely!' Kitty was amazed.

The shop was poky and dingy. But up here it was spacious and light. At the front where the living room was, the sun poured in through two long windows, each dressed with the prettiest floral curtains. The kitchen was surprisingly large, with a breakfast area at one end and a range of new pine units fitted round three walls; there was a round pine table with four ladder-back chairs and a wide shallow window that stretched almost the whole length of one wall. 'I could live here all right,' Georgie exclaimed, running from room to room.

There was one large, tastefully furnished bedroom, and a small bathroom, tiled from top to bottom in soft grey tiles, with a carpet to match. 'I could live here myself,' Kitty declared. 'It's like something out of a magazine.'

The shopkeeper was delighted. 'My wife is the one with the taste,' he said. 'Give me an old sofa and a pair of slippers and I'm happy as Larry.'

'Will I meet her?' Georgie asked.

He grinned from ear to ear. 'I reckon you've already met her, ain't yer? She's the one who said you had a tongue like a sewer rat.'

When he saw their faces fall, he assured them. 'She don't often make her way here, and even if she did, I'm the one in charge of letting the flat, and I say if you want it, it's yours. Pay three months in advance and you can move in whenever you like.'

Terms were discussed and Kitty got out her cheque book. 'We'll pay *six* months in advance if that's all right,' she said. At the back of her mind was the idea that it might take all of six months for Georgie to get herself organised. Meanwhile Kitty didn't want her to feel that if she hadn't secured a job and the money to carry on with the rent, she might be thrown out on the streets again.

'You ain't got a job going, have you?' Georgie asked the shopkeeper, 'I'm good on the till, and I don't mind getting up early of a morning to see to the paper round.'

'As a matter of fact, I just might be able to put a few early-morning hours your way,' he answered, 'but the pay ain't much. The shop isn't a goldmine and, thanks to the missus, I've got a new mortgage round my neck.'

Georgie was thrilled. 'It's a start,' she told Kitty. 'That's all I need, a start.'

For the next two hours they traipsed the shops, buying towels and linen and anything Georgie might need in her new home. 'I can't believe it.' Georgie gave Kitty a big grateful squeeze. 'What did I do to deserve a friend like you, eh?'

'It works both ways,' Kitty reminded her as they went to have a scone and tea at a corner cafe. For a while she was deep in thought. They had found Georgie a place to stay, but there was still the moneylender to deal with and she would be on pins until Jack turned up. What if he should change his mind? After all, twelve thousand pounds was a small fortune.

Friday morning came, and so did Jack. Tired and irritated after his long drive, he swept into the foyer and thumped his fist on the desk. 'Mr Jack Harpur for Kitty Marsh. Let her know I'm here,' he instructed, and the clerk took an instant dislike to him.

The three of them sat in the lounge, Jack stretched out in a big soft armchair, Kitty seated next to him on the edge of a settee, and Georgie next to her, nervous and anxious. 'I'm sorry to be such a burden,' she told him. 'It's reallly good of you to let me have the money, but it's only a matter of time before I pay you back, I promise.'

Jack gave her a frosty look. 'Best not to make promises you can't keep,' he said. 'But no matter, because I'm really doing this for Kitty, so I don't want the money back.' He looked at Kitty as much as to say, 'I'm having her instead'. But he merely smiled and touched her hand; his smile fading when Kitty visibly cringed. The incident did not go unnoticed by Georgie.

While they chatted, the morning sped by. Jack treated them to lunch in the main dining room. Georgie ate heartily and Jack too had a healthy appetite, but Kitty merely picked at her food. She had other things on her mind. Soon she would be standing before God making her promises to a man she could never love. Yet she would do it, because she had given her word, and Jack had kept his.

In the afternoon, Jack went to the bank, and Kitty took Georgie round the shops again. 'You need some new clothes,' she said. And she needed to put a distance between her and Jack, at least for the time being.

At five minutes to eight Kitty and Jack made their way down to the foyer. Georgie wanted to accompany them, but Kitty asked her not to. 'There's no need for you to face him,' she said. 'Let me and Jack deal with it.' Georgie knew it made sense.

The moneylender was already waiting as they came into the foyer. Addressing Kitty, he demanded, 'Got the money, have you?'

Jack moved forward and took the fellow by the lapels. 'Watch your mouth, you creepy bastard!' he hissed, pushing him backwards until he fell into an armchair. 'The money's here.' He raised the briefcase. 'But first, I want any papers that were signed.'

The man sneered. 'I've got them here.' He patted his breast pocket. 'We're not criminals, you know ... just honest blokes trying to make a living.'

Kitty spoke calmly, though she could easily have hit out at him. 'Whether you're a criminal or not is a matter for discussion,' she said. Turning to Jack she said, 'Wait a minute. Don't hand anything over just yet.' As she walked away she heard the fellow complaining about how he hadn't got time to waste 'buggering about'.

When Kitty returned with the hotel manager, Jack was

puzzled. The moneylender guessed her intention. 'No need for any of this,' he said.

'Oh, I think there is,' she answered. At the desk she had explained what was going on to the manager, and though he was indignant that such a transaction should take place in his hotel, he was even more indignant about the moneylender's trade. 'I'm well aware of what's going on here,' he told him in a hostile voice. 'Let this be the last time you set foot in this establishment.'

It took only a few minutes to make the transaction. When he was certain that the amount of money tallied with what he had to collect, the moneylender gave up the papers that Mac and Georgie had signed. Satisfied, he was about to leave when Kitty called him back. 'Haven't you forgotten something?'

Without a word he reached into his breast pocket and produced a printed receipt-pad. After scribbling the date and sum received, he handed it to her. 'You're wasting your time anyway,' he declared with a wry little smile. 'They'll be back for more. Once we have them in our clutches, they always come back.'

'Not this time,' Kitty said, putting the receipt in her handbag alongside the papers. 'I think you'll find you've seen the last of this little source of income.' She hoped so. Dear God, she hoped so! But, with Georgie, you could never be sure.

On Saturday, Georgie moved into her new home. 'Normally I would want to clear the cheque,' the shopkeeper said, 'but I trust you. You've got an honest face.' His remark was directed at Kitty.

After the groceries were unloaded, Jack was eager to be away. 'We've got a long drive ahead of us,' he moaned, 'I don't like travelling the motorways in the dark.'

'Take care of yourself,' Kitty told Georgie.

'I won't let you down,' she promised. 'And I'll never forget what you've done for me.'

She gave her heartfelt thanks to Jack who hinted, 'I'm a businessman. If I pay out, I expect something to show for it.'

At first Georgie took that to mean he expected her to prosper with the excellent start she'd been given. But after he and Kitty climbed into the car and she was waving them away, she caught sight of Kitty's face peering out of the window. It was a sad face, a face that told a story, and it set her thinking.

Kitty had little to say on the way home. She felt desperately unhappy. Wasn't it strange how life turned out? she thought. She and Georgie had come a long way since the children's home. Now she was going back to a life of luxury, while Georgie was settling into a flat above a newspaper shop. And, as the car carried her away from Georgie and nearer to the day of her wedding, Kitty would gladly have changed places.

PART FOUR

1981

Winners

CHAPTER SIXTEEN

The phone had been ringing some minutes when Harry came into his office. Throwing off his mac, he grabbed up the receiver. 'Jenkins' Haulage.' It always gave him a rush of pride when he said that.

There was a slight pause at the other end, before a man's voice crackled over the line. 'Harry? Harry, is that you?'

Harry recognised the voice as belonging to one of his main customers. 'Mike!' Harry was relieved. 'Am I glad to hear your voice! I've been trying to get hold of you all week.'

Based in the south of England, Michael Norden owned a string of garages throughout the country. Against more established hauliers, Harry had won the contract for distributing spare parts far and wide. 'What's the urgency, mate?' As a rule Michael Norden was friendly and chatty. This time he seemed impatient, almost irritated.

'I still haven't had this month's despatch sheets,' Harry told him. 'Is there a problem?'

Taking the phone with him, he sat in the chair behind the desk. He was shivering with cold. The weather had taken a turn for the worse. All night it had been pouring with rain, and since four o'clock that morning he had been up to his neck in axle grease and filth. One of his drivers had called him out after a breakdown on a country lane in the middle of nowhere. 'What with one thing and another, I'm late in planning the schedule,' he explained, 'so I need those sheets like yesterday.'

'Late in planning your schedule? It sounds to me like it's *you* that's got the problem.'

Harry was not about to confess he had lost contracts that had been his bread and butter. 'It's nothing I can't handle,' he affirmed. 'I can take the schedule over the phone now, and you

291

can send the paperwork on. I'll get the deliveries out today. One of the lorries is in dock right now, but I've another returning this afternoon. If needs be, I'll do the job myself.'

He picked up a pencil and began scribbling. 'If I remember rightly, you were waiting on a delivery to the Cambridge depot? It would have been done by now, but like I say, I couldn't get hold of you, and no one seemed to know where you were.' He laughed. 'If I didn't know better, I'd say you were giving me the runaround.'

The silence at the other end set off warning bells in his mind. In a worried voice, he said, 'Mike? What's going on?' Still no answer. 'All right. Out with it. Am I still on your books or what?' His jaw worked in anger. There was something funny happening lately, and he couldn't quite put his finger on it. 'Answer me, Mike. Do you want the job done or don't you?'

'It's not up to me, Harry.'

'What do you mean, it's not up to you? It's your company, isn't it? Who the hell else is it up to?'

'I have to answer to the bank, you know that.'

'As we all do.' Harry retaliated, trying to inject some humour into the situation. 'You can't tell me you're getting some other haulier to do it cheaper than I do? Christ! If I did it any cheaper, I'd have to *pedal* the stuff about.'

'Sorry, mate. I've no more work for you.'

'Are you having me on?' It seemed inconceivable that this contract should be ended. He had never once let this man down, and always kept his rates trimmed to the bone to accommodate him.

'I've decided not to renew the contract.'

'And that's it?' Harry couldn't believe his ears. 'Can we sit round the table and discuss it?'

'Sorry, mate. I won't be renewing your contract and that's an end to it.' The phone was replaced and Harry was left looking into the receiver. 'What the hell's going on?' Carefully replacing the receiver he went to the filing cabinet and took out a batch of papers. Spreading them on the desk, he glanced through them. 'There's something very strange about all this,' he muttered. 'That's the third contract I've lost in as many weeks.'

Taking a towel from the cupboard, he rubbed his hair dry and poured out a measure of brandy. He needed to think rationally about this business, and for the minute he was both angry and confused. 'Calm down, Jenkins,' he told himself. 'Don't go jumping to any conclusions. There has to be an explanation.'

After a while he began to thaw. He worked on his ledgers and balanced his books ready for the accountant, and even there he could see how drastically his orders had dropped. Another thing was the silence. Lately, the phone didn't ring either. 'It's like I've got the bloody plague!'

When the Tautliner returned at five o'clock he waited until the driver had gone home then locked up the office and checked the yard before making his own way home. 'A hot bath and a good meal,' he sighed. 'Afterwards I'll try and work out what to do.'

One thing he did know, he would have to watch the pennies for the time being. Thanks to Susan's extravagant style of living, money was pouring out, and less of it was coming in. That was disaster to any business. And right now, it was the business he was most concerned with.

Not wanting to worry Susan unnecessarily, he kept his main fears from her, though he did tell her she might have to forego the idea of her latest new toy. 'You're talking a lot of money,' he explained, 'and you don't really need it. Leave it for a few months. We can talk about it then.'

She greeted the suggestion with rage. 'Why can't I change my car for a new one?' she demanded. 'Anybody would think we were counting our pennies.'

As usual there was no meal on the table; nothing cooking in the oven. It didn't bother Harry. He had become used to looking after himself. In fact, he preferred it. That way he didn't feel obliged to her.

'I'm talking to you,' she snapped. 'Why can't I change my old car?' As he crossed the room, she followed him. 'I've already ordered it. You'll make me look a fool if I cancel it now.'

He was cold to the bone, his stomach rumbling with hunger, and what with the contracts being cancelled one after the other and not knowing the reason behind it, Susan's selfishness was the last straw.

Swinging round, he took her by the shoulders. 'For Christ's sake, what kind of woman are you?' Yanking her towards him, he held her tight, his dark eyes blazing into hers. He saw how beautiful she was, how feminine and seductive; he recalled the many times she had satisfied the sexual need in him, and wished to God he had never met her. There were men who would give their right arm to have her, but they didn't know what lay beneath that sweet sugar coating. Susan was hard and cruel, a bitter woman with a wicked tongue and an insatiable desire to bend everyone to her own will.

Her voice was suddenly warm and persuasive, her anger temporarily forgotten. 'Don't look at me like that, Harry,' she softly pleaded, 'it only makes me want you more.' When he was in a rage like this, with those dark brooding eyes looking into her soul, her passion was fired as always. Harry Jenkins was more man than she had ever met. When they made love he took her to the very heights, yet when it was over he was gone from her. Like a wisp of smoke he drifted away and she could never get a grasp on him. In her heart, she suspected he yearned for someone else – Jack Harpur's woman maybe, but she wasn't certain. How could she be certain? 'Let's do it here ... on the rug,' she whispered, her pretty eyes looking up at him. 'I've been lonely today. You were gone so long, Harry. I always miss you when you're away.'

'You surprise me.' Releasing her so suddenly that she stumbled backwards, he drew himself to his full height, still looking down on her, wishing he could sit and discuss the worrying side of his business with her, like any other man might do with his wife. But she was not that kind of woman and he had to accept that. 'I've never refused you anything,' he murmured, 'but as far as your changing a car that's not yet a year old, I'm sorry, but we can't do it. Not yet anyway.' He had no wish to dash her hopes altogether.

Flouncing away, she turned on him again. 'Bastard! Why are you doing this? What's behind it, eh? Is it because you saw me making eyes at the salesman? For God's sake, Harry! It was only a bit of harmless flirting. I thought it might get me a few extras on the car. What's wrong with that?'

His smile infuriated her. 'If you want to make a fool of yourself, who am I to interfere? As for getting you a few extras on the car, all it will get you is a bad name.'

'Don't play games with me. I'm only concerned about the car. Why can't I have it?'

Taking a deep breath, he stared up at the ceiling. Why couldn't she just leave things the way they were? Why couldn't she accept his judgment?

'Answer me, damn you!' Like a dog with a bone, she wouldn't let go.

'You'll just have to trust me.'

'That's not good enough, Harry. I want to know what's behind all this?'

Tired and irritable, he slowly brought his gaze to bear on her. 'All right. I had hoped to save you the worry, but work isn't as easy to get as it was. Contracts are drying up, and I can't yet figure out why.'

Her eyes grew round with horror. 'Losing contracts? I don't believe you.'

'Well, you'd better try, Susan, because I've no reason to lie. I'm losing contracts hand over fist, and I've no idea why. I'll get to the bottom of it, though, I can promise you that.'

She smiled slyly. 'It has to be a mistake. You'll get the contracts back, I know you will. You've said yourself there isn't a haulier in the country who can match your rates. You make certain every load is delivered on time, and you've never had one single complaint.' She sidled up to him, 'I know it's expensive, but we can afford it . . .'

'The car is out, Susan. It's a luxury we'll have to put on hold.' He hated piling this on her shoulders. He supposed it was her nature to be more extravagant than thrifty; the real trouble was, she didn't care where the money came from as long as it kept coming. Now she had given him no alternative but to spell it out, and, to tell the truth, it was a blessed relief to actually talk to someone about it. 'You said just now anyone would think we had to count the pennies.' His voice was serious, and he could see that the truth was getting through to her at last. 'If things go on the way they are, that's just what we shall have to do.'

He didn't say anything. Instead he gave her a look that drove the message home. Then he went to the kitchen, where he rummaged about in the fridge.

'What do you think you're doing?' She followed him to the kitchen door and stood there, hands on hips, impatiently fidgeting.

Harry wasn't in the mood for an argument. 'I'm famished ...
getting myself something to eat.' Lifting a huge steak pie from
the shelf, he took it to the table where he sliced off a chunk.
Sliding it on to a plate, he smiled at her. 'Want me to cut you
a piece?' He felt lighter of heart. The worst was over. He had
spilled out his worries. Later he would work out a solution.

She grimaced. 'What I want is for you to put that bloody
thing back and get changed.'

'I'll shower and change when I've put this on to heat.'

'No! I mean change into your best clothes. I thought we might
go and try that new restaurant in Langho.'

He put the pie under the grill and took a long hard look at
her. He hadn't noticed before but he saw now: she was dressed
to kill. Wearing a tight blue dress and stiletto heels, she was
painted in rouge and mascara. In a slow deliberate voice he
told her, 'At four o' clock this morning I was on my back under
a lorry, with water and grease pouring down my neck. I've
had a lousy day, I'm dog-tired, and all I want is a bath and a
hot meal. After that I thought I might put my feet up, and the
two of us could talk.'

'I don't want to talk. I want to go out.'

'Then I'll get you a cab and you can go out on your own.'
He wondered how long he could put up with her cat and mouse
games.

'Will you talk about me having the car?'

'Nope.'

'Then there's nothing else for us to talk about.'

He gave a wry little smile. 'You're right,' he admitted. 'We
don't seem to have much in common these days, do we?' A
wave of regret came over him. 'But then, we never did have,
only I was too blind to see it. In fact I've been too blind to see
a lot of things. Happen we should call it a day.'

'You're a wicked bugger, Harry!'

He despised her at times. She was a money-eating machine.
Never satisfied, no matter what he did. ' "Wicked"?' He shook
his head. 'I don't think so.'

There was a world of emotion in his voice. He didn't love
her. He never had and he never could. But he had always tried
to do his best by her; always given her what she wanted, whether
it be material things, companionship, or sex of a kind that left

them both exhausted. Not once had he refused her anything if it was in his power; it was almost as though he was compensating her in every other way for what she could never lay claim to: his heart. Kitty had that. It would belong to her until he drew his last breath, and beyond, if such a thing was possible.

Sensing that she had gone too far, Susan changed tack. 'I didn't mean to yell,' she lied, 'and I'm sure things will come all right at work.' Sitting at the table, she looked up with soft pleading eyes. 'I don't like it when we fall out,' she purred. 'It's just that I don't understand things like contracts and income and expenditure. I've never had the need to know about these things.' Crossing her legs, she drew her skirt up so her thighs were showing.

'I'm sorry I had to put you in the picture. It can't be easy for you to accept we have to curb our spending for the time being.' He was aware of her little ploy to seduce him. He was also aware that she had splendid thighs. It was just a pity she had no heart or substance.

She watched him as he took a plate from beneath the grill. 'What about Jack Harpur?'

He was sitting at the table now. The mention of Kitty's future husband made him frown. 'What about him?' His voice hardened as he pushed the plate away. Suddenly his appetite was gone.

Susan noticed his change of mood and though her suspicions were fired with regard to Kitty, she was wise enough not to make mention of it; she had other ideas on how to deal with that little matter. 'I was just wondering, that's all.'

'Oh? Wondering what in particular?' He was wondering too. Wondering whether she had perceived his longing for Kitty.

'It isn't Jack Harpur who's cancelled contracts, is it?'

'Not yet, but the way things are going, I wouldn't rule it out.'

'Would it be bad if you lost his work?'

He gave a small laugh, but it was without mirth. 'Now that really *would* break the bank.' Losing his contract with Harpur would be bad in more ways than he cared to admit. It wouldn't happen if he had his way. Not only was Harpur one of his biggest customers, he was also a vital link with Kitty.

Susan was very quiet. Jack Harpur had been on her mind for some time, and now that Harry's business was taking a battering, he somehow grew in importance. She gave a secret little smile, before asking, 'Are you coming out?'

'Not tonight. When I've had a shower, I've got some serious thinking to do, and maybe a few phone calls to make.'

'And you really don't mind if I go out?'

He thought about that a while, and when he gave his answer it had a ring to it. 'I'd like you to think about what I said, Susan. Maybe it would be better if we went our separate ways anyway.'

She came to him and kissed him long and hard. Running her fingers up his leg and into his pocket, she caressed the end of his penis through the silk lining. 'There's still time before I go,' she suggested, pushing her tongue into his mouth.

He was only a man after all, and she was a sensuous, beautiful woman. He could feel himself growing hard, growing bigger with every stroke. The feel of her tongue in his mouth made his senses race. She was smiling then laughing, confident that she had him just where she wanted him. 'Make love to me,' she cooed, licking his ear and softly giggling.

He was burning. His loins were so tight he felt he would burst. 'Thought you wanted to go out?' he said. Taking hold of her wrists, he thrust her away, a coolness coming over him as he stared at her with an expressionless face.

'You really are a bastard after all,' she muttered. Then she kissed him again and departed. 'See you when I see you,' she called as the front door opened. 'I might be back. I might not.'

'Whatever,' he murmured. He'd grown used to her strange little games.

He went up the stairs two at a time. In the bedroom he stripped naked, smiling at himself when he passed the mirror and saw that he was still erect with passion. 'You're a bloody fool if you think you can ever have Kitty,' he told himself. 'Maybe you should take it where you can get it.' But his heart told him something else. It told him that rather than spend his life with a woman he didn't love, he would spend it alone.

Showered and dressed, he ran a comb through his thick dark locks and returned to the lounge. Sitting in the chair by the fireside, he stretched out his long legs and mulled over the events of the evening. 'You and Susan will never make a happy marriage,' he murmured. 'End it now, before it cripples you both.'

Stretching out his hand, he took their wedding photograph from its place on the coffee table. For an endless moment he stared at it, at Susan in her beautiful gown, at himself in a dark suit looking far more serious than any groom should look, 'Why the hell did you do it?' he demanded, placing the photograph face down on the table. 'It wasn't fair to you or her.'

Leaning back in the chair, he closed his eyes and pictured Kitty in his mind. A smile came over his handsome features as he recalled all the good times they had shared. It seemed so many years ago that they were just children; sharing a garden swing, etching their names on the tree trunk, playing footie with Kitty as goalie. He remembered the time when he had kicked the ball a little too hard and it canoned into Kitty, sending her down the garden with it. He had been horrified, but Sarah, his sister, thought it hilarious. Kitty laughed it off and they all settled for an ice-cream when the van turned up. In his mind he could see the sparkle in Kitty's eyes. He could hear her laughter, and it tore him apart. As a boy he had loved her. As a man she had become his very life. In the nights, when he couldn't sleep, he still treasured her. In his dreams she was there, always elusive. Every waking moment, when he was in the office or walking along a lonely street or driving along the highways, he treasured her. But she wasn't his to treasure. That was what hurt. Kitty was someone else's woman now. That had been her decision and, however painful it was to him, he had no choice but to live with it.

Suddenly he felt weary, as if the weight of the world was on his shoulders. 'Susan's right,' he admitted, 'you're working every hour God sends, and for what?' Even when he was home he couldn't sleep. But it wasn't sleep he needed. It was Kitty. She was the reason he drove the roads and kept away from the house as long as he could. She was the reason he pushed himself so hard. He had to keep busy or be swamped by the reality of losing her forever. While he was busy he could cope, but the minute he was given time to think, he could only think of her.

Suddenly she was all around, in his mind, in his heart, touching him, whispering to him. 'Leave me be, Kitty,' he moaned. 'You've made your choice. Now leave me be.'

Getting out of the chair, he went to the mahogany filing cabinet. From it he took out a folder containing his bank statements. Fingering through them, he realised again how serious the situation was. 'Worse than I thought,' he muttered. 'Work is dwindling fast. If Harpur pulls his contract now, I'd really be struggling.'

Another thought entered his mind. 'You should have had this month's despatch sheet through from him and it still hasn't arrived.' He had not been unduly worried because often they were late, but they always turned up. 'Ring him,' he said aloud. 'Put your mind at rest.' He had something else on his mind, too. He could also ask about Kitty.

He went quickly to the hallway. For some time now he had meant to put a telephone in the lounge, but had never got round to it. Probably because Susan objected. 'It would ruin my television viewing if the phone started ringing right here in the room,' she complained. It didn't really bother Harry one way or the other so a phone in the lounge had slid to the bottom of his list of priorities.

Consulting the directory, he dialled Jack's home number, pen at the ready to take down details of any new jobs coming his way.

The phone seemed to ring for an age, and when finally someone answered it came as a shock to Harry, because it was Kitty's voice on the other end. 'Oh!' Momentarily lost for words, he didn't know how to respond. 'I'm sorry, Kitty. I didn't realise you would be there.' He felt like a fool. Of course she would be there! They were a couple after all, weren't they? He had the pen in his hand and without even thinking he wrote her name on the pad.

'It's lovely to hear your voice, Harry.' The sweet sound of his name on her lips made him gasp. 'How are you?'

'I'm fine. Busy, but happy in my work.' His voice was soft and light, hiding the pain beneath. 'Are you keeping well, Kitty?'

There was a brief silence, and for a moment he wondered if she might be thinking the same thoughts that were passing through his own mind. Was she experiencing the same yearning? The same awful loneliness? The same anger at Fate for driving them apart? Again and again, in a subconscious outpouring from his heart, he wrote her name on the paper beneath his fingers.

It was on the tip of his tongue to confess all, to tell her how much he loved and needed her, but he knew it would be to no avail. Besides, it would place Kitty in an impossible situation and that wouldn't be fair. It took every ounce of his strength to suppress the words that rose to his lips.

It gave him a shock when Jack's voice came on the line. 'All right, Kitty darling, I'll deal with it.' There was a click as she put down the extension. 'Kitty's upstairs,' Jack explained. 'We're just getting ready to go out, and she got to the phone before me. I expect she's putting on a face. You know what these women are.' He laughed. 'I keep telling her she's beautiful enough without make-up. Anyway, I expect it was me you wanted to talk to, wasn't it? Fire away. I've got a few minutes.'

Harry was bitterly disappointed. He hadn't expected Kitty to answer the phone in Jack's house, but when she did it was both shocking and wonderful, and now she was gone, he felt more empty than ever. 'It's about next month's runs,' he answered. 'Are there any deviations, or is the schedule the same as before?'

'The same . . . with the exception of the engines going to the West Coast. They've postponed because of refurbishment.'

'It's a good job I rang then, because I was already allocating a truck for that delivery.'

'No problem. I'll probably have another job to take its place before next week.

'I'll need the despatch papers.'

'You'll have them in a few days. Meanwhile, I have a very lovely lady waiting for me. Talk to you soon.' The receiver went down, and so did Harry's hopes. For one anguished moment he was tempted to ring her back, but thought better of it. 'Be happy, sweetheart,' he murmured. 'Don't make the same mistake I did.'

It was gone midnight when Susan returned. Though she didn't deserve it, Harry had waited up for her. When she came into the room he was sprawled out in the chair, lapsed into a deep sleep. The first he realised she was back was when he felt the flies of his trousers being undone. 'I'd have to look a long way before I found another man like you,' she whispered in his ear. 'So you don't get rid of me that easily.' While he struggled to his senses, she began giggling. Her breath smelled of booze and it was easy to see she'd had more than enough.

'The place for you is bed,' he announced. Pushing her off, he did up his trousers, slid one arm round her waist, the other beneath her legs, and with one effortless movement collected her into his arms and was on his way up the stairs.

While he was undressing her, she made several attempts to seduce him, but to her fury, he dismissed each one. 'What the bloody hell's wrong with me then, eh?' she demanded in a slurred voice, 'Aren't I as pretty as a picture?'

'Prettier.' Tugging off her silk stockings, he laid them over the back of a chair.

'Don't you love me any more?' She was pouting now, acting the little girl lost.

Not wanting to hurt her unnecessarily, he had to think about his answer. 'I love you as much as I ever did.' At least he wasn't lying, because he had never truly loved her.

Turning nasty, she struggled to get up but was too drunk. 'Make love to me, you bastard!'

With calm deliberation he stripped off her dress and petticoat, slid her nightgown over her head, and tucked her unceremoniously under the covers. 'Sleep it off,' he said. 'You'll feel better in the morning.'

She wriggled and poked about under the bedclothes, grumbling at him, a deep frown on her face. 'You've left my knickers on.'

'I thought it might be as well,' he remarked dryly.

'Bastard!'

'So you keep saying.' He turned to leave.

'Aren't you coming to bed?' She could hardly keep her eyes open.

'Later,' he lied. He wouldn't be sliding in beside her. Not tonight. Not with Kitty's voice still echoing in his mind.

'You said we never talk. We can talk now if you like.'

'Go to sleep. We'll talk in the morning.'

When he saw her eyes close and her breathing settle into a deep rhythm, he gazed at her for a while. 'I'm sorry,' he murmured. Then he went downstairs to secure the house, before making his way up to the guest room.

He couldn't rest. His mind was too alive with thoughts of Susan; his marriage; his work; the contract cancellations; and Kitty.

More than anything, his mind was alive with thoughts of her.

There was an urgent need in him, a driving urge to travel south and confront Jack Harpur. Harry would tell him: 'Kitty's mine. She always has been. I've come to claim her.' He laughed at himself. 'The pair of them would show you the door! And you'd deserve it.'

With all of that on his mind, he closed his eyes to a fitful sleep, disturbed by dark invasive dreams that became terrible nightmares.

In the morning Susan looked at him across the breakfast table. 'You look worse than I feel.'

They sat in silence for a while, picking at their breakfast, each burning with things to say, but not knowing how to say them.

The moment of truth came when the telephone rang and Susan went to answer it. 'It stopped before I could pick it up,' she explained coming back to the table.

'If it's important they'll ring back,' he answered, finishing off the dregs of his tea.

'Were you hoping it might be Kitty?' Her voice was flat and trembling, and it made him look up in astonishment.

'What makes you think that?' He could feel the hairs standing up on the back of his neck.

'Explain this, you devious bugger!' Flicking a piece of paper towards him, she pointed a manicured nail at the name written there at least eight times. It was Kitty's, and it was written by Harry. His heart sank when he saw it there. 'You can't deny that's your writing.' The pen strokes were bold and confident. Like him.

Picking up the paper, he folded it and put it in his pocket. 'I'm not denying it.'

His honesty knocked her back, and it was a moment before she demanded in a quiet, harsh voice, 'Tell me I mean more to you than she does.'

His dark eyes appraised her face. The last thing he wanted was to hurt her, but he wouldn't lie. 'I'm sorry, Susan. I can't do that.' His expression told her everything. The time for living a lie was long past.

With one great sweep of her arm she swept the breakfast crockery from the table. It crashed to the floor and broke into a million fragments. As she stared at his honest dark eyes, she saw everything she had schemed for slipping away. 'How can she mean more to you than I do? What have I done wrong?'

'You've done nothing wrong. It's me who's at fault. I should never have married you in the first place, not when I was in love with someone else.'

'She won't have you, I'll see to that!'

His mouth turned up in what might have been a smile. 'She doesn't want me.' Kitty wanted Jack. Like Jack, he too wanted Kitty, and Susan wanted him. Fate was cruel.

'Dump me, Harry Jenkins, and I'll take you for every penny you've got!'

Getting out of his chair, he spread his arms wide. 'Take it,' he offered. 'If that's what you want, then you're welcome to it.'

His gesture had a sobering effect on her. 'It's *you* I want,' she said. In fact she wanted the best of both worlds: Harry and his money-making talents.

Leaning over the table, he told her, 'I would think long and hard about that if I were you. No woman wants a man who can't give her his best.'

'Piss off then!' When she talked like that she was ugly.

'That might be a good idea,' he answered quietly. 'Give us both time to think.' With that he strode out of the room, and out of the house. In the fresh air he could breathe, and think, and plan a way out of his nightmare.

Kicking away the broken crockery, Susan went to the sink where she filled the kettle to make herself another pot of tea. She had woken with a blinding headache, and now she was in turmoil. 'I can't lose him,' she muttered, 'I love him.' In truth she didn't know the meaning of the word. What she 'loved' was a lazy way of life, to cover herself in glamour, go out when she pleased, and spend money whenever the fancy took her. Harry provided such luxuries.

Harry also gave her reason to be possessive and proud, for he was a strikingly handsome man. Whenever they went to functions or out to dinner with his clients, the women always made a beeline for him. Any one of them would have fallen into his arms, or his bed, but he remained untouchable, always charming and attentive but never persuaded by their womanly wiles.

She had been foolish enough to think it was her he wanted above all others. 'Now I know why he never strayed!' she snarled. 'It wasn't me he was being faithful to, it was Kitty Marsh.'

When a new thought came to her, it was like a bolt out of the blue. 'Of course! Why didn't I think of it before?' It was a devious, spiteful idea, but she believed it might be the answer to keeping Harry.

It took only a minute to locate Jack Harpur's work number, and less than that to dial it. She was delighted when he instantly recognised her voice. 'I thought you might have forgotten me?' she cooed. 'After all, we only met for a short time.'

'Once seen, never forgotten, Susan. I've only got a short time now, I'm afraid, so what can I do for you?'

There was a world of spite in her voice. She didn't see any need to disguise her reason for calling, so she came right out with it. 'I thought you should know my husband is in love with your fiancée.'

Though her news shook him to the core, his reply was deliberately matter-of-fact. 'I wouldn't worry about it.'

'You mean you knew?' This put a different complexion on things.

'Kitty's always been honest with me. Apparently this affection between Harry and her goes back a long way. It's over now.'

'Not as far as he's concerned.'

'Don't bother yourself about it. In fact, it might ease your mind to know that Kitty and I are to be married very soon.'

She actually smiled. 'I'm pleased to hear that,' she said. 'Congratulations. I'm sure it will come as a blow to Harry. But for myself, it couldn't be better news.' Harry was an honourable man. Now he would have to accept that Kitty was truly beyond his reach.

Jack's thinking was much on the same lines. Even so, he had known for some time that Kitty was still in love with Harry Jenkins. With confirmation that he was just as restless for her came a very real threat to Jack's plans. 'I think it would be better for all concerned if you didn't mention any of this to Harry,' he suggested. 'It might push things to a head . . . if you know what I mean? If Kitty so much as suspected Harry Jenkins still wanted her, she would drop me in a minute.'

He was under no illusion that she was marrying him for any other reason but to repay him for helping Georgie out of the moneylender's clutches. If this should ever come to light, Harry Jenkins would find a way to release her from the debt, leaving her free to choose between them. Though Kitty had a strong sense of right and wrong and would consider Susan's feelings too, Jack suspected love would win out and both he and Susan would be left high and dry.

It was a risk he dared not take. 'Keep this conversation to yourself,' he urged. 'As far as the wedding is concerned, there will be time enough for him to know about that when it's over . . . when the vows are made, and my ring is safe on Kitty's finger.'

She nodded. 'I understand.' The quicker those two were married and Kitty was Mrs Jack Harpur, the better, she thought vindictively.

In her haste to be rid of Kitty, she couldn't see the truth: that Harry was already bringing their own marriage to an end, and that however much she might want to cling to him and all he could provide, it was too late. She had already lost him.

CHAPTER SEVENTEEN

Jack studied Kitty as she bustled about. It was on the tip of his tongue to ask her about Harry, but he was afraid of the answer she might give. He couldn't bear to lose her. Not now. Not after all his scheming and waiting. Next Saturday couldn't come soon enough for him though he suspected Kitty would wish it away for ever if she could.

He had been here ten minutes and she had only spoken a few words. 'Aren't you well?' he asked. Getting up from his chair, he went to her side. 'You really don't have to cook for me, darling,' he said in a patronising voice. 'We can go out if you prefer. As a matter of fact, I *want* to take you out. We can try that new restaurant alongside the river.'

'No, thanks. I'd much rather stay in.' She continued chopping parsley. 'Besides, the vegetables are almost ready, and the casserole is cooking nicely. All we need are the rice to finish cooking, and that bottle of red wine you brought . . . open it, will you, Jack?' As she turned he went to kiss her, but she avoided him.

She wanted him to leave. She wanted him to say he didn't intend holding her to her promise; he couldn't marry her when her heart so obviously wasn't in it.

With every day it became more and more obvious Jack Harpur was not about to let her go, and anyway she had come to believe that it really didn't matter. Not with Harry settled and his wife about to have their first child. There was no longer any reason to fight the direction her life was taking. And even if there was, she was trapped, just as surely as if Jack had fastened her in chains.

One good thing had come out of all this. In spite of the fact that Mac had not yet contacted her, Georgie was content, really content for the first time in a long while. She had a temporary job with Marks and Spencers in Liverpool, and they were so pleased with her that she had been given the promise of her job back after she'd had the baby. 'I had a letter from Georgie today,' Kitty told Jack. 'She'll be on the four-fifteen train tomorrow afternoon. I've arranged to meet her at the station.'

'I thought she was working now?'

'She is, but she's had this week booked off ever since I told her the wedding date.' She beamed with pleasure at the thought of having Georgie here. 'I'm thrilled she's agreed to be my maid of honour. It was the devil's own work getting her to say she would do it, but as I told her, with the right dress it won't be too easy to spot that she's pregnant.'

Jack felt neglected. 'When was all this arranged? And why wasn't I told?'

'You would have been told, it's just that I hadn't got round to it, that's all. What with racing all over the town with Mildred, in and out of the shops, and chasing every little detail every hour of every day, I've been rushed off my feet. Honestly! I don't know where the time's gone. Saturday seems to have come upon us with a vengeance.' But it was good to keep busy, because whenever she paused for thought, she was panic-stricken. Once that ring was on her finger, there would be no turning back.

Jack appeared to read her thoughts. 'You should have had plenty of time. I mean, you've postponed the wedding three times already. The first date was set for April, and now we're into May. Anyway, what do you mean "Saturday's come up on you with a vengeance"?' He forced himself to smile. 'That's hardly a flattering comment, darling. I've spent a small fortune to make Saturday the most wonderful day of your life. Instead of that, you talk as if you're about to be given a life sentence.'

'I'm sorry. I didn't mean it to sound that way.' All the same, he was right. She *was* about to be given a life sentence.

Seating himself at the table, he waited to be served. 'It'll be the best wedding Bedford's ever seen.' He looked very pleased as he congratulated himself on his own efforts towards the wedding. 'I've done my share of organising. The newspapers have been notified; the honeymoon's booked . . . the best suite in the most expensive hotel on Mauritius, I might tell you. We'll be chauffeur-driven to the airport and collected in style the minute the plane touches down at the other end. And just wait until you see what I've bought you for a wedding present!'

'I can't wait to show you off. When you walk down that aisle in your wedding gown, I'll be the proudest man on earth.' As he gazed at her, she imagined she saw a tear, and was filled with guilt.

Going across the room, Kitty placed the dish of rice in the centre of the table. 'Jack, are you quite sure you want to marry me?' It wasn't the first time she had asked him that, but his answer was always the same.

It was now. 'I want you to be my wife more than I've ever wanted anything.' He knew why she asked, and he knew the answer she wanted. But he was not about to give it. 'Please don't ask me that again.'

'I just wish you hadn't invited half of Bedford to the wedding.'

'That's an exaggeration, and you know it.'

'What! All forty members of your sailing club, and every customer you've ever dealt with?' She paused there, because Harry was large in her mind. 'It's a pity Harry and his wife couldn't make it.'

'I know, but I did ask him,' he lied. 'Apparently he and Susan have made other plans for that date.'

'Thank you for that,' she acknowledged. To be truthful, she thought it might be as well they couldn't come. In one way it would have been nice to have Harry there. In another, she didn't think she could bear him to listen while she gave her vows to another man. The fact that he had chosen to be elsewhere told her a great deal.

Jack complained then that he couldn't see why she hadn't accepted his invitation to move into his house. Kitty made her excuses for the umpteenth time, and quickly changed the subject.

She had stayed in the flat because she wanted to be on her own. She needed time to adjust to the changes that were looming. She had to come to terms with the fact that soon she would be Mrs Jack Harpur. She chastised herself for being reluctant because after all he was a good man. He was wealthy, her life would be much easier, he had promised to show her the world, and obviously adored her. What woman wouldn't be thrilled at the prospect of marrying him?

The meal was eaten, the wine was drunk, and Jack wanted to make love. 'It's been a whole week,' he moaned, 'I can't wait until Saturday.' Standing behind her chair, he slid his hand down the neck of her blouse. 'You're enough to drive any man mad.' The tips of his fingers found her nipples. 'I want you so much,' he sighed, softly caressing her. 'Let me take you ... right here on the floor.' Bending forward, he licked her ear and pressed his face to hers. 'I can't wait much longer,' he whispered. 'I'm in agony. You wouldn't turn a man down when he's in agony, would you?'

Kitty tried so hard not to dislike him. He didn't deserve that. He had always treated her well, and though his reasons were not unselfish, he had come to Georgie's rescue. Yet she couldn't love him. Not the way he wanted.

She could feel him all over her; his hands; his mouth; the touch of his tongue on her neck. In a way it was good. Someone needed her. Someone prized her above all others. This man was prepared to spend the rest of his life with her. That had to count for something. Besides, these past few days she had felt incredibly lonely, aching inside, wondering if she could ever be content again. She could hear him whispering in her ear, soft and persuasive. He needed her. She needed him. Besides, she had needs too. A spiral of anger rose in her. What was wrong with taking love where you could find it?

Now he was groaning as though in agony, his probing fingers caressing her thigh. Her legs were open. She felt vulnerable. For one brief moment she was tempted to yield, to let him invade her. 'Just once more before we're married,' he urged excitedly. 'After Saturday we'll be together for always.'

The temptation subsided. 'After Saturday' he'd said. And Saturday was only a few days away. Suddenly she was cold inside. 'No, Jack,' she said softly. 'The wine's gone to my head, and I'm heavy with sleep. Saturday will soon be here.' She forced herself to smile at him. 'You'll just have to be patient.'

Lurching away, he made a growling sound in the back of his throat. 'You've got me too excited to wait until Saturday.'

Kitty inched away. 'You've got *yourself* excited.'

'You're a hard woman, Kitty Marsh!' His eyes were glittering brightly. 'I ought to take you anyway, whether you want it or not!'

Kitty was quickly on her feet. 'If you tried that, it would be the first and last time.'

He bowed his head. 'Sorry, darling,' he apologised. 'I was only joking. I would never do that, and you know it.'

After that he couldn't do enough for her. He helped her clear the table. He washed the dishes while she dried, and afterwards, when she told him she was tired, didn't put up an argument. Instead he went quietly. 'I'll see you tomorrow then?'

'Not tomorrow,' she said, reminding him that she was collecting Georgie from the station. 'After I've got her home I shall feed her and get her settled, then we'll just sit and talk till the cows come home.'

'Wednesday then?'

'Not Wednesday either. There's still so much to be done,' she reminded him. 'On Wednesday there's her dress to be fitted, her shoes to be got, a hair appointment to be made for both of us, and all the other little last-minute things.'

His face fell with disappointment, but he didn't argue. 'Thursday, then,' he said, smiling from ear to ear when she nodded her agreement. 'But it will seem like a lifetime until then.'

After he'd gone, Kitty sat with her feet up and a mug of hot chocolate clutched in her hands. 'You're wrong, Jack,' she muttered, recalling his parting words. '*Saturday* will seem like a lifetime. And every day after that.'

At midnight she went to bed. At six she was downstairs again, unable to sleep any longer, excited that Georgie would soon be here. She had a slice of toast and a cup of strong tea, then washed the crockery, tidied her bedroom, hoovered the entire flat and scrubbed the kitchen floor. That done, she put on her coat and went into town.

It was still only eight-thirty by the time she got to the florist, but they were open and just setting out a splendid pavement display. 'I'll have two bunches of white chrysanthemums,' she told the assistant. 'And another bunch of those lovely pink roses.' The colours would mix wonderfully well, she thought.

On her way back, she remembered Georgie's weakness for eccles cakes. Calling in the baker's she bought half a dozen, oozing with currants and with pastry so flaky it fell off like a snow shower when the girl put them into a bag. Kitty also bought a french loaf, six large crusty baps, and some naughty chocolate eclairs. 'You'll get fat,' the girl laughed.

'I should be so lucky,' Kitty replied with a glance at her trim shapely figure. She wouldn't mind being fat, if it was fat of a kind that would produce a baby at the end. That was something else she was concerned about, a niggling little worry at the back of her mind.

Right up to the hour before she was due to meet Georgie, Kitty kept herself busy. She took delight in arranging the flowers; a huge vaseful in Georgie's bedroom, more in the sitting room, and even in the bathroom. She washed the bathroom from top to bottom, she polished every windowsill in the flat, and even had a go at cleaning the windows. It was a beautiful day. The sun shone in through the windows and Kitty's heart was happier than it had been in a very long time.

The hours sped by, and soon it was time for her to make her way to the station. She thought it too lovely a day to go by bus so decided to walk; along by the river and through the Arndale Centre, with its splendid old façade and busy thoroughfares.

Pausing now and then to gaze in the shop windows, she saw the most beautiful brooch in a corner jeweller's; it was a blue red-eyed rabbit, a bright cheerful creature with long floppy ears. She had already bought a present for the maid of honour, but as soon as she saw the rabbit, she knew Georgie would love it.

It took only a few minutes to purchase the brooch, then she was on her way, her steps quickening as she approached the Midland Road station. 'Due in a few minutes,' the clerk confirmed. 'Meeting someone, are you?' Kitty had only bought a platform ticket so he knew she wasn't travelling.

As she walked away, his appreciative gaze followed her, from the top of her shining dark hair to the shapely lines of her ankles. Kitty was wearing a short beige skirt and long-sleeved blue blouse. She had on her blue high-heeled shoes, and the whole outfit showed off her figure to perfection. 'Nice eyes too,' the clerk muttered with a saucy wink. 'Wish I were thirty years younger.'

Kitty sat on the wooden-slatted bench, a small forlorn figure on that lonely platform. She watched for the train and tried to push all thoughts of Saturday from her mind. Oh, but it would be wonderful to have Georgie for a whole week. She missed her. She missed having a friend to talk with, to share her fears and hopes with. She remembered the old days, when she and

Georgie were younger. In spite of the unhappy reasons that had taken them to the home, Kitty still cherished the memory of those times as some of the best in her life.

Just as the clerk had predicted, the train was on time. The last few minutes before it came speeding into view, a multitude of people crowded the platform.

Kitty pushed her way through to watch the train as it came into the station, her eager eyes searching every carriage as it went by. For a minute she thought Georgie had changed her mind as she often did, and her heart fell like a lead weight inside her. 'Don't let me down, Georgie gal,' she muttered, smiling with embarrassment when a big ginger-haired woman gave her a funny look. As the wary woman hurried on to the train, Kitty couldn't help but chuckle. 'She must think I'm a brick short of a load!'

All the passengers had boarded and still Kitty couldn't see any sign of Georgie. Disillusioned, she turned to leave when a familiar voice chirped out, 'Some bleedin' friend you are, Kitty Marsh! Invite a gal to your wedding then ain't got the decency to see her safely off the train!'

Kitty swung round and there she was. 'GEORGIE!' With open arms she ran to her, hugging her as if she never wanted to let go. 'I didn't see you get off,' she laughed. 'Oh, Georgie. I'm so glad you're here.' She gulped back the joyful tears. For one awful minute she'd feared she would have to walk down that long, lonely aisle on her own. Now Georgie was here and the world was a brighter place.

'Bleedin' hell, gal!' Dropping her suitcase, Georgie let herself be swung round. 'Are you after strangling me or what?' But she was thrilled to be here. She had so much to tell Kitty, and there was so much she wanted to know in her turn.

They took the bus as far as the top of the market, then walked the rest of the way. 'We'll go by way of the embankment,' Kitty said. As they walked along arm in arm, with Kitty insisting on carrying the suitcase, she couldn't keep her eyes off her old friend. Georgie looked so much better than when Kitty had last seen her. There was a spring to her step, and a twinkle in her eye.

Georgie gave her a sideways look. 'What the 'ell are you gawping at?'

Kitty squeezed her arm with affection. 'I'm "gawping" at you,'

313

she answered. 'You look ... different somehow.' She couldn't quite put her finger on it, but there was something very new about Georgie, like a light shining from inside her.

Georgie made a wry little face. "Course I'm different,' she pointed out with exaggerated patience. 'I'm fat and heavy, and I'm carrying a bleedin' monster.'

'No, you're not,' Kitty corrected. 'You're very smart and light of foot, and being pregnant suits you.' It must be that, she decided. She couldn't help but wonder whether being pregnant might suit her too, but suddenly there it was again, that little nagging worry at the back of her mind.

'You never told me you lived in such a posh place,' Georgie remarked as they strolled along the riverside. 'It's beautiful.'

They sat on the bench and watched the riverlife. Graceful white swans glided by with multi-coloured ducks following in their wake. Children played on the bank beneath the watchful eyes of their parents, and all along the riverside graceful willows bent to the gentle breeze. 'It's like paradise,' Georgie said, mesmerised.

Kitty knew exactly what she meant. 'It is beautiful,' she murmured. 'But it isn't paradise to me.'

Something in the tone of her voice made Georgie turn to look at her. Quietly she said, 'For someone who's getting wed in four day's time, you seem a bit down in the mouth, gal.'

'Let's go home,' Kitty said, picking up the suitcase. 'You must be tired.'

As they completed the journey to Kitty's flat, Georgie kept sneaking a look at her quiet companion. She had been bubbly and bright, but now she seemed preoccupied. There was a deep frown on her lovely face, and a heaviness to her step.

Though she was concerned that it was she who had dampened Kitty's spirits by her thoughtless remark, Georgie decided to say nothing about the swift change of mood. But she began to wonder. And when she wondered, certain things began to make sense. And when she began to put two and two together, she didn't like what it all added up to.

In better mood by the time they reached home, Kitty flung open the door to her flat. 'Welcome to my little abode,' she said proudly. She had put a great deal of love and effort into this place, and now she wanted to show it off to her one and only

314

true friend. 'What do you think?' Dumping the suitcase by the door, she waited for Georgie's reaction.

Georgie's blue eyes stood out like hatpins. 'Bloody Nora, gal!' she cried. 'Let me get me foot in the door first!'

As she took off to carry out a closer inspection, Kitty picked up the suitcase and padded behind her.

They went into the kitchen first, then on to the bathroom. 'Getting above yerself, ain't you?' Georgie said on seeing the freshly filled vase. 'Flowers in the loo? La de da!' When she winked, Kitty knew she approved.

They went into Kitty's bedroom. It was a bright cheerful room, with lots of scatter cushions and pretty floral curtains. 'You always did have good taste, gal,' Georgie assured her. 'That's the first time I've ever seen a wicker chair in a bedroom, let alone covered in brightly coloured cushions.' She chuckled. 'Mind you. I wouldn't want a wicker chair in *my* bedroom, thank you very much.'

Kitty was intrigued. 'Why not?'

'Because I have a tendency to run about in the nuddy. You know how forgetful I can be? If I should plonk myself down on a wicker chair like that, me arse would be scratched to buggery!'

Kitty had forgotten what a tonic Georgie was. Laughing out loud, she dragged her away. 'Come and see the room I've got ready for you.'

'You ain't got no wicker chair in there, have you?'

'See for yourself.' Kitty remained at the door while Georgie went inside.

'By! You've really gone to some trouble, ain't you, gal?' Georgie's surprised gaze travelled the room. Kitty had painted it the softest shade of blue because she knew that was Georgie's favourite colour. There was a soft blue shade hanging over the light, a blue chequered eiderdown, and a blue vase filled with pink and yellow flowers. Georgie shook her head. 'It's really lovely,' she murmured. 'It's like a real home, that's what it is.' Turning to look at Kitty she said softly, 'Why do you do it, gal? Why do you go out of your way to please me, when I don't do nothing but bring you a heap o' trouble?'

'Because I love you.' Georgie would never know how much, Kitty thought fondly. She couldn't possibly realise what she had come to mean to her over the years.

Lost for words, Georgie looked round the room once more. 'It's lovely,' she said again. 'Really lovely.' She came to Kitty then, her blue eyes glittering with tears as she told her in a hoarse whisper, 'I love you too, gal, and it ain't easy for a hard-boiled egg like me to say that.'

Kitty didn't want the past to swamp them, as it swamped her every time she let her mind wander back over the years. Going to the bed, she flung the suitcase down. 'First of all, we'll hang your clothes up, or they'll be creased like concertinas, then you'll go into the sitting room and rest your feet, while I make us something to eat.'

'Don't want nothing to eat, gal.' Georgie began unfastening the suitcase. 'I had a cheese sandwich on the train and I couldn't eat another crumb. Besides, if you intend stuffing me full of food, I'll look like a bleedin' turkey instead of a maid of honour.'

Later, Kitty managed to persuade her into enjoying a small salad and a portion of salmon. 'This is what I call style,' Georgie joked, and Kitty was content to see how at home she was making herself.

'How's Mildred getting on with her old man?' Georgie asked, in between sipping at her tea.

'She seems really happy.' With her legs stretched out and her feet resting on the fender, Kitty looked very relaxed. It seemed so right with her and Georgie together again.

'Do you reckon they do it?'

'Do what?'

Georgie winked. 'You know! Roll about in bed, him on top of her . . . her on top of him?'

'I expect they do. I hadn't really thought about it.'

'I do. All the time.'

'Do what?' This conversation was taking a very funny turn Kitty thought with a little amusement.

'Think about it. On the train on the way here, I kept looking at people, older people mostly.'

'What for?' She was just beginning to follow Georgie's train of thought.

'You know . . . just wondering if they did it or not. There was a couple sitting opposite me, and they kept looking at each other, like a pair of sweethearts might do.'

'What's wrong with that? I expect they *were* sweethearts.'

'I can't see how they could still do it, though.'

'Why not?'

Georgie giggled. 'Because he was ninety if he was a day. She was short and he was tall, and they were both fat as barrels. I mean ... how would they ever get it together?'

Kitty crumpled with laughter. 'Serves me right for asking,' she said.

'Mildred and her bloke are coming to see you wed, aren't they?'

'Try and keep them away,' Kitty replied warmly. 'Mildred's already helped me organise the woman's side of things, and as I haven't got a father or anyone else to give me away, Eddie's volunteered his services. They're coming over on Friday morning, and staying with Jack for the night.'

'I'm glad she's made up to you for the wrong she did.'

'She's more than made up for it, Georgie. She's been a real godsend.'

'What about Miss Davis? Is she coming?' Georgie rolled her eyes. 'God! Seeing that old biddy again will bring back memories.'

'I haven't had a reply, yet, so I don't know whether she'll turn up or not. I expect she's off on one of her globe-trotting adventures.'

Georgie gave her a sly little look. 'What about *him*?'

Kitty knew straightaway who she meant. 'Harry won't be coming. He and his wife have other commitments on that day.' She tried to sound casual, but the deepening flush on her face gave her away.

'Shall I tell you what I think?'

'You will anyway.'

'I think he won't come to the wedding because he couldn't bear the sight of you walking down the aisle to another man.'

How Kitty wished that was so. 'You couldn't be more wrong, Georgie. Harry has carved out his own life. He has a thriving haulier's business in Blackburn, and he's very happily married. He'll soon be a father, and I know how thrilled he must be at the prospect.'

But there were doubts in her mind. Since her party there had been doubts, only they were confused. *She* was confused. How could she know what Harry was feeling? The last time she had seen him, he had said certain things, looked at her in a certain way. But how could she know? How could she be certain? They were friends before they were lovers, and friends were allowed to say affectionate things to each other, weren't they?

'Why are you marrying Jack?'

Georgie's question took Kitty unawares, and she didn't really know how to answer it. Instead she posed her own question. 'Why shouldn't I marry him?'

'Because you don't love him. You've said so yourself.'

'I'm fond of him,' she answered truthfully. 'I know it can work, or I wouldn't even contemplate it.' She didn't want Georgie to know it was her debt to the moneylender that had finally tied the knot between herself and Jack.

Georgie's sigh echoed round the room. 'Look here, gal, I know I shouldn't poke my nose in, but you've had such a lousy life, and you've no real family to speak of. I only want you to be happy, you know that, don't you?'

Kitty's smile should have wiped away all her fears, but it didn't fool Georgie. 'Stop worrying. Jack's a good man, and I'm lucky to have found him.' In a way she was, because without him it really would be a lonely future. 'When I make those vows on Saturday, I will mean every word.' And so she would. But it still wouldn't stop her from wishing it was Harry standing beside her.

'All right, gal. Have it your own way. But I want you to know something.' As she looked into Kitty's dark brown eyes, Georgie's expression was intense. 'I can't help feeling you're marrying him as a kind of reward for paying off that debt. If I thought that was the case, I swear to God, I'd find the money somehow ... by one means or another.'

Kitty grasped her hand. 'You can put that out of your mind right away,' she said sternly. 'Like I said, I'm very fond of Jack. I'm marrying him because he loves me, and because I think I might come to love him in time. Jack's been good to me. He's kind and thoughtful, and he would never knowingly hurt me.' She smiled reassuringly. 'I promise you, Georgie, once Jack and I are married, I'll do everything in my power to make it a good marriage. I've always wanted children, you know that. At the minute Jack doesn't feel the same way about that, but he will, I know he will.'

She prayed he would. Up to now he had shown little incli-
nation towards starting a family. Then there was that niggling
worry again. The anxiety at the back of her mind that they had
made love without protection and she had not fallen pregnant.
Not that she had wanted to fall pregnant out of marriage,
because not taking precautions was a very foolish thing, but the
question remained – why hadn't she fallen pregnant? Was it
the wrong time of the month? Was it her? Was it Jack? Did
it mean that a family was out of the question? She daren't even
think about that.

'I don't want to hear any more about me and Jack,' she told
Georgie. 'It's you I want to talk about. Are you carrying that
baby well? Isn't the job too much for you right now? You said
in your letter they've offered you a permanent position after
the birth. If you take it on, who'll mind the baby?'

'Bloody Nora! Talk about nosey!' Georgie laughed. 'Everything's fine with the baby. The doctor says there's no problems.
I'm enjoying my work, and yes, I will take the job on afterwards,
'cause I have to eat and pay the rent. And no . . . I will not
take any more little "gifts" from you. I'm a grown woman, and
now that you and Jack have freed me from the moneylenders,
I have to look after myself. If I do take the job on permanently,
the shopkeeper's wife has promised to look after the baby.
You'd be surprised how friendly she is. After she said I had a
mouth like a sewer, I thought she was a right old cow, but she's
not a bad old stick once you get to know her.' Her gaze dropped
to the floor. 'And no, I still haven't heard from Mac.'

Kitty was surprised. 'I thought you had. I mean, you've got
that look about you . . . like a woman happy with her man.'

'Naw.' Georgie made one of her faces. 'There ain't no man in
my life, gal.' She patted her stomach. 'Only this little fella, and
he's brought his own sunshine.'

'How do you know it's a fella?'

'I just know, that's all.'

Kitty reached out to the small drawer in the coffee table.
Taking out a blue velvet box she handed it to Georgie. 'Just
now you said you wouldn't take any more gifts from me, but I
want you to have this. It's your present for being maid of
honour.'

Georgie was thrilled. 'It's lovely, gal,' she said, gently fingering
the blue rabbit. 'I'll pin it in pride of place on my fancy dress.'

She gave Kitty a peck on the cheek. 'Talking about fancy dress, when do I get to see it?'

'Tomorrow. When we go shopping.' She couldn't be certain whether Georgie was deliberately using the term 'fancy dress', implying that Kitty's marriage to Jack was little more than a façade, or whether she was just being Georgie. Kitty decided it didn't really matter anyway. 'I've lined up three shops that specialise in wedding wear and fast alterations, in case they're needed. I hope we can get what we want quickly, because I don't want you doing too much and wearing yourself out.' She cast a glance over Georgie's figure. 'I shouldn't think we'll have any trouble fitting you out, though.'

'I don't want frills and bows,' Georgie declared. 'I like straight-fitting frocks. As a matter of fact, though I'm over four months gone, my bump ain't that big.' She rubbed the small mound with the flat of her hand. 'Little sod knows how to kick though.'

When Georgie gave a long-drawn-out yawn, Kitty glanced at the mantelpiece clock and was horrified to see it was already midnight. 'Good God! Look at the time. We'd best get you off to your bed, my girl.'

'You sound like Miss Davis.'

'Less of your cheek.' Collecting the empty crockery, Kitty took it into the kitchen, where she placed it on the draining board. 'That can wait until the morning.'

'A gal after me own heart.' Georgie stood at the bedroom door. 'Goodnight, sleep tight,' she told Kitty.

'We're up early in the morning, so mind you get a good night's sleep,' Kitty warned. There was so much to do, and time was racing away.

Content to know Georgie was only a short distance away, Kitty soon fell into a deep restful sleep, the like of which she had not enjoyed since she was a small child.

Georgie waited her time. When she was certain Kitty must be sleeping, she crept out of her room and made her way to the hall. 'It ain't right,' she muttered as she cautiously switched on the light. 'It just ain't right.'

First of all, she checked Kitty's personal telephone book, a small leatherbound volume lying on top of the main directories. She couldn't find what she wanted. Disappointed, she replaced it, took up the receiver and dialled the enquiries operator.

While it was ringing she glanced towards the sitting room. Good, there was no sound, no sign that Kitty was awake. 'Hello? I'd like a number for Blackburn, Lancashire.' A pause, then, 'Jenkins... Harry Jenkins. It might be listed under Jenkins Haulage.'

Another pause. 'No, I'm sorry. I don't know the address.' Georgie crossed her fingers. She had to talk to Harry. She just had to! Suddenly the operator was talking again. Georgie picked up the pen lying by the phone and jotted down the number, 'Thank you so much.' Exhilarated, she replaced the receiver, and studied the number. 'Midnight. What if *she* answers?'

She toyed with the idea of waiting until morning, 'I might not get a chance,' she muttered. 'And there isn't much time.'

Nervously, she dialled the number. It seemed to ring for ages. Just as she was about to put it down, a woman answered. 'Who the hell *is* this?'

It was on the tip of Georgie's tongue to make some excuse for ringing at that time of night, to say she worked for some company or another, and that they were in urgent need of a truck and driver, when the woman's voice yelled: 'WHO ARE YOU? WHAT DO YOU THINK YOU'RE PLAYING AT, RINGING AT THIS HOUR? ANSWER, DAMMIT!'

Georgie's nerve went and she dropped the phone as if it was burning her fingers. 'You bloody coward!' she chided herself. Then she chuckled. 'That's unnerved the little cow! She'll not sleep a wink tonight.'

Keeping the paper on which she'd written the number, she returned to her room. 'Somehow or other, I'll find a way to ring him early in the morning,' she decided. 'If that other bugger answers, I won't be so quick to drop the phone again.'

It was six o'clock the following morning when Georgie tried again. Kitty was still sleeping. 'He's bound to get up early for work,' she reasoned.

She was out of luck because the woman's voice answered again, yelling at her in the same abusive manner. Georgie was bitterly disappointed. 'Get back to sleep, you miserable bugger!' she yelled back, and when there was a stunned silence at the other end, slammed the receiver down. As she turned she was astonished to see Kitty standing there, bleary-eyed and tousled.

'Who was that?' Kitty asked, stifling a yawn.

'God knows!' Georgie exclaimed. 'Some drunk, I expect. I'll wring his bloody neck if I ever lay hands on him . . . getting me out of bed at this unearthly hour.'

'You go back to bed,' Kitty told her. 'I'm wide awake now so I might as well stay up. I'll call you in about an hour, after I've cooked us a bit of breakfast.'

Georgie groaned as she plodded back to her room. 'How on earth am I gonna reach Harry Jenkins?' Convinced that he was the answer, she was determined not to give up.

It was Thursday evening. Harry waited for the men to return from their various journeys. It had been a strange day, unlike any other because today he had let it be known to those who might be interested that his business was on the market.

The men knew the score, and bore him no grudge. When they came back, there would be no despatch notes for them to scrutinise, no schedules for them to keep the next day. Like Harry they had seen it coming, and now had reluctantly accepted the inevitable.

As they came in he handed them their last wages. 'I'm sorry,' he told them, 'you're good men. If I could keep you on, you know I would, but you've seen for yourself how things have gone from bad to worse. Now I'm back where I started, with only enough work for one man and his truck.'

John McCabe was a strapping Scotsman with arms like cabers and a look that would frighten even the fiercest dog. But he had a soft heart and generous manner that earned him many friends. He had great respect for Harry and loathed the idea of him going under. 'At least you're shrewd enough to get out while you're still a working concern,' he commented. 'I know you've been trying to get to the bottom of why the work's been drying up, but you know as well as I do, there ain't that much to go round at the minute. It seems to be a case of first come, first served.'

Harry agreed up to a point. 'What I can't understand is how the other hauliers have managed to undercut me. It's as if they must know my going rates, or how could they do it time and again?' It was a real puzzle, and so far there were no answers.

This time it was the other man who spoke, a little fellow

wearing a cloth cap and sporting a jagged scar from ear to temple. 'Whether you sell up or keep going, I wish you the best of luck, but I'm certain you'll make a success of whatever you decide to do. If you're ever looking to take on again, count us in. You're the best boss we've ever had.'

Harry thanked them. 'I'll remember that.' Handing them each an envelope he said, 'You might need these references. You've certainly earned them.'

When the men were gone, he looked round the office. 'You're right to get out while you can, Jenkins,' he decided. 'All the contracts are gone, with the exception of just one.' He thought a moment, his face darkly serious. 'And I'll have to end that one myself. After all, I can't be dependent on the man Kitty chose over me.' The idea was repugnant to him.

He locked the filing cabinet, bolted the door, and took the telephone off the hook. Then he plucked his overcoat from the back of the door and settled down on the couch. It seemed right that he should stay here, with his work, with his thoughts. Tomorrow he might have a clearer mind.

The night was bitterly cold. He couldn't sleep. He just lay there, wondering what the future might hold.

Three times he glanced at his watch; midnight, then two o'clock, and now it was almost three in the morning. He knew then he could not delay what he had to do. At three-fifteen on Friday morning, he made his way home.

After spending too many hours on the couch at the office, Harry was not in the best of moods. As he came up the drive to the house he saw the lights on. When he came through the front door she called out, 'If that's you, Harry, you can piss off back where you've come from.'

He knew it would not be easy. 'We have to talk,' he said as he went to the door of the breakfast room. Surprised to find her still up, and by the look of it, drowning her sorrows in a bottle of wine, he made no attempt to go in. Instead he stood at the door, his dark eyes regarding her with a look of sorrow.

'Where the hell have you been?' She was on her feet now, ranting and raving, accusing him of neglecting her. 'I've been out of my mind with worry. I tried the office number and couldn't get through. Some maniac's been ringing here. I couldn't sleep, and now you just turn up as if nothing's happened.' She looked at him and saw a man at the end of his tether. She knew he had never wanted her, but she didn't care. She wanted him. That was all that mattered. 'I *want* us to talk,' she told him. 'I *want* to sort out this little problem between us, because I don't want our marriage to break up. I love you, Harry.' She had tried one tack, now it was time to try another.

'You don't love me,' he answered soberly. 'You love this house, the wardrobes stuffed with clothes, and the life of luxury you've enjoyed since the business took off. That's what you love. If I should walk out of this door right now and never come back, you'd manage well enough. Besides, you have every right to what's left of the business, *and* this house. At the end of the day you'd have a fairly healthy bank balance. Losing me wouldn't be the end of the world.'

She suddenly realised what he was saying. He actually meant to end it. She stared at him in disbelief; at his tall strong figure and the easy way he leaned against the doorjamb. She took in the fact that nowhere would she find such a man as Harry Jenkins. It wasn't just that he was the most handsome man she had ever met, with his dark sensuous eyes and wonderful lop-sided smile; it wasn't even the way he made her feel when he held her in his arms, making love with such passion that it took her breath away. There was something else about Harry – a unique strength of character, a caring tender side that she had not seen in other men. From the very first moment she had met him on the railway station, she had felt he was the one for her. For whatever reason, she still felt that. 'Please, Harry. I want our marriage to work.'

He looked at her for a while and his heart was heavy. He had never meant it to end like this, but he had come to a point where he had to wipe the slate clean, to give himself a chance, to give her a chance. 'It's over, Susan. You know it and I know it.'

'Don't do this to me, Harry.' She had awful visions of having to start again, of having to exercise her charm and ensnare another man who might provide her with all the things she had grown used to. Suddenly it seemed like too much effort, too much of a gamble, and she wasn't getting any younger. Her looks were not as fresh and blooming as they once were. It took longer in the morning to put on a face and present herself to the world as a bright young thing, full of adventure and bubbling with life.

Harry knew her too well. He had learned to see through her little charades. 'You're fooling yourself if you believe we can go on the way we have. Look, Susan, I've had plenty of time to think, and I've come to some very important decisions. I'm selling the business before it buckles under me. This house can be sold, or you can stay in it. That's up to you. When everything's settled, I'm going away. I need to find fresh pastures, new challenges.'

He had been foolish enough to believe Susan could be a substitute for Kitty, and he wouldn't forgive himself for that. Now he had to let her go, so that she too could make an honest life away from him. It was the fairest thing he could offer her.

'You're not going anywhere without me. I won't let you!'

'I'll leave you well provided for, don't worry.'

All pretence over, she was screaming at him, the way she always did: 'You bastard! Why did you marry me in the first place?'

He looked at her and wondered whether she really could take the truth. 'Let's just leave it the way it is,' he warned. 'There's been enough bad feeling, Susan. Let it be. There's no point in crucifying ourselves.'

Flinging herself at him, she demanded, 'It's *her*, isn't it? Kitty Marsh! I've been right all along. Tell me the truth, or I swear you'll be sorry.' Her fists pounded his stomach as she spoke.

Filled with a terrible rage, he took hold of her. Propelling her across the room, he sat her down. Leaning over her, said, 'You're right. It is Kitty Marsh. It always will be. You want to know why I married you? Well, seeing as you seem hell bent on knowing, I'll tell you. I married you because you were there, and because I believed it would work. I wanted a family, a reason for living, someone to come home to at the end of the day, someone who would share not only the good things but the bad. Someone like Kitty, who knows how to laugh and love, and give as well as take. I married you because she wasn't there for me, because I was foolish enough to think you could help me forget her. And because, God help me, I believed I could be everything you wanted me to be.'

Susan's face twisted with hatred. 'You had no right to marry me when you still loved her!'

'But you knew that from the start,' he argued. 'I never lied to you.'

'You never told me the whole truth either!'

Grabbing her hand, he held it out. 'I put that ring on your finger, Susan, with all the best intentions in the world. I wanted to take care of you, to be with you, to honour and obey like I promised in the wedding vows. But you wouldn't let it happen. Marriage is a two-way thing, but you couldn't see that. You didn't want to work at it, and now I'm glad because it makes my leaving that much easier.'

Her eyes narrowed and in a voice so heavy with loathing he could hardly recognise it, she hissed, 'Go on then. Get out. I won't play second fiddle to anyone. Especially not to Kitty Marsh.'

He merely nodded. There was nothing left to say. As he turned, she scraped her finger nails against his neck, drawing blood. 'I hate you.'

He felt ashamed. 'I honestly didn't want to hurt you,' he whispered. With the tips of his fingers he stroked her face; it was silky soft, like the ears of a cat. 'You'll be better off without me,' he said. 'When you get used to the idea, you'll realise that.'

On slow heavy footsteps he went upstairs and began to pack a bag. She followed him, ranting and raving, shaking her fists and threatening all kinds of retribution. He made no comment, just went on packing, thinking it was better for her to get it out of her system before he left, because once he went through that door he was never coming back.

He had the suitcase in his hand and was walking across the room when the telephone rang. He didn't answer it. Neither did she. Instead she stared at him, blocking his way. 'Aren't you going to answer that?' she taunted. 'It might be your precious Kitty Marsh. Or it might be that maniac who called while you were out, making your devious plans.'

He merely smiled and pushed his way past. He hadn't wanted it to get ugly. He knew that when the dust was settled, she really would be better off without him. 'I'll let you know where I'm staying. I won't be leaving Blackburn for a while. There's a deal of tidying up to do before I can shut shop altogether.' The phone was still ringing, its insistent tones buzzing in his brain. When she flung out her arm and sent it flying across the room, he simply reached down, picked it up and replaced the receiver. He could hear a woman's voice at the other end of the line, frantic and high-pitched. He assumed it was one of her drinking cronies. They all tended to be hysterical.

As he went down the stairs, the phone rang again. This time Susan snatched it up, yelled something obscene into the receiver and threw it down again. 'Where are you going?' she cried as he left her. 'It's four o'clock in the morning, for pity's sake. You can't leave me like this. What will people think?'

He shook his head at that. So it *was* her pride that was hurting? He'd had her figured out right after all. If he knew anything for sure, he knew she would come to no harm. Susan was a taker. More often than not it was the takers of this world who came out on top.

Outside, he threw the suitcase into the back of the car. He didn't want to waste time opening the boot. The sooner he was gone from here, the sooner the two of them could begin again. 'Damn!' He had forgotten his jacket, thrown it over the banister as he went into the house earlier. 'Left my wallet, credit cards . . . everything!'

He glanced back, thinking she might be standing at the door. To his relief there was no sign of her. Leaving the car door open he raced up the path. The front door was open. Susan was on the telephone, her face flushed bright red as she screamed down the receiver: 'If you ring here again, I'll call the police and have you locked up!'

At the back of his mind he recalled her saying something about a 'maniac' ringing when he wasn't here. He couldn't leave it like that. While Susan was still his wife, he counted himself responsible for her welfare. Calmly taking the phone from her, he demanded in a firm voice, 'Who is this?'

At the other end, Georgie gave a sigh of relief. 'Thank God!' she cried. 'I've been trying to get you for two bleedin' days. Your office number's been engaged for most of the time, and just now there was a madwoman on the end of this line, threatening to have me jailed for life. If that was your wife, I feel sorry for you, because it's *her* who wants sodding well locking up!'

It took a while before Harry realised who talked in a cheeky voice, interspersed with swear words and a warped sense of humour. He glanced sideways. Susan was pacing the sitting room, out of earshot. 'Georgie?' he asked in a whisper. 'Is that really you?' His solemn features broke into a smile.

'Who the bleedin' hell d'you think it is? Look, I ain't got much time. I've crept out me bed and I'm standing here half naked, but I just had to ring you. Kitty's getting married to Jack Harpur tomorrow. She's said herself she doesn't love him. She loves you, she always has. She's marrying him because he paid off a huge debt to get me out of the moneylender's clutches. She says it's nothing to do with that, but I know it is. You've got to stop her from making the biggest mistake of her life. Even if she can't have you, she mustn't ruin her life ... You can make her see sense, Harry. You've always been able to talk to her. Please! Get here as quick as you can.' She gave him Kitty's address, and then with a little gasp added, 'I can hear her moving about. I've got to go. If she finds out I've phoned you, she'll have my bleedin' guts for garters.'

Excited and worried all at the same time, Harry went from the house at a run. Behind him he could hear Susan's voice. 'Go on then! You'll be back. You'll want me before I want you.'

He was two miles down the road before he realised he still hadn't collected his jacket. 'How the hell can I travel the best part of two hundred miles without any money?' he wondered. Nearing the local garage he flicked out the indicator and steered his car to the pumps. Filling the tank to the limit he told the young man behind the counter, 'Put it on my account, Mike.' He had no immediate cash; even the petty cash box at the office was empty. He could have made a phone call and borrowed money, but that would waste time. Anyway, what did he want money for? He had the means of getting to Kitty, and that was all he cared about.

The M6 was busy as usual, vehicles haring up and down like there was no tomorrow. 'Tired of living some of them,' Harry muttered threading his way into the fast lane. Once there he put his foot down, but didn't get very far. Three miles along the road was jammed solid, with traffic at a standstill and no sign that it would soon be moving. 'This is all I need!' Harry moaned. If he could only get to the slip-road he could leave the motorway and make his way south by another route.

For the moment there was nothing he could do but wait. Minutes passed, then half an hour. Suddenly the traffic edged forward and he breathed a sigh of relief. It stopped again, and he cursed out loud. A white van behind him was too close for comfort. He hung out of his window and flagged for the driver to keep his distance. All he got for his trouble was two fingers in the air. 'Crazy bastard!' Harry muttered, quelling the urge to get out and give him a piece of his mind.

When the flow of traffic picked up speed he went with it. The white van was on his tail, dogging him every inch of the way, too close for comfort, making his blood rise. Ahead he could see the warning lights flashing. He slowed down, glanced at the dashboard clock, and saw that already it was half-past five, and he was only as far as Manchester. He had to get to Kitty. He had to tell her the way things were. Maybe there was a chance for them after all. Dear God he hoped so!

The driver of the white van was too close. 'Are you blind or what?' Agitated, Harry glanced in his mirror, deliberately pumping his foot on the brake. He had to let the fool know there was traffic built up ahead.

Cars were swerving from one side to the other, searching for the faster moving lane. When an articulated lorry almost took him with it, Harry slammed on his brakes. 'Jesus!' He shook his head, thanking his lucky stars he hadn't been dragged to an early grave. No sooner had he put a distance between himself and the truck than there was an almighty crunch from behind and he was hurtled backwards and forwards, feeling as though his neck had been wrenched from the rest of his body. But he wasn't hurt. He was angry. White-hot, raging angry as he got out of the car and saw the damage. The back end of his car was squeezed like a concertina. The driver of the white van got out of his cab. A burly unshaven man of about thirty years old, he sauntered over to see the damage. 'I'll 'ave you for this,' he threatened. 'You're a bloody menace on the roads!' Taking out a piece of paper from his pocket he began writing down Harry's registration number. 'I'll want your insurance details as well.'

Harry couldn't believe his ears. 'What the hell are you talking about?' he demanded. 'I think your brains must be be scrambled. You've hounded me every inch of the way . . . pushing up close to my boot and hemming me in whenever the traffic slowed. Never mind about damaging my car and wasting my precious time, it's a wonder you haven't caused a major incident!'

The big fellow's face hardened. 'Are you saying I'm a bad driver?' He took a pace forward, leering menacingly at Harry and obviously trying to intimidate him.

Because of the obnoxious smell that emitted from the man's filthy clothes, Harry would have taken a step back but he was burning inside. 'No, I'm not saying you're a bad driver,' he corrected. 'I'm saying you're a danger to every other driver and should never be allowed on the roads.'

With surprising agility, the man lurched forward. Grabbing Harry by the shoulders, he made to lift him from the ground. In that split second Harry caught sight of cruel eyes and thought the man really *was* mad. He thought of Kitty too, and that was the spur he needed. With one mighty effort he freed himself from the man's grasp. Drawing his fist behind him, he brought it forward with alarming speed. When it crashed into the man's grinning face it made a sickening sound and, for a moment, he was stunned. But only for a moment. Harry saw he was after blood and neatly sidestepped a series of clumsy blows. 'Good on yer!' shouted a passing driver, and there was a chorus of cheers as the traffic began moving on.

Suddenly Harry found himself being arrested. 'Causing a fracas on the highway,' said the officer. 'We'll have the pair of you in the car . . . now!'

At the station, he was almost out of his mind. 'I've got to get to Bedford,' he told the officer. 'I'll sign whatever you want, but I've got to get out of here.'

'You should have thought of that before you caused an accident and then decided to beat up this fellow.' He pointed to the big man who was skulking in the corner. 'You're nicked. You're *both* nicked.'

Suddenly the big fellow lunged forward, sending the officer flying to get at Harry. He gave as good as he got, and it took two other officers to separate them. In a minute they were being marched out. 'The pair of you can cool off in a cell,' they were told. Fortunately for the big man, he and Harry were locked up in different areas.

Kitty came into the sitting room and set the tray down. Looking up, she saw that Georgie had her head pressed to the window again. 'I don't know what you find so fascinating out there,' Kitty laughed. 'You've had your nose stuck to that window all evening.'

Edgy by now, Georgie came away and sat in the chair opposite. She gratefully accepted the cup of chocolate and seemed to relax when in fact she was desperately praying for that knock on the door, the knock that told her Harry was here and Kitty would be made to see what a terrible mistake she was making.

Kitty was intrigued. 'What's wrong with you? You're not nervous about tomorrow, are you?' It was a funny thing, but now that the day was almost on her she had somehow come to accept her future role as Jack's wife.

Instead of answering the question, Georgie apologised. 'I'm sorry I didn't want to go out tonight,' she said. 'I hope you didn't mind too much, gal?'

Kitty shrugged her shoulders. 'We can always have another night out, another time,' she promised. 'It doesn't have to be a hen night.' In fact she wasn't too bothered herself about going out. Accepting her marriage to Jack was one thing. Celebrating it was another.

'Are you sure you still want to go through with it?' Georgie asked softly. 'It still isn't too late to change your mind.'

Before Kitty could answer another voice intervened. 'Of course she's still going through with it.' Mildred came in from the kitchen. Placing a plate of cakes on the coffee table, she told Georgie in a tone of reprimand, 'Any girl would give her eye teeth to be in Kitty's shoes when she walks down that aisle tomorrow.'

Georgie could understand why Mildred was so in favour of Kitty being wed to a wealthy man like Jack Harpur, but still hadn't forgotten how she had cheated Kitty, and it showed in her voice as she replied, 'In my book, a girl doesn't marry a man unless she loves him.'

Mildred sat down, her expression giving nothing away as she

said sweetly, 'Love isn't everything. Jack Harpur is a good kind man, and he thinks the world of Kitty.' She smiled at her niece, who was taking it all in. 'He'll give Kitty a good life . . . take care of her. When a family comes along, he'll be a splendid father too.'

Georgie looked at Kitty. 'Are you happy, though? When you walk down that aisle tomorrow, will you be content?'

Kitty thought about that. In fact she had thought about nothing else for weeks now. 'I'll be as content as anyone has a right to be,' she answered.

They drank their chocolate and ate their cake and toasted each other with a little drop of champagne that Jack had sent over. 'I'd like to see you in your dress,' Georgie said, hoping that if Kitty actually put it on again, it would drive home the seriousness of what she was about to do.

Mildred went into the bedroom with her and Georgie stayed in the sitting room. 'Make a grand entrance, gal,' she urged. When their backs were turned she ran to the window and looked out again. 'Where the hell are you, Harry?' she muttered. There was no time! No time!

Kitty looked magnificent. The gown was a mass of lace and silk, decorated with the tiniest of pearls and fitting her like a dream. 'By! You're a real beauty,' Georgie breathed, reverently touching the gown.

'When Jack sees you, he'll love you all the more,' Mildred sighed.

Kitty went to the mirror and saw herself there. She had to agree the gown was beautiful, and the shoulder-length veil, and the crescent head-dress. She recalled the dream when she had seen her wedding dress and the face of the man who was waiting at the altar. This was not the gown. Jack was not the man. In her mind his name echoed over and over . . . Harry . . . Harry. She pushed it away. Harry was gone. This was her life now! 'I've made the right decision,' she said to Mildred's delight. 'You're right, Jack is a good man. I know we'll be happy.' She saw Georgie's face fall. 'I mean it,' she promised. 'Like Mildred said, he'll be a good husband and father.' Something hardened inside her. There it was again. That little niggling worry. She so much wanted a family, lots of children to fill her lonely world.

At ten o'clock, Eddie came to collect Mildred. 'I'll be back first thing in the morning,' she said. 'Now you two get off to bed. We've got an early start.'

Neither Kitty nor Georgie could sleep. Kitty lay awake while Georgie kept creeping out of bed to stare out of the window. 'Bugger you, Harry Jenkins!' she moaned. 'You know who your real friends are when you need them.' She even tiptoed out to the phone but decided against ringing his number. 'If you don't care enough to come when she needs you, then you'd best stay away,' she whispered. Then she went back to bed where, like Kitty, she slept fitfully until the dawn lit up another day.

At six they were both in the kitchen drinking tea and going through the list of things that should all have been done. 'There ain't nothing else for you to do but tie the knot,' Georgie said sarcastically. 'Gawd help you.'

Kitty understood her fears. 'You know how I felt about Harry, so I do know how worried you are that I've made the wrong decision,' she said. 'But it's made now, and you're not making things any easier for me.'

Georgie was mortified. 'I'm sorry, gal. It's just that, well, in the home, when you used to talk about all your dreams and the way you felt about Harry, it was like I was dreaming with you. Now it's all gone, and I feel we've both been cheated.' Her voice broke. 'I'm sorry, gal.' A tear ran down her face. 'I ain't much use to you, am I?'

Kitty shook her head. Her lips trembled as she came to Georgie and took her in an embrace. 'Oh, Georgie! Georgie! Don't ever talk like that,' she murmured. 'You'll never know what you mean to me'

They cried quietly, the two of them together; for the precious things that had passed into a time they would never see again, and for what the future held. They cried for all they had lost, and for all they had found in each other, and they laughed through their tears when Georgie suddenly said, 'Christ Almighty, gal! That bloody Mildred will be here any minute. We'll have red noses and swollen eyes and she'll have us under the cold water tap till the cows come home!'

Fortunately, by the time Mildred arrived at eight o'clock, order was restored; the flat had been cleaned from top to bottom in a fever of nerves; Kitty's honeymoon case was packed and standing in the hall; Georgie had accepted that Harry was not coming after all, and as Kitty had asked, she put on a smile and got caught up in the excitement of the day though deep down her every thought was with Kitty, for she knew her love for Harry was as strong as ever.

At eleven o'clock, Mildred insisted that they all had a bite to eat. 'Settles the nerves,' she said.

Kitty found that she was actually hungry. She ate two slices of toast and a spoonful of marmalade, then drank another two cups of tea and afterwards soaked in a hot sudsy bath, emerging blossom fresh and wishing the hours away. At last she was resigned to her fate. Once this day was gone, a new one would begin. With Jack. She *wanted* to make it work. She *had* to make it work.

At midday the flowers arrived. Kitty and Mildred helped to get Georgie ready, 'Look at me,' Georgie declared, twirling in front of the mirror. The dress was a pale blue calf-length creation, fashioned empire-style so as to disguise the fact that she was pregnant. 'Wish Mac could see me,' she murmured. When her smile dipped, Kitty put a comforting arm round her and all was well again.

When Georgie was ready, Kitty was dressed. 'You look so beautiful,' Mildred cooed. Georgie merely smiled. It was still in the back of her mind that Harry might turn up, but that was up to him now.

At twelve-thirty Eddie arrived. Fifteen minutes later, Georgie was looking out of the window for the wedding cars when a big white van drew up outside; its front bumper was badly dented, and the big ugly fellow driving it looked like he'd been in a fight. He looked up with a sorry expression. 'Bloody cheek!' Georgie cried, throwing open the window. 'Get that scruffy thing out of there. There's a wedding going on, bugger you!'

Kitty came to the window to see. 'Who is it?' she asked, craning her neck to see over Georgie's shoulders, and heard her friend cry out, 'IT'S HARRY! WELL, I'M BUGGERED. HE TURNED UP AFTER ALL!'

Kitty's heart almost stopped. 'It can't be,' she muttered, backing from the window. 'It can't be.' In just one minute her whole world was turned upside down. How could Harry do this to her? How could he turn up on her doorstep just a few minutes before she was going to church where Jack was already waiting?

She was desperately afraid. 'Send him away,' she told Mildred. 'I don't want him here.'

It was too late. Harry was coming through the door. 'You won't find that easy,' he said softly, his dark eyes pained at the sight of her in a wedding gown. 'I love you, Kitty.'

So many emotions sped through her then: anger, regret and love. Oh! Such deep abiding love. But Harry had left it too late. The anger was overwhelming. 'If you want to come to my wedding, you're in the wrong place. You should be at the church with the other guests.' Her calm voice belied the tumult of panic inside her. He looked wonderful; the same tall dark handsome man who had claimed her heart all those years ago; the same tumbling unruly hair and those wonderful dark eyes. But it was too late. Too much had happened. Too many people would be hurt.

Turning to the other three, he asked them, 'Please ... we need a minute alone.'

Mildred hesitated, with Eddie standing beside her. Georgie dragged them away to the kitchen where they peeped from behind the kitchen door. 'Pray she goes with him,' Georgie urged. 'It's the only way Kitty will ever be truly happy.'

Harry stepped towards her. 'You and I belong together,' he murmured. 'We can never be happy with anyone else, you know that.'

'Aren't you happy with Susan?' Kitty's astonishment betrayed itself in her voice.

'No. Not with Susan, and not with any woman but you.' His fingers touched her face, sending shivers through her. 'I want you to come with me, right now. Nothing else matters. Just you and me. I love you, sweetheart, and I know now I can't live without you.'

Before she could answer, there was a knock on the door. When it opened a cheery face peered in. 'Wedding cars,' he said. 'Best get a move on. The traffic's building up and I'm a bit late.'

Kitty collected her bouquet. 'Jack's waiting,' she told Harry, and in a softer voice, 'Susan too. I'm sure she's waiting.' How could she talk so calmly when her heart was fluttering like a million butterflies let loose? 'It's too late, Harry,' she said. 'Perhaps it was never meant to be for us.'

As she walked by him, he grabbed her arm, his dark eyes disbelieving as he told her, 'You're so wrong, Kitty. It was *always* meant to be. It's just that we lost our way for a while.' His grip was like iron on her arm.

A flash of anger lit her eyes. 'No, Harry! My plans are already made!' With that she almost ran out of the flat and down the stairs, where she stumbled into the taxi.

Harry would have followed, but Georgie stopped him. 'Let her be,' she said. 'Let her think it through. Stay here a while.' She noticed how weary he was. 'Kitty's been through a bad time. I didn't realise before, but some things go very deep and can't be overturned in a minute.'

'Tell her I'll wait,' he said. 'I'll be at the railway station for an hour. After that, I'll be gone and I won't bother her ever again.'

'All right. But you have to tell *me* something, Harry.' Georgie was never more serious. 'Is it really all over between you and Susan?'

'It was never really on.' His tone spoke volumes.

'What will happen to the child?'

Now he was astonished. 'What child?'

Her suspicions had been right. It was a ploy by that wife of his. 'Forget it.' She smiled. 'You've told me all I want to know.'

Downstairs she pulled Eddie aside. 'Let me travel with her to the church. You go with Mildred in the other car.' Mildred would have intervened but Eddie walked her away, softly talking to her, and she seemed to accept that there were happenings here beyond her control.

Climbing into the taxi, Georgie slammed shut the door. 'Shift your arse up, gal,' she told Kitty. 'Don't forget I'm a bit wider now.'

Kitty raised a smile, but kept her gaze firmly fixed on the taxi floor. As it moved away, she asked in a forlorn voice, 'I wonder if I had him wrong all along, Georgie?'

'Meaning?'

'How could he do that? How could he even think of leaving Susan when she's carrying his child?'

There was a little smile in Georgie's voice. 'I think you should ask him that yourself.'

Kitty turned to look at her. 'I can't do it, Georgie. I daren't hope any more. It's too painful.'

'You never struck me as the type of person who was afraid of pain.'

Kitty toyed with her bouquet, absent-mindedly picking at the petals and showering them to the floor. 'Why couldn't it all have come right in the beginning? Why did I have to send him away all that time ago?'

'Because there's a right time for everything, and when you sent him away, it was the right time for that. Now it's time to put the record straight. Marry Jack Harpur and I swear to God you'll live the rest of your life regretting it!'

Kitty knew that what Georgie was saying was right. But what about Jack? What about Susan, and Harry's child? 'How can we take our own happiness at the expense of others?'

'Because if you don't, you'll *all* end up miserable.'

Soft silent tears flowed down Kitty's face. 'It really is too late now, isn't it?' she whispered. 'Because I've sent him away again.'

Taking hold of her hand, Georgie asked her in a mischievous voice, 'Did you think he would go as easily as that, gal?'

When Kitty turned stricken brown eyes to her, Georgie went on, 'He's waiting for you, at the railway station. But you'll have to be quick or this time you'll lose him forever.'

Kitty let out a cry. 'Oh, Georgie! I can't let him go again. I just can't!' Leaning forward she called excitedly to the driver, 'We're not going to the church! We're going to the railway station . . . as quick as you can, please.'

The driver went at a fast pace, through the town and on towards Midland Road station. Behind him the two women urged him on, telling him to go ever faster. 'I'm going faster than the old engine's been before,' he complained. 'If I'm not careful I'm bound to get a speeding ticket.' When Kitty promised to pay any fine he might incur, he took off his cap, scratched his head, gave a big sigh, and with a boyish grin was caught up in all the excitement. 'Hold on to your seats then!' he cried and off they went.

Harry's train had just pulled in. He looked up and down the platform one more time. 'She's not coming now, Harry boy,' he told himself. But then he looked up again and there she was, hair blowing in the wind as she ran towards him. 'HARRY!' She was laughing and crying all at the same time. 'DON'T GO, HARRY!' The hem of her wedding dress was held bunched in her fists as she passed all the staring passengers. She didn't care that she was showing more leg than a lady ought to show, and she didn't care that they had crowded to the windows to cheer and clap as she and Harry ran towards each other. All she cared about was that he was here, and he was hers. She could hardly believe it. At long last, he was hers.

On 15 June, 1982, Harry's divorce was made final.

Exactly one month later, Kitty walked down the aisle to her beloved man. Everyone said they made a splendid couple. This time Kitty had chosen to wear a completely different style of dress to the one she had almost wed Jack in. But it was magnificent – a long plain creation with little pearl buttons at the throat and a gentle slit at the hem. She carried a posy of pink rosebuds and wore a small round veil that fell just below her cheekbones.

Georgie walked behind her, proud and pretty in a loose-fitting cream dress. Slim now, and happier than she had been in a long time, she had her own life to cherish. 'Just look at the pair of us, Kitty gal!' she whispered as she walked sedately behind. 'I'm buggered if we ain't as proud as models on a catwalk.'

Among the well-wishers were Harry's family. His sister Sarah had grown away from him over the years, but now after a long period working abroad, had come to value her family, and rekindle her old friendship with Kitty.

Miss Davis watched from the pews, her face smiling and proud. As Kitty walked by, she whispered her blessing. When the service was over she was off to Australia to visit a longlost cousin who lived in the outback.

Beside Miss Davis stood a red-haired man, well presented in a smart suit and wearing a tie in which he appeared to be very uncomfortable. Mac was home. Subdued by a longer term in prison, and realising that he must mend his ways, he now had a job which paid enough to rent a good house and to keep his little family. In his arms was a child, a beautiful baby girl by the name of Katherine. This was Georgie's daughter, and what other name should she give it than that of her darling Kitty? It wasn't a boy as Georgie predicted, but in a way, she was glad.

Many surprising and wonderful events had taken place in the last year. Susan and Jack consoled each other after their partners walked out on them; so much so that they were now planning a wedding of their own.

Harry had discovered it was Jack who had been deliberately causing the damage to his business by revealing his rates to other hauliers who then undercut him to win the contracts themselves. Jack had hoped to make Harry's business dependent on his own company so that he would never be able to try to win Kitty back.

But that was all behind them now. Outside the church bells rang. Harry swept his bride into his arms, and swore he would never let her go. 'This day is the start of our lives,' he said.

It was also the start of their family; a son in the following year and twins two years after that, a boy and a girl.

When the photographs were taken, Kitty took Georgie aside while Harry and Mac disappeared. Kitty kept Georgie talking until after a few minutes she took her by the shoulders and turned her round. 'Look, Georgie,' she said. And when she saw what Harry and Mac had brought to the gates of the church, she burst out crying. It was a minibus. The brightest blue minibus she had ever seen.

'It's for you, sweetheart,' Kitty said. 'For being the best friend a girl could ever have.' In all these years she had never forgotten Georgie's cherished dream.

In the years to come, Harry's business would thrive. He and Kitty's plan to have a big four-bedroomed house in the suburbs of Blackburn was realised. Georgie and Mac would build up their minicab business to include another four vehicles, and their children would grow up to be fast friends, just like their parents before them.

But for now, on this wonderful summer's day, Kitty looked up into her husband's dark eyes. 'I love you, Harry Jenkins,' she whispered.

Kissing her tenderly, he enfolded her in his arms, and she vowed that nothing would ever again tear them apart, only the Good Lord above when the time came.

But there was a whole lifetime until then. A lifetime they would live to the full, until they were very, very old, and their children had children of their own.

'Come on, you lovebirds!' Georgie's voice sailed across the lawns. 'If you like, you can climb into the back of my minibus, and I'll take you to the reception in style.'

The black cars were dismissed. Everyone clambered into the minibus, with Miss Davis up front. They sang all the way to the reception and Georgie was still merrily singing when Kitty put her to bed three hours later. 'You're a disgrace, Georgie gal,' she murmured, kissing her on the forehead before covering her with the blanket. 'You swear like a trooper, and don't give a damn, and you still can't take your wine without giggling and falling asleep.'

She turned out the light and softly closed the door, saying with a contented smile, 'But, so help me, gal, I wouldn't change you for the world.'